AUTHOR	CLASS
PINCHER, C	F

TITLE The private world of St. John
Terrapin

THE PRIVATE WORLD OF
ST JOHN TERRAPIN

The Private World of
of
St John Terrapin

A Novel of the Café Royal
by
CHAPMAN PINCHER

SIDGWICK & JACKSON
LONDON

First published in Great Britain in 1982
by Sidgwick and Jackson Limited

Copyright © 1982 Chapman Pincher

ISBN 0-283-98849-5

Printed in Great Britain by
Biddles Ltd, Guildford, Surrey
for Sidgwick and Jackson Limited
1 Tavistock Chambers, Bloomsbury Way
London WC1A 2SG

TO LORD FORTE
WHO PRESERVED THE FABRIC
AND THE SPIRIT

CONTENTS

FOREWORD

by Chapman Pincher

The voluminous diaries and papers of the late Mr St John Terrapin were passed to me by his only surviving relative in the hope that they could be worked up into a readable book. I was unable even to read them completely until my retirement from Fleet Street, and since then have done what I can with this remarkable material, presenting it as though it had indeed been written by Mr Terrapin and retaining his occasionally quaint style as far as practicable. That, I am sure, is what he would have liked, as indicated by his introduction, which was all that he had managed to complete before being overtaken by terminal illness.

How much he has added to what is already on record it would be impossible for me to discover without research for which I do not have the time. Certainly, many of the statements he deciphered from the lips of Oscar Wilde eventually appeared in that writer's plays and books, because Wilde used his conversations to generate his aphorisms and polished them up later. The same may have happened with other Café Royal habitués, for many of them, even those who were painters like Whistler, Augustus John and William Rothenstein, also wrote books.

It is sometimes difficult to know from Mr Terrapin's records whether the events he describes took place in the Domino Room, in the Restaurant or elsewhere in the large building, so I may be responsible for errors there. Mr Terrapin himself has certainly taken some liberties. However, the events which he records in beautiful copperplate handwriting presumably occurred somewhere in his beloved Café Royal, where so much happened that I have had to be selective in this book, so the precise location is of small consequence. Perhaps he regarded a deliberate mislocation as justifiable licence, having acquired from 'friends' like Wilde, Harris and Chesterton a feeling for the joys of the unreal semi-fictional world as having greater appeal than stark, restrictive reality.

Clearly, Mr Terrapin also used his wide reading of his subjects' biographies and other writings to fill gaps in his daily records. So, on his behalf, I should pay his posthumous acknowledgement to any writers and publishers on whom he may have drawn. When sufficiently stimulated, he moved outside to examine locations, attend funerals and witness events like criminal trials, in which he expresses an almost morbid interest, especially when murder was involved, though this is common enough.

What is extraordinary is that this strange little man, in many ways almost a recluse, was able to claim insight into the characters of many of the most notable figures of his long life and, in recounting some of the dramatic events in their lives, was able to say, 'I was there'. The way he achieved this must surely be unique. But perhaps the documents, which record events in almost Proustian detail, provide the deepest insight into the character of Terrapin himself. The determination with which he set about educating himself so as to be able to take advantage of the extraordinary 'university' in which he had accidentally found himself, and the effort this required in his peculiar circumstances, are most impressive. The effects which this strange hobby produced on his character are not without interest. The tone of his diary entries increasingly suggests that he came to believe he had a right to invade the private lives of other people, so much so that he was, I suppose, what might be called an 'Eavesdropping Tom'. I sense that for all his humility and self-effacement, Mr Terrapin had a deep-seated urge to be recognized and appreciated, though without much hope as regards his literary effort. As he says: 'It is one of the lamentable things of life that there are no prizes for a worthwhile try.'

Whether I saw him or not I cannot say. I was a fairly frequent evening attender in the Brasserie, as the Domino Room was renamed after the alterations, when I was a student at London University in the 1930s and occasionally after the war. I have a vague recollection of a little, elderly man wearing an oversize, old-fashioned stiff collar, who seemed to be something of a fixture in the place, but having read so much about him in preparing this book it is possible that my memory is playing tricks.

His last diary entry was made on the day that the Brasserie closed in January 1951. I quote it verbatim here, because nothing could better describe the intense feelings of this strange man, who had shown so much courage and resolution, at that crucial moment in his life.

'I have chosen to publish my own work now because the Domino

Room, later called the Brasserie, has been finally closed down and converted to a restaurant. I am one of the last few survivors of its great days. Max Beerbohm, now Sir Max, is still alive but has lived for many years in Italy, while Augustus John, now a rather battered old gentleman, seems tied to the public houses in Chelsea; there are a few others, but most of my subjects have passed on.

'I have seen so many come and go, some of them tragically young, but that is the way God made it – without death there cannot be life – and there now seems little point in my remaining when what was my whole world has ended. It is as though I have been deprived of my home and my few remaining friends at one blow. Most people find that the attention one must give to one's friends, if one wishes to keep them, is time-consuming; the attention I gave mine consumed all my time. Now they are gone I have time on my hands. But it may not be much time, for during the past few weeks I have been experiencing the kind of pain which, after a lifetime of false alarms, tells me that something is really wrong.

'I had such zest for living, even if vicariously, that I never believed I would ever want to go, but now I am not so sure.'

He clearly suspected then that he was mortally ill, and died within the year. It may be that with the end of Bohemianism, which the closure of the Brasserie signified, St John Terrapin had simply lost his purpose in living.

London 1981

1

THE HUB OF MY UNIVERSE

This book, my first and only work, which represents a lifetime's patient observation, is a record of events, collected mostly at first hand, concerning some of the most illustrious and notorious men and women of the last half-century from the 'Gay Nineties' onwards — artists, sculptors, poets, writers, musicians, politicians, businessmen, crooks, actors and actresses, lords, dukes and even kings.

In explaining how I, St John Terrapin, formerly known as William Baynes, have come to publish it at the advanced age of eighty-seven, I am driven to confess my most intimate secret — that for some sixty years I have lived in a world of absolute silence. It is a confession because I have every reason to believe that throughout most of that time very few have been aware of my total deafness — an achievement in which I take considerable pride. I lost my sense of hearing at the age of twenty during a vicious attack of scarlet fever, from which I nearly died. Its effects on my future and on my personality were, of course, devastating. I had always been gregarious, needful of human companionship, and after a reasonable education at a modest boarding school had developed special interest in those activities demanding hearing of high quality, such as music, drama and conversation. (I had always hated organized games, pleading my mother's conviction that I had a 'weak chest', which might have been true, for I was susceptible to coughs and colds and was never allowed out of the house in winter without a muffler, a habit I still retain.)

Suddenly I found myself alone, deprived of easy communication with my friends and without the sympathy and assistance that is invariably extended to those who have lost their sight. My mother, to whom I had been deeply attached, was dead and my father old, ill, and remote as he had always been. As the only child I had few relatives. Loneliness, that ever-besieging enemy of the deaf, which loomed so menacingly, filled me with dread. To live in the solitude of absolute silence might appeal to a religious fanatic but to me it would have been a living death. For people to have to write their answers to my questions would, to my perhaps peculiar nature, have been shameful and I determined that I would either overcome my disability or end my life.

Fortunately, the good Lord usually offers recompenses for disaster and in my case it was the endowment of most excellent eyesight – still quite good, thank God – and an iron determination to succeed. I do not think I am being immodest in claiming that few have been able to lip-read with my facility. Of course, one cannot detect what people are saying unless one is able to see their lips moving. But there is a compensation for this – one can see what people are saying when they are so far away that those dependent on their ears cannot hear more than a mumble of sound, especially in a crowded room. Background noise does not affect the lip-reader. Further, the truly expert lip-reader can glean additional insight into what a distant person is saying by his body gestures, the use of the hands, leaning to whisper, facial expression and the glance of the eyes. Even when privy to only one partner's conversation, the expert can construe much of what the other is saying. Being totally deaf, in fact, makes one extremely observant of what, I suppose, could be called 'body language'. Lip-reading is something I would make essential in the training of every spy. Indeed I wonder if it already is.

In retrospect I suppose I experienced something of the thrill of being a spy, but one whose purpose was never baneful and who, until now, reported only to himself. I could be accused of infringing privacy on a rather massive scale, but I console myself that, as almost all of my 'targets' are dead, any breach of their confidentiality is now academic. I have kept their secrets until now, and were I to wait any longer I should be dead myself. I cannot, however, in all honesty dispose so easily of the resolution I made when I first began my diaries, namely that I would never take financial advantage of anything I overheard. Sadly, such is human greed that this resolution was soon broken, for I found I was able to overhear conversations between leading lawyers, City financiers and others which enabled me to buy a modest number of shares and take advantage of projects which were then confidential. This unexpected bonus considerably improved my financial circumstances. Now here I am proposing to publish all in the hope of some financial reward, however meagre, for, as I quickly learned from listening in – more accurately watching in – to so many writers, every author worth his salt wants his effort to be bought. I have witnessed so many authors insisting that they write to please themselves. I do not believe them and I am, I fear, as vain in this respect as any of my subjects.

A further dispensation I enjoyed from the Almighty was that my father, with whom I had never been on close terms, died soon after my medical misfortune. The modest legacy I inherited made me independent, provided that I lived reasonably simply and denied myself the pleasure of a wife and family, which, because of my disability and what it did for my character, did not have much appeal for me. Without that financial independence I should not be writing now because, like most people who lead dull lives in furtherance of earning their living, I would have had no exciting subjects to write about.

I should perhaps explain how I came by my strange name. For reasons which may seem unaccountable to others I was so ashamed of my deafness that I cut myself off from all my previous friends and, to assume a different identity, changed my name by deed poll as soon as I was twenty-one. The reason I chose Terrapin has been a secret until now. It so aptly described my being – a creature confined within a shell but able at intervals to shoot out its head and then retract into its peculiar privacy. Tortoise or turtle would have sounded too ridiculous. As for St John, I liked the sound of 'Sinjon'. It had a distinguished ring about it, and as an avid reader of the Holy Bible, my favourite book is that of Revelation from the hand of St John the Divine.

Nothing worthwhile is achieved in life without effort, and my ability to 'oversee' what others were saying was the result of countless hours of practice in front of a mirror in the modest lodgings I took in Guilford Street, Bloomsbury, followed by observations of those sitting near me in the cheap restaurants and bars I frequented. I developed a reputation for looking people straight in the eye when I spoke with them, but in reality I was looking them in the mouth. Some men get their pleasure out of interest in things – their gardens, their stamps, their models. I have always been more interested in people. So I found it highly intriguing to know what others were saying when they believed they were speaking in private. It was like having a hidden microphone which, if it had been invented, was not then available for eavesdropping purposes. At first I indulged this pleasure only among people who might be described as 'ordinary', though their private conversations were often interesting enough, sometimes frighteningly so. Thus did I secure at least a partial victory over the enemy of loneliness.

Then one day, while soaking in a hot hip-bath – the long bath and
gas geyser were later innovations in my life – an idea for turning my
adversity to advantage suddenly occurred to me. If I could insinuate
myself into the company of illustrious people, without their knowing
it, I could record conversations which might add up to a diary of such
interest that one day, perhaps like that of Samuel Pepys, it might be
found worthy of publication. But how could I, with my modest
means and background, possibly do that?

Again I have to thank good fortune. Some time in the spring of
1886 I read in the *Evening News*, then one of London's several
halfpenny papers, about a place called the Domino Room in the Café
Royal near Piccadilly Circus. The reference was in an article about the
Café Royal by one of its habitués, a man called Frank Harris, who
turned out to be the *Evening News*'s editor. He had achieved this
exalted position at the age of only twenty-eight, and kept it by
boosting the circulation, mainly by printing the full proceedings of
police court cases with all their pathos, humour and, on occasion,
sexual implications. He named some of the people to be seen in the
Café Royal and revealed that, though it could be expensive, there was
a place called the Domino Room where it was possible to linger
among those illustrious people for the price of a glass of beer and a
boiled onion! I decided to go there.

The façade of the Café Royal with its main entrance in that part of
Regent Street called The Quadrant, abutting on Piccadilly Circus,
was known to me: I recalled its four pillars, pendant lamps and oval
medallion bearing its name. I knew too from what I had read of
Harris's writings that the establishment, which had become the most
famous in London for its food and wine, had been developed from
very small beginnings by Monsieur and Madame Daniel Nicols who
had emigrated from France. They had opened a little café-restaurant
in Glasshouse Street, the short thoroughfare behind Regent Street, in
1865, and by acquiring leases on property, expanded it forwards,
into Regent Street itself. It may be remarked that 'Nicols', which was
boldly displayed over the entrance, does not sound French, and in fact
the name of the proprietor, who became very rich, was really Daniel
Nicholas Thévenon. He had changed his name after decamping from
Paris following his bankruptcy, which was a criminal offence in
France. He was also quick to change the name Café Nicols to the more
prestigious Café Royal, which I feel to have been fully justified, for it
was indeed the haunt of royalty and it provided me and many others
with so many right royal days.

On the sunny afternoon when I first arrived there, shortly after 1 p.m., I found a knot of people by the Regent Street entrance with the uniformed commissionaire striving to keep them in order.

'What's going on?' I asked a workman who was craning his neck to see through the swing doors.

'They reckon the Prince of Wales has just gone in there with that Lillie Langtry woman.'

Lillie Langtry (whose name is so often mis-spelled Lily) was, of course, the Prince's first public mistress. It was well known that Albert, Prince of Wales, known to his friends as 'Bertie', was as lecherous as a monkey and that no woman was safe from his seigneurial advances, especially if she happened to be the wife of one of his friends, who were banished from the royal presence if they declined the honour he was offering. But Lillie, daughter of the senior clergyman in Jersey, was the first 'fancy woman' he had flaunted in public. They had been 'friends' for about ten years and it was commonly believed that they had produced an illegitimate daughter who had been hidden away in Jersey, but this turned out to be only half true, as I will later explain.

Understandably there was some sympathy for his mother, Queen Victoria, though there were strong rumours that she had a 'fancy man' in a Scottish ghillie called John Brown, who took great liberties with her. But the deepest sympathy was felt for the Prince's beautiful Danish wife, Princess Alexandra, for whom I had a special feeling since she was known to be going deaf. Bertie had been married to her for fourteen years and had five children by her, plus others on the wrong side of the blanket, when he met Lillie. There could be no doubt that the Princess was aware of his promiscuous activities and was even obliged to accept Lillie and some others of the presentable mistresses in her entourage.

Still, such is human nature that, while the Prince's behaviour was deplored, more women copied Lillie Langtry, who was exciting, if wicked, than emulated the Princess, who was virtuous but dull. For a brief period some fashionable women walked with a limp in emulation of the Princess, who had a slight leg deformity following rheumatic fever when she was expecting her third child – what women will do to be 'in vogue' – but Lillie's coiffure, her clothes, her mannerisms were the rage, and the number of children named after her was legion because, I suppose, she was believed to be the most beautiful woman in the world. I was therefore very interested in getting a close view of Lillie if I could, having already seen the stout and bearded Prince who wisely was to take the name Edward, on succeeding his mother, thereby avoiding comparison with his father, 'Albert the Good'.

Some raucous woman in the crowd – for the numbers had been quickly swollen with passers-by, including ladies of easy virtue who plied their trade in that area – was insisting that she had seen 'the pair of them' alight from a hansom cab, among the many which were always clippity-clopping up and down Regent Street. But, as the Prince's eating habits with his fondness for many courses was well known – as many as ten for dinner, it was said – it was obvious that we would have to wait for hours if the two had just gone to lunch. So, summoning up more courage than I had thought I might need, I elbowed my way through and asked the commissionaire the way to the Domino Room. I feared he might think that a person like myself could have no business there but he was most courteous, called me 'Sir', and pointed out the way, which was very easy because it was on the ground floor.

I was quite unprepared for the impact of the Domino Room as I first entered through the green swing doors. The place was garish, the walls being adorned with long, gilded mirrors flanked by numerous plaster caryatids and garlands, and the ornate turquoise ceiling, from which depended glass chandeliers, being supported by blue pillars wreathed in golden vine leaves. The customers sat on crimson plush banquettes and ate and drank off marble-topped tables, which also served for the games of dominoes regularly played there. The clatter of ivory dominoes being shuffled or plonked down was a feature of the room, but one of the sounds which I would never 'oversee'. As the room was not large, and little attention was paid to ventilation, there was a constant aromatic smell of the smoke of cigars and Turkish cigarettes, occasionally overlaid by the garlic scent from some chafing dish for, though it was mainly a drinking den, it was also a popular place for 'putting on the nosebag', as we used to say in those equestrian days.

I looked around for the Prince but, while there were several stout, middle-aged, bearded gentlemen with attractive ladies, none was likely to have been mistaken for the Prince, though many men deliberately copied his style. Then, of course, I realized that the Prince and Lillie were probably in some even grander, more formal, part of the building, perhaps in the Restaurant upstairs, which Harris had also praised.

For me, however, the Domino Room was lavish enough. If the

character of an age is reflected in its furniture it was certainly true of that enchanting room, which captivated me from the moment I entered it. Such became my affection for the place that I was to derive pleasure just from touching the tables or the garlanded marble columns, as I hung my bowler hat on one of the cast-iron coat hooks, which I came to regard as my own. The ceiling, which Oscar Wilde described as 'deliciously pagan', was divided by gilded beams into large squares, some simply with gilded swags on a turquoise background, others bearing paintings of ladies in classical poses. But it was the reflections of the big mirrors which became my absorbing interest. Ah, if only some scientist could invent a way of recovering them now! What a gallery of celebrities we should see – a gallery the like of which, I believe, will never be seen again, for those mirrors have reflected Whistler, Wilde, Beardsley, Shaw, Paderewski, Toulouse-Lautrec, Lawrence (both D. H. and 'of Arabia'), Rossini, Caruso, Verlaine, Rimbaud, Augustus John, Marie Lloyd, Lillie Langtry, Margot Asquith, Nina Hamnett, Enid Bagnold, Nancy Cunard, Virginia Woolf, and a host of others who were only names to most people but who, without knowing it, shared their intimacies with me. I remember 'hearing' Max Beerbohm, the caricaturist and writer, explaining an idea he had for a novel about a magic mirror which retained the impression of each scene which had ever been reflected in it. The idea had come to him during one of his many visits to the Domino Room and, sadly, he had to abandon it because he could not make it credible to the reader, though an occasional visitor, H. G. Wells, might easily have done so. For me the mirrors had a much more practical significance. I quickly learned to use them in reading lips which I could not directly see.

There was an unparalleled collection of eccentrics, a few of them loners like myself, but most of them humanly gregarious enough to form coteries with names like the Decadents, the Bohemians and the Bloomsburyites. Some were *poseurs* determined to draw attention to themselves, but others were merely incapable of conforming with the customs of the day and enlivened the scene with their odd behaviour – a flavour missing today when eccentrics seem to be in short supply.

Quite frequently the extremely rich Marquess of Clanricarde, dressed in filthy clothes, including a battered stovepipe hat, almost green with age, and carrying a ruptured umbrella, would wander in from his flat in the Albany across the road. (Everything seemed to be so near to the Café Royal.) He would then sit down, open a dirty-looking parcel containing fish-paste and demand a bread roll to

spread it on! On one occasion an irascible man violently disagreed
with the general view that Mistinguett, the French dancer, wittily
described in the Domino Room as 'a rose-red cutie, half as old as
Time', had the most beautiful legs in the world. He took off his own
wooden leg and hurled it towards her admirers, suggesting that it
was better!

I was present when a man who had been quietly sitting at a nearby
table crept up behind Willie Crosland, the poet—journalist, who was
gossiping animatedly with a friend called Townley Searle and a
couple of others. Expecting some practical joke or other, I just
watched, and then was horrified to see the man pull out a knife and
make to stab Willie in the back. Fortunately Searle, perhaps hearing
my cry of alarm, saw him in time and knocked the knife from his
hands. But the waiters were never more astonished than the day I
remember so well when Aleister Crowley, the self-styled 'Magus',
walked slowly through the room in a star-spangled conical hat,
utterly convinced that his cloak, adorned with zodiac signs, made
him completely invisible. I should point out that Crowley was not
alone in appearing in outlandish garb. There was one gentleman who
almost invariably dressed in the fashion of Dr Samuel Johnson,
wearing knee breeches and a long, brown, square-cut jacket, waistcoat and cravat. He was Percy Wood, a noted sculptor and one of the
earliest art photographers, producing photographs at the turn of the
century which to me seemed every bit as beautiful as paintings. Some
of the habitués like Aleister Crowley, who also called himself the
'Beast', Frank Harris and Horatio Bottomley might best be described
as villains. But what villains! And how dull life would be without its
share of them!

Then, of course, there were the ladies, if one could call them so –
French and German as well as English. Scores of prostitutes and
'enthusiastic amateurs' appeared in the Domino Room with various
men who had picked them up, sometimes prior to their departure to
one of the private rooms upstairs. What they talked about and the
terms in which they discussed it should surprise nobody, I suppose,
for many had known no better since childhood, but I was astonished –
I might say appalled – at the subjects which some ladies of quality
and intellectual attainment discussed and at the language they used. I
have never known much about women but it is my belief, after my
long trespass into their secret nature, that many men who think they
do are in the same predicament.

That first day I selected a table which commanded a view of almost the whole room but was least likely to be attractive to anybody else. It was close to both the kitchen and the bar, where the Misses Cheswick and Sunderland, always dressed in tight-laced black, dispensed drinks and cigars; so there was always a clatter of plates, trays and glasses and a buzz of waiters' banter – none of which could possibly worry me. I sat down and ordered my beer and boiled Spanish onion and made friends with the waiter, whose name was Jules, one of about eighteen needed to serve that busy room. I told him about the crowd on the pavement outside and asked him if it was true that the Prince and Mrs Langtry were in the building. He replied that they did patronize the Café Royal occasionally, though usually in a private room, and that he would find out for me. He soon told me that they were not, but my disappointment was quickly overcome by the sight of a man of much greater interest to me, whom I fancied I recognized from his photographs which were forever in the newspapers and magazines.

'Is that Horatio Bottomley?' I asked, nodding towards a fat man with a squarish face sitting alone at a table not far away.

'It is, sir', Jules replied. 'He lunches here regularly. Here or in the Restaurant, but never alone. He must be expecting somebody. Probably a lady, if I know him,' he added with a wink.

Though I was never to meet Horatio Bottomley, he was one of the people I got to know really well. There's no denying that he was a rogue. But what a rogue!

Bottomley was already a heavy man but he was to become enormous, being described then as 'stout' rather than 'fat', due to the belief in those days that to satisfy a hearty appetite was healthy and that being heavy implied both physical strength and stability – the style of John Bull. Though only about five feet five inches he eventually weighed about eighteen stones. His charm – for he had that in too great a measure for his own good – resided in his large head with its heavy jaw and strong forehead, and in the remarkable brain behind it. He was, I suppose, further evidence that little men tend to be both aggressive and successful. But I also am small and came to nothing!

I think that one of the reasons I soon warmed to Bottomley was because I learned from Jules that he too had found the Café Royal by accident and immediately made it his second home. Like me he had been living in digs in Bloomsbury and stumbled on the place, some time in 1879, I believe, when he was a shorthand writer at the Law Courts, a position which taught him so much about the machinations of the law and how he might manipulate it. When he acquired money, which was quickly, he found the unique wine cellars of the Café Royal greatly to his liking, especially the famous vintages of champagne to which he became completely addicted. Indeed he claimed that without 'bubbly' he could not live. He certainly could not work without it, and the 11 a.m. clinking of champagne bottles being taken into his offices in King Street became known as 'The Angelus'. Pommery was his favourite and he never drank less than two bottles a day, starting at breakfast, when he liked to accompany it with kippers!

He shared, in good measure, the commonest characteristic of the Domino Room habitués – vanity. He literally was as vain as a peacock and was never so happy as when in full view of a large audience with two or more pretty girls round him at the table helping him to drink his champagne. Like many excessively active men in many fields of endeavour he would turn to the fair sex when in need of light relief after some exhausting bout of effort, and usually had girls housed in flats at his expense. As Frank Harris put it, quoting some German writer whose name I never grasped, 'Man shall be educated for war and women for the recreation of the warrior'. Sadly, Bottomley was also very greedy and it was a combination of greed, compulsive gambling and irresponsibility about the feelings of others which brought about his ruin, which was every bit as great and as sensational as Oscar Wilde's.

As I watched him in the Domino Room that first day, enthralled to be at such close quarters, he was joined by a man who looked for all the world like a lion-tamer. He had a squat, powerful frame, a rather fierce and swarthy square-jawed face, protruding ears, a German-style moustache – up-curled, I learned later, to make him look like Bismarck – and black hair parted almost in the middle and plastered to his scalp.

'Not a lady!' I whispered to Jules as I called him over to order another beer, not wishing him to think I was a one-glass customer.

'Not a gentleman, either,' Jules replied. 'That's Frank Harris, the rudest man in London.'

So this was the very man whose fulsome writing had brought me to the Domino Room! What a stroke of good fortune that I should have chosen that afternoon. But, as I was soon to discover, something was always happening in the Domino Room – or about to be. I was tempted there and then to walk over and thank Harris for the great service he had done me but, as I always would, I refrained. Though I was eternally indebted to him, Jules's remark was well justified. Harris treated the waiters abominably, even making them break the law by the sheer brute force of his personality and aggressive vanity. I remember how, at a later date, when it was long past the licensed time for serving drinks, Harris demanded whisky, summoning the waiter with a flourish of a hairy hand that bore two, or sometimes three, large rings. When the waiter drew his attention to the time Harris bawled 'Nonsense! It is I, Frank Harris, who am here. Telephone the Commissioner of Police and you will see that it is all right. Then bring me a large whisky and soda.' On another occasion, at a dinner given *in his honour*, he said, 'I have never encountered younger wines or older jokes.' That day, however, Harris was well behaved, perhaps because he was Bottomley's guest. Bottomley's purpose was to discuss how he could raise money for the company which he called the Hansard Union. I heard him mention Lord Folkestone and someone called Kennard, of whom I had never heard.

'Get me those two names for my board of directors, Harris, and I'll give you a cheque for £10,000.'

'A nice round figure,' Harris responded, not a bit taken aback, as I was, by the mention of such an enormous sum, as it was in those days. 'But what have you paid for all the companies, and what is the capitalization?'

Bottomley passed him a paper, and after perusing it Harris said, 'These figures mean you are buying the businesses for £200,000 and selling them to the company for £1 million!'

'I may even make it a quarter of a million more, with debentures,' Bottomley said, unabashed at this outrageous personal profit. He could charm money out of anybody's pockets, rich or poor, and did so on an enormous scale until his downfall. Like Harris, he had started in journalism in a small way with publications like *The Draper's Record* and *Mother's Magazine*. They both achieved great success and Bottomley, who also founded the *Financial Times* and later produced the immensely successful *John Bull*, was to become the most widely read journalist in Britain, one of the most influential and possibly the highest paid. They were also both adept at spending money on good food, wine and women, so had a great deal in common, not forgetting their joint claim that they had been educated in 'The University of Life', which for Bottomley had started at Sir Josiah Mason's orphanage in Birmingham.

'I have often wondered, Bottomley, but are you related in any way to Charles Bradlaugh?' Harris asked, referring to a politician who was a fine speaker, though he alienated many with his atheism and opposition to the monarchy. With Bottomley's deep upper lip and hair brushed back without a parting the resemblance was indeed close.

'I am indeed,' replied Bottomley. Then, leaning across the table, he added, 'Strictly in confidence, he is my father.'

I had no means of knowing it at the time, but this was a bare-faced lie. As was eventually to emerge, Bottomley, who hailed from Hackney, was the son of a tailor's cutter who had died soon after he was born.

'I take it that you yourself have political ambitions,' Harris said.

'That is correct. I have my eye on a constituency. Meanwhile journalism is my game.'

'Writing about what in particular?'

'Anything that will bring the money in. I'll write about anything from gee-gees to Jesus, so long as it's well paid.'

'Yes, I have heard that you are a betting man,' Harris said. 'It's said that you would bet on a couple of flies crawling up the window-pane.'

'I would, too,' Bottomley averred, adding with a sly smile, 'if I knew that one of them was wearing a lead boot.'

At this I noticed the waiter smile. I was to be told later that both men had loud, resonant voices which made their conversations carry, a feature not unconnected with their short bodies, for it seems that a bass voice, along with a lusty sex drive, are common compensations for lack of height.

Harris was clearly warming to his new-found friend, especially as he was in need of the money being offered.

'I'm sure I can help you,' Harris said as they set to their food in earnest. He was a fast eater but not in the same field as Bottomley, who gulped his food as eagerly as he guzzled his champagne.

As they stood up to leave I saw that Bottomley was even an inch shorter than Harris, but then I noticed that the latter was wearing shoes with built-up heels — a further expression of the vanity of the man. For such a forceful figure, this seemed quite unnecessary. Why can't short men realize that their really vital statistic is that measurement from the neck up?

Harris and Bottomley left together at about 4 p.m., seemingly none the worse for the enormous amount of alcohol they had imbibed, and no doubt convinced that they were 'in business' as Harris was fond of putting it. During their long lunch Jules had pointed out to me a few other celebrities who were already in the room, explaining that each tended to have his own table where he would be joined by his regular friends – and woe betide the waiter who offered such a table to a stranger. Some were playing dominoes, but most were talking and a few were writing. The Domino Room was prepared to provide writing materials free, which I gather was a custom in French cafés frequented by writers. I have seen the great G. K. Chesterton writing one of his stories standing up in the Domino Room, Arnold Bennett scribbling down ideas in his fat, leather-bound notebook, and Ernest Dowson composing a poem on the back of an old letter, but throughout the many years that I was able to scribble there, I always brought my own lined notebooks, which in those delightful days cost only a penny.

In the first few hours I spent in the Domino Room – the most important of my life – I was able to convince myself, after my success in 'hearing' almost everything that Harris and Bottomley had said, that I could become a member of almost every coterie yet not one of them would know. I would be 'the fly on the wall'! It was an entrancing prospect, for that very afternoon, artists, some of whom were to become famous, were hawking their paintings round the tables either for sale or for criticism, budding playwrights were discussing their efforts with possible impresarios, and authors' manuscripts were being handed over to publishers, who used the Domino Room almost as an office. The Domino Room lived up to all my expectations and more. Of course there were occasions when the clientele was dull, but there were many more golden days when it was full of fascinating personalities providing an ever-moving panorama of the period. Relaxing in that hot hip-bath when the inspiration had come to me, and reading that article by Harris, were two of those moments – 'mutation moments' I call them – which can completely change a way of life and give it new purpose.

The 'Forum of London', as Crosland called the Café, was more educational than any university could ever have been. My seat of learning was to be the University of Life and the Café Royal, as Augustus John said, *was* life. Only Jules, the waiter at my table, who became a valued friend, knew what 'the man at table ten' was doing when I made notes in my book which was always open in front of me. He was so helpful to me, filling in gaps in conversations I could not overhear by listening to the gossip of his comrades, revealing what went on in the Restaurant, in the Grill Room and even the private rooms. I have lost count of the times when Jules whispered to me that some important, perhaps royal, figure was about to descend the

marble Grand Staircase, giving me time to stroll out to the entrance
hall where I could see them at really close quarters while pretending
to be browsing at the French bookstall. Dear Jules! I can see his
friendly face now alight with pleasure as he pretended to wipe my
table with his napkin while imparting some titbit of gossip.

When I stared at people I suppose they imagined I was looking
into space for inspiration, or more likely they regarded me as just
another eccentric whose main occupation was preoccupation. The
reader will see that if I must be judged eccentric then the Domino
Room was my natural home, so much so that when any little coterie
struck up the old Café Royal song – rendered to the tune of 'Green-
sleeves', which fortunately I knew before I went deaf – I could join in
with all sincerity:

> *Jove be with us while we sit*
> *On these crimson, soft settees,*
> *Drinking beer and liking it*
> *Most peculiarly at ease . . .*
> *That for life and this for love,*
> *'B' for bliss and 'P' for pain*
> *Not till midnight will we move —*
> *Waiter, fill 'em up again!*

As Oscar Wilde might have said, had he thought of it (or had he
heard someone else say it), 'Familiarity breeds contentment'.

While the Domino Room regulars were respecting my apparent
need for solitude, little did they know the extent to which their
minds, as well as their words, were open to me. I heard them on their
guard and in their unbuttoned moments. I did not only hear Oscar
Wilde talking about himself, I heard Whistler talking about Oscar
behind his back. I listened to Augustus John when he was buoyant
and when he was depressed; to Marie Lloyd when she was acting a
part and when she was her sad little self; to Frank Harris when he
was flush and when he was broke; to Virginia Woolf when she was
confident and when in dread of incipient insanity. I eavesdropped on
swindlers and pranksters plotting their next coup; on couples in love
and in hate; on the talented young, near-starving and desperate for
success, and on the old who had found scant satisfaction in it.

The reader may ask how one man could learn so much from so
many. Fortunately, I started young, so I had more than sixty years in
which to acquire my knowledge!

Looking back, it was an enormous advantage that I never actually met my Domino Room 'friends'. As they never knew me I never had to take sides with any of them, and so remained friendly with them all. This alone made me unique among that throng, since they were forever falling out, sometimes even resorting to fisticuffs, as I shall also relate. In fact in retrospect I could say, as Oscar might have done, 'There's nothing like keeping one's friends at a distance for retaining their fidelity.' Had they known what I was up to I am sure they would have judged me an excellent listener – the best in the world perhaps, for some of them, like Frank Harris, were so vain that they resented any intrusion into their monologue.

Nevertheless I occasionally did get my oar in, so much so that I began to believe in telepathy. The very question I was dying to ask was so often asked for me by somebody else that mentally I may indeed have been taking part in the conversations, or so it seemed. In any case, as often as not I got my answers. These I noted down when I could, but I was always assisted by an excellent memory for which I believe I must thank my mother, who, according to my father, '. . . never forgot a damn thing'. Nevertheless, to improve my capacity for my secret task I took lessons in Mr Gregg's new shorthand and became so proficient at this time-saver that I was able to make verbatim notes without taking my eyes off the moving lips of my subjects, disciplining myself to make my shorthand outlines without looking at my notebook. And of course I became an avid reader, for to understand their literary conversation I had to make myself conversant with some of the writers and philosophers whom they discussed, and to this end the *Saturday Review*, which Frank Harris edited, was a most useful source.

With encouragement from Jules, who had friends among the staff in the Restaurant on the first floor, I ventured there for an occasional lunch, which was not too extravagant provided one had not more than two courses and no wine. I could not afford to make a habit of eating there, even frugally, but Jules was able to tell me when an interesting group of my 'friends' was to lunch or dine there and he would arrange for me to have a convenient table on my own.

Each night, back in my modest lodgings when I had returned from the Domino Room, usually after 11 p.m. and often after midnight, I would convert my notes to longhand in my diaries, which were to become not only an account of the age in which I had the good fortune to have lived but the intimate story of my strange life. It was during those lonely yet delightful hours, when I often wrote so far into the night that I heard the horses trotting to Covent Garden market, that I first appreciated the truth of Oscar Wilde's dictum, 'All art requires solitude as its companion' – not that I would lay any claim to literary ability myself, mark you. Even when I finally got into bed I would spend some time meditating over the day's events, with a pencil and pad handy by my candlestick. Little happened in the Domino Room before mid-day, so I lost nothing by sleeping in next morning beyond the sacrifice of my breakfast egg. And I was able to observe my rule that one should never go to bed on the same day that one gets up.

In the later years, when the Domino Room took on a Bohemian air, I indulged myself privately in my room, though never in public, by dressing in Bohemian garb in the style of Augustus John with a large black hat and floppy black cravat. In my imaginary arguments with the characters in my work, whom I never addressed in real life, I supposed I resolved my need for conflict, but my purpose was to clarify my understanding of these remarkable people who were such strange mixtures of good and evil, vanity and humility, generosity and avarice.

Geographically, the Domino Room could not have suited me better. As I walked back to my lodgings that first day I realized I had entered a new world, and, since the candle of my life was then, I hoped, long, with the exuberance of youth I counted on many years in which to explore it. My usual route took me past the British Museum to Tottenham Court Road, then down Charing Cross Road to Shaftesbury Avenue and Piccadilly – all so very different from their appearance today with their clinical electric lights. It was cosier then, I think, with the gas lamps, the naphtha flares in the fogs, the jangling barrel organs, the clatter of horse-drawn, iron-tyred carriages and drays and the air smelling, not of petrol fumes, but sweetly – yes, I do remember it was sweetly – of horse manure! And on a frosty night what scent was ever so appetizing as that of hot potatoes gently roasting in the chimneyed, kerbside ovens? If Piccadilly was the hub of the universe, as it was in those great British days, then the Café Royal was to be the hub of St John Terrapin's.

2

THE BUTTERFLY AND THE LILY

James McNeill Whistler was the uncrowned king of the Domino Room when I first began to frequent it in 1886. He would then have been about fifty-two and was established as both a portrait and landscape painter; his very restrained pictures, especially those of the Thames, enjoyed a considerable vogue, though many of the critics, whom he despised, regarded his work as rubbish without meaning. A jaunty little man, with a swarthy complexion, hooked nose and longish black curly hair with a single white lock, which he greatly cherished, he was so convinced of his genius that on being asked by an American collector who had called at his Chelsea studio, 'How much for the lot?' he answered 'Five million.'

'What?' the collector exclaimed in amazement.

'My posthumous prices,' Whistler explained.

His vanity extended to his appearance, and I have seen him pause before entering the Domino Room to remove his flat-topped hat with its very wide band and adjust his hair, smooth his bushy eyebrows, his moustache and the little imperial beard he had cultivated as a cadet at the West Point military academy – he was an American – and re-position his monocle. Perhaps the ultimate expression of his vanity was his repeated expression, 'Men of genius stand so far apart that they are laws unto themselves.' Whether he really believed that I doubt, but regrettably others to whom he preached it, such as Oscar Wilde, not only believed it but put the precept into practice, with savage consequences.

He was gifted with a waspish wit and could not resist scoring off his friends, many of whom as a result became estranged. The weird poet Algernon Charles Swinburne, a bird-like creature with red hair who occasionally patronized the Café Royal, felt so strongly about this that he criticized Whistler for it in a poem, having previously championed his work in another poem, 'The Little White Girl'. When Wilde had been married, four years previously, Whistler had sent a telegram to the church saying, 'Fear I may not be able to reach you in time for the ceremony, but don't wait,' to which Oscar claimed he had replied, 'Neither shall we wait for the dear Queen. In this fine weather I asked her to remain at Osborne.' Such was the sadistic pleasure which Whistler secured from insulting his friends as well as his enemies that he published a book called *The Gentle Art of Making Enemies*!

As you may imagine, a conversation between Whistler and Wilde, who were close friends for a year or two, was entertaining in the extreme. Both were excellent raconteurs, though the painter was more long-winded than the writer, who had an outstanding facility not only for making a scintillating remark in the minimum number of words, but for producing the apposite anecdote and telling it with the simplicity and brevity of a biblical parable.

I remember one particular lunch in my early days in the Domino Room when the signs of the final fracture in their friendship appeared. The two artists — Wilde always referred to himself as an artist — had arrived by appointment for one of their regular lunches at which the older man always took command, whoever was the host. They could hardly have been more dissimilar in appearance, for Wilde was a huge, shambling man with a large head, heavy eyelids, thick lips and a fleshy jaw.

Whistler had discovered a cheap claret in the Café Royal's enormous cellars, Château des Mille Secousses (Castle of a Thousand Shocks) and found it such outstanding value that he would drink nothing else there, though he was making a great deal of money from his paintings. He and Oscar almost always ate chops with it; though Whistler ate much less than his companion, the food had to be perfect. Wilde's appetite for wine was also much greater because Whistler was one of those unfortunates (as I am myself) on whom a little alcohol has considerable effects.

Luckily for me they sat, as most people did, side by side on banquette seats, so provided they were facing my table, as they were, I could oversee everything. Hoping for some pleasant constructive talk from which, perhaps, some usable epigrams might emerge, Wilde opened by paying his friend a compliment.

'On one of my rare walks, Jimmy, I happened to see old Battersea Bridge in the moonlight. I must say it did look like that *Nocturne* of yours which led to your libel action against John Ruskin.'

Whether he did not relish reference to the libel action, in which he had been awarded a farthing damages and no costs, after the critic Ruskin had accused him of charging 200 guineas for 'flinging a pot of paint in the public's face', or could not resist a riposte, Whistler answered sarcastically, 'Yes, Nature's creeping up. I take it you agree with me, Oscar, that Nature usually has it wrong? Nature contains the elements, in colour and form, of all pictures as the keyboard of a piano contains the notes of all music. The artist is born to pick and choose as the musician selects his notes. To say to the painter that Nature is to be taken as she is, is to say to the player that he may just sit on the piano.'

'As you well know, Jimmy,' Wilde replied, lowering his loaded fork though not putting it down, 'that is entirely my view. Nature is a foolish place to look for inspiration, but a charming one to forget one ever had any. I deplore your choice of a musical analogy, though. Apart from being the most expensive of all noises, music has the unpardonable disadvantage of interfering with conversation. Musical people are absurdly unreasonable. They always want to be perfectly dumb at the very moment when one is longing to be absolutely deaf. I agree with Bernard Shaw that Wagner's music is the most satisfactory. It is so loud that one can talk the whole time without other people hearing what one says. Still, I concur in principle. Nature is almost always wrong. That is why it is so important for artists like us to put it right.'

Whistler was clearly irritated by his companion's description of himself as an artist, believing that the written word was not to be compared with the painter's brushstroke.

'I remain surprised, Oscar, that you know so little about art – real art, I mean,' he said in a voice which Jules told me was high-pitched and rather raucous. 'You seem to have no more sense of a picture than of the fit of a coat.'

This remark was guaranteed to nettle Wilde, who was as much a dandy as Whistler, regarding himself as being 'exquisitely over-dressed' in his frock-coat with its huge collar and check trousers, the bunch of Parma violets in his buttonhole and the scarab ring on his finger. It was a fact that Wilde's clothes did not fit his huge and overweight frame like the smart linen duck suits the little artist affected and which were tailored faultlessly. But the comment was uncalled for.

'The true author has every right to call himself an artist,' Wilde proclaimed, unconsciously – or perhaps consciously – laying his finger on his chest as though indicating himself. 'Indeed the poet is the supreme artist. A painter can place any daubs he likes on a canvas and announce that is how he sees things and how others should see them. The writer's words must at least make sense.'

I almost had to restrain myself from applauding the way Wilde had seized the entirely justifiable opportunity of siding with the critics who ridiculed Whistler's paintings as meaningless daubs, particularly as Whistler was one of those who could not bear criticism, though he was forever handing it out to others.

'Is it true, as rumour has it, that you are now charging *three* hundred guineas for two days' labour?' Oscar continued, deploying what I was to discover was his usual gambit of introducing a new subject to avoid repartee against what had gone before.

'More than that,' Whistler replied, screwing up his deeply lined face. 'Though as I said at the trial, I ask it not for two days' work but for the knowledge of a lifetime.'

At that point Wilde produced a poem which he had written on very thin paper, and handed it to the artist.

'That took me two days to write,' Wilde said, 'What would you think *that's* worth?'

Perking himself in his chair and inserting his monocle with a theatrical gesture, Whistler read it slowly, then, balancing the paper as though weighing it on his palm – he was eloquent with his hands – he remarked, 'I'd say it's worth its weight in gold.'

Hastily helping down a large mouthful of food with a swig of wine, Wilde forced a smile at this sally, which had been accompanied by the artist's peculiar nasal laugh with his head thrown back, said to be so fiendish that Sir Henry Irving copied it for use on the stage. But he never forgave Whistler.

Whistler was clearly in a particularly irritable mood that day, because when a lady at a nearby table sneezed, perhaps because of over-liberal use of the pepper mill, he turned sharply and commented, 'Spare me your microbes, thank you. I've enough of my own.'

Wilde would not have been so rude to a stranger, especially to a lady. He had no need to, for he possessed the extraordinary ability to insult people and the institutions they held dear without provoking their anger, though on rare occasions he risked being cruel rather than resist the opportunity for a *bon mot*. I remember one such when a rather moderate poet was complaining to Oscar about his lack of recognition and the failure of critics to review his books.

'There's a conspiracy of silence against me. What should I do?' he asked.

'Join it,' Oscar advised.

As regards his relationship with Whistler, it was the age-old story of a young man with talent overtaking an old one, and the inevitable resentment.

'Seen anything of Lillie lately?' Whistler asked with studied art-lessness, knowing that this lady was something of a bone of conten-tion between them. 'I hear she's telling everybody you are a terrible bore and that you use her friendship as a means of publicizing yourself.'

'Ah, it's only those we love who can betray us,' Oscar replied, with unconscious prophecy of the terrible events to come. 'Frankly though, Jimmy, the Lily herself is becoming a bore. She is like so many people, who pass out of one's life as soon as one has invented them.'

'*You* were not present, Oscar, when Lillie was "invented". *I* was.'

'You mean at the dinner where she met Millais?' Oscar said, winding his Egyptian cigarette around his head, a common habit of his in conversation, as I soon found out.

'Met me — and *then* Millais, among others. I know you have claimed to be the first to call her the Jersey Lily, but that was Millais, and you know it.'

'Her name is of no importance, Jimmy. It was her character I moulded. It was I who educated her, gave her so much of the knowledge on which she now dines out with princes. But only fools expect gratitude. It is a tedious sentiment, anyway.'

'Lillie's social success is not due to education by you or anyone else,' Whistler answered sharply. 'She is the centre of attraction because she isn't English.'

'Meaning that the Channel Islanders are really French?'

'Exactly! So she looks and acts like a real woman, a sensuous woman who could easily be undressed without having to grapple with a portcullis of whalebone. The ordinary Englishwoman succeeds, as no other could, only in obliging men to forget her sex.'

'One is certainly aware of the Lily's,' Oscar agreed with a hint of a sigh.

'You betcha,' Whistler replied, using one of the Americanisms which Wilde deplored to emphasize his suggestion of the utmost intimacy with Mrs Langtry. 'That is why we artists were immediately interested in her, at the dinner to which you were not asked,' Whistler continued, 'when she came in wearing a clinging black dress and her

hair looking as though it could be fondled without causing a catastrophe. The rest of the women there were all hairpins and corsets.'

'You imply that there is a touch of the vulgar in Lillie?' asked
Oscar, implying, perhaps, that such a trait would naturally appeal to
an American.

'Maybe, Oscar. Maybe. But it is a touch of vulgarity that makes
the whole world kin.'

'Not the whole world, Jimmy. So far as I am concerned vulgarity is
the conduct of others. But Lillie certainly has been copied. Coiffure,
shoes, little black dress and all. . . .'

'Yes. Most women are unaware of the strong sexual attraction of
black – a colour, or lack of it, of which I am very fond. Black is the
particular paradise of fair women. I have given some thought as to
why. The attraction must lie in the ultimate contrast of black with
the alabaster white of a good female body.'

Oscar was clearly irritated, as he fiddled with his scarab ring.
Aware that Whistler was drawing attention to his rumoured sexual
success with Lillie, who was later to state that she had found the
young Wilde's colourless, podgy face with its unhealthy, sallow look
and dirty fingernails, physically repulsive – he picked up his lavender
gloves and cane as an intimation that he wished to leave.

'I'll tell you one thing, Oscar, about the likes of Lillie,' Whistler
said, studying the bill. 'Any man who made merry with the lower
half of my wife could damned well have the half that eats.'

He laughed to himself as he signed the bill in his usual manner, a
monogram of his initials in the design of a butterfly, with which he
signed his pictures and also had worked on his handkerchiefs.
Though Oscar always appeared distressed by any coarse remark, the
two seemed to part on a friendly note, though from that point they
showed their mutual enmity openly.

'What has Oscar in common with art,' Whistler asked, 'except
that he dines at our tables and picks from our platters the plums for
the pudding he peddles in the provinces?'

After that they ceased to meet but continued to attack each other in
conversation, much of which I overheard, such as Oscar's remark,
'Small men have no dignity. Whistler is always pretending he was
born in St Petersburg. I can tell you he was born in a no more
romantic place than a one-horse town in Massachusetts.' The two
would now sit as far away from each other as possible, if they
happened to be in the Domino Room together, and though Whistler
had taken a studio across the road in Regent Street he soon ceased to

patronize the Café Royal, as though unable to bear the sight of Oscar on his old throne there.

3

VISITATIONS OF VIOLENCE

Of all the habitués who were or became famous, one of the most rivetting for me was an artist who had been a pupil of Whistler – Walter Sickert. He was a fascinating man of about twenty-eight when I first saw him: handsome, tall and a brilliant talker who could hold his audience spellbound, partly, perhaps, because he had undergone professional training as an actor with no less a tutor than Henry Irving, another occasional visitor to the Domino Room.

There was a particular reason why I enjoyed hanging on his every word over the many years I knew him – he was obsessed with unsolved murders and especially with the most intriguing murder of all time, that of the man known throughout Britain and, indeed, the world, as Jack the Ripper. Such was Sickert's knowledge of the case and his need to talk about it that I have always suspected that he knew the killer's true identity, and I believed that one day I might hear him reveal it in some confidence or other. But first I must set the scene. . . .

Towards the close of my vintage summer of 1888, on 31 August, occurred the first of a series of macabre events which were to plunge all London into fear. The newspapers of the following day revealed that the freshly killed body of a woman in a most horrific state of mutilation had been discovered in Bucks Row, a sordid little thoroughfare off Whitchapel. *The Star* reported that the victim, a middle-aged vagrant called Mary Nichols, had first been killed with a razor or sharp knife, which had almost severed her head, and the body had then been ripped upwards twice from the groin to expose all the internal organs.

Neither I nor anybody else in the Domino Room paid much attention to the event, for brutal murders were common enough in the East End, which was the haunt of all manner of criminals, including rough seamen and other foreigners. But eight days later the same murderer killed again, leaving his terrible signature on the body of Annie Chapman, another woman so destitute that she could exist only by selling herself to men for a few coppers. Her savaged remains were found in a backyard off Commercial Street, only a few hundred yards from the scene of the previous murder. Examination of both bodies revealed that the man must be a fiend of ferocity unprecedented in modern times because, in addition to the mutilations, he grovelled about in the steaming entrails in search of the womb and other parts.

Ever quick to seize on such a sensation, the newspapers soon had an unforgettable name for the unknown killer, 'Jack the Ripper'. As I remember it, the murderer gave himself this name by signing it on a letter to a news agency, which passed it to the police who reproduced it on a poster in the hope that somebody might recognize the handwriting. Whatever its origin, 'Jack the Ripper' became a token of terror for all London women, dissolute or respectable, who might have occasion to go out at night.

Being not far from Scotland Yard, which was at the bottom of Whitehall, the Domino Room was occasionally patronized by senior detectives. The managers of such establishments were always keen to remain on good terms with the police since brawls and other minor breaches of the peace might otherwise attract their attention, and over the years I saw many off-duty senior officers of the Criminal Investigation Department and other policemen enjoying themselves in the Domino Room, no doubt at the management's expense. Soon after the second Ripper murder the Commissioner of the Metropolitan Police himself, Colonel Charles Warren, who was to be knighted, came in for a quick lunch with a colleague who, I realized later from his picture in the newspapers, was Inspector Abberline, the head of the big team of detectives assigned to the case. The pictures of both men were often in the newspapers, and over the years I was to see Warren arriving and leaving for various functions in the Freemasons' Temples housed in the Café Royal. He was very unpopular among the radicals in the Domino Room because they held him responsible for 'Bloody Sunday' the previous year: about a hundred thousand unemployed had converged on Trafalgar Square for a protest meeting, to find themselves confronted not only by police but by soldiers called in by Warren. In the ensuing squabble one man had been killed and about 150 injured.

It transpired from the conversation that the two police officers had come straight from a meeting at Scotland Yard and would be returning there for further discussion. The murders were causing even greater public concern than they merited because at least three previous killings were being attributed to the Ripper, though the bodies of those victims had not been ripped open and could have been the work of other violent men. The Home Secretary of the day, a certain Mr Henry Matthews, was being held publicly responsible for the failure of the police to catch the Ripper, and for the spate of false arrests of suspects who were being pulled off the streets on the flimsiest pretexts. I recall, for instance, how after some newspaper suggested that the way parts of the body were removed implied some surgical knowledge on the part of the Ripper, anybody seen carrying a black bag was subject to harassment. Anyone known to the police to have sexual habits involving violence was also suspect, and this net even enmeshed an occasional visitor to the Café Royal, the poet Algernon Swinburne, who was addicted to flagellation by women. Fortunately for him he was by that time safely in the custody of the writer Theodore Watts-Dunton, who for his own good kept him almost incarcerated in a house in Putney.

It soon became clear from the tenor of the conversation between Warren and Abberline that the Home Secretary, described by the *Daily Telegraph* that very day as 'helpless, heedless and useless', was venting his anger on them.

'This business is getting hopelessly out of hand,' Warren said between mouthfuls of omelette, always his favourite lunch. 'It's these blasted mutilations that have incensed the public. They are so unnecessary.'

'I agree, sir. What is the point of them?'

'That, Inspector, I am not permitted to explain. We'll just have to go on living with these horrors, though not for long, I hope.'

Abberline shrugged resignedly. 'It's just that, having seen the state of these bodies, it makes me wonder what they'll do next.'

They! Did Abberline know that the Ripper was not a lone killer, but a gang? If so, what sort of gang? Self-righteous people fanatically opposed to prostitution? Though the phrase was hardly applicable to me, suddenly I was 'all ears'.

'Whatever *they* do, I know what *we're* going to do,' Warren said emphatically. 'We shall have to go through the motions of using bloodhounds.'

Abberline looked doubtful as Warren, a dapper figure with his smart suit and monocle, smoothed his military-style moustache.

'I'm afraid it will be obvious that bloodhounds could do no good in Whitechapel, sir. It's full of alleys already stinking to high heaven with stable yards, slaughterhouses and earth closets.'

'I have been to the scene of the murders,' Warren reminded him loftily. 'At least the public will see that we are trying everything. Another thing we can be seen to be doing is eliminating all the doctors in the area from our inquiries. Particularly left-handed doctors,' he added with a sage wag of his finger. 'We need to keep that theory going in the newspapers.'

Abberline nodded, and I wondered why the police would want the public to believe that the Ripper was left-handed simply because his victims' throats had been slashed from left to right. Surely that would be the way a *right-handed* man would do it if he grabbed a woman from behind?

'We've covered all the doctors in the immediate vicinity,' Abberline said. 'Apart from that Russian lunatic Michael Ostrog, who doesn't seem to be in the area, I see no suspect.'

'Well, track down Ostrog if you can, but don't arrest him. Just keep tabs on him until these killings are finished. Then he could be a godsend. And don't relax your watch on Cleveland Street. That woman could still turn up there.'

It sounded as though both Warren and Abberline *knew* that the Ripper would strike again. And why were they looking for a woman in Cleveland Street? The only Cleveland Street I knew had nothing to do with Whitechapel: it was in 'Fitzrovia', the artists' quarter round Fitzroy Square, off Tottenham Court Road.

The mystery was compounded when, while waiting for his bill, Warren remarked with a heavy sigh, 'All hell is going to be let loose when the next body is found.'

When the next body is found? Not *if*.

All hell *was* let loose on the night of Saturday 1 October when the Ripper killed *two* prostitutes. The Sunday newspapers told us that he had not mutilated his first victim, apparently because he had been disturbed, but had then directed his thwarted ferocity on the second woman, whose body was found not far away in an appalling state of dismemberment. Never in my recollection had the newsboys had such bloodcurdling contents to exploit as they shouted, 'More 'orrible murders in Whitechapel . . . two disembowelled women found . . . mutilation murders special . . .' Once again, in spite of the bloodbath, the Ripper had vanished on a clear, early autumn night.

At lunchtime that day Walter Sickert was in the Domino Room wearing one of the rigouts which he said he favoured so that he could not possibly be confused with the Decadents, led by Oscar Wilde. It was a Norfolk jacket and breeches topped by a long tweed coat and a deerstalker cap. As he took his seat he was a perfect match for the description of a young man, alleged by the newspapers to have been seen leaving the scene of one of the murders! I also knew from his conversations that he regularly haunted the Whitechapel area, making sketches for his paintings. The Domino Room was convenient for Sickert because his studio happened to be in Cleveland Street. So here was a further connection with the Ripper inquiries. Coincidences, of course — surely his background ruled out any connection with the crime. I had heard him tell how his father and grandfather had been court artists in Denmark and how, as a result, he had met Princess Alexandra since she had come to live in England.

That day Sickert was joined by George Moore, then a little-known Irish writer with a chubby face, pink cheeks and a receding chin. Immediately he tried to interest Moore in the Ripper case but with no success, even when he hinted that if all the facts were known they could be made into the novel of the century.

'You might find royalty involved,' Sickert said, darkly.

'Royalty has been overdone,' Moore replied. 'I prefer to write about the predicament of ordinary people.' This, of course, he did to great effect a few years later in his novel *Esther Waters*, about a servant girl.

I could have hit Moore on the head for his lack of interest. With a little more encouragement Sickert might have said far more. What had he meant by royalty? There was already a crazy rumour that the Ripper was Prince Eddy, the Duke of Clarence, the elder and rather backward son of the Prince of Wales and Princess Alexandra who was know to the public, affectionately I believe, as 'Collar and Cuffs' because of his habit of wearing very deep, starched collars to hide his over-long neck, matched with shirt cuffs protruding several inches from his jacket sleeves. Eddy was a wild young man, but the suggestion that this future heir to the throne of England could be a homicidal maniac was preposterous. The rumour seemed to be based on nothing more than a much reproduced photograph showing the Prince wearing a deerstalker!

Following the double murder the public outcry became so

deafening that there were demands for the resignation of the Home Secretary and the appointment of someone who would get something done. These views were reiterated through the Domino Room by intellectuals who would normally have held themselves aloof from such muck-raking. There were also those customers with their own theories about the murders, the most interesting being that of the young Scottish author, Arthur Conan Doyle, later to become immortal as the inventor of the greatest detective of all time, Mr Sherlock Holmes. Conan Doyle, who was soon to use the Café Royal in a Holmes novel, *The Illustrious Client*, was already a frequent visitor to the Domino Room and had made a considerable name for himself with novels such as *A Study in Scarlet*. His theory, which was taken seriously, was that the Ripper disguised himself as a woman, so that he could not only approach his victims but escape without arousing suspicion.

Another Domino Room theory suggested that the Ripper must be a Freemason who was killing his victims according to Masonic ritual. This was supposed to be why each victim's throat was cut from left to right and the entrails were slung over the shoulder. Apparently, according to Masonic legend, three apprentices who killed a Master Mason building Solomon's Temple were executed in this manner. I did not pay much attention to this theory because I knew that the man propounding it was an Irish Catholic who detested Freemasonry.

George Bernard Shaw, another occasional customer, made use of the murders in a characteristic way – to draw attention to the dreadful social conditions in the East End where, it was alleged, eighty thousand women were driven to live by prostitution. (This figure, announced by some bishop or other, caused a tremendous outcry but did not surprise me because the whole of London was infested with such women, even children being available in the side-streets off Haymarket.)

Meanwhile Commissioner Warren's experiments with blood-hounds had degenerated to farce. After specially selected dogs had been quickly trained, with the fullest publicity, they were let loose for a trial run on Tooting Common. Instead of following the trail which had been laid, the bloodhounds ran off and police everywhere were looking for them instead of the Ripper!

Shortly after the double murder Inspector Abberline came in with a stranger who turned out to be another policeman transferred to assist him with the Ripper case. By that time every murder of any woman in London was being attributed to the Ripper, and the strain was showing on Abberline's face.

'What an extraordinary room,' the stranger remarked as Abberline motioned him to the table he had booked for a quick 'working lunch'.

'Yes. But it has advantages,' Abberline replied. 'We don't get a bill. I thought I would bring you here privately to mark your card. The fewer who know in the office the better. Nobody can overhear us at this table, but watch it while the waiter's about.'

I could scarcely resist a smile at this remark as I briefly transferred my gaze to another part of the room.

'I can't tell you too much, but you already know that there's politics behind all this?' Abberline continued.

'Vaguely. But why bring me in at this stage? I thought that four was the finish.'

'It should have been, but the bloody fools got the wrong woman. The one that matters most, Mistress Kelly, is still alive. They thought the last one was Kelly but she just happened to be living with a man called Kelly. But what would you expect with amateurs?'

'So the case shouldn't last much longer?'

'I hope not, but with all this outcry we have to go through the motions – carry on hauling in the doctors and all that stuff. As a matter of fact I called you in because the Queen has suddenly intervened.'

'The Queen!'

'Yes. She's cottoned on to the theory that Jack the Ripper is a slaughterman and a foreigner, so she wants us to check out on all the cattleboats.'

'So though it's a waste of time, we'll have to be seen to be doing it?'

'For a while,' Abberline replied.

'Surely the Queen can't know the full truth,' his companion observed. 'Does she know about the P.A.V. connection?'

Abberline looked startled. 'How did you hear about P.A.V.?'

'On the Yard bush telegraph.'

Abberline shook his head despairingly. 'Well, for God's sake don't mention it to anybody else. His name must be kept right out of it. And any mention of Cleveland Street or Annie Crook. Warren and the Home Secretary are in enough trouble.'

'What's Warren like to work with? At close quarters, I mean.'

'He's all right, but it's of no consequence now. He's going to resign.'

'Resign! The Commissioner! But why?'

'He just can't take any more of this revolting caper, and I don't blame him. The Assistant Commissioner is taking over – anything for promotion.'

It was all most intriguing information. There was Cleveland Street again! Who was the woman Kelly? How did they know that someone had been murdered in mistake for her? Who was Annie Crook? What was the extent of Queen Victoria's involvement? And who or what was P.A.V.?

For the rest of the day and in bed that night I racked my brains for an answer to the last riddle, with no success. Then next morning, without conscious thought, the meaning came to me. Prince Albert Victor! That was the official title of Prince Eddy, the Duke of Clarence. So Collar and Cuffs *was* mixed up in it! What had I got my nose into! Or rather my eyes?

Sure enough Warren resigned, and on that very day, 8 November, Jack the Ripper perpetrated his most wanton orgy. When I saw the billboard headlines and heard the newsmen calling I could not part with my halfpenny quickly enough to see the victim's name. There it was – Mary Kelly! Her body had been so ripped and cut to pieces that it had to be taken to the mortuary in parcels. So the murders *had* been arranged. The police *had* somehow known about them in advance. And, somewhere, Prince Eddy *had* been involved. But who had committed the dreadful mutilations, and why? The obvious explanation that they were to prevent identification of the body could hardly be correct, for Mary Kelly was not killed on the street but in her hovel of a home!

Such was the public revulsion at the Ripper's deeds and the failure of the police to catch him that thousands of people thronged to the funeral of poor Mary Kelly, for whom nobody had cared much in life. A few days later a drawing of 13 Miller's Court, the dreadful slum dwelling where the murder had been committed, appeared in the *Penny Illustrated Paper*, which I read in the Café. It showed a poorly dressed young woman letting in a top-hatted man, obviously well-to-do and carrying a black bag. Because of my secret knowledge I could not resist going down to the East End to see the murder room. I was not alone when I entered that dreadful alley off Dorset Street: there were a dozen equally curious people trying to peer through the broken window into the squalid little room where Mary Kelly had taken the Ripper and had met her end. Looking round at their questing faces I felt that some of them might be wondering whether I was the wanted man, who had been unable to resist the compulsion to return to the scene of his ghastly crime.

I wandered around the area to some of the other places where the Ripper had struck. It became obvious that he, or they, must have had a house or rooms nearby into which to sneak to wash and dispose of clothes, unless the departure from the scene had been facilitated by the police and accomplished, perhaps, in a cab.

The memory of that dreadful area, the like of which I had never seen before, remains vivid to this day, as does any place which one explores with a purpose rather than merely for sight-seeing. As I walked westwards from the Whitechapel Road I felt confident, from my inside knowledge, that the Ripper would not strike again. And if he did not it would be proof that some appalling mission with official backing had been completed.

My hunch was justified. After some months without a recurrence the police let it be known, through the newspapers and rumour sources, that their chief suspect had committed suicide. They refused to name him because of the effect it would have on his innocent relatives. One rumour had it that it was an insane Russian doctor, whom I assumed to be the man Ostrog mentioned by Inspector Abberline, but Walter Sickert circulated a different story in which he gave the Ripper a name like Drewitt, which I did not hear him spell. This Drewitt was supposed to have drowned himself in the Thames less than a month after the murder of Mary Kelly.

I also overheard policemen putting this Drewitt tale about, but if it were true why did Sickert go on talking about the Ripper mystery year after year, always with the emphasis on the murder of Mary Kelly? To me it seemed to be a cover story for the truth which I knew to be much more complicated, and a false explanation of why the police had abruptly ended their inquiries into the killings.

My suspicions were intensified when the police raided a male brothel where a relay of GPO telegraph boys offered their services. Though the authorities tried to hush up the scandal it soon became known that several prominent men had been among the haul of regular patrons. They included Lord Arthur Somerset, Lord Euston and, most important of all – Prince Eddy. Further, the brothel was situated in Cleveland Street, near Sickert's studio, so once again there was a connection between Prince Eddy, Cleveland Street, Sickert and sex.

By 'coincidence' the policeman in charge of this case was my old friend Inspector Abberline and, once again, the main villains of the piece were allowed to escape prosecution. Prince Eddy was sent on a naval cruise to get him out of the way, while others moved to the Continent for a few months. Yet another cover-up to protect top people!

Clearly, Prince Eddy enjoyed the pleasures afforded by young boys, but if the rumours about him had any foundation he was interested in women too. I heard more than one artist allege that he had an illegitimate daughter by one of Walter Sickert's models. Jacob Epstein even called the model Annie Crook – the very name which had been mentioned by Abberline in connection with the Ripper murders. So Sickert must have been connected with them, along with Prince Eddy.

I have spent many hours trying to solve this intriguing riddle, believing that I was on the brink of the solution, but got no further than the conviction that the murders had been politically inspired in connection with some event in Prince Eddy's private life which had to be concealed. As for the horrific mutilations, they could have been a cold-blooded part of the cover-up – to throw the blame on some unknown madman. In that case, of course, the letter alleged to have been sent by a man calling himself Jack the Ripper may have been fabricated by the police.

If Collar and Cuffs was privy to the truth he died with the secret. Homosexual or not, he became engaged to the beautiful Princess May of Teck who was half-English, being the daughter of Lady Mary Cambridge by the German Prince of Teck. But two weeks before the proposed wedding, in February 1892, Eddy caught pneumonia and died, aged only twenty-eight. By then it was rumoured that he had other complaints acquired from his habits, which seem to have been bisexual, and though appearances can be misleading he certainly looked dissipated. The Princess, who eventually married Eddy's younger brother George instead and later became Queen Mary, may have had a very lucky escape.

It was just as well for Bertie, the Prince of Wales, that his son's possible connection with the Ripper was never publicly substantiated for, as I will relate, he was soon to be in enough serious trouble himself.

I recall hearing only one further mention of Prince Eddy in the Domino Room, some ten years later. Aleister Crowley had somehow acquired a few incriminating letters from the dead Prince to a boy who had lived in Cleveland Street, and I heard him discussing the prospects for using them to raise money from those who might want them suppressed.

I continued to hang on Sickert's words for any mention of Annie Crook, but without success. Like the rest of the Ripper saga, the truth was locked away in the minds of a few who are already dead or soon will be.

Editor's Note

Mr Terrapin's bewilderment seems to have been recently resolved by the exhaustive researches of Mr Stephen Knight, a resourceful journalist who secured first access to the secret files on the Ripper case held both at Scotland Yard and at the Home Office. His well-documented book, *Jack the Ripper: The Final Solution*, published by Granada in 1977, claims that, through friendship with Walter Sickert, Prince Eddy fell in love with a young model called Annie Crook, who lived in Cleveland Street. They had a daughter and went through a form of marriage. Mr Knight alleges that when this became known to Queen Victoria's Prime Minister, Lord Salisbury, in 1888, drastic steps were taken to end the relationship because, though the marriage was illegal, Annie was a Catholic and this could have exacerbated the anti-Royalist feeling which might have intensified the substantial threat of revolution. Eddy was sent away and Annie was certified insane and kept in asylums for the rest of her life.

A girl called Mary Kelly, employed by Eddy as a nanny for his infant daughter, escaped to Whitechapel, where the search for her was soon suspended. Unfortunately she turned to prostitution to survive and fell in with three seasoned whores who, on hearing her story, realized the possibilities of royal blackmail. When this became known the authorities, without involving the Queen, decided to silence all four, who were killed by two or three men acting with police protection. The ringleader, according to Mr Knight, was Sir William Gull, the Queen's physician. A fifth prostitute was killed in error.

Mr Knight adduces convincing evidence that the mutilations were part of some Masonic ritual required by those who had agreed to carry out the assassinations, but Mr Terrapin may well have been right in assuming that they were also a deliberate ploy to strengthen the public belief that the murders had been committed by a maniac.

The child, Alice, survived and eventually became Sickert's mistress, bearing him a son who is alive at the time of writing and has been interviewed by Mr Knight.

It would seem, then, that rumours that Prince Eddy was actually involved in the murders were untrue but, unwittingly, he was the cause of them.

4

PECCADILLOES OF A PRINCE

It used to be said that if you stood long enough in Piccadilly Circus you would see everyone that mattered in the world. By simply waiting inside the entrance to the Café Royal you could have achieved that objective in a fraction of the time. In that way I eventually caught many close glimpses of the Prince of Wales and saw his physical condition gradually decline, no doubt through the kind of life he led, with his inveterate late-night gambling, drinking, smoking — he always smelled of cigars — and excessive womanizing. I was also continually surprised by the guttural tone of Bertie's voice, especially in the pronunciation of his r's, which stemmed, so I was told, from his parents' habit of speaking in German.

In the early 1890s if there was anyone who could have claimed to be the person in the popular music-hall song which ended, 'I'm the bosom friend of Albert, Prince of Wales', it was a Portuguese diplomat called the Marquis de Soveral, more popularly — and affectionately — known in the Café Royal as 'The Blue Monkey', because of his heavy five o'clock shadow which made his face look permanently blue. The chefs were unanimous in agreeing that he was a great epicure who really knew about food, and they accepted his strictures if a meal was not up to his exacting standards. His comment, however, was usually high praise for the food, wines and manner of presentation, so he often brought with him the Prince, who had appointed him his honorary adviser on gastronomy, doing Britain a service by setting a fashion for more refined and more elegant meals in the great houses as well as in restaurants.

I therefore saw Bertie leave the Café Royal on many occasions with the Blue Monkey, whose taste in clothes was equally elegant — a black frock-coat, shiny topper, gloves, cane, spats, monocle, the whole set off by a white gardenia and a black 'Kaiser Bill' moustache, heavy eyebrows and the tiniest of black beards in the middle of his chin.

I mention the Blue Monkey, who was later to become the Prime Minister of Portugal, because it was through him that I eventually received my first close-up of Lillie Langtry after he had brought her to lunch in the Restaurant in 1892. I have to say that I was rather disappointed, even though she was thirty-nine by that time, and concluded that her beauty had been somewhat exaggerated, as it was with so many beauties of the stage, and later of the screen, who appeared in the Café Royal. She had a flawless complexion, with gold hair shading to auburn and nice violet-grey eyes, and she walked well, but her nose was not quite straight at the tip and her chin, with its hint of a dimple, was rather firm. She certainly looked sensuous – meaning, I suppose, that she gave the clear impression of being a full-blooded woman who would enjoy sex. That she did so there was no doubt in my mind nor in the public's in general. At the time she was even having a love affair with the Blue Monkey, for Bertie did not mind if his friends sampled his women as long as he could return the compliment. As became apparent, much later, her illegitimate daughter had been sired not by the Prince but by Louis Battenberg, a distant cousin of Bertie's who later changed his name to Mountbatten, and she was apparently conceived in the cabin of a warship anchored off Cowes!

Lillie had love affairs – possibly in her case lust affairs would be more accurate – with many men, usually rich or with titles.

It was from the lips of Margot Tennant, of whom more anon, that I heard a first-hand account of the scandalous public fight between Lord Lonsdale and Sir George Chetwynd for Lillie's favours. A couple of years or so before I began to frequent the Café Royal, Margot had been riding in Rotten Row in Hyde Park and happened to be near the Achilles statue when she saw two men, who were both horse-mad and hot-tempered, insulting each other while still mounted.

'Why the hell are you hanging about here, Lonsdale?' Chetwynd asked.

'I have an appointment with Mrs Langtry.'

'So have I, the sly bitch,' Chetwynd said, with some justification for it later transpired that Lillie had mischievously set the two men against each other and deliberately organized the confrontation.

'Don't you speak like that about my Lillie,' Lonsdale shouted in a voice that the gathering crowd could hear.

'*Your* Lillie!' Chetwynd bawled. 'Take that!' He slashed at Lonsdale with his crop and knocked his hat off.

'What the bloody hell's got into you?' Lonsdale cried angrily.

'Don't meddle with my Lillie,' Chetwynd warned, and struck him across the shoulders with his whip.

Lonsdale, who was in his late twenties, struck back with his own whip at his assailant, who was a few years older but more heavily built. Soon the two men were in joust, while the crowd began to cheer them on. The horses became so frightened and unruly that the adversaries were forced to dismount and fight with their fists, before falling to the sand, wrestling and thumping each other mercilessly.

Two men whom Margot recognized as the Duke of Portland and Sir William Cumming went in to separate the great lovers, who by this time were both bleeding from the nose and had made a ghastly exhibition of themselves. As mounted policemen dispersed the crowds, who should she see there, heavily veiled and not dressed for riding, but Mrs Langtry herself, no doubt delighted with the whole affair!

Though I greatly regretted not having witnessed this encounter, I could visualize the scene vividly because, like so many other Londoners in those days, I often went to watch the parade of riders in the park, both those who were mounted and those in their carriages. By choosing the time correctly it was possible to see Bertie, on his horse with its distinguishing red noseband, Princess Alexandra in her deep red, open carriage drawn by two bays with coachmen and footmen up in plush breeches, and the rest of High Society. It is difficult for people now to imagine the care that went into the design and turnout of the carriages. They were so much more wonderful to look upon, with their liveried servants, than any motor car, and the horses themselves were of such high quality and so magnificently groomed. 'Spanking tits,' they were called when they were of that quality; the phrase produced no snigger in those days, when 'tit' was a common slang name for a horse.

Margot, who clearly did not approve of Lillie, had an explanation for the fight which was probably correct. 'I can only assume that Lillie organized the fight for the publicity, which she certainly got. The newspapers carried a full description of it, naming her as the romantic cause, and I am sure it was no coincidence that she happened to be acting in a play at the Prince of Wales Theatre; an unfortunate name, perhaps, in view of her all too well-known association with the Prince of Wales to whom she did so much harm. I had been to see the play and did not think that Mrs Langtry was very good. In fact I thought she was very hammy. I have seen far better acting in the literary charades we play at our weekend parties.'

Margot was never one to mince her words but whether Lillie was a good actress or not she always managed to keep her name in the forefront of the public mind, which seems to be one of the ingredients essential to stage success.

Perhaps it is not surprising that Lillie should be lusty, for according to Sir John Millais, the great painter who had connections with Jersey and occasionally patronized the Domino Room with his fellow artist Will Rothenstein, Lillie's father, the Dean of Jersey, sired so many bastards on that island that it was a public scandal there. Indeed he was later removed for these offences by the ecclesiastical authorities, being transferred to work in London's slums as a penance.

Lillie was nothing more than a high-class prostitute who, I suppose, in earlier times would have been dignified by the euphemism 'courtesan'. She slept with men for money or for access to High Society which brought the equivalent of money, if not money itself, as in her relationship with Bertie, who had set her up in a fine house near Bournemouth, unbeknown to her husband, Edward Langtry.

Before she became a successful actress, as she eventually did, the only asset she had was her body and she set about making it into a business in every way she could. She sold the monopoly on her photographs. She shocked her society friends by selling her name to Pears' Soap, which issued advertisements with her signature claiming, 'For the hands and complexion I prefer it to any other.' And, as I have already said, perhaps too bluntly, though I can see no point in hiding it, she sold her body carnally. Of course, she was by no means alone in this. I once heard the earthy Frank Harris say that another 'professional beauty' was contemplating a biography to be entitled *My Life under Five Sovereigns*.

I cannot leave the subject of Lillie at this juncture – I will have more to say about her later – without dealing with the occasion when she is alleged to have dropped ice or ice cream down the back of the Prince of Wales's neck. I have heard Captain Nicols-Pigache, then the owner of the Café Royal, assure customers that it did occur and happened on the first-floor landing of the Café Royal. Lillie herself denied it in her memoirs and said the legend arose out of such an event at the Folly Theatre, but the impulsive lady concerned was Kitty Munro. I have to say that I could never find a single witness to the event among the Café Royal staff, and Lillie was far too clever to have risked her friendship with the socially powerful Prince. Further, Pigache was totally incorrect in his claim that after the event the Prince terminated his friendship with Lillie. They remained close friends, if no longer lovers, though I suspect that occasionally happened as well.

For all his faults, Bertie was a kind man who liked to remain on affectionate terms with his former mistresses. I say 'former' as regards Lillie because in 1889 Bertie had begun a long and passionate affair with a woman who, although from the top ranks of Society, was every bit as abandoned as Lillie. Her name was Lady Frances Brooke, the wife of Lord Brooke, heir to the earldom of Warwick, but from childhood she had always been known as Daisy.

I had seen her only once in the Domino Room in the company of Margot Tennant, as I shall relate later. Daisy was one of those peaches-and-cream beauties with light brown hair, dark blue eyes and, in those days, such an expression that one would think that butter would not melt in her mouth. She was proud of her descent from Nell Gwynne, and within a few years of her marriage she began to behave like that famous courtesan and was to be involved in one scandal after another for the rest of her long life.

Her first affair became the talk of the Domino Room because it involved poor Bertie long before he himself had laid hands on the lady. It was a liaison with a fiery public figure called Lord Charles Beresford, a naval officer known to be a close friend of the Prince of Wales and with an enviable reputation as a ladies' man.

I frequently saw Beresford because he was a regular customer in the Restaurant, where the waiters liked him because he made them laugh with his great fund of dirty stories, which they then brought down to the Domino Room. Other customers were not so amused because Beresford was going deaf, and as his voice became proportionately louder some of the ladies were embarrassed. One husband demanded an apology when Beresford rounded off some joke, about a girl who had been drinking gin in the hope of aborting an unfortunate pregnancy, with her doctor's remark, 'You might just as well rub your belly with vanishing cream.' But most were not prepared to tackle this peppery character, especially when he was soaked in brandy, which was usually the case. (I had some sympathy for his lordship because it is difficult for a deaf person to gauge the volume of his voice. In my case it is impossible, my appreciation of what my voice sounds like being totally restricted to my mind's ear.)

I also saw Daisy's husband, Lord Brooke, from time to time when he dined in the restaurant with the Blue Monkey, who seemed to know everybody. Brooke was a fine-looking man, dark, with a firm, resolute chin and strong moustache with the ends fashionably waxed with pomade. It may therefore be asked why this man, who would soon be the Earl of Warwick, a title of historic distinction, put up with his wife's infidelities. The answer is that in the eighties and nineties in High Society it was an accepted practice that wives and husbands should have extra-marital lovers. A girl had to be chaste, or appear to be, before her marriage, but afterwards it was something of a free-for-all with only one serious penalty – there must be no scandal so serious that it could end in divorce. For the aggrieved spouse as well, divorce meant social death, and every sacrifice was made to avoid it.

Like Edward Langtry, Lord Brooke succeeded in avoiding an appearance in the divorce court, and in judging them as spineless cuckolds one must not abstract them from their time. In those circles it seemed that a man was judged to be a cuckold only if he did not know about his wife's affairs. If he knew about them, and condoned them because it suited him or to avoid a family scandal, he lost no respect.

Lord Brooke was no fool and he must have known what was going on because he and Daisy and the Beresfords were often asked to the same weekend house parties, where what might be called 'musical beds' rather than musical chairs seemed to be part of the entertainment. From what I heard, Daisy's affairs suited her husband, for he was like Edward Langtry in one respect: he regarded a day's fishing or a day's shooting as the most satisfying way of spending his time, and would leave his wife to her own devices while he indulged himself on river and moor. As Oscar Wilde, who knew a lot about fishing and shooting, once remarked, 'While the joys of the sports of the field no longer appeal to me, I do recall that the pleasure of them lasts rather longer than the pleasure of the marital bed and is more vividly remembered.'

Daisy's problem was that she was so passionate by nature that, unlike Lillie, she fell in love with her various men and became jealous to a dangerous degree. As a result she was absolutely furious when Beresford went back to bed with his wife after a lapse of several years and gave her another child. Daisy was foolish enough to complain about her lover's 'infidelity' in a letter which fell into the hands of Beresford's wife, who, not being promiscuous herself, determined to get her revenge on her rival. By this time Daisy was friendly with the Prince of Wales, though only on a social basis, and dragged him into helping her recover her letter. Heaven knows how these intimate encounters leak out, but Bertie's kindness landed him in a confrontation in which Beresford called him a blackguard and was said to have raised his fist at him. For this the Beresfords were exiled from the Prince's presence for many years.

Bertie had failed to recover the letter, but he resolved Daisy's problem for her by taking her on as his own mistress, when she was twenty-eight and at the peak of her beauty, and he was twenty years older and looked it. Once again Lord Brooke put up with the arrangement, partly no doubt because he was not prepared to offend his friend Bertie, who invited him and his wife to Sandringham for the shooting.

Daisy felt so honoured that she was indiscreet and her position soon became the talk of London, as it had been with Lillie, plus the added spice that Princess Alexandra, who knew all about the Beresford affair, would not accept her as she had Lillie.

Even if Daisy had been more discreet, the ordinary public would soon have heard all about it because of a dreadful scandal in which, in fact, she really had no part. This was the notorious Tranby Croft Affair which took place in September of 1890 but was not common knowledge until a court case arising out of it the following year involved Bertie up to the hilt.

I was among the first to hear about the affair through the gossiping tongue of a young officer whose name, I believe, was Berkeley Levett, and who had been one of the guests at Tranby Croft, a large house near Doncaster where the Prince and others had been staying for the races. Speaking to another somewhat older man, with whom he was having a late afternoon brandy, Levett told a most extraordinary story.

'I was put into a terrible position about the Colonel,' he explained rather nervously. 'I didn't think I should talk about it in the club, sir. That's why I asked you to come here.'

'The Colonel? How come?'

'Well, you know that the Prince of Wales was one of the guests? He played some baccarat, not for high stakes, and held the bank. Well, the Colonel was accused of cheating.'

'The Colonel? I don't believe it!'

'I'm afraid it's true, sir. After young Wilson, the son of the chap we were staying with, drew my attention to it, I saw it for myself. The Colonel won more than £200, mainly from His Royal Highness.'

'Good God! What was he doing?'

'He was palming the counters – increasing his stake when he

thought he was going to win and reducing it when he could see he was going to lose. It was hot, I can tell you!'

'I still can't believe it, Levett. The Colonel, of all people! What happened? Surely the Prince wasn't told?'

'I'm afraid he was, sir, because the Colonel insisted on seeing him. It was a dreadful business. Five people said they had seen him cheating.'

'What did the Prince say?'

'Just that as five people were accusing him it had to be true, and the best thing the Colonel could do was to sign a pledge never to play cards again. If he did that, then everything could be kept quiet.'

'And did he sign?'

'Yes, once he had been assured that the incident would never be mentioned again. But it's bound to get out, sir. That's why I thought, as second-in-command, you should know.'

'Thank you. If it becomes public the Colonel will have to resign. It will be terrible for the regiment. I take it I have your word that you will never tell anybody else?'

'Absolutely. But I shall be surprised if somebody doesn't blab. There were quite a few women there. . . .'

I heard nothing more of the matter for two or three months, but by the New Year journalists in the Domino Room had got wind of the affair and knew that the Colonel concerned was Lieut-Colonel Sir William Gordon-Cumming, a baronet in the Scots Guards. Though I had never seen him, I knew quite a lot about him because he had such a reputation as a womanizer, being credited with the vain boast, 'All the married women try me.' (It was inevitably assumed that Daisy had been one of them.)

As the rumour circulated, Sir William found that he was being cut by friends and, feeling that he had to do something to rebut the charges, he brought an action for slander against the five people who had accused him. Nothing could have been worse for the Prince of Wales who was subpoenaed as a witness after his friends had failed to stop the action.

The case opened before Lord Chief Justice Coleridge on 1 June 1891 and lasted nine days. I managed to get into the public gallery for only one day, the crush being so great because of the Prince's involvement. Unfortunately I was not there when the Prince was cross-questioned, courageously, by Sir Edward Clarke, who was defending the Colonel, but I did see Lillie Langtry in the court. She had a special interest, because after Daisy Brooke had declined to accompany Bertie to Tranby Croft, he had asked Lillie, who could not go because she was acting in *Anthony and Cleopatra* at the Prince's Theatre. Of course I also saw Bertie, who never looked at the witness box when Sir William was in it but simply gazed ahead, though they had been close friends for years. Later Bertie told the court that, while he had seen no sign of cheating, it would have been difficult for him as banker to do so. Nevertheless he had to accept the word of five independent witnesses.

On 9 June the five who had been accused of slander were acquitted by the jury after only brief deliberation. Poor Sir William, who had a fine, smart bearing with his slim, erect build and military-style moustache, was cashiered from his regiment, expelled from all his clubs and virtually exiled to his Scottish estate. Still, he was nothing if not resilient. He soon married a rich American to whom a title presumably meant more than the scandal.

Sadly, the damage to Bertie's reputation was far greater. He had appeared in a squalid case involving gambling and it was wondered whether, when the time came, he might gamble with the interests of the nation. He was of course a compulsive gambler but, when the testing time eventually came, he proved himself to be highly responsible in political affairs, growing into the job as so many men do when they are saddled with command.

Religious organizations were not alone in condemning him for sleazy habits, especially as the playing of baccarat was illegal. *The Times* accused him of indulging in 'questionable pleasures' and the foreign press went much further. One German paper on sale in the Café Royal, and handed round the Domino Room with guffaws, showed the Prince of Wales's crest with 'Ich Dien' replaced by 'I deal'. By all accounts the Queen was greatly distressed and only the delightful Princess Alexandra was sympathetic.

Daisy Brooke was too angry to be helpful. She had been accused by her enemies of leaking the secret and, as a result, was known for a time as Lady Babbling Brooke. She denied this publicly by pointing out that the death of a near relative had prevented her and her husband from being guests at Tranby Croft, but she must have heard about what went on there and her tongue may well have wagged.

While Bertie was earning the title which Frank Harris had given him, 'Edward the Caresser', Lillie Langtry in turn was playing the field, and since she had reached the peak so far as Society was concerned she was concentrating her attention on money. Nevertheless it was a great shock to me and to others to learn from bookies in the Domino Room that she had taken up with 'The Squire', of all people. The Squire was a blackguard called George Abington Baird, who had inherited a huge fortune – at least £3 millions – mainly based on coalmines under his Scottish estates. He was so pugnacious that he had been expelled from Eton for threatening to strike anyone who attempted to give him a flogging, which had been ordered for some misdemeanour. After that he consorted with grooms and pugilists, and though apparently he did get into Cambridge he did not work there, expending his efforts on gambling, horse-riding and cock-fighting. A keep-fit fanatic, he liked nothing better than a brawl, though he was short, spare and boyish in appearance. He never lacked courage but he always fought foul, and usually took the precaution of being accompanied by a few bruisers and fairground fighters. One in particular was a pugilist of considerable fame, or perhaps I should say notoriety – Charlie Mitchell, who only weighed about eleven stone but took on anybody on the principle 'The bigger your man the better your mark'.

The Squire was hated in the Domino Room but could not be barred because he and his cronies, most of whom had criminal records, would have wrecked the place if asked to leave. Fines meant nothing to him, and after being arrested for bar brawls he always managed to buy himself out of going to prison. His favourite trick for picking a fight was to throw drinks over other people, but Charlie Mitchell had a more dangerous habit: he seemed to be expert in throwing bottles and decanters so that they struck his opponents in the groin.

According to those who had witnessed the meeting of this little sadist with Lillie, he literally 'bought' her by pressing some of his racecourse winnings into her hand. He showered her with jewels and cheques and she earned it all – not only on her back but because of the vicious beatings he gave her through insane jealousy and possessiveness. On one occasion, when he caught her with another man in Paris, he almost killed her, but though this caused a public scandal in the newspapers she forgave him when he bought her a yacht. It was called the *White Lady*, but was soon being referred to by Domino Room wags as the *Black Eye*! When asked why she was prepared to make herself a punchbag for this little swine she answered – with commendable honesty – 'Because every time he does it he gives me a cheque for £5000.'

Maybe, as with Oscar Wilde, there was some animal pleasure in 'rolling in the mud' with a person like Baird, but there can be no doubt that money was the main attraction for her. She was also not averse to the publicity, believing, again like Oscar, that for anyone connected with the stage bad publicity is better than no publicity at all. In her autobiography, published in 1925, which caused a few old lovers to quake before they read its harmless pages, she made no mention of Baird but she did confess, 'In life I have all that I really wanted very much – a yacht, a racing stable, a theatre of my own, lovely gardens.'

There are those of us who know how she got them and what she had to endure to keep them. (When Baird hired the Haymarket Theatre for her he set up a rat-pit in the foyer with dozens of his pals betting on which terrier could kill the most rats!) I have never had any of those material possessions but I would imagine that my life has been equally rewarding, if not more so, for people are surely more interesting than things.

Lillie and the Domino Room were delivered from Baird by his early death in America when he was only thirty-two. As I had heard him say so often, he had long had an ambition to find a British boxer who could beat the seemingly invincible American world champion John L. Sullivan. Charlie Mitchell had been matched with him in France in 1888, and after 106 rounds the bare-knuckle fight had ended in a draw. Finally, in September 1892, Sullivan, the slugger, was convincingly dispatched by another American, 'Gentleman Jim' Corbett, who won through boxing skill under the new Queensberry Rules. The Squire saw his chance to pit Mitchell against Corbett but unfortunately, as we all knew, Charlie was once again in prison. When he duly emerged, a match with Corbett was arranged and, after a riotous celebration in the Domino Room, Baird, Mitchell and an entourage of boxers and hangers-on set off for the United States via Liverpool, beating it up all the way. The fight never materialized because Baird caught pneumonia and within a fortnight he was dead.

I am sorry to have to admit that I heard the news with some relief. So, I suspect, did Lillie, even though his demise deprived her of a seemingly bottomless pot of gold.

How did this woman manage to take London and later America by storm, and so achieve a position where she could meet rich and influential men? I think that, as with my discovery of the Domino Room and the social world it opened up for me, she was exceptionally fortunate in experiencing what I have already called a 'mutation moment' – a chance encounter which completely changed her life. It happened at a dinner to which she and her husband had been invited and which happened to be attended by a number of artists including John Millais. The family origins of Millais in Jersey formed an immediate topic of conversation after his introduction to Mrs Langtry, and he suggested that she should model for him. Frederick Leighton and others present followed suit, the most important for Lillie's future being the poorest artist there, a magazine illustrator called Francis Miles, who had the habit of exposing his person to small girls and, after being arrested for it, eventually died in a madhouse. Miles made a sketch of Lillie on the spot; later he made a better one and sold it to a printer who pushed it into the shops.

I remember seeing some of his prints myself in the windows of the little shops in Museum Street and elsewhere. A newspaper critic remarked that the best of them, showing Lillie's head in three positions, reminded him of paintings by Botticelli. I had never seen any of the Italian artist's work so I paid a special visit to the National Gallery in Trafalgar Square where I agreed with the comment, though I reversed this judgement after seeing the lady in the flesh. The drawing *was* like a Botticelli model. Lillie was not.

It was the fashion in those days for ordinary people to frame such prints and they happened to sell in thousands. In that way Lillie was established as a professional beauty and it was inevitable that she would be put at the Prince's disposal by one of his friends anxious to curry favour by obliging him.

The fine oil portrait eventually completed by Millais did even more for Lillie in the social realms which she was determined to invade. As a play on her name, he had conceived the idea of painting her holding a lily, alleged to be the special flower of Jersey, and the title of the picture, *The Jersey Lily*, ensured that it would become the centre of attraction, as it deserved to be, when it was shown at the Royal Academy, a short walk from the Café Royal. It drew great crowds and much comment in the newspapers and art magazines. It also raised the rumour that Lillie had granted her favours to Millais.

I have seen scores of women every bit as beautiful as Lillie walking about in London – shop girls and the like – but they did not have her luck or her ruthlessness; nor, perhaps, her intelligence, for which I have the authority of George Bernard Shaw who said, 'I resent Mrs Langtry. She has no right to be intelligent, daring and independent as well as lovely. It is a frightening combination of attributes.' She was also fortunate in having married a man who was either extremely stupid or uncommonly compliant – possibly both. I suspect that he put up with his wife's infidelities because of the social benefits it brought him.

Lillie's attributes would have fitted her to join the ranks of the Domino Room but, so far as I am aware, she never entered it, not even with Oscar Wilde, with whom she became close friends through Francis Miles. Only the upper reaches of the Café Royal, including the *salons privés* with comfortable sofas so that other activities could follow a luscious meal, were of interest to her.

5

GREEN FAIRY AND SCARLET MARQUESS

By 1892 I had seen Oscar Wilde enter the Domino Room or the Restaurant scores of times and it was always an event, particularly since he had become a symbol of unnatural vices following publication in 1891 of his novel *The Picture of Dorian Gray*, which many regarded as dangerously immoral. Some of those habitués who disliked him affected not to notice him, but even the way he walked commanded attention, for he was a very tall, heavy-jawed, powerfully built figure with a cat-like tread, elegant in bowler hat, frockcoat with buttonhole flower and striped trousers and carrying the long, gold-headed malacca cane favoured by the dandies of the day. Wilde believed or pretended to believe that the reformation of the rather dull established dress was far more important than the reformation of religion.

'As an artist, I myself should be a work of art,' he proclaimed. 'I find an ever-growing difficulty in expressing my originality through my choice of waistcoats and cravats.' And like so many others he came not only to see, but to be seen. He was on stage every moment that he was in public, and I once heard him say, 'I regard the year as a splendid drama with three hundred and sixty-five different acts.' Even in the street, to further his affected loathing of exercise he would take a cab just to cross the road, provided enough people were looking, just as he would lean on a friend's arm to cross a crowded room. He was, I suspect, after watching him so long, a frustrated actor. It was no coincidence, then, that he wore his hair, which was brown and usually artificially tinted with auburn, either long in its natural waves or, occasionally, dressed in the style of Nero. He fancied himself as living in the style of a Roman emperor, fawned on and self-indulgent to the extreme, though when he proclaimed that 'Nothing succeeds like excess' I am sure he was referring to the publicity value of being noticed; he was so successful at this that he had been lampooned by W. S. Gilbert in *Patience*, in the song containing the lines:

> *As you walk down Piccadilly*
> *With a poppy or a lily*
> *In your medieval hand . . .*

Oscar was always at pains to explain that he had never done such a thing, and had immediately scored off Gilbert with his widely quoted riposte, 'Caricature is the tribute which mediocrity pays to genius.' He was later to admit, however, that he had courted the publicity by saying, 'The difficult thing was to make people think I *had* done it.'

There was always interest, too, in the guests who accompanied him to the rather chipped marble-topped table in the Domino Room where he normally held court, dispensing the epigrams and aphorisms which he eventually used in his books and plays. They could be established figures like James MacNeill Whistler, with whom I had seen him there in 1886 at the start of the dissolution of their friendship, or the bombastic Frank Harris, each of whom had their favourite table and held their own courts. They could be personalities just beginning to be heard about, like the music critic George Bernard Shaw or the daring young artist Aubrey Beardsley who, with Wilde and others, formed the group calling itself the Decadents.

A child prodigy in pen draughtsmanship, Beardsley was introduced to Wilde by Oscar's friend Robert Ross. I remember seeing them early in their acquaintance in the spring of 1892. Like Oscar, Beardsley, who of all things had been a clerk, was made for the Domino Room: 'Pure rococo,' he declared with delight as he entered it for the first time. His appearance was striking because of his oddity: slightly built, he wore his tortoiseshell hair plastered on to his forehead where the parting continued down to the bridge of his aquiline nose. His face was gaunt, his eyes sunken and his complexion sallow from the ravages of the tuberculosis which was to kill him at twenty-five. A dandy like Wilde, he wore floppy bow ties, a cutaway coat, lemon gloves and a white gardenia, carried a silver-topped cane, and spoke in what Jules confirmed was an affected, effeminate manner, with restless movements of his bony hands which were, perhaps, another consequence of his awful illness.

'What a dear day; how perfectly enchanting,' he would say on arrival at Oscar's table, speaking at a rate which always tested my powers of lip-reading.

The strange exterior concealed an even stranger character. He was obsessed with sex — it was even rumoured that his relations with his sister Mabel were incestuous — as his drawings showed. They were regarded as the epitome of decadence but none could gainsay his genius, least of all Beardsley himself. His drawings for an edition of *Morte D'Arthur*, with their unique writing-like quality and economy of line, started quite a craze and he became such a success that he was appointed art director of the fashionable *Yellow Book*, an illustrated quarterly, when he was only twenty-one. He and Oscar could have been made for each other and to begin with their friendship blossomed.

'When I have before me one of your drawings I want to drink absinthe, which changes colour like jade in sunlight and takes the senses in thrall, and then I can live myself back in imperial Rome, in the Rome of the late Caesars,' I heard Oscar say.

'Don't forget the simple pleasures of that life, Oscar,' Aubrey replied. 'Nero set the Christians on fire, like large tallow candles; the only light the Christians have ever been known to give.'

This was the kind of badinage which delighted Wilde who needed little persuasion by Robert Ross to commission Beardsley to do the illustrations for his play *Salome*, which was considered so blasphemous that it had to be published in France.

'Absinthe is stronger than any other spirit. It is just like your drawings, Aubrey,' Wilde said, raising his aperitif, which he called 'the green fairy' and was indeed three times stronger than brandy. 'It gets on one's nerves and is cruel. Baudelaire called his poems *Flowers of Evil*. I shall call your drawings *Flowers of Sin*.'

The drawings were brilliant but Beardsley, who had a vicious streak, could not resist including some malicious caricatures of Wilde in them. Oscar was perhaps unduly sensitive but his reaction, which I overheard him make to Ross, was that the illustrations were

'. . . cruel and evil, so like dear Aubrey himself, who has a face like a silver hatchet'.

Beardsley's animosity increased when he heard that Wilde was telling people he had 'invented' him, which was, of course, quite untrue. Though influenced by the painters Burne-Jones and Whistler, Aubrey had invented himself. His response was to ensure that Wilde's work never appeared in the *Yellow Book*, but Wilde secured his revenge, albeit unwittingly. When Oscar was disgraced Beardsley was dismissed from the *Yellow Book* because its directors considered him too closely identified with Wilde in the public mind.

Poor Aubrey! He lived in such dread of death, and in the spring of 1898 he knew he was dying. A letter urging a friend to destroy 'all obscene drawings' was headed: 'In my death agony'. I have often wondered whether there was some connection between Aubrey's obsession with sex and his tuberculosis. I once overheard a conversation between two doctors in which one of them stated that the increased body temperature engendered by the infection stimulated sexual desire and interest. Indeed they made a joke of it concerning some consumptive woman patient who had an abnormal appetite for men. Tuberculosis of the lungs was known as 'phthisis' in those days, and I remember one of the doctors remarking, 'Whoever heard of a phthisical icicle?'

Though Wilde's association with someone as young as Beardsley caused some comment, it was other young men who were to bring about his downfall – coarse, uncultured creatures like stable boys, clerks and layabouts; they were dangerous liaisons which Oscar flaunted, for it has to be admitted that he boasted of his vices, saying that he had 'had' five telegraph boys in one day.

'There is a dreadful youth waiting for me in Regent Street,' I heard him remark to his friend Vincent O'Sullivan. 'He is pacing up and down before the door like a wonderful black panther. Do go and see. If he is there I shall go out by the side door.'

However on a certain October day in 1892 the young man who arrived for lunch with the 'Master' was of a different class, clearly cultured, with the insolent air of the aristocrat born to do no work – 'the arrogance of the useless' – and so strikingly handsome with his pale, oval face looking as though it had never needed to be shaved, his honey-coloured hair and slim figure, that he would have made a good-looking woman. This was a feature not lost on those of Oscar's detractors who saw in this relationship further expression of his predilection for young men, though he himself was married and had children.

Perhaps five feet nine inches in height, the young man seemed smaller as he walked in the Domino Room alongside Oscar in a beautifully tailored grey suit, silk shirt with large-knot tie and lace-up boots, carrying a straw boater and gold-headed cane. He looked no more than nineteen, though I knew him to be twenty-two, for this was Lord Alfred Douglas, youngest son of the Marquess of Queensberry, that fiery patron of the pugilistic art who was to be remembered as the originator of the Queensberry Rules of boxing, which converted vicious slugging into what some regard as a noble, manly sport.

I had seen them there together before and knew that they also frequently dined in the Restaurant, where Oscar was later to record that they lived on '. . . clear turtle soup, lucious ortolans wrapped in their crinkled Sicilian vine-leaves, amber-scented champagne, pâtés procured directly from Strasbourg, washed down with the special *cuveés* of Perrier-Jouet'. I had discerned that Lord Alfred, whom his friends called by the nickname 'Bosie' – a corruption of 'Boysie' – already had aspirations to be a poet and was later to declare himself 'The Genius of the Sonnet' and the author of 'some of the finest poetry in the English language'. Such immodesty was regrettably common to the whole Wilde circle. On entering America to give a series of lectures a few years previously, Wilde himself had greatly amused customs officials and reporters there by announcing, 'I have nothing to declare but my genius.' They took it as a joke, but I have no doubt that Wilde believed it.

Oscar and his Lordship were all smiles as they sat down, but I was soon to see that relations between them were far from happy. Normally, Wilde made sure that his conversations were overheard, and I was told that his speaking voice, described by others as a 'beautiful tenor', carried well; but though, of course, I could not judge the volume of their voices, I could tell by their manner that he and Bosie were speaking quietly, as though anxious that their words should remain private. They were acting like any husband and wife who are in the throes of bitter disagreement but do not want the world to know it. In particular they kept their gaze on each other or on the table, whereas normally Wilde had the habit of looking round the room for any person of note who might be welcomed to their table, and basking in the flattery of being able to captivate such a handsome young man – he was becoming rather bloated himself at that time, being thirty-seven and, as Bosie put it, 'too fat for beauty'.

Wilde's snobbishness was a factor in Douglas's attraction for him. He liked the way the waiters called his guest 'Mi'lord' and often turned the words 'Lord Alfred Douglas' over on his tongue, saying on one occasion, 'Even your name is like a flower', a compliment which delighted his companion; I was surprised to discover eventually that in Bosie's case 'Lord' was purely a courtesy title. It was simply because his father had inherited various titles that this younger son was called 'Lord', and, like so many other sons of noble houses who 'lord' it through life, he was never a peer, never a real lord.

The waiter brought Wilde his ritual absinthe, which I am sure he drank only as part of his Bohemian pose, for this bitter extract of wormwood was associated with the Parisian artists and writers who called themselves Bohemians, because of their gipsy-like scorn of social conventions, and drank it in the belief that it sharpened their artistic perception. His lordship drank white wine, which Oscar always insisted on calling yellow, which, of course, it was. Then after lighting yet another Egyptian cigarette from one of the several cases he carried in his capacious pockets, and which he never offered round, Oscar summoned the chef, to whom he gave his customary instructions for the meal and wine in great detail. To some this seemed ostentatiously out of place in the Domino Room, and to me, for whom food was never much more than body fuel to be consumed sparingly, was an endless source of astonishment. Unlike Frank Harris and some others Oscar was kind to the waiters, though he could be cross with them if they fell below his exacting standards. 'When I ask for a watercress sandwich I do not mean a loaf with a field in the middle of it', I heard him declare on sending back an order which was not to his delicate taste.

The formalities completed – Wilde always paid for every meal I ever saw him and Bosie eat together, though that, perhaps, was natural when he was so much the older man, and the richer – his eyes narrowed and he tore into his guest, speaking purposefully through his sensual purple-tinged lips.

'You are shallow, Bosie, shallow. And shallowness is the supreme vice. You are also unpardonably vain and greedy for money though you do little, if anything, to acquire any.'

Lord Alfred's normally pale face flushed at this renewal of an onslaught which had obviously been going on before they had entered the Domino Room. Though he made no reply his expression showed that he regarded the accusations as unfair, for he believed that through his birth, '. . . with more than a thousand years of true aristocracy behind me', as he put it, he was entitled to everything, and that anybody should consider it a privilege, even an honour, to provide it. As I once heard Oscar chide him, 'You ride the high horse so well and so willingly it seems a pity that you have never tried Pegasus!'

Oscar's remarks were fully justified. It would be no exaggeration to say that Bosie sponged on his friend, whose books were selling well at that time, for his father had stopped his small allowance when he had refused to end his association with Wilde. I have myself seen him ask Wilde for money, which was passed to him surreptitiously under the table. As in so many enduring relationships, one needed to give and the other was a born taker, demanding and receiving almost imperiously. So I suppose it could be said that they were made for each other.

'You should have learned by now, Bosie, that these scenes and rows you generate are so destructive of my talent,' Oscar said, acidly, as he savoured the bitterness of the absinthe. 'The trouble is, you and your family seem to thrive on them.'

'Oh, you are harping on that again,' Bosie said petulantly.

'Not again; still,' Oscar said sharply. 'You will never be anything of consequence, Bosie, until you rid yourself of this dreadful hatred of your father.'

'I can't help but hate him, not just for the way he has treated me but for the way he has treated my mother – like a beast.'

'All that may be true, but can't you see that your hatred is ruining *you*, not him? And it could well ruin me, too. Your only thought is to see your father "in the dock", as you put it, and I have a terrible presentiment that I am going to be the one who suffers most.'

'But how can that possibly be?' Bosie asked incredulously. 'I can't see what he could do to you.'

'You can't see because hate is blinding you.' Wilde toyed with his empty glass. 'I can't see it myself but I wake at night in a sweat fearing that I shall be the catspaw in this evil quarrel. Why should the sins of you and your father be visited on me?'

Before Lord Alfred could answer there was a turning of heads and a silence which made both aware that something connected with them had suddenly occurred. Indeed it had. The Marquess of Queensberry, 'Q' himself, a little terrier of a man with a long nose and a red-whiskered, sullen face, pinked by drink, full of self-conceit and violent temper, a face almost guaranteed to respond to a smile with a glare, had stalked into the room and sat down, his hands on the knob of his stout cane, his jaw thrust out ferociously, eyeing his son and Oscar.

There were few in that room who were unaware of the conviction of the Scarlet Marquess, as he was called, that Wilde was a pouncing homosexual whom, he had said, he intended to thrash in public for seducing his son.

Sensing the danger, Lord Alfred rose immediately and went across to greet his father. The air was electrified. All eyes were on father and son. Those, like Horace de Vere Cole, who loved to see a fight, especially if there was a chance that they could join it, were intensely interested; while the bookmakers and touts, easily identified by their loud check suits and coarseness of manner, who frequented the far end of the Domino Room near Glasshouse Street, were betting that the object was to enable Wilde to make a dash for it – but they were wrong. I assume that there was a gasp of astonishment as the Marquess rose, accompanied his son to Wilde's table and shook the author's limp hand. Wilde had a flabby handshake which the Marquess did not like, but in no sense was he afraid. The Marquess had been a lightweight amateur boxing champion but he would have been fighting far outside his weight, for Wilde towered over him, was far stronger and could probably have picked him up and thrown him over his shoulder for, as his Oxford associates have since testified, he was not short on physical courage.

As all eyes watched, the Marquess accepted a whisky from Wilde and eventually joined the two for lunch, being quickly captivated by Oscar's manner and conversation. Most of the people in the room seemed relieved, but I feel that not a few were disappointed that the promised horse-whipping had not materialized.

I am convinced from his manner and brusqueness that when Queensberry came in he had every intention of confronting Wilde there and then, but Oscar immediately mollified him with his charm – a considerable feat, for there was no point in being subtle or sophisticated with the Marquess. Soon Queensberry was laughing as the epithets and aphorisms tumbled out of Oscar's mouth in the rich voice which Jules described to me as, 'Plummy, Sir. Definitely plummy.'

'Give me the luxuries, Marquess, and anybody can have the necessities,' he quipped as he savoured his wine. 'The hardships of the poor are necessities, but talk to me of the hardships of men of genius and I could weep tears of blood.'

'You seem to think very highly of yourself,' Queensberry remarked.

'My admiration of myself is a life-long devotion, sir. You see the only thing that consoles me for the stupid things I have done is the praise I give myself for doing them.'

'And you have every justification for doing so,' Bosie concurred.

Oscar nibbled at his knuckles, as was his habit when thinking what to say next, and replied, 'Oh, dear. You know, Marquess, whenever people agree with me I always feel I must be wrong.'

'I have heard it said that at heart you are a Socialist, Mr Wilde.'

'It depends on what you mean by Socialist, Marquess. I believe that Socialite is a commoner jibe, but if Socialism means the bludgeoning of the people by the people for the people, then I am opposed to it. It is much to be regretted that a portion of our community should be practically in slavery, but to propose to solve that problem by enslaving the entire community is childish.'

'I am much relieved to hear you say that,' the Marquess said. 'Equality is being championed far too freely. Dangerously, I'd say.'

'I agree with you,' Oscar replied enthusiastically. 'Were equality possible it would be the death-knell of the nation. There are three kinds of despot, you know. There is the despot who tyrannizes over the body. He is called a Prince. There is the despot who tyrannizes over the soul. He is called the Pope. And there is the despot who tyrannizes over body and soul alike. That despot is called the People.'

The Marquess, who was clearly slow to appreciate anything but the obvious, smiled broadly, and Oscar completed his mollification on the political score by adding, 'Of course we must all want a world where liberty is not just a cause but the common condition. On the other hand common people do not appeal to me. Surely everyone prefers names like Norfolk, Buckingham and Queensberry to Jones, Robinson or Smith.'

'You seem to cultivate the aristocracy, Mr Wilde,' Queensberry said, seeming to suggest that Oscar's friendship with his young son was part of his social climbing.

'Not cultivate, Marquess. Fascinate! My purpose is to entertain the working classes, enrage the middle classes and fascinate the aristocracy. To get into Society one either has to feed people or to shock people. The latter is much cheaper. I would not deny that I enjoy visiting their beautiful homes, but it is the beauty which attracts me rather than the owners. The only person in the world I should like to know thoroughly is myself, but I don't see any chance of it, just at present.'

'Oscar had a beautiful place himself, in Ireland,' Bosie interposed. 'Marvellous fishing!'

Wilde then proceeded to surprise the sporting Marquess with his knowledge of fishing and shooting, which he had practised in Ireland on his father's estates, for they were hardly activities associated with the effeminate.

'Do you still have your properties in Ireland?' Queensberry asked.

'Heavens, no! I got rid of them at the first possible opportunity. I have no sense of property. Property not merely has duties but so many duties that its possession to an artist is a bore. Man will kill himself to secure property. To me the important thing is not to *have* but to *be*, and so far as land is concerned I think that man is made for something better than disturbing dirt.'

'You certainly have a point there, Mr Wilde,' said the Marquess, no doubt remembering the vast properties he had inherited but sold.

'Yes, indeed.' Oscar smiled, displaying the black teeth which marred him and may have had an ominous origin, as I shall later divulge. 'To live is the rarest thing in the world because most people just exist. As an artist, I live all the time.'

'Obviously you don't believe in conforming to custom.'

'Absolutely not. Every impulse that we strive to strangle broods in the mind and poisons us.'

'Are you suggesting that artists stand above the law?'

'I am not just suggesting it, Marquess, but insisting that they do. For any man of culture, and especially for any man of genius, to accept the standard of his age is a form of the grossest immorality.'

This was Queensberry's chance.

'I am glad you mentioned that word, Mr Wilde. As you must be aware, there is a great deal of talk about your own immorality – talk which disturbs me very much.'

'All envy and malice, Marquess, I assure you. Enemies come with success. Indeed, my old friend Whistler, who now seems to be my greatest enemy, though I have done more than anyone to make him successful, has written a tract on the subject. There are, of course, exceptions like Mr Bernard Shaw, who has no enemies but is immensely disliked by his friends.'

Oscar waited for the smile but there was none. Instead the Marquess insisted on treating the subject seriously, or trying to. 'I should warn you that you do have enemies, Mr Wilde. Many of them. . . .'

'Ah! I wonder who they are?' Oscar interrupted flippantly. 'A man cannot be too careful in his choice of enemies. However, I never take notice of what common people say, any more than I interfere with what charming people do. Mediocrity always detests ability and loathes genius. To me the sphere of art and the sphere of ethics are absolutely distinct and separate.'

'Few good people would agree with you,' the Marquess countered.

Oscar must have wondered what a man with 'Q's' reputation knew about good people. He knew, for instance, that his wife had divorced him after he had suggested that he should bring his young mistress to live with them both. But all he said was, 'Ah, good people exasperate one's reason. It is bad people who stir one's imagination. Anyway, if I am insulted why should I care? On the whole, in England, an artist gains by being attacked. His individuality is intensified. He becomes more completely himself.'

'You call yourself an artist, Mr Wilde. I thought artists were painters.'

'I am a painter, Marquess. A painter in words, beautiful words, both by hand and by mouth, conversation being the surpreme art. Beautiful words are the privilege of the artist, like beautiful things and beautiful sins are the privilege of the rich.'

Bosie, who was deliberately leaving the field to his more lo-quacious companion, nodded his approval as Oscar continued, 'Just like a painter, when I look at Nature I cannot help seeing all her defects. As he puts them right with a brush, I do it with a pen. Isn't it fortunate for us all, Marquess, that Nature is so imperfect, otherwise we should have no need of Art at all.'

'I have no need of art and no interest in it – except for the "noble art" – boxing, I mean.'

'Ah, but you are confusing skill with talent. I would like to convince you that real art is absolutely essential. It is our gallant attempt to teach Nature her proper place. Your world is a world of facts; mine a world of fantasy. And it is infinitely preferable. Who would go out at night to meet Tomkins, when he could sit at home with the characters of Balzac, or of mine? The loveliest things never happen – never become facts. That is what Romance is about – creating a fantasy world which is so much more pleasant than the real world, and above all more beautiful. To me the eye of a toad is a jewel, as it was to Shakespeare, not just a pigmented bag of water.

Every fictional story is a lie. The art of lying is something we should all cultivate. And we should disregard facts. We are a degraded race because we have sold our birthright for a mess of facts.'

Queensberry was clearly confused by this outpouring. 'But how could you even find your way home without facts?'

'It might take longer, but it would be far more interesting.'

The Marquess could not resist a smile, and shrugged as though convinced that Wilde, with his green scarab ring and foppish manner, was essentially just a harmless and highly entertaining showman who deliberately tried to shock and to attract notoriety as part of his stock in trade. It must have been plain to him too that Wilde was of good breeding.

At this point, round about 3 p.m., Bosie, in his typically petulant way, left the table and the Café Royal, irritated by being excluded from the conversation. Oscar shrugged at his departure and he and the Marquess relaxed and continued their drinking and talking, mainly about Christianity and atheism, which Queensberry professed. The subject had arisen following a quip by Wilde, an Irishman, which appealed to the Scot in Queensberry — 'Only the English have the miraculous power of turning wine into water.'

From the New Testament Oscar switched to the Old, securing the Marquess's agreement that the banning of his play about Salome was preposterous.

'You seem very knowledgeable about the Bible, Mr Wilde,' Queensberry said.

'Ah, the Bible! Yes, it is beautifully written but very predictable. As it begins with a man and a woman in a garden, it naturally ends with Revelations. I must read it more often.' This, too, was a prophetic remark, because for many months the Bible was to be almost his sole reading in prison.

It was almost 4 p.m. by the big clock over the bar when the Marquess stomped out with his cane, in rare good humour. Oscar had the extraordinary ability of admiring some quality in everyone, even in the Marquess, and of convincing them that his admiration was sincere. He was, I suppose, an outstanding exponent of what the Irish call blarney, a mixture of fable and twisted truth. Queensberry had certainly been captivated, if only temporarily, and was to write to Lord Alfred admitting that Wilde was a 'wonderful man'.

When Bosie returned to the table after seeing his father leave Regent Street he was radiant. 'You were simply wonderful, Oscar. You have charmed him completely. I thought you were brilliantly restrained – especially when he raised the subject of immorality. How dare he, of all people, even mention the word. . . .'

Oscar smiled at the praise from his favourite. 'I think that at least we established a useful basis of misunderstanding,' he quipped. Then he turned to call the waiter to bring a bottle of Irish whiskey and a soda siphon, his favourite drink after taking wine, and, in the relief of his success with the Marquess, they proceeded to demolish it, staying at the table until past 5 p.m.

Playing to the gallery, after the Marquess had left, he cried, 'Bring on the dancing boys!' It was a remark overheard by several who, while happy to be entertained by him, were not his friends and were likely to make such a remark much more dangerous in the retelling. I use the word 'dangerous' advisedly because, while the London of the eighties and nineties was a vicious city – far more so than Paris, for all its reputation – there was an uncompromising hatred of sodomy as a bestial act, worse, perhaps, than murder. Indeed the reader should understand that until 1861, only thirty years previously, sodomy had been a crime carrying the death penalty under British Law, and could still result in life imprisonment.

The more Oscar was criticized, the more strongly he would argue his case, with more and more outlandish remarks and behaviour. Earlier in his career, when he had been castigated as being effeminate in an age when masculinity was held in greater regard than it is now, he exacerbated public reaction by dressing in knee breeches and silk stockings and wearing on his coat green cornflowers or carnations and gilded lilies.

6

A GATHERING OF PANTHERS

An astonishingly accurate forecast of the fate awaiting Oscar Wilde was made by young Max Beerbohm, the up-and-coming caricaturist, who called into the Domino Room almost every day: 'Oscar will be taken for "certain kinds of crime" in the Café Royal. Bosie, being an excellent runner, will escape.' Max, who had known of them at

Oxford (where indeed Bosie had been an excellent middle-distance runner), belonged to the Decadents, and though I suspected that he might be a homosexual, like so many of the others, I was apparently mistaken. I heard him say that he disliked 'the heavily perfumed atmosphere of homosexual flirtation' and he eventually married, though he never produced any children.

A slightly built young man of Dutch-German ancestry, he had a large head with bulging brow, saucer eyes, small mouth and thick black hair, parted in the middle and brushed back; he looked older than his years, Oscar saying of him: 'The Gods have bestowed on Max the gift of perpetual old age.' Max had first been brought to the Domino Room by his elder brother Julius, a poet of some distinction himself, and fell in love with the Café Royal atmosphere. As Oscar did with his plays, and other writers with their novels, Max used the Café to collect subjects for his drawings and was forever scribbling descriptive notes in a little book. In turn he brought with him his then more famous half brother, Herbert Beerbohm Tree, the impresario who had changed his name for theatrical reasons.

Max seemed to have an enormous capacity for friendship and managed to retain Oscar's, though he caricatured him savagely, exaggerating his excessive weight and bloated face. Indeed he spared none of his friends, on the principle I heard him enunciate: 'It is the business of the caricaturist to seize mercilessly upon the points of his subject's features, expression and general appearance which lend themselves to burlesque and to emphasize them for all they are worth, with frank disregard for the feelings of the victim.' The existence of this streak of ruthlessness behind such bland, rather immobile features led Oscar to remark to a mutual friend: 'Tell me, when you are alone with Max does he take off his face and reveal his mask?'

None agreed with Max about the harshness of good caricature more heartily than Aubrey Beardsley, who was even more savage with his subjects. Sharing their delight in draughtsmanship, the two would go off together after a snack in the Domino Room to watch the sport at Angelo's, a fencing school in St James's Street, where I never had the nerve to venture, feeling that this was a class barrier I could not breach.

'Max', as he signed himself on his drawings, was also regularly in the Café Royal with Will Rothenstein, a phenomenally dynamic little Jew from Bradford who, by sheer effort and force of personality, had made himself a figure in the art world of Paris. Originally he had gone there without money, but was making himself quite rich with drawings and lithographs of famous British university figures, politicians and the like. He was immediately noticeable for his thick spectacles and mass of black hair combed down on to his forehead. With Beardsley, the two made an outstandingly talented trio, and they would talk and talk until poor Aubrey would fall asleep through sheer exhaustion, his hatchet head sunk into his breast.

Another Domino Room crony of Beerbohm's at this time was Ted Craig – Edward Gordon Craig, who later became a distinguished stage producer after years of regarding himself as the neglected 'genius' of the theatre, and writing a much praised book called *The Art of the Theatre*. He was what was described as a 'love child' of Ellen Terry, the much adored actress, who herself occasionally graced the Domino Room, though never in the company of an artist. She had been briefly married at sixteen to the painter G. F. Watts but, hating the life, ran away from him to the stage. She then set up house with a man called Godwin, an architect who designed Whistler's strange house in Tite Street and later did the interior decoration for Oscar Wilde's house close by. Before she left him to return to the stage at the age of twenty-seven she bore Godwin two children, a girl called Edith as well as Ted, who both took the name Craig.

Godwin was before my time in the Domino Room, but some of the waiters remembered him there with Whistler. Had Craig's mother been a nobody he would have been described more bluntly in those days as a bastard, and would have carried some stigma through his illegitimacy, but in upper-class and 'artistic' circles a much more tolerant view was taken. Miss Terry made no secret of Craig's existence. Indeed, when he produced the first child of his own large family – several of them illegitimate – she let it be generally known that she was afraid she would get no more parts because she was a grandmother, a fear which, happily, was not realized.

Ted Craig, who had inherited his mother's fair, good looks, followed her lead in scorning respectability and in pursuing a stage career, being a member of Henry Irving's company at the Lyceum Theatre for several years. He was very likeable, but nobody could approve of the way he sponged on his mother who helped to support his children throughout her working life.

Max seemed to specialize in friends born 'on the wrong side of the blanket'. Another whom he introduced into the Domino Room on occasion could usually claim to be the ugliest person present, and I once heard him do so. This was Reginald Turner, the illegitimate son of some rich man widely believed to be Lord Burnham, a fat little fellow previously called Levi Lawson, the proprietor of the *Daily Telegraph*. I gather, however, that it is more likely that his father was Burnham's uncle, a gay old bachelor called Lionel Lawson, who built the Gaiety Theatre in the Strand, eventual home of the famous Gaiety Girls.

Reggie, as he was always known to his many friends, had an enormous mis-shapen nose, thick lips and a wrinkled skin and was forever blinking his eyes. His compensation from the Good Lord was an acute sense of humour and, while he seldom smiled himself, he had the capacity for keeping Max and others in fits of laughter. On one occasion Reggie had watched two young men who had sat together for hours in the Domino Room without exchanging a word. 'I suppose that when you two cherubs are together neither of you can get a silence in edgeways,' he said as they stood up to leave.

While observing the capacity of men to attract women, I have come to the conclusion that the ability to make them laugh is a commanding asset. This must also be true of homosexuals, for in spite of his ugliness Turner was 'loved' by several men, including, I believe, Oscar himself – Turner could not have been more unlike Bosie in appearance, yet Wilde was attracted to both.

Had Wilde restricted his homosexual activities, to which he later fully confessed – to men like Reggie Turner and Lord Alfred, and had he behaved more discreetly, he might have gone on to even greater success and acclaim than he achieved over the next two years. But he was in fact already doomed by a habit which seemed so out of character – his need for sexual relations with coarse, working-class youths like jockeys, stable boys and others who might be described as guttersnipes.

I remember one late afternoon in 1893 when Frank Harris, then, at thirty-eight, owner and editor of the prestigious *Fortnightly Review*, was sitting in his favourite corner playing chess with Ernest Dowson, a rather grubby poet whose general knowledge of poetry in several languages, like Harris's knowledge of literature, was extraordinarily wide. Harris who, like me, had rented a cheap room in Bloomsbury when younger and then taken an enduring fancy to the Domino Room, was often in the company of poets and other aspiring con-tributors to his periodicals. Dowson was a very careful player for whom time seemed of no consequence, and while waiting for him to make his next move Harris walked out to the men's room. While he was there Wilde arrived with two rough-looking young men, who looked as though they might be grooms, and sat at his usual table.

Harris stopped by Wilde's table to pass the time of day on his return. At that moment Wilde was in full, eloquent flood over his absinthe, telling the two youths, who turned out to be Cockneys (my lip-reading skill was such that I could often discern accents), how at the Olympic Games young athletes wrestled, ran races and threw the discus, all without any clothing.

'You mean they was nykid?' the younger of the two boys asked.

'Of course. Nude. Clothed only in sunshine and beauty.'

'Oh my,' the lad giggled, to Harris's obvious disgust. 'I couldn't stand that.'

Oscar, who always found it 'tedious' to be interrupted, completed his conversation with the youths before acknowledging the presence of Harris, whom he had known for ten years; during that time they had lunched together at the Café Royal every fortnight, and many of the remarks which Wilde put into his plays had first been coined in their conversation. I saw Harris shaking his head in disbelief at the intellectual level of Wilde's companions as he returned to his chess game, and it was clear from Dowson's expression, or what could be seen through the smoke cloud of his black cigar, that Harris told him what he had heard.

The slightly built and somewhat stooped Dowson, who was well known to be a patron of the tarts in the Domino Room and in the pubs and music-halls he frequented most nights, made a grimace of distaste – though he himself had his sexual peculiarities, having, as his friend Arthur Symons said, 'a curious love of the sordid'. He had fallen in love with a twelve-year-old girl, though he never got the chance to be intimate with her, had he so desired, which I suspect he did.

It was also soon clear from Harris's expression that he was not pleased when Lennox Pawle, a most eccentric friend of Dowson, sat himself beside them. As could be guaranteed, once Pawle had been set up with a drink, he produced a box of wax matches and commenced his favourite procedure for drawing attention to himself. While watching the game he would soften the dead end of a match with his fingers and then press it against his cheek or chin until it stuck there, gradually building up a forest of white matches which looked like whiskers. Then, when he saw that enough people were watching him, he would set the matches alight so that his head appeared to be going up in flames. Somehow he always managed to put out the fire with his hands before it burned him and, while the management and the waiters hated the exhibition, it delighted most of the customers, except for those regulars like Harris and Wilde who were bored with it and thought it infantile.

The pin-thin Dowson, who was so tuberculous that he was to die emaciated and destitute at the age of thirty-three, had seen it so often that he seemed not to notice the conflagration any more, and in any case was such an eccentric himself that he probably regarded it as normal behaviour. Though he had rooms, he would sleep on anybody's couch or armchair rather than go to them; as a result his clothes always looked as though they had been slept in, because indeed they had been. A devout Catholic convert, he used to produce a small gold cross on a chain from his waistcoat pocket and dip it into each glass of absinthe before sipping it. This was a frequent performance because he drank to an extent which undermined his health, sometimes being so intoxicated that the more elegant habitués like Aubrey Beardsley loudly expressed their disgust.

Pawle was about half-way through the build-up of his matches when Oscar bid goodbye to his boys, looked at his fob-watch, ordered another drink, lit a cigarette and called for writing paper on which he began to scribble. This gave Harris his excuse to escape.

'I must speak to Oscar. Would you finish the game for me?' he asked Pawle. 'You should be in a winning position.'

Pawle did not seem so convinced of the prospects of victory, perhaps suspecting that Harris was opting out of losing, which he hated on any occasion, but nevertheless obliged.

I was delighted because Harris, who before taking up a literary career claimed to have been a cowboy, bootblack, butcher and bouncer in a gambling saloon, was almost as brilliant a conversationalist and story-teller as Wilde; the two coruscated, the hard metal of Harris's comments striking showers of sparks from Oscar's flint. Naturally I was never able to hear the tone of Harris's speaking voice, but Jules assured me that it was rich and resonant, 'like a bass bell', and I was later to hear Aleister Crowley, of whom more anon, proclaim that he had never heard a voice so full of power and passion combined with control and delicacy of expression.

'Ah, Frank, do sit down and tell me what you think of this verse,' Oscar said warmly as he held up the writing paper. 'I should first explain its background. There is a member of my club by name the Viscount Molesworth, the title being Irish and going back a couple of centuries or so. He is very grand and deprecates the recent election of a certain Mr Molesworth, who is self-made and obviously no relation. Such are the noble lord's sentiments about his humble namesake that I propose to pin on the Club notice board the following brief verse:

> *There are two moles of equal worth*
> *But not, alas, of equal birth,*
> *For he whose blood is very blue*
> *Is far the bloodier of the two.*

'Very good, Oscar,' Harris said with a guffaw. 'You are beginning to show promise as a poet at last.'

'Just a trifle, Frank.' Oscar smiled with a wave of the lavender gloves he usually held to accentuate his utterances. 'Tossed off while I wait for Bosie Douglas who, as you know, is always late. One gets quite lonely . . .'

'It would be better if you stayed that way rather than consort with trash like those two who have just left you,' said the aggressive little editor, who was never one to mince his words. 'I tell you as a friend that you are doing yourself enormous harm being seen with them. It's the talk of London. I can't go into a club where it's not mentioned. Are you trying to destroy yourself just when you are becoming so successful?'

Harris, who was later to go far towards destroying his own literary reputation with his sexually shocking *My Life and Loves*, was, however, perceptive about the faults and weaknesses of others, and had spotted the self-destructive streak in Wilde's otherwise creative nature.

'I suppose I could limit myself to consorting only with other writers, but there is a dire penalty for that. I should have to read their works.'

'For God's sake be serious for once, Oscar. I am giving you good advice.'

'Oh Frank,' Wilde protested wearily as he beckoned the waiter. 'You know my tastes are catholic. It gives me particular pleasure to dine with a duchess one evening and with a corner boy the next. Any serious writer must give himself maximum exposure to all levels of human nature and particularly with the young. Besides, the only way to get rid of a temptation is to yield to it.'

'But why can't you see that kind of riff-raff in private?'

'Upstairs, do you mean?' Wilde asked mischievously, referring to the *salons privés* where Harris, who was tormented by sex, took his women, especially when bent on a first seduction. 'I suppose the danger is half the excitement. It's rather like feasting with panthers. I feel like the snake charmer when he lures the cobra from the reed basket.'

'But doesn't Douglas mind?' Harris asked, ordering a whisky in his peremptory, discourteous manner.

'Why should he? I only demand that freedom I willingly concede to him and to others.'

'A woman would still be jealous.'

'Frank, you are speaking about a subject you have always claimed to know nothing about – the love between men, which is the highest form of love.'

'I hope, please God, that I shall remain in ignorance of it, Oscar. Nobody believes more strongly than I do that sex is the gateway to life, but it has to be natural sex.'

'Nothing that I do or that any other true artist does is unnatural, Frank. For me what you would call promiscuity is a natural sampling of what the world has to offer. We insult Nature by not taking all she offers from her cornucopia.'

Harris, who could not resist groping round the private parts of any woman who stimulated him, regarded promiscuity as the natural right of all men, not just of artists, but it had to be with women.

'The world is full of exciting women, Oscar. Stimulating women. I just cannot understand why they aren't enough for you. Surely the female cleft holds sufficient mysteries and delights?'

Wilde, who was averse to the slightest hint of crudity, answered quietly, 'It didn't for Alexander the Great, for Caesar, for Leonardo, for Erasmus, for Michelangelo. . . . What you call vice is as good to me as it was to them.'

And while Harris fingered his moustache Oscar added mis-chievously, 'It was as good for Shakespeare, too.'

The man who regarded himself as the world's greatest authority on Shakespeare, who in fact almost identified himself with the bard, as Oscar did with Christ, thrust out what he called his 'fighting jaw', braced his muscular shoulders and snapped, 'You know that I don't agree with you on that score.' Then he added with a smile, 'I have to admit, however, that while I have no experience of homosexuality, if Shakespeare had asked me I would have had to submit.'

It was a remark that I was to hear Harris repeat more than once, *bon mots* in the Domino Room being rarely lavished on a single airing.

'There are others who might have seduced you, Frank,' Oscar said, warming to his theme. 'Are you aware thàt Christopher Marlowe's lines, "Come live with me and be my love, and we will all the pleasures prove", was written to a young man?'

'Of course I am aware of it, but the public will hardly regard that as evidence that it gives *you* licence to prove any pleasures which take your fancy, especially if they happen to be against the law.'

'Oh Frank, surely you believe that every great artist must have licence to plumb any depths he desires to further his experience of human emotion and passion so that he can express his feelings with greater force and confidence? I need to drift with every passion till my soul is a stringed lute on which all winds can play.'

'Huh,' Harris grunted. 'I find it difficult to imagine what worthwhile depths of passion or emotion you could experience with scoundrels like those two who were sitting here a few minutes ago.'

A lesser man might have reacted irritably to such a reference to his friends, whatever they looked like, but I never heard Oscar raise his voice in the Domino Room, where angry words, which sometimes ended in blows, were so common. All he did was to shrug resignedly. 'What is called the vice of the upper classes is really the pastime of the working classes. These lads have their peculiar appeal which offers a new experience, and I would sacrifice anything for a new experience. One can never pay too high a price for any sensation.'

'*You* could, Oscar, *you* could,' Harris insisted. 'The Marquess of Queensberry. . . .'

'That oaf,' Wilde interrupted. 'If you limit passion in any way you impoverish life, Frank. You weaken the mainspring of art and narrow the realm of beauty.'

'And you think that something special attaches to the homosexual passion?' Harris asked, determined to stick to the subject.

'As I have told you before, there certainly seems to be a link between the love of men for each other and artistic achievement. Whether it sharpens man's perception and stimulates his creativity I do not know, but I reject entirely the common assumption that it is depravity.'

'Would you admit that it may be a malady, even a madness?'

'If it is, it appears to attack the highest natures.'

Harris must have sensed that his well-meant warnings were falling on deaf ears, and did not pursue them after their conversation was interrupted by a gasp from the strangers and a cheer from some of the habitués as Pawle's wax 'whiskers' finally went up in flames.

'Is it true you are going to sell the *Review*?' Oscar asked. 'I do hope so. Bernard Shaw is right, you know. Journalism is not for people over forty.'

'I'm not forty yet,' Harris replied testily.

'In any case you should get out of journalism,' Wilde insisted. 'You are made for better things, Frank. Your work should be on shelves, not wrapping meat.'

While Harris was vain enough to agree to the compliment, he was proud of his journalistic achievements. He had built up the circulation of the *Fortnightly Review*, in which he had published some of Wilde's essays, just as he had raised that of the *Evening News*.

'At least I've never yet been driven to edit a woman's paper,' Harris retorted, referring to Oscar's brief reign as editor of *The Woman's World*. 'But I take it that, as something of a journalist yourself, even though you lacked the self-discipline to hold the job down, you see a great difference between the merits of journalism and book literature.'

'Perhaps there isn't all that much difference. With a few exceptions, including my own articles, the former is unreadable while, again excluding my own volumes, the latter is not read.'

Harris could not resist a broad smile at the sally. 'I must slip out now,' he said. 'I see that scoundrel Bottomley has arrived.'

He nodded in a direction behind him where Horatio Bottomley was drinking champagne with a blonde lady much younger than himself.

Harris had remained friendly with Bottomley until he had heard that the financier, who was intensely anti-Semitic, had called him a 'Polish Jew'. After that he described Bottomley as '. . . someone with whom to eat, drink and be wary'.

'I thought Bottomley had been acquitted,' Oscar said, referring to one of his many appearances in court, where, as usual, he had conducted his own defence.

'He was – but by a gross miscarriage of justice. The trouble with the law, Oscar, is that while the villains often go free the honest end up in prison. Remember that. I bid you good day,' and he strode out of the Domino Room purposefully, five feet five inches of pugnacity with the spats, high cuban heels, high choker collar, heavy gold albert and generally flashy dress of the deliberate showman he was.

I do not imagine that Harris's pointed remark about prison caused Wilde to think that he might end there as he sat waiting for Douglas. If it did, it had no effect on his behaviour. Oscar continued to base it on the principle that: 'To be master of one's moods is exquisite, to be mastered by them more exquisite still.'

Of course Wilde was not alone in desiring recourse to lower-class sexual partners. Augustus John, the painter, for instance, consorted occasionally with women who could only be described as sluts. I believe the French have a phrase for the strange drive which makes some men do this — *'nostalgie de la boue'*, a longing for the gutter. Usually, however, this weird requirement tends to be satisfied in private, but I suspect that Wilde derived an exhibitionist pleasure out of being seen with rough youths. Later Wilde was to blame Bosie for introducing him to these gutter pleasures, saying, 'I allowed myself to be lured into the imperfect world of coarse passion.' I can testify, though, that he was patronizing working-class boys and bringing them into the Café Royal before he ever met his lordship; so much so that the women flower-sellers in Piccadilly, who missed very little of what was going on around them, would insult him if he passed them in the company of a young man.

I am as certain as I can be that it was an earlier friend, Robert Ross, a Canadian, slim of body, with a rather bulging forehead and slightly upturned nose, who introduced Wilde to the homosexual prostitutes and enthusiastic amateurs who haunted the Piccadilly area.

Ross, a journalist, had been a practising homosexual when Oscar first met him in 1886 — in a public urinal according to Harris, for such a location, known to the queer fraternity as a 'cottage', was a common place for such encounters. He was, in fact, known to the police for importuning in Piccadilly and, though thirteen years younger, may well have seduced Oscar, for I heard him claim with some pride after Oscar's death that he had been his first 'lover'. In that case he has much to answer for, though I should point out now, as I will in greater detail later, that Ross proved to be Oscar's truest friend in his extremity, along with his bosom companion, whom I also assume to have been homosexual, William More Adey, one of the first translators of Ibsen's work into English.

It is clear from conversations I overheard that Wilde tried sodomy, and the other things homosexuals do, as part of his 'drifting with every passion', and liked it. But for this to happen there must have been some germ of mental abnormality already there. I did not know it at the time, but I discovered later that his mother had treated him in a way which may have been responsible. This formidable woman, herself a writer who became known as Speranza, her pen-name for the inflammatory anti-British articles and poems she wrote in support of

Irish independence, had longed for a girl and was greatly disappointed when Oscar arrived. She kept him in skirts until he was almost five, which according to the modern science of psychology covers the period when warped attitudes to sex can be ingrained.

I am in no doubt that he was 'in love' with Bosie, and indeed could be said to have been besotted by him. From the tone of their conversations I am in little doubt that when they met in private they kissed each other on the lips. I think it perfectly sensible for men who are really close friends to embrace as a gesture, as many Europeans do, for after all one shakes hands with a complete stranger, but the relationship between Oscar and Bosie was at a passionate level. In Bosie's autobiography which he published in 1929, when he was fifty-nine, he admitted homosexual 'practices' with Wilde but insists that they never indulged in 'the sin which takes its name from one of the Cities of the Plain' – meaning sodomy, of course. However, in view of their passion for each other I find that as hard to believe as the claim of a girl who, after cohabiting with a man, might say she had not lost her virginity.

Whatever they did in their private sessions, Wilde was undoubtedly the male partner and I have heard him describe their relationship as like that between the Emperor Hadrian and the boy Antinous, with whom the Roman practised sodomy. In the rather lurid love letters he wrote to Bosie, which were eventually to be so disastrous for him, and to Bosie himself in a much later libel action, he treated him as a normal man would treat a woman and made his passion plain.

It is therefore extraordinary that, although Bosie seemed to be infatuated with Wilde, he did not seem to mind the infidelities with other boys, and I have overheard them discussing Oscar's conquests. I have reason to believe that Bosie was unfaithful himself, probably with Reggie Turner, but I never saw him in the company of the kind of riff-raff Oscar favoured.

I have, on occasion, been able to overhear the conversations between Wilde and young men he brought into the Domino Room. So much so that, had the prosecution been aware of it, they could have subpoenaed me as a witness in the case against Wilde. And a damaging witness I could have been, though in fact nothing would have dragged the truth out of me at that time. I recall one particular young man called Edward, whose full name became known to me only at Wilde's trial: it was Edward Shelley, and Wilde had picked him up on a visit to his publisher, where he served as office boy. He was a rather tall, heavy fellow with a square jaw, and not in the least effeminate in appearance. Wilde brought him into the Café Royal more than once, the first time I saw them together being shortly after the meeting with Queensberry which I have already described. The next time they drank together in the Domino Room it was in less friendly circumstances. I heard Shelley demand money from Oscar, while reminding him of '. . . the sins we have committed together'.

A much more odious and more dangerous youth whom Wilde chose to meet in the Café Royal was called Alfred Wood. He was fair-haired and quite pleasant to look at, but I could discern from their conversations that he was a bad lot and, as it transpired, a sneak thief and a blackmailer. It seems to me that the real danger of homosexuality lies not so much in the habit itself, which, as I am told, may be something a man cannot help, but in the vicious nature of many of those involved in it. This, of course, may be due to the fact that, being a crime as well as a social sin, it is bound to attract blackmailers, and this is exactly what two of Wood's other friends were. I mention them because they were instrumental in bringing about Oscar's downfall. These two professional blackmailers, William Allen and Robert Cliburn, made use of youths like Wood to steal letters from the men with whom they had homosexual relations.

Wood was already a friend of Bosie, who took him to stay with him in Oxford. There Wood extracted a number of letters from Wilde to Bosie and showed them to Allen and Cliburn. They thought them so damaging that they decided to try to get money out of Bosie for their return. As usual Bosie simply turned the responsibility over to Oscar, to whom he had passed Wood on for homosexual purposes. Oscar decided to see Wood personally and, in spite of what he had done, invited him to meet him again in the Café Royal. I witnessed the meeting and, though I was not then aware of the background to it, I could see that they began on rather cold terms and discussed the matter of the letter. Though Wood admitted that, as a result of his villainy, or stupidity as he claimed, the issue was now in the hands of his criminal friends, Wilde not only forgave him over their dinner but, perhaps under the influence of the wine, invited him back for the night to Tite Street, where his long-suffering wife presumably did not know the purpose of the visit.

Oscar was soon to learn that, through Wood's villainy, events were in train that would prove disastrous. In April 1893 he was joined at his table in the Domino Room by Max Beerbohm's half brother, Herbert Beerbohm Tree. Carefully putting his top hat and gloves on the table, for he was as dandified in his way as Wilde, Beerbohm Tree

said, with much truth, 'I always think that anyone who wants to see
the English people at their most English should come here, where
they are trying their hardest to be French.'

For a while they discussed Wilde's play, *A Woman of No Importance*,
which the impresario Tree was rehearsing at the Haymarket Theatre.
Then Tree produced a letter from his pocket. 'This has been sent to
me and presumably to other people. It purports to be a letter from
you to Lord Alfred Douglas.'

Looking slightly shocked, Wilde looked at it and said, 'Yes, it is.
What of it?'

'What of it? That sentence about those red-leaf lips being made for
kisses. That is open to misconstruction, to say the least.'

Oscar dismissed the possibility with a smile. 'My dear chap, Bosie
Douglas and I are both poets and we express our sentiments in poetic
terms. This letter is nothing more than a prose poem. If put into
verse it would be worthy of inclusion in any respectable anthology.
Frankly I don't give a damn who sees it.'

Beerbohm Tree shrugged his disagreement. An inveterate womanizer, who took every advantage of his stage connections in that
respect, he would have little time or sympathy for homosexuals, for
such men with large heterosexual appetites seem to be the most
virulent of all against what they regard as abnormal.

By now almost two years had elapsed since Oscar's mollification of
Queensberry, which the latter had clearly come to regard as only the
first round of a contest he intended to win by a knock-out. The
Marquess had soon come to suspect the worst of the relationship
again, and, as might be expected, when Wilde refused to give the
blackmailers a further £10 for a particularly dangerous letter, having
already paid them £30 for the return of all those he believed they had,
it was duly sent to Queensberry. When the Marquess read it his face
must have justified the adjective 'Scarlet' so often applied to him:

'My own Dear Boy,
    Your sonnet is quite lovely and it is a marvel that those
red-leaf lips of yours should have been made no less for music
than for the medium of kisses. Your slim, gilt soul walks
between passion and poetry. . . .'

It was certainly a letter capable of being misinterpreted and it duly
was, by almost everyone who eventually heard about it.

The Marquess's reaction was to write to his son demanding an immediate end to the friendship with Wilde, making it clear that he had been brooding over the situation and had entirely reversed his opinion about it: '. . . Your intimacy with this man Wilde must either cease or I will disown you and stop all money supplies. . . .' Bosie's response was to exacerbate the dangerous situation by sending his father a telegram calculated to infuriate him: 'What a funny little man you are.' Bosie also took a further precaution which was to cause something of a sensation a few days later in the Domino Room for those of us who witnessed it.

'You remember your letter complaining that ". . . it is intolerable to be dogged by a maniac"?' he asked Oscar.

'Indeed, dear boy, and so it is,' Oscar replied.

'Well, I am doing something about it.' He put his hand in the pocket of his dove-grey jacket and produced a small, pearl-handled pistol which he aimed at the head of the nearest caryatid with his mouth contorted with hate. Those at the table below the figure took evasive action, but Oscar resolved the situation calmly by asking to see the weapon. He checked that it was loaded, removed the bullets, put them in his own pocket, and gave the gun back to Bosie.

As a precautionary move Wilde asked a friend to convert the contents of the leaf-red lips letter into a sonnet which was published in the Oxford magazine, *The Spirit Lamp*, run by Bosie, so that he could claim that the original had been a 'prose poem'. This turned out to have been a mistake, for having read it the Marquess pronounced it 'disgusting' and told his friends that if he ever found Oscar with his son he would strike him with his cane and wreck any restaurant where they might be.

Late in 1894 I was sitting at my table in the Domino Room when the Marquess strode in, complete with cane and accompanied by a bruiser; he glowered round the tables, clearly looking for the couple. The Marquess sat for a few minutes, hoping that they might appear and leaving the rest of his audience in no doubt of his intentions. In truth many of them hoped the two would enter so they could enjoy the fun. Even Ernest Dowson, who was busy, as was his practice, drafting some verses on the back of an envelope, an activity usually quite undisturbed by background noise or events, watched expectantly. Queensberry then went up to the Restaurant with the same intent and warned both the head waiters there – as Bertrand, my waiter friend there told me – that they were not to serve Wilde and his son if they appeared together. Otherwise he would cause a fight and wreck the place.

On his way out of the Café Royal he glowered into the Domino Room once again but, to the disappointment of most of the habitués, the offending pair did not appear that day. I feel sure that many in that room would have relished the smash of the pugilistic Marquess's fist on those full, sensual lips, but it is my bet that it would have been Queensberry's 'claret' which would have been 'tapped', as the boxing fraternity put it.

There was the additional exciting possibility of a shooting affray, because all the Domino Room habitués now knew that Bosie was carrying a revolver and that he was hot-headed enough to use it. A couple of days after flourishing it in front of me he had pulled the trigger in the Berkeley Hotel in Piccadilly and shot away part of a chandelier. His explanation to the manager there was that he needed practice in case his father walked in and attempted to shoot Oscar, as he had threatened. I for one, at least, was glad that Wilde and Bosie did not appear to provide a sordid spectacle ill fitted to the nature of either of them.

7

THE IMPORTANCE OF BEING OSCAR

It was not often that I could afford to go to the theatre, because it was essential for me to sit in the expensive front row seats to 'hear' the dialogue; however, by booking well in advance I was able to be present at the memorable first night of Wilde's greatest success, *The Importance of Being Earnest* at the St James's Theatre in King Street, just off St James's Street, on a February evening in 1895.

It was a glittering social occasion, for which I had to hire evening dress, the first time I had ever worn one. I hired it from the firm of Moss Bros, whose shop in Bedford Street, near Covent Garden, I had often passed. I hired everything, very cheaply I thought, including the stiff collar, irreverently known in those days – because of the angel-like wings – as a 'come-to-Jesus' collar, and, believe it or not, an opera hat and a cape. I should really have hired a coat because that winter of 1894–5 was the bitterest I can remember. It seemed to go on and on, with the snow never beginning to thaw.

The suit did not fit very well, which was probably my fault as I did not have the figure for it, but eyes turned as I walked up Guilford Street that evening, though nobody took any notice once I had reached Kingsway since, from then on, 'toffs' in dinner jackets or tails were common enough.

I had left my lodgings, where my landlady, Mrs Moffat, had expressed delighted surprise as I descended the staircase, in plenty of time to walk to the Domino Room so that I could call in there for a beer before going to the theatre – hoping, I must confess, that some of the regulars might see me. Though I was a non-smoker, partly because of my weak chest but also to protect my precious eyesight, I stopped at the 'Cigar-divan' in Piccadilly to buy a small cigar, thinking that I might light it while walking round the foyer during the interval, even if I could not smoke it properly. This little shop was patronized by the toffs and was acclaimed in a popular song called 'Millie's Cigar-divan', which contained the suggestive line: 'And if Millie bites the end off it costs a shilling more!'

I remember walking through the swing doors of the Café Royal past the commissionaire, who saluted, but I do not think that he recognized me. It is strange how clothes are such important recognition signals. I have even passed Café Royal waiters in the street, realizing that I knew them well but unable to place them out of their usual uniform of short black jackets, white shirt and tie and long white apron down to the ankles. Of course Jules was the only one who passed any comment, assuring me that evening dress suited me so well that I should wear it more often. 'It improves the appearance of any gentleman, sir,' he said, which I doubted in my case because, while clothes may make the man, they can hardly make the mouse.

The Domino Room was fairly full but there were few of my favourites there. Frank Harris was in animated conversation with Julian Beerbohm, half brother of Max, who I knew was away in New York. I spotted Arthur Symons, long-faced with his drooping moustache, alone, staring at a piece of paper and looking miserable, for it later transpired that he had fallen passionately in love with a ballet dancer he had seen at the Empire, and had already written many poems about her. Perhaps, that night, he was drafting another. Anyway he had no eyes for me or for anyone else. Also in evidence was George Grossmith, the little man of Gilbert and Sullivan fame who could sing at such astonishing speed. As usual he was with a very pretty girl and never took his eyes off her.

Having shown myself I walked out in leisurely style, carrying my cloak and hat until I reached the exit, for I feared that had I put them back on in the Domino Room it would seem that I was deliberately trying to attract attention. It was a particular joy for me to walk through some of the most elegant and fashionable parts of London, even though more snow had begun to fall, and to linger in the foyer of the theatre among so many people of quality. I stood for a few minutes, as though waiting for some friend, watching them alight from the broughams, hansoms and beautifully varnished barouches, many with crests and armorial bearings, before I drifted inside to my seat, as though used to the procedure.

I have to admit that I felt self-conscious. In the same row as myself, though they were in the centre while I was far at the side, I recognized Whistler, Aubrey Beardsley and Robert Ross. I looked round for Bernard Shaw but he was not there, and we would have to wait a further day for his review, which turned out to be scathing. In the box facing me was the Prince of Wales himself, stout and bearded and wearing one of the decorations he loved to sport, possibly having arrived direct from some diplomatic function. With him, sitting openly, was Lillie Langtry, beautifully dressed in the height of Paris fashion. I knew that she was no longer there as his chief mistress of the bedchamber, for Daisy Brooke had supplanted her, and was herself being replaced, but she was making the most of being seen in the royal company.

There was, of course, no sign of Princess Alexandra, who was becoming more and more withdrawn from such entertainments through her deafness. Oh dear, what I could have taught her! With my experience I am sure I could have made her into a lip-reader of sufficient skill to enjoy a play with the help of opera glasses, for, while she was not stone deaf, as I was, an ear trumpet, then the only artificial hearing aid, was forbidden to a royal personage in public, especially one as pretty as the Princess. Poor Alexandra! She had much to bear: she not only walked with a limp and when riding her horse side-saddle had to sit to the right, but also had to wear high collars or a jewelled band to hide a bad scar on her throat. On top of all that she had to put up with Bertie's habits, though I understand he was not unkind to her in other ways and she always forgave him.

Lillie was still friendly with Oscar Wilde and it was natural that she would want to be at the first night, especially as at that time she was nursing secret ambitions to do some more acting. Originally, some twenty years previously, Oscar had been much taken with her chocolate-box beauty. When interviewed in New York, where he happened to be on a lecture tour when Lillie chanced to arrive, he had told waiting reporters, 'I would rather have discovered Mrs Langtry than have discovered America.' He had also written an over-effusive poem about her called 'The New Helen', which I had heard him read in the Domino Room. Later he had written *Lady Windermere's Fan*, his first big stage success, in the hope that she might act in it; but, when he had told her quite artlessly that it was about a woman with an illegitimate daughter, she had refused even to read it. As I looked up at Lillie that night Helen seemed a suitable name, for that lady too had been abducted from her husband.

Glancing up at Bertie, as most of the audience were from time to time, with his rapidly receding hair and hooded eyes and the luxuriant beard hiding a weak chin, I wondered what Lillie could see in him except, of course, the royal aura. It was this, I suppose, which induced men to copy his mannerisms. Once the Prince started drinking hock and other white wines thousands followed suit. I remember hearing Frank Harris explain how the Prince had changed the drinking habits of the upper and middle classes by introducing cigarette- and cigar-smoking at the table; this reduced the consumption of port, which, apparently, does not go as well with tobacco as brandy does. When Bertie left the bottom button on his waistcoat undone, either accidentally or because of the pressure of his paunch, which must have reached a girth of fifty inches and had given him the nickname of 'Tum-Tum', it started a fashion which persists to this day. After he turned his trouser bottoms up to avoid mud one day men began wearing trousers with turn-ups – quite useless save to the odd character who used a turn-up as an ash depository when sitting cross-legged, to avoid having to reach to the ashtray. Despite the Tranby Croft affair, I had to agree with Frank Harris when I heard him say, some time after Bertie's death, 'King Edward was loved by the English because he had all the aristocratic vices, whereas King George is disliked because he has all the middle-class virtues.'

Before the Prince had arrived – I took my seat early to see as much as possible – there was a commotion in the foyer of the theatre. The Marquess of Queensberry, intent on his habit of causing a public disturbance and on angering Oscar, arrived with a bouquet for the author. Characteristically, for he had behaved in this way at other theatres, mainly to draw attention to himself, it was a huge bunch of carrots and turnips which he intended to throw at Wilde at the end of the play while delivering an insulting speech about him to the audience. Fortunately, having heard that 'the screaming Scarlet Marquess', as Oscar had named him, had booked a seat, Wilde had asked the management to refuse him admittance, while he himself remained discreetly backstage. The police had also been informed.

The play itself was a resounding triumph for Oscar, containing some of the wittiest lines ever heard on the London stage:

> 'If the lower orders don't set us a good example, what on earth is the use of them? . . .'
> 'To lose one parent, Mr Worthing, may be regarded as unfortunate; to lose both looks like carelessness. . . .'
> 'All women become like their mothers. That is their tragedy. No man does. That's his. . . .'

Though I greatly enjoyed the play, many of the lines were already familiar to me, though perhaps in cruder form, for Oscar had produced them in his various conversations, then refined them. It was commonly said that he refined other people's remarks as well, which to me seemed fair enough; after all, Shakespeare borrowed plots and situations from previous writers. As both he and Oscar showed, it is not so much what an author says as how he says it that makes for theatrical success.

The audience was loud in its praise, with sustained insistent cries of 'Author! Author!' and 'Speech! Speech!', but Wilde did not appear. Perhaps he still feared that the Marquess might somehow get in, and it was just as well that, for once, he was discreet. Too many remembered his performance at the first night of *Lady Windermere's Fan* when, wearing the smile which Max Beerbohm had described as 'half-fatuous', he had told the audience, 'I congratulate you on the great success of *your* performance, which persuades me that you think almost as highly of the play as I do myself.' No doubt he had been playing his usual part, but it had been overdone in the circumstances and, while it had produced a few laughs and titters, especially from the front row, it had also engendered hisses and catcalls from those who felt the remarks to be not only arrogant but insulting. What Oscar still had to learn, and learn it in the most terrible way, as it proved, was that an audience's love can quickly turn to hate. I have heard Oscar remark that the reason for the link between love and hate is that the people you love are in the best position to hurt you. He was soon to discover that this also applied to his most enthusiastic fans, if I may use that modern word. While the fickleness of the public must have been apparent to such a keen observer, Oscar was subject to the delusion which seems to be an integral part of the human make-up: 'it could never happen to me.' In Oscar's case this blinding weakness was compounded by two other factors which corrupted his judgement – his inherent vanity and his stunning success.

The Importance of Being Earnest was quickly seen as being a classic comedy of its kind, and the author was hailed as a playwright not only of great skill but of an entirely new kind. Society lionized him more than ever, and hostesses tumbled over themselves to include him in their great parties. Conversationally, he rose to the occasion with an unending flow of the paradoxes and epigrams which were his hallmark. Max Beerbohm, who, as I noted earlier, had missed the first night of the great play through being in America, saw it on his return and brought Oscar to lunch at the Domino Room to congratulate him. 'Thank you, dear Max,' Oscar responded. 'Anyone can sympathize with the sufferings of a friend, but it requires a very fine nature to sympathize with a friend's success.'

Frank Harris also congratulated him with a lunch and, being a strong man who set much store by physical fitness, warned his guest that he was allowing himself to become prematurely old through over-indulgence. 'You are going to seed, Oscar, and you won't retain an active mind without a healthy body. Nobody enjoys his food and drink more than I do, but I take care to keep myself fit.'

'Ah, Frank', Oscar replied languidly. 'To win back my youth there is nothing I would not do – except take exercise, get up early or be a useful member of the community!'

If only Wilde could have been more down to earth and more serious about his work, instead of being obsessed with the importance of being Oscar. What he might have left us! But then he wouldn't have been Oscar at all. And we should have been denied such withering comments as his remark, when encountering a critic who had been unkind to him, 'You will pardon me. I remember your name perfectly but I cannot recall your face.'

There was a third factor in the gathering circumstances of the tragedy – the nature of Lord Alfred Douglas. While he may at one time have loved Oscar 'in his fashion', to misquote the best-known poem of Ernest Dowson, he more than anyone was responsible for his friend's downfall, as I shall relate. I do not believe that he ever felt sorrow about it, because he was so conceited that he could never bring himself to believe he could have behaved so selfishly; otherwise why would he have written, years later, 'My motto has always been "Give, give, give"', when for years all I saw him do was Take, take, take? Douglas remained spoiled, immature and naive to the end of his long life in 1945. In his autobiography he wrote, 'When you go to heaven you can be what you like, and I intend to be a child.' I have no doubt he believed this. He blamed Wilde for all the social problems which originated in his own nature, claiming that he came to realize that Oscar was 'a very wicked man'. He may well have been, in some respects, but I have to record myself as being in agreement with another occasional visitor to the Café Royal, Lord Birkenhead — known in the Domino Room as 'Lord Burkeandhare', after two notorious body-snatchers. He was heard to remark of Bosie, 'It is said that the gods' favourites die young, but the real tragedy is sometimes that their life is long.' Was the real truth that the relationship between Wilde and Douglas was of the type which psychologists now call sado-masochism? Douglas certainly enjoyed inflicting distress on his older friend, and Wilde endured it to such an extent that it is not inconceivable that he may have enjoyed it.

8

PRELUDE TO DISASTER

In the afternoon of 18 February 1895, only four days after Oscar's great theatrical triumph, Queensberry called at Wilde's club, the Albemarle in Albemarle Street, and left a card with the porter bearing the mis-spelled statement, 'To Oscar Wilde, posing as a somdomite'. Instead of tearing up the card with the contempt it deserved, Oscar was greatly angered by it, regarding it as the ultimate in what had become a tiresome campaign of denigration and threats by Bosie's father. Over the next few days he discussed it with friends, who, with two exceptions, urged him to ignore the Marquess's stupidity. After all, the porter would not have known what a 'somdomite' was and nobody else had read the card.

The exceptions were Robert Ross, who recommended a lawyer, and the man who should have been most solicitous in guarding his friend's interests – Bosie himself. Seeing the opportunity to achieve his ambition of putting his father in the dock, he urged Oscar to issue a writ for criminal libel. One true friend above all did all he could to divert Oscar from the course which, to everyone but himself and Bosie, was so obviously suicidal. That was Frank Harris who, first at a dinner at the Café Royal, then at a lunch, worked hard in Oscar's interests.

On 1 March Wilde applied for a warrant for the arrest of Queensberry, who appeared on a charge of criminal libel at Marlborough Street Police Station the following day. With the names of both men being so well known, particularly in London, the event attracted enormous publicity.

A few days afterwards – my diary says it was a Monday – Harris, who already had a lunch appointment with Bernard Shaw, whom he had just hired as drama critic for his *Saturday Review* at £6 a week, had invited Wilde to join them later if he wished; the Café Royal was at that time just about the only restaurant where Wilde was still welcome because of the gossip about him. I had overheard the conversation, in which Wilde asked if he could bring Bosie. Harris had replied in his forthright way, 'I would rather you did not, but it is for you to do just what you like. I don't mind saying what I have to say before anyone.' Harris, who proved to be extraordinarily far-sighted over the whole affair, was fully aware of Douglas's destructive intent and was determined to warn Oscar about it.

Unfortunately the lunch was in one of the private oak-panelled rooms, but by good fortune the wine waiter happened to be my other good friend Bertrand – he of the large black side-whiskers preserved for posterity in a drawing by Aubrey Beardsley – who not only told Jules what he had heard but gave me a personal account. Frank Harris was later to write in detail about the meeting and, though much of his reminiscences has been dismissed as fiction, he certainly seems to have recorded that event with accuracy, and I have drawn on his words and my previous glimpses of Shaw in the Domino Room with Harris and others.

The conversations between Harris and Shaw before the arrival of Oscar would have been fascinating enough to me. The two could hardly have been more dissimilar: Harris, short, loud-voiced, almost pugilistic in his physique and aggressiveness, and with jet-black hair, which I suspect he dyed, and his Germanic moustache; Shaw, tall, stringy, with a high-pitched brogue and waspish, his red hair and beard contrasting sharply with his chalk-pallid, rather pitted face, for he had contracted smallpox during the epidemic of 1881. They were also opposed in their attitude to dress, for Harris considered his idea of smartness to be most important while Shaw, regarding clothing as no more than a warm covering, wore rough tweeds which were purposefully unpressed so as to give them what he called 'human shape'.

Like Wilde, Shaw never used really crude language in his speech ('Not bloody likely' in *Pygmalion* being something of a liberty for him), whereas Harris peppered his talk with profanities. While Harris was besotted with sex, considering women and wine the two best things in the world, Shaw seemed sexually passionless, though I had heard him assuring Harris in the past that he had indulged in what he called 'fornication', though not before he was thirty. Harris was a gourmet while Shaw, a vegetarian, was almost as abstemious with food as he was with drink, being a life-long teetotaller because his father had been a drunkard.

Though Shaw's main literary accomplishments were still to come, he was an established critic in the musical world and touched with as much vanity as Harris in his certain belief in his genius, rating his mind above that of Harris's idol Shakespeare. He was to write: 'With the single exception of Homer, there is no eminent writer, not even Sir Walter Scott, whom I can despise so entirely as I despise Shakespeare when I measure my mind against his. . . . It would positively be a relief to me to dig him up and throw stones at him.'

Harris claimed to have 'found' Shaw, and when they lunched he invariably challenged him to prove that he was the greater authority on Shakespeare. Harris's memory was certainly phenomenal, and he could not only recite great slabs of the plays but produce the telling quote for the right moment. As I was to witness, Harris retained a low opinion of Shaw. Later I heard him pronounce, 'Shaw is the most over-rated man today. He will never be remembered in the twentieth century. His plays are all full of Shaw. In one play he assumes a dozen different names but the characters are all Shaw. Furthermore, all his thoughts come from the head, while all really great thoughts come from the heart.'

Shaw's general opinion of his host was equally unflattering: 'He is neither first-rate, second-rate nor tenth-rate — just his horrible unique self. He is unable to distinguish between what is true and what is false.' This view was endorsed by Max Beerbohm, who said, 'Harris tells the truth when his invention flags.'

Lunch had proceeded in the usual Harris fashion. He sent back the hors d'oeuvre with a fierce 'What do you call this?' to the waiter, and when the steak appeared cried, 'This is horse-flesh – more probably donkey-flesh. Take it away. It's not fit for a Christian gentleman!' If Harris's purpose was to impress Shaw he was singularly unsuccessful. The Socialist and future dramatist, who knew well enough how Harris praised the Café Royal cooking in his writings, sat half amused and half angry at this unnecessary behaviour towards the waiter, which I interpreted as deriving from the fact that Harris had once been a waiter himself among the many other jobs he had tried when he was young.

Shaw had a plate of macaroni and Apollinaris water, but had to wait while his host waded through the usual three courses including a quite enormous entrecôte, which eventually arrived cooked to his satisfaction. He liked to prolong a meal to give the maximum time for conversation, having learned the art – for art it was – of being able to talk while eating at the same rate as his table companions, a feat which once led Wilde to remark that Harris's mouth was always either full of words of full of food.

Harris firmly believed that steaks were essential to the maintenance of his virility, and once, when eating a huge porterhouse, I saw him turn to a woman at a table nearby and cry, 'We do this for your sakes, you know!' He made the same point concerning Shaw's lack of interest in sex at the particular lunch I am describing.

'How you hope to write without intimate knowledge of women I cannot understand,' he said. 'Passion is the forcing house of talent. That is why so many of the creative men have been hag-ridden by sex.'

'I have no doubt I shall manage,' Shaw replied. 'I agree with you that sexual intercourse can produce a celestial flood of emotion and exaltation of existence. But it is too fleeting. Intellectual exaltation has more appeal. In my view the ideal love affair is one conducted by post.'

'By post!' Harris scoffed. 'I agree that words are important in sexual affairs, but they need to be uttered during the act – the coarser the better for most women. Verbal images excite them.'

Shaw's response surprised him. 'That was part of my trouble during my limited sexual experience. I talked all the time, but not as you would. Frankly, in retrospect, the sex act seems so indecent that it is a hopeless basis for marriage. How any self-respecting man and woman can face each other in the daylight after spending the night together I don't understand.'

'No problem,' Harris replied. 'They do it again in the daylight. But seriously, don't you think that Shakespeare derived much of his drive and achievement from his passion for the Dark Lady?'

'I believe my works will disprove your theory,' Shaw answered, stretching backwards in his chair, for he was always very restless.

Harris, who had probably heard one lady's description of Shaw's love-making as 'passion served up with cold sauce', was not impressed. 'I am sure it's that food you eat, Shaw. Next time you come to lunch with me let me order for you. I have a special aphrodisiac meal devised by Nicols, the owner here. I would reveal the secret to few, but you are a particularly needful case. It is hors d'oeuvre with caviare, the tail-piece of cold salmon trout, then a cold grouse, finished off with wild strawberries and of course the right wines and brandy. I can tell you it works – especially when the lady eats it too.'

Shaw winced. 'I find the whole prospect revolting,' he said, toying with his macaroni, which he claimed that he never enjoyed in the Café Royal because it was so expensive and no better than in a restaurant where he could get it for tenpence.

Harris laughed uproariously, lifted his glass of Chambertin, held it to the light and said, 'Now this is like the woman of thirty. More body than claret, more generous, with a finer perfume, but very intoxicating and must be used with self-restraint.'

'You are incorrigible,' Shaw remarked as Harris drank the glass which had followed several previous draughts, not only of burgundy but of white wine and aperitifs.

'Nevertheless you would do well to mark my words, Shaw. Copulation is more important than literature. The penis is mightier than the pen, or even the sword!'

Shaw turned his grey-blue eyes in horror towards the ceiling, but before he could reply Oscar entered with Bosie in tow behind him. Harris's moustache which, it was alleged, he curled by sleeping with it wrapped round a paper clip, seemed to rise with his obvious annoyance at the sight of Douglas; and Shaw, who had never met Bosie, offered to leave. It was Wilde, however, who begged him to stay after introducing him to his friend. Harris immediately sent for the brandy bottle again, poured three and waited for Wilde to take the initiative.

'Frank, I intend to go ahead with this case against Queensberry and I want you to give evidence for me.'

'I will gladly do so, but you are going to lose the case, whoever gives evidence for you,' Harris retorted.

'No, Frank, I am going to win it. As you know, Queensberry is a professed atheist, a rabid supporter of Bradlaugh. He will refuse to take the oath, and call it "Christian tomfoolery", as he did with the oath of allegiance in the House of Lords. That will alienate the court, who will already be aware that he is mad after his behaviour at the St James's Theatre, which was widely publicized. Then Bosie will show the court what a beast his father is and it will have no sympathy for him.'

Harris shook his head emphatically, being clearly unimpressed with anything Douglas might do, and being quite convinced that he was present purely to ensure that Wilde was not swayed by anybody else's advice.

'Look, Oscar, we start from the certainty that you are going to lose this case. I take it, since we have had the police court proceedings, that you have seen the particulars of justification?'

Wilde nodded without replying verbally.

'Do they have hard evidence against you?' Harris asked.

'They think they have,' Oscar replied airily.

'Then,' declared Harris with a flourish of his hand, 'you must give it up. Drop it at once.'

Bosie's face flushed with anger and Wilde sighed despairingly.

'Look, Oscar, I know the law,' Harris boomed in his know-all way. 'If they have evidence – and I happen to know they have – the Director of Public Prosecutions will have to proceed against you.'

'But I have Sir Edward Clarke, the leader of the Bar, as my counsel,' Wilde protested.

'Yes, and I hear that the defence has managed to induce Edward Carson to act for Queensberry,' Harris said.

Oscar, who had known Carson, the first Irish QC to come to the English Bar, when they were at Trinity College, Dublin, dismissed the suggestion by saying, 'What does old Ned Carson know of literature or life?'

'You may think that he is your inferior intellectually, but he has already proved his power of advocacy by successfully defending another idiot Marquess, Clanricarde.'

'That scavenger of dustbins,' Wilde said scathingly, referring to the wealthy Marquess's habit of stealing food from waste bins outside restaurants to save a few pennies.

'What he can do for one eccentric he can do for another,' Harris warned, almost heatedly.

Sensing the mounting tension, Shaw attempted to provoke the conversation on to a higher level. 'Tell me, is *The Importance of Being Earnest* a pot-boiler or not?'

Such a remark would normally have produced a stinging rejoinder from Wilde but, apart from giving Shaw a look of intense disappointment, he paid no attention to it.

'Frank, I want you to testify that *Dorian Gray* is a highly moral work,' he said earnestly, referring to his novel which contained arguments that many found distasteful.

'You are clutching at straws, Oscar. Whatever I testify or don't testify you haven't a dog's chance of securing Queensberry's conviction. And then where will you stand? . . . I will tell you,' Harris went on without waiting for his question to be answered. 'You will stand in the dock yourself.'

Fearing that Wilde might be swayed by the argument, Douglas attacked Harris. 'If you say that you are no friend to Oscar.'

'My advice is entirely friendly, Douglas. And furthermore it is sound. Oscar must not only drop the case but get out of England.'

Douglas was horrified as he saw his chance of seeing his father in the dock slipping away, and rose to leave, but sat down again since Wilde remained at the table.

'Don't you agree, Shaw, that it is my duty to proceed with this case, to show the world what a terrible man this Marquess is?' Wilde asked his silent fellow Irishman.

I was thrilled by the prospect of an argument between Wilde and Shaw, for I had heard Oscar say to another of his fellow countrymen, W. B. Yeats, 'We Irish are the greatest talkers since the Greeks.' Shaw did not disappoint me. Rubbing his hands vigorously, his mannerism when getting words out, he said, 'When a stupid man does something he is eventually ashamed of he always declares that it was his duty.'

'You should go abroad,' Harris interrupted, 'and, as your ace of trumps in view of Queensberry's assertion, you should take your wife with you.'

'No,' Douglas almost shrieked at the mention of Oscar's wife; his voice was as shrill as Queensberry's and his face as contorted.

'Yes,' Harris insisted firmly. 'Then for the excuse you should write a letter to *The Times* such as you alone can write. You should set forth how you have been insulted by the Marquess and how you naturally went to the courts for a remedy, but then found out this was a mistake.'

'It would not be a mistake,' Douglas interjected hotly.

'It would be a mistake and it *is* a mistake,' Harris reiterated, thumping the table. 'It was a mistake, you point out, an error of judgement, if you like, because you now realize that no jury would give a verdict against a father. The only thing for you to do, therefore – the only sensible course left open to you – is to go abroad for a couple of years and leave the ring, with its gloves, its sponges and pails, to Lord Q. You should say that you are a maker of beautiful things, not a fighter, whereas the Marquess of Queensberry takes joy only in fighting. You refuse to fight with a father under such circumstances.'

Wilde paused, as though considering the proposition. Harris poured three more brandies, cost being of little importance to him since most of his meals were set against the bill for advertisements which the Café Royal placed in the *Fortnightly Review* to encourage a literary clientele.

'What do you really think, Shaw?' Wilde asked eventually.

'I think Frank is absolutely right. You are putting your head in a noose. . . .'

'Then such advice shows that you are no friend of Oscar's either,' Douglas declared. 'It would be running away. . . .'

'The best thing Oscar could do,' Harris insisted. 'I tell you I *know*. If he goes on with this case it will reach a certain point where he will find himself in the dock, himself the man on a criminal charge being asked dangerous questions. . . .'

Though my judgement was of little consequence to anyone when I heard the arguments, I felt in my bones that Harris was right, and found it hard to avoid writing to Wilde, urging, 'Take his advice, go to the Continent with your wife. Cast the vile Douglas out of your life, you stupid fool!'

The very idea, me calling Oscar Wilde a fool! But my arrogance was justified by secret knowledge. On a previous occasion in the Domino Room I had overheard Wilde telling Robert Ross that when he had instructed his solicitor to proceed with the case he had been asked for an assurance that there was not a word of truth in Queensberry's libel. Wilde had given this so affirmatively that the solicitor had replied, 'If you are innocent then you should succeed.' This was an honest opinion but, after his downfall, Wilde misused it to claim that it was on his solicitor's advice that he had brought the action.

Sadly Wilde was putting far too much faith in swaying the jury by having Douglas in the witness box to destroy his father's character before he himself was subjected to cross-examination. Further, Harris was talking in terms of hard, inescapable facts which never appealed to Oscar. Indeed he hated facts and always preferred fantasies. So Harris's advice was doomed to be rejected without serious consideration, for their minds operated in different ways and in conflicting realms. As I once heard Wilde say to Harris, 'I am like a Persian, who lives by warmth and worships the sun, talking to some Eskimo, who answers me with praise of blubber and nights spent in ice houses!'

Finally Oscar rose wearily and said, with sadness in his voice, 'It is not friendly of you Frank. It really is not friendly.'

'Don't be absurd,' Harris countered.

'No, Frank, it's not friendly.' It was a sentiment with which Bosie, from his half-smile as he finished his brandy, clearly agreed.

Harris, who was not easily hurt, stood up and said, 'I hope you don't really doubt my friendship, Oscar. You have no reason to.'

Wilde, who had not touched his second brandy, did not reply but walked slowly to the door, followed by Douglas. It was a sad moment for all of us, for it was Oscar's last exit from the Café Royal, where he had held sway for eleven years.

As the two disappeared Harris held up his hands in despair. 'It is not only Oscar who will be on trial, Shaw, but a whole way of life. It will rub off on all of us who come here. We are all involved.'

'Not I, Harris. Not I,' Shaw said sanctimoniously.

'But you agree with me that he is doomed?'

'I do. One man who has a mind and knows it can always beat twelve men who haven't and don't,' Shaw said, thinking of the jury Oscar would face. 'But in this affair Wilde has no mind. He is letting that revolting little creature do his thinking for him. It's unusual for an Irishman.'

'How come?' Harris asked.

'Because an Irishman likes to know what he is doing and why. There's nothing an Englishman hates more.'

Harris, who had been born in Galway, managed a faint smile.

'Wilde is behaving like so many unsuccessful litigants before him,' Shaw continued. 'He thinks it will be as easy to convince a court of strangers as it is for him to convince a circle of his chosen friends.'

There was, without doubt, a self-destructive streak in Oscar's nature, and he was so aware of it that I once heard him say, 'Sometimes I think that the artistic life is a long and lovely suicide.' He was certainly not alone in this. Over the years I noticed this streak in many of those who professed to be creative. Such people, like Virginia Woolf, literally destroyed themselves. Others let their friends destroy them. Douglas was such a destroyer by nature that he was the worst type of person that a soul like Wilde could have encountered, especially when Oscar was to convince himself that Bosie was his inspiration, which may of course have been true, or at least partly so. While Oscar was a generous giver, Bosie was a born taker, and it is my considered view that those on the make, like Frank Harris, are preferable to those on the take, like Bosie Douglas.

When I say a 'born' taker I mean it literally, because Bosie believed that being an 'aristocrat' entitled him to special treatment and deference. He frequently used that word about himself and his family, in spite of the abominable behaviour of his father and some other of his ancestors. I once heard him use it in a way which demonstrated the depth of his self-delusion: 'Through more than a thousand years I have inherited all the instincts of the true aristocrat, the chief of which I take to be generous and open-handed.' The Wilde – Douglas relationship was like the situation, common enough among aristocrats and ordinary people alike, where a man is besotted by a woman, then victimized by her, but still cannot resist her and puts up with all her tantrums, rages and misdemeanours. Those of us who have never experienced it cannot understand it, are sure that we would never tolerate it, and despise the man that does.

I suppose that Wilde's loyalty to Douglas to the point of self-ruination deserves some merit, but it showed profound lack of judgement. Clearly his judgement had been corrupted by his love for the younger man, who, for all his faults, was loaded with that indefinable quality called charm. Douglas, of course, was so vain that he could never see his faults. When things went badly for him he blamed the curse which he genuinely believed had been laid on his family, the historically notorious 'Black Douglases' of Scotland. But, as Oscar had seen, the curse lay in Bosie's black hatred of his father. Anyone so motivated by loathing would be likely to divert some of it to other targets, as Douglas did throughout his life, bringing one stupid law suit after another.

I have my own views – a theory, if you like – about the real root cause of Oscar's determination to take Queensberry to court, but I shall reserve this for a later chapter. Some may think it incredible, but the more I dwell upon Oscar's character, as unfolded to me personally over the years, the more I believe I am right.

9

TRIAL OF IRISH WITS

Queensberry's trial opened at the Central Criminal Court – the Old Bailey – that grim building, since demolished and rebuilt, from which so many had been sent to death or imprisonment, on 3 April 1895. I had queued for a place since 3 a.m., taking my little folding stool which, in those days, could safely be left while one slipped off for a coffee at the stall near Smithfield meat market, but the case attracted such interest that I only managed to secure standing room in the court, for even the gangways were packed. Of course many well-to-do men – there were no women in court – had somehow managed to secure reserved seats, I believe by bribing the ushers, and jokes were being made about 'The Importance of Being Early'.

There was a murmur as Wilde entered, elaborately dressed, as usual, in a long Melton overcoat, carrying a very tall, conical silk hat and wearing a white buttonhole flower – the badge of innocence. Everyone stood as the judge, Mr Justice Collins, an Irishman, entered, followed in the customary manner by the High Sheriff of London bearing a sword representing justice. Oscar's counsel, Sir Edward Clarke QC, who had cross-questioned Bertie during the Tranby Croft trial, looked most impressive and dignified, a small man but with the stout build and very long side-whiskers which at that time were somehow associated with strength of character and reliability. Like Wilde's solicitor, he too had been assured of his client's total innocence. Mr Carson, another Irishman and later to be Lord Carson, famed in politics for helping to found the Ulster Parliament, looked in his gown and wig and with his great protruding lower jaw like the relentless inquisitor he proved to be.

The clerk called for silence and the Marquess of Queensberry entered the dock, his red whiskers contrasting sharply with a light blue hunting stock.

'John Sholto Douglas, Marquess of Queensberry,' the Clerk of Arraigns recited, 'you are charged with contriving and maliciously intending to injure one Oscar Fingall O'Flahertie Wilde and to excite him to commit a breach of the peace and to bring him into public contempt, scandal and disgrace on the eighteenth day of February in the year of our Lord one thousand eight hundred and ninety-five. What have you to say on this charge?'

'That I am not guilty, my lord,' Queensberry replied. 'The libel is true. I consider it for the public benefit that it be published in this court.'

There was discreet applause from Queensberry's supporters, then the jury was sworn in.

'The libel was published in the form of a visiting card left by Lord Queensberry at the club to which Mr Wilde belonged, and it had written on it certain words,' Sir Edward explained. 'You will appreciate that the leaving of such a card openly with the porter of a club is a most serious matter and one likely gravely to affect the position of the person as to whom that injurious suggestion was made. What we have to settle now is whether or not this libel is true in regard to Mr Oscar Wilde.'

In fact Wright, the porter at the Arts Club, was later to testify that, while Queensberry had handed him the card, he had not understood what a 'somdomite' was, had put it back in the envelope, and given it to Wilde with no chance that anybody else might have seen it. No libel had therefore been committed and, had not Oscar taken the bait, nobody need have heard about it.

As Carson rose to speak, in a slow, melodious and very expressive brogue, as the newspapers reported it, it soon became clear that this sharp-witted Irishman was determined to turn the defence into a prosecution, as Frank Harris had predicted. In later years Carson was to be castigated by admirers of Wilde's works for being the means of sending such a sensitive man to prison, but at the time of the trial I overheard it stated authoritatively by people concerned with the case that he had originally refused to take the brief because he detested the raking up of a public man's private affairs, especially as there seemed to be no evidence that could be brought into court. He accepted the brief only after detectives searching a flat in London had found letters associating Wilde with many reprehensible youths. He had been so horrified by the letters that he agreed to defend Queensberry, in the belief that Wilde was a disgrace to society and to his native Ireland. What had finally swayed him was the argument of Queensberry's solicitor, Mr Charles Russell, that if Wilde won the case he would claim it as proof that a man of genius was above the moral and national laws — as I knew he fervently believed — and might then write a play on that theme.

'My Lord, gentlemen of the jury,' Carson began. 'As you are aware, the whole of this lamentable inquiry has arisen through the association of Mr Oscar Wilde with my client's youngest son, Lord Alfred Douglas. Lord Queensberry has in his possession certain letters written by Mr Wilde to Lord Alfred. I ask the court to read these letters and to say whether the gorge of any father ought not to rise. Lord Queensberry has drawn from these letters the conclusions that most fathers would draw. It remains for this court to decide whether these conclusions are justified. My client, in his dealings with Mr Wilde, has been influenced by one hope alone — at all risks and at all hazards to save his son from an association he feels to be disastrous.'

There was enthusiastic applause as he sat down.

When called into the witness box Wilde stared around the court like an elegant gazehound as Sir Edward cross-examined him, rather prosaically, ending with the question, 'Is there any truth in these allegations?'

'There is no truth in any of them,' I heard Wilde reply, a statement on oath which I knew to be a lie, as both Oscar and Lord Alfred were to confess in later years.

Mr Carson then rose to cross-examine a man whom he knew personally, and scored immediately by correcting Oscar who had given his age as two years younger than it was, a stupid vanity which reduced his credibility. Carson then asked, 'It appears that you are in the habit of associating with certain classes of young men — grooms, valets and the like. Now what can a gentleman like you have in common with low-class youths?'

'I delight in the society of people younger than myself. I recognize no social distinction of any kind and to me youth, the mere fact of youth, is so wonderful that I would rather talk to a young man for half an hour than be cross-examined in court.'

This brought the first laughter as Carson asked, 'Do you give them wine?'

'What gentleman would stint his guests?'

'Do you drink champagne?'

'Yes. Iced champagne is a favourite drink of mine – strongly against my doctor's orders.'

'Never mind your doctor's orders, sir.'

'I never do,' Wilde replied, amid further laughter.

I watched the Marquess's face screw into a scowl as he saw Wilde scoring point after point, but I felt that, like me, he knew they were superficial points being scored by painless jabs as his adversary bored in with damaging body blows.

Using his hand theatrically, Carson made much of the fact that Wilde was forty while Douglas was only twenty-four, then passed to Wilde's novel, *Dorian Gray*. 'You talk about one man adoring another. Did you ever adore any man?'

'No, I have never adored anyone but myself.'

The crowd roared with laughter.

Then Wilde continued. 'There are people in the world, I regret to say, who cannot understand the deep affection that an artist can feel for a friend with a beautiful personality.'

Carson then read an extract from *Dorian Gray*: ' "Your slim gilt soul walks between passion and poetry." Is that a beautiful phrase?'

'Not as *you* read, Mr Carson. You read it *very* badly.'

Carson was unperturbed by the ensuing laughter, and suggested than any illiterate person getting hold of *Dorian Gray* might put a decadent construction upon it.

'The views of illiterates on art are unaccountable,' Wilde replied. 'I have no knowledge of the views of ordinary individuals.'

This passage on *Dorian Gray*, which Wilde had defended so brilliantly, ended with the author's disdainful statement, 'I don't know what you are talking about.'

'Don't you?' Carson replied grimly. 'I hope I shall make myself very plain before I have done.'

It was already clear to me that Oscar had made a grave mistake in stinging Carson, himself a master of invective, with his biting ripostes, and would be made to pay for it.

Replacing *Dorian Gray* among his exhibits, Carson picked up a slim magazine and said, 'I have a sonnet of yours referring to ". . . a hidden love that dare not speak its name". I really must ask you to explain those lines to the court. What is this love that dare not speak its name?'

'The love that dare not speak its name in this century is such a great affection of an older for a younger man as there was between David and Jonathan, such as Plato made the basis of his philosophy, and such as you find in the sonnets of Michelangelo and Shakespeare. It is that deep, spiritual affection which is as pure as it is perfect. It is beautiful, fine, the noblest form of affection. There is nothing unnatural about it. It is intellectual and it repeatedly exists between an older and a younger man when the older man has intellect and the younger man has all the joy, hope and glamour of life before him. That it should be so the world does not understand. The world mocks at it and sometimes puts one in the pillory for it.'

This noble statement, so beautifully rendered, brought loud applause, though there was some hissing from those determined to support the Marquess and mock the writer.

Carson then read a letter from Wilde to Douglas containing the words: 'Bosie, you must not make scenes with me. They kill me, they wreck the loveliness of life. I cannot see you, so Greek and gracious, distorted by passion. I cannot listen to your curved lips saying hideous things about me. I must see you soon. You are the divine thing I want, the thing of genius and beauty; but I don't know how to do it. . . . Why are you not here, my dear, my wonderful boy?'

Wilde said it was no more than an expression of tender admiration for Douglas, but I could see that many people present thought differently.

Carson, rather superficially I thought, then tried to make capital out of the fact that Wilde burned joss sticks in his house, presumably on the grounds that this was an effeminate habit, though I, for one, could not see why it should be when millions of virile Chinamen did the same.

My legs were beginning to ache – and my fingers too, with my efforts to make shorthand notes – as Carson left the scene of literature for Wilde's more dangerous activities with what Harris had called his riff-raff friends, but he had not got very far before the court was adjourned until the following morning.

Immediately Wilde, smiling and bland, was surrounded by friends congratulating him on such a witty performance, but even as unworldly a person as myself could sense that his sallies had not impressed the jury and could well have alienated it. He had behaved as though he was there for the laughs, when it was clear to everyone else that the situation could hardly be more serious. He had even mimicked Carson's Irish accent, as I read later, and the fact that the barrister was speaking with a heavy cold, which was obvious to all of us from his frequent recourse to his handkerchief, and while this raised a cheap laugh or two it was to prove dear the following day.

I knew Wilde had perjured himself, but my sympathies were still with him as I walked back to my lodgings, sad at heart and quite exhausted by the concentrated effort of continuous lip-reading over such a long period.

The following session was altogether different in atmosphere and, whether Oscar's conscience had been stricken during a sleepless night or not, he seemed far less sure of himself as Carson tore into him about his sordid relationships.

He concentrated first on a man called Alfred Taylor, an educated person of good family, who had sumptuously furnished premises in Little College Street which had been raided by the police who found women's clothes provided so that 'clients', who were what are now called transvestites, could derive sexual satisfaction through dressing up in them. It was inevitably presumed that they were also used in other sexual acts, and it was to transpire that Taylor functioned as a ponce by inviting messenger boys, newsboys and other low-class youths who could be induced to perform homosexual acts for money.

'Has Taylor been to your house and to your chambers?' Carson asked.

'Yes.'

'Have you been to Taylor's rooms to afternoon tea parties?'

'Yes.'

'Did Taylor's rooms strike you as peculiar?'

'They were pretty rooms.'

'Have you ever met there a young man called Wood?'

'On one occasion.'

My heart sank at the mention of this name, for I knew from what I had heard myself in the Café Royal that Wood, a tall, fair-haired youth, was not only a sodomite but a blackmailer, in touch with even more hardened villains who would do anything for money. I recalled that evening when Wood had confessed to Wilde in my 'hearing', while they dined together, that he had secured incriminating letters from him to Bosie. If Carson had these in his possession Oscar was undoubtedly lost, whatever wit he might still conjure up from the increasing despondency which seemed to surround him in the witness box.

'What was your connection with Taylor?' Carson asked almost aggressively, while Oscar began to show his nervousness by twiddling his big scarab ring.

'Taylor was a friend, a young man of intelligence and education: he had been to a good English school.'

'Did you know Taylor was being watched by the police?'

'No.'

'Did you know that Taylor was arrested with a man named Parker in a raid made last year on a house in Fitzroy Square?'

'I read of it in the newspaper.'

'Did that cause you to drop your acquaintance with Taylor?'

'No. . . .'

'How many young men has Taylor introduced to you?'

'Five in all.'

'Did you give money or presents to these five?'

'I may have done.'

'Among the five men Taylor introduced you to, was one named Parker?'

'Yes.'

'Did you call him "Charlie" and allow him to call you "Oscar"?'

'Yes.'

'Did you know Parker was a gentleman's servant out of work, and his brother a groom?'

'No. I did not.'

'What was there in common between you and Charlie Parker?'

'I like people who are young, bright, happy, careless and original. I do not like them sensible, and I do not like them old.'

Oscar raised a laugh with this remark, but it was dearly bought as Carson, who was forty-one, continued with his remorseless and damning recital.

'Had you chambers in St James's Place?'

'Yes, from October '93, to April '94.'

'Did Charlie Parker go and have tea with you there?'

'Yes.'

'Did you give him money?'

'I gave him three or four pounds because he said he was hard up.'

'Did you give Charlie Parker a silver cigarette case at Christmas?'

'I did.'

That was by no means the end of it.

'When did you first meet Fred Atkins?' Carson asked.

'In October or November '92.'

'What age was he?'

'Nineteen or twenty.'

'Did you go to Paris with him?'

'Yes.'

'Did you give him money?'

'Yes.'

Carson continued to press him about his relations with another boy formerly employed by Bosie in his rooms in Oxford.

'Did you ever kiss him?' he asked.

'Oh, dear no. He was a peculiarly plain boy. He was, unfortunately, extremely ugly. I pitied him for it.'

The whole idea of one man kissing another was intended to revolt the jury, and I could see by the jurymen's expressions that Carson, who was proving his mastery of cross-examination, was producing the desired effect.

And where was Bosie as the tragedy unfolded? In the court, yes, but not in the witness box where, according to both Oscar and himself, he was to have swung the case by branding his father as the dreadful man he undoubtedly was. Having seen and spoken to Douglas, Sir Edward Clarke was convinced that he would be a bad witness. He also knew that the judge would not have permitted him to blacken his father's character because this was irrelevant to the case at issue. So he did not put Bosie in the box before Wilde, as both, apparently, had expected. Wilde's only other witness was the porter from the Arts Club, and Carson was allowed to present Queensberry as a noble father, a 'pathetic old man' though he was only in his early fifties.

After Carson broke Wilde with his final question, asking him if he would know a certain waiter in a Paris hotel, where detectives had been making inquiries, Sir Edward Clarke rose to re-examine, reluctantly making use of some letters that Queensberry had sent to his son and which expressed malice to many people and mentioned leading public figures. But any effect of this was far outweighed by his apparent failure to put Bosie into the box, which probably made a bad impression on the jury. Throughout his life Bosie insisted that Clarke had promised to put him in the witness box so that he could give evidence against his father, and claimed that he could never understand why this was not done, because he believed he could undoubtedly have swung the case in Oscar's favour. Sir Edward later denied that he had ever promised to put Douglas in the box, and it would appear that he had quickly realized that his client was guilty and had lied to him, and that his prosecution might follow.

I left the court on the second day as depressed as Oscar must have been. Nobody could deny that all the honours had gone to Carson for his dazzling display, and the result of this on Oscar's so-called friends was appalling: most of them slipped quietly out of the court; only one or two had the loyalty to speak to him – as I venture to say I would have myself, had I really known him.

The next day sealed Oscar's fate, for Carson produced several of the young men he had mentioned and encouraged them to tell their stories. It was not long before Sir Edward Clarke spoke privately with Carson. Then, after talking to Wilde, he withdrew the prosecution. Quite properly Carson then insisted that this withdrawal must mean that Queensberry's plea of justification had been upheld. The judge and jury agreed, in these tragic terms:

> *Clerk of Arraigns*: 'Gentlemen of the jury, do you find the plea of justification has been proved or not?'
> *Foreman*: 'Yes.'
> *Clerk*: 'And do you find the defendant not guilty?'
> *Foreman*: 'Yes.'
> *Clerk*: 'And Lord Q may be discharged?'
> *Judge*: 'Certainly.'

As Queensberry stepped down, having been granted costs which spelt financial ruin for Wilde's family, there was wild applause, cheering and cries of 'Long live the Marquess!' which the judge made no effort to restrain, even when it was accompanied by shouts of 'Down with Oscar Wilde!' The cheers and jeers were echoed in the street especially by prostitutes, who believed that Wilde and so many other homosexuals were undermining their trade. My suspicion that Queensberry had hired a claque, part of which had managed to get into the court, was strengthened.

As Napoleon said, 'Providence is on the side of the big battalions.' The big battalions had been on the Marquess's side, but Oscar had really been his own executioner. All Wilde could do was to issue a statement to the press declaring:

> 'It would have been impossible for me to have proved my case without putting Lord Alfred Douglas in the box against his father. Lord Alfred Douglas was extremely anxious to go into the box, but I would not let him do so. Rather than put him in so painful a position, I determined to retire from the case and to bear on my own shoulders whatever ignominy and shame might result from my prosecuting Lord Queensberry.'

Queensberry, true to form, could not resist exulting in Wilde's extremity. As soon as the trial was over he issued a message to Wilde through a news agency declaring: 'If the country allows you to leave, all the better for the country. If you take my son with you I will follow you and shoot you.'

10

LONDON SHAME

Immediately after the case Wilde was urged by well-meaning friends to flee to France, but his mind was already befogged by his ordeal and, understandably perhaps, he drank a great deal in a hurry, as desperate men may do. He withdrew a considerable sum of money from his bank, as though intending to escape, but dithered too long and, accompanied by Bosie and Robert Ross, went round to the room at the Cadogan Hotel in Sloane Street where Bosie was staying. As their cab trotted off from the precincts of the Old Bailey towards Holborn just before mid-day, I noticed a man who must have been a detective clamber into another cab which took off in the same direction and at the same speed as Oscar's.

That afternoon government officials decided that Wilde had to be arrested and charged. Sadly they included the husband of one of his former friends – Herbert Asquith, then the Home Secretary, married to Margot Tennant, and a former customer of the Café Royal.

Oscar, who had been joined in his extremity by the ever-sympathetic Reggie Turner, was picked up at ten minutes past six that evening. Bosie was out, trying to see his cousin George Wyndham at the House of Commons on Wilde's behalf, when two detectives arrived to apprehend his lover and take him to Scotland Yard to be charged. After drowning his fears in hock he was probably too intoxicated to appreciate the implications of the charge of 'committing acts of gross indecency'. It could, of course, have been far worse. Had he been accused of sodomy, for which there was much evidence, it would have carried the possibility of life imprisonment. From Scotland Yard Oscar was then taken to Bow Street where he faced someone he had certainly seen before, even though he may not have noticed him: this was the magistrate Sir John Bridge, who was quite a frequent visitor to the Café Royal as it was so conveniently near to the Bow Street court. Many of those who knew Sir John to be fair and good-hearted, as I did, were disappointed when he refused to grant bail, but, as so often happens in life, his attitude became much more understandable when the full facts were known. Some months later Sir John was lunching in the Grill with a friend and one of my informants gave me the following account of the conversation.

'I gave Wilde a sporting chance, which he hardly deserved, but he declined to take it,' Sir John explained. 'When I was asked to issue the warrant for his arrest I took the trouble to find out the time of the boat train to France, where I felt sure he would go. It left about five, so I held up the issue of the warrant until it had gone. It meant adjourning the court for almost a couple of hours and the Treasury solicitor didn't like it, but Wilde had given me a lot of enjoyment and I could see no good purpose in sending him to prison.'

'It could kill him, I suppose,' the friend remarked.

'I doubt that – unless he kills himself. But I knew he would certainly suffer more than most men.'

'Pity he didn't grasp the opportunity, John.'

'Yes. Trials like that do the country no good at all. But once he arrived at Bow Street I couldn't risk allowing him bail in case he took off. I knew by then that Whitehall wanted a conviction.'

'Ah, political motives! I suppose the government thought it expedient to go along with public opinion, which wanted an example made of Wilde.'

'That, no doubt, was a factor,' Sir John agreed. 'But there was another that was much more pressing. You may recall that before the Queensberry trial there was a serious leakage of information from the grand jury that had to consider the facts first.'

'Yes, it was all over the French papers. Rosebery was supposed to be involved, wasn't he?' the friend replied, referring to the man who had become Prime Minister.

'Well, I hope this never gets out, but there was some question about a homosexual relationship between Lord Rosebery and another of Queensberry's sons – Lord Drumlanrig.'

'Isn't that the fellow who was killed in a shooting accident?'

'The same, but there's some doubt about whether it was an accident. His shotgun was supposed to have gone off accidentally, but if you know anything about shooting you know that an experienced shot like Drumlanrig would never point his gun at himself or attempt to clean it when it was loaded.'

'So you suspect it was suicide?'

'I do. And not unconnected with the possible scandal of his alleged affair with Rosebery. Drumlanrig had been an MP and had been Parliamentary Secretary to Rosebery when the affair, if there was one, was supposed to be going on.'

At this point Sir John's friend had looked quite startled. 'But if Queensberry knew all that, it explains why he was so vicious against Wilde. Having lost one son through a homosexual affair, he was determined not to lose another.'

'Exactly! Of course, I don't know whether he was aware of it or whether there's any certain truth in it. But of one thing I am certain – the government was terrified that it might all come out in court.'

'Then for God's sake why did they prosecute him? Why did they bring a court action at all?'

Sir John smiled. 'Governments are queer fish. They were even more fearful of the consequences if the newspapers, who were howling for Wilde's blood, said that Wilde had been allowed to escape trial in order to cover up for the Prime Minister.'

The friend had shaken his head in bewilderment. 'The machinations! If Wilde had fled while you delayed the warrant, the government would have been in the clear because the newspapers could hardly have blamed it for that.'

'No comment,' Sir John replied.

'Yet obviously you could not grant bail once he had been arrested, because then the government would have been blamed.'

'No comment on that either.'

Poor Oscar! I wonder if he ever learned that a potential political scandal for which he had no responsibility whatever had helped to settle his fate.

The news that Oscar was at Bow Street after his arrest soon reached the Domino Room, and I could not resist making the short journey to the police station, the original home of the famous Bow Street Runners. There I found a dreadful mob, including scores of prostitutes, howling for Oscar's blood. It must have been extremely frightening, and perhaps it was as well that he was too drunk to understand that if he were allowed outside on bail he might have been lynched – a further reason, perhaps, for Sir John Bridge's uncharacteristic action.

I was pleased to return to the relative calm of the Domino Room, for I fear nothing more than a mindless mob, but even there the intensive discussion about the case led to several angry exchanges, and there were few who could summon up any sympathy. On the contrary I have to record that many of the habitués expressed themselves more than pleased with Oscar's perilous predicament. The ordinary mind appears to take some natural satisfaction from seeing the mighty fallen. Perhaps it comforts us for our mediocrity: like death, disgrace is a leveller, for there are so many who can exalt themselves in the social order only by the fall of those with talent.

Wilde was taken to Holloway Jail, which in those days was a prison for men. Robert Ross and his other homosexual friends quickly fled the country, mainly to France, but the robust Frank Harris made the long journey by hansom cab to Holloway to visit him and to bring him cheer. After his return I heard him say that Wilde was being treated as though he were already convicted.

Further, because the flow of cash from Wilde's royalties was held up and his creditors panicked, he was hurriedly sold up by the bailiffs. His beautiful books and other treasured possessions were put up at auction, which I attended out of sympathy as much as curiosity, though it did at last give me a chance to see inside the house with its lemon yellow- and scarlet-enamelled rooms. It was a pathetic occasion, for even the children's toys went under the hammer. A Whistler painting went for a shilling. For twice that sum I bought one of Wilde's less expensive walking sticks, which was too long for me and has stood in a corner of my room ever since, as I felt it almost sacrilegious to cut it down. I saw Will Rothenstein buy a picture by an artist I had never heard of, called Monticelli, and I was not surprised later to learn that he sold it and kept the money for his old friend. Mrs Wilde had understandably left London with her two boys, whose surname was later changed to Holland, to get away from the scandal. The bailiffs took no care of the Tite Street house, allowing it to be broken into by thieves and hooligans, who looted manuscripts and a writing table which had belonged to the Scottish writer, Thomas Carlyle, whom Wilde had admired.

While these terrible things were happening I wondered if Oscar was reminded of his quip: 'It is only by not paying one's bills that one can hope to live in the memory of the commercial classes.'

Of course Lord Alfred Douglas did not appear in the Domino Room, or in any of his old haunts. He crossed the Channel to France on 25 April, but later I heard him claim that he had visited Oscar daily during the three weeks that he was held in Holloway and that

Wilde and Sir Edward Clarke had urged him to get to France before
the trial began. Whatever the truth, Bosie disappeared from the
scene on the day before Oscar's trial opened. His departure marked
the end of the Decadents as a group in the Domino Room, though
fortunately for me some of them, like Max Beerbohm, continued to
attend regularly with other friends, and most of those who had fled
returned eventually. I was thankful to see that these included Reggie
Turner who, after a sojourn in France, came back and took a writing
job with the *Daily Telegraph*. This meant that we were not denied the
benefit of his charming and generous nature in the Domino Room –
at least not for a while. As he was independent financially, he was to
spend most of his later life in France and Italy, enjoying himself but
also writing twelve novels which, as he mournfully prophesied, were
not very successful.

Oscar knew that he had no hope of acquittal, being condemned by
the public before the trial began. There was a flush of obscene stories
and rhymes – retailed all round the Domino Room – like the parody
on 'Casa Bianca':

> *The boy stood on the burning deck*
> *His back towards the mast. He would not turn around again*
> *'Til Oscar Wilde had passed. . . .*

Happily, in those days, such obscenities did not get into the newspapers (except for that strange journal known as 'The Pink 'Un'), but
journalists were allowed greater licence then to pillory a man before
his trial, and did so. I remember seeing one terrible cartoon showing
Oscar already in a prison cell, which must have been a contempt of
court. And the pornographers, who are always with us, hawked the
juiciest evidence of the previous case, highlighting what chambermaids said they had discovered on bedsheets, in crudely illustrated
pamphlets, of which I still retain two copies. This all served to
incense the public further, and many of Wilde's friends feared that if
he were released he would be hunted down like a fox. No murderer,
not even Jack the Ripper, had he ever been caught, could have
aroused such animosity.

When the *Daily Mail* revealed that the police were watching the
haunts of other well-known homosexuals not connected with the
Wilde case, more of the queer fraternity quietly quit the country, 'to
take the waters' or on other trumped-up excuses. Others joined
cricket clubs, apparently thinking that this manly sport associated

with good, clean living would make them safe from suspicion; this move would have amused Oscar, had he been capable of laughter then, for I had once heard him remark: 'I never played cricket because the attitudes of the fielders are so indecent.'

The plea by Wilde's defence for a postponement to give the lawyers more time, which is usually granted, was refused. The trial opened at the Old Bailey on 27 April 1895 and this time, though I arrived at the court at 2 a.m., I was by no means the first in the queue. Clearly it was going to be something of a Nero's Circus, and many wished to witness the ritual slaughter. I noticed several other Domino Room habitués in the public gallery, such as Frank Harris and Max Beerbohm who, I am sure, were there out of sympathy rather than morbid curiosity.

Once again, for reasons I found hard to understand, Oscar had agreed to be defended by Sir Edward Clarke, who, he believed, had made such a hash of the first case, and by Mr Travers Humphreys, later a famous judge, who had also assisted in the Queensberry hearing. On Queensberry's instructions all the evidence and a shorthand note of the libel action had been sent to the Director of Public Prosecutions. I was later to learn from friends of Mr Carson, lunching in the Café Royal, that he had refused to have anything further to do with prosecuting Wilde and indeed asked Sir Frank Lockwood, the Solicitor General, a position Carson himself would eventually hold, if the prosecution could be abandoned. 'Can't you let up on the fellow, now?' he had asked. 'He has suffered a great deal.'

Lockwood said he would have preferred to, but could not for the political reasons which I was to hear Sir John Bridge mention. Lord Rosebery, then the Prime Minister, and Mr Gladstone had been named in those letters of Lord Queensberry which had been read out by Sir Edward Clarke in the libel action, and Lockwood had argued that if the case were abandoned the public might think it was to cover them. So in introducing those names Sir Edward had, albeit unwittingly, made a further tactical error which may have been instrumental in sending Oscar to prison.

Listening to the evidence of Charles Parker, who said quite openly that Oscar '. . . had committed sodomy with him and paid for it', to Alfred Wood recalling that evening when I had seen him drinking with Oscar in the Domino Room, and especially to the revolting testimony of the chambermaids, I was sure that Oscar was sunk. He had not put up a convincing performance in the witness box, and his one witty sally was in my opinion stupid. When asked about his expensive habit of giving silver cigarette cases to rough youths he answered, 'It is less extravagant than giving jewelled garters to ladies.' This scored off the questioning barrister, who had some reputation as a womanizer, but I thought it would convince the jury that the gifts to either sex were in pursuit of sexual favours.

I was delighted to find that my judgement was wrong. Sir Edward Clarke spoke so eloquently for two hours in Wilde's defence that he swayed some of the jurymen, though unfortunately not all. A new trial had to be ordered and Oscar faced the whole ordeal again.

At first bail was again refused, but mercifully a judge in chambers granted it and for a couple of weeks Oscar tasted freedom again, but a freedom that was very circumscribed. Few hotels or restaurants would have him in the place, and when he found a room under an assumed name Queensberry went there, denounced him and had him turned out.

In desperation Oscar sought refuge with his brother Willie in Oakley Street in Chelsea. His whereabouts were kept secret but I soon learned them because his friend, Robert Sherard, came from Paris to see him and visited the Domino Room where, in greatest confidence, he told Max Beerbohm where Oscar was and that he should visit him. Sherard said that Oscar hated being with his brother, who was an alcoholic and with whom he had fallen out long ago, but that a more comfortable sanctuary was in sight. Oscar's staunch old friends Ada Leverson, a plain but pleasant woman whom he had always called 'The Sphinx', and her Jewish husband were to take him into their home in Courtfield Gardens.

Max Beerbohm reported that he had duly visited him there and found him not only in high spirits but still flippant enough to say: 'The working classes are with me – to a boy!' Left in peace, he duly surrendered to his bail and found himself under a different judge, Mr Justice Wills, who proved to be a bad choice for him.

To save the Leversons from embarrassment he moved back to Oakley Street for the few days of the trial and there he was visited by Frank Harris, who recounted the experience to several people in the Domino Room:

'I called for him in a hansom and tried to persuade him to come to lunch at the Café Royal, but he couldn't face that. Still, he did venture out, and we had a good long talk in a quiet place I knew in Great Portland Street. He then told me that all this wretched evidence about stains on the bedclothes had had nothing to do with him. The other person in the bed with various youths had been Bosie Douglas! I did all I could to get him to induce Clarke to bring that out, but Oscar refused because it would be letting Bosie down. For God's sake! Letting Bosie down! Anyway there was no shifting him, and then Oscar said something which shattered me:

'"You talk with the same passion and conviction as if I were innocent."

'"But you are, aren't you?" I asked.

'"No, Frank, I'm not. I thought you always knew that."

'As soon as I heard that I knew that his case was doomed . . . so I urged him to get out of the country and jump his bail while he still could. I told him I could borrow a yacht from an MP friend of mine and could quickly get a carriage with fast horses to take him to Erith, where it was lying. But he refused.

'All he would say was, "Oh, Frank, how wonderful; but how impossible. I couldn't live with my conscience if I let down my sureties for my bail. How could I live in France fearing all the time that the policeman's hand might clamp on my shoulder? That would kill me in a month."'

Such then was Harris's story. Knowing his fondness for Oscar and his generosity of spirit, I believe the part about the yacht, though others thought he invented it to make himself look heroic. Even if it had not been true, the resourceful Frank would assuredly have organized something similar, had Oscar agreed. But I do not believe that he ever thought Oscar to be innocent. I had heard him too often castigating Wilde for consorting with scruffy youths and warning him of the danger. He knew that Wilde was a practising homosexual, so how could he genuinely have thought that he was innocent? Bernard Shaw attributed Oscar's obstinacy to the fact that he was not only Irish but an Irish gentleman. So, having given his word to surrender to his bail, he could not possibly bring himself to break it. Still, I think Oscar's main reason for remaining was wrapped up in my private theory about his downfall, which I will reveal later.

Oscar's third and final legal ordeal opened on 21 May, and once again I managed to secure a place in the public gallery, though with greater difficulty than ever, even though I had risen even earlier. Even the Marquess of Queensberry, intent on seeing justice done, had to stand. I can see him now, his face a cauldron of vindictiveness, gnawing at the rim of his flat-topped bowler hat. A few days previously he himself had been apprehended by the police and bound over to keep the peace for fighting with another son, Percy, at the corner of Bond Street and Piccadilly, after Percy could endure his father's insults no longer.

Also standing, when he should not have been, was poor Ernest Dowson, who by this time was deeply in consumption's grip and had allowed himself to go to pieces after the death of his mother, to whom he had been deeply attached. He was there out of genuine friendship, demonstrating his trade as a fellow poet by wearing a crumpled green jacket and a floppy bow tie, attached round his neck as usual by tired elastic which was always visible. Like myself, he felt he owed a debt to the defendant, because when Oscar had heard some of his work he lunched him at his Domino Room table, a symbol in those days that Dowson had arrived as a poet.

Alfred Taylor, a pleasant-looking man in his thirties, had undoubtedly procured youths for Wilde but, to his eternal credit, refused to give evidence against him. He was quickly convicted and received two years' hard labour. Charlie Parker, on the other hand, testified on oath that Oscar had committed sodomy upon him, and from that moment there could have been little if any doubt about the verdict in the minds of the jury.

The trial dragged on for four days, during which the foreman of the jury asked the very reasonable question as to whether a warrant for arrest had ever been issued against Lord Alfred Douglas. He was told that there had been no suggestion of arresting Douglas, and then bravely argued that if any guilt was to be deduced from various letters which were read in evidence then it would apply equally to Lord Alfred. Mr Justice Wills curtly commented that Lord Alfred was not involved in the trial. Indeed, his involvement had been studiously avoided and, while I believe that Oscar was pleased about this at the time, there could be little doubt that Douglas was being spared only because he was the son of a peer of the realm. Douglas should certainly have been tried, but in his case justice was neither done nor seen to be done.

Sir Edward Clarke attempted to persuade the jury that since the evidence rested on the words of blackmailers and other criminals it should all be rejected, but it was a poor effort. He followed up by begging them to allow such a distinguished man of letters to continue to give pleasure to so many people through his plays by remaining free, so enabling his genius to mature.

The jury quickly returned the only verdict they could: 'Guilty on all counts.'

The judge showed the bias he had demonstrated throughout the case by the malevolence not only of his sentence, but in his manner of announcing it.

'That you, Wilde, have been the centre of extensive corruption of the most hideous kind among young men, it is impossible to doubt. I shall, under the circumstances, be expected to pass the severest sentence that the law allows. In my judgement it is totally inadequate for such a case as this. The sentence of the court is that you be imprisoned and kept to hard labour for two years.'

This was much more severe than it sounded, for in those days 'hard labour' not only meant what it said but also meant solitary confinement, with only one letter per quarter, an horrific prospect for anyone so gregarious and needful of friendship. There were some cries of 'Shame', and I was near to tears as I saw Oscar limp and dejected in the dock as he realized what this was going to mean to him. For such a kind and highly sensitive man to be incarcerated with common criminals, and above all to be deprived of books, was a savage penalty. As he was taken down to the cells by policemen – roughly, I thought – I could only hope there would be some appeal which might mitigate the sentence.

Every aspect of the trial and the official and public attitudes to it had been arrayed against poor Oscar. It was particularly nauseating for his few friends to observe how those male prostitutes, then known as 'renters', and their pimps, who had given evidence against Wilde on the firm promise that, in return, they would not be prosecuted, were permitted to flaunt themselves in their usual revolting, effeminate way outside the court room.

Those of Oscar's friends who were recognizable were booed and jeered as they left the court. Of course nobody took note of me, but I recall a whore pointing a finger at Ernest Dowson and shouting, ''Ere's another of the dirty buggers!' Presumably she had assumed from the floppy tie he wore to advertise his Bohemianism that, being an artist, he was homosexual. In his case nothing could have been further from the truth. When in funds he was one of the 'light ladies'' most regular customers.

I was never so depressed as I was that night sitting in the Domino Room, looking at the empty table from which Oscar had so often regaled me with his wit and wisdom. But the prostitutes who haunted the Café Royal were jubilant at this public blow to their competitors in sexual trade, and they sang and danced, as so many who regarded themselves as pillars of propriety had done outside the

Old Bailey when the verdict became known. I recall one painted creature crying, ''E'll 'ave 'is 'air cut reglar nah!'

I should have mentioned, for my diary records it, that during the trial Wilde's name was erased from posters advertising his plays, which were showing to packed houses at the St James's and Haymarket Theatres. The owners and managers wanted no association with him, but were not prepared to lose the money which removal of his plays from the stage would have entailed. George Alexander, who had refused to stand bail for Oscar after earning so much from his plays, later claimed that his name had been taken off the billboards so that his family could continue to draw royalties, but I have never believed this.

The day after Oscar's public disgrace banquets were held to celebrate it and actors and actresses, who owed him so much for the memorable lines he had put into their mouths, attended them. Indeed Charles Hawtrey, one of the most prominent actors of the day, gave a dinner to the wretched Lord Queensberry, while it later transpired that another envious actor, called Charles Brookfield, had gone out of his way to supply Queensberry with evidence about Wilde's homosexual activities, including the crucial information about the male brothel run by Taylor.

Only a tiny minority of the acting profession, which was to go on owing Oscar so much, felt any sympathy. They included Ellen Terry who had sent him a bunch of violets during his trial with a note: 'To bring you luck'. A few others took a neutral view; for instance Mrs Patrick Campbell, Shaw's friend, who remarked, 'I don't care what these men do as long as they don't do it in the street and frighten the horses.' But most of the mummers, as Wilde sometimes called them, were loud in their condemnation. To parody poor Oscar, 'Nothing recedes like success.' Frank Harris was one of the few people who felt sorry for Oscar and had no qualms about being identified with him, believing perhaps that, with his reputation for seducing women, nobody was ever likely to brand him as a homosexual.

We soon learned that Oscar had been incarcerated in the dreadful Newgate Prison next to the Old Bailey to await removal to a more permanent address. From Newgate, which was also soon to be demolished, he had been transferred, handcuffed, to Pentonville Prison near King's Cross. He remained there until July when he was moved to Wandsworth, from which he was required to attend the hearing of the bankruptcy forced on him by Queensberry, who was demanding his costs for the expensive libel action which Wilde had brought against him. This was harrowing enough for Oscar, but a more scarifying experience befell him when he was eventually transferred out of London to the gaol at Reading in November. He and his warders had to change trains at Clapham Junction, and while he was standing there in the rain in his prison dress with its broad arrow marks, his head shorn and his hands shackled, some of the travellers on the platform recognized him. To their eternal shame they jeered at him and derided him with cat-calls, one so-called gentleman even spitting in his face.

It was at Reading that Harris visited him, and 'Forceful Frank' was in a rare old temper when I heard him describe his experience on his return to – of all people – Horatio Bottomley, with whom he had made a temporary armistice.

'Oscar told me that Dante never imagined any hell like an English prison. In the lowest circles of his Inferno people could at least move about and hear each other groan. There was some companionship in human misery. "Here I am alone, half-starved, in a windowless cell deprived even of pen and paper."'

As some of his fellow prisoners realized and told him, prison life was a much severer sentence for him than for them. He could not stomach the food, and the plank bed and hairy blankets were alien to his way of life. As one who has known such deep loneliness, I felt particular sympathy for him and, often, when lying awake at night, would conjure up an image of Oscar in his cell. I knew that it would be in sleeplessness, in the small hours, that his ordeal would be most severe. Why is it that personal problems and fears, which are manageable in daylight, loom so much more menacingly in darkness? Is it simply that silence and solitude can force the mind to concentrate upon them without distraction? Or is it a manifestation of some primitive terror of the night in all of us? All my life I have been subject to night terrors, sometimes about the most trivial affairs. What Oscar must have suffered as he lay there contemplating a present that was unbearable and a future as an outcast from society, without which he knew he could be nothing.

Being the man of action he was, Harris moved to secure a petition to have Wilde's sentence reduced, but almost everyone he approached refused to sign it. They included the artist William Holman Hunt, who had painted the popular picture of Christ with a lantern called *The Light of the World*. As I heard Harris say, 'He was always painting Christian pictures but he had little Christian forgiveness in his nature.' Hunt's response had been, 'I must repeat my opinion that the law treated him with exceeding leniency!'

Even Harris's attempts to improve Oscar's conditions in prison by allowing him to have books and a light so that he could read at night were fruitless. Bernard Shaw and George Meredith were among the several men of letters who refused to sign a petition to the Home Secretary, though Max Beerbohm and a few others did so. I was later privy to a Domino Room conversation in which More Adey and Robert Ross were organizing another petition, which I understood had been drafted by Bernard Shaw. It was all ready to send when the Home Office declared that it could see no grounds whatever for the mitigation of Oscar's sentence. Eventually, however, the persistent and charitable Harris managed to induce a new Governor of Reading Gaol to improve Oscar's conditions, for which we are ever in debt to both of them. Without their help we should all have been denied the pleasure of reading *De Profundis*, the moving book Wilde wrote on blue prison paper in the form of a long letter to Lord Alfred Douglas, his last work in prose. But what prose!

11

HIS OWN EXECUTIONER

My poor friend Oscar Wilde was released from prison on 19 May 1897. I would dearly have liked to be among those waiting to welcome him back, but the details of his release were kept secret by his friends to spare him from harassment by the press. Like me, the newspapermen thought he would be released from Reading Gaol, but in that we showed our ignorance of the law, for in those days a prisoner had to be released from the gaol to which he had first been committed. So it was from Pentonville that he emerged on that May morning to be met by More Adey, the friend who had managed Oscar's affairs during his imprisonment, and a clergyman who had always been kind to him and had offered the safety of his home until Oscar could leave the country for France.

As I was to learn later, from various conversations, Oscar had suddenly decided that he would rather go into some kind of Roman Catholic monastery for a few months, even though arrangements had been made for him in France. He startled More Adey, who recounted the episode, by asking the clergyman to send a letter to the Jesuits in Farm Street, near Berkeley Square, asking for sanctuary. It seemed an odd request to me when I heard about it. A further withdrawal from society after two years of it! But then Oscar was a sensitive person and he may have been suddenly overcome by fear of the outside world. As he should have realized, the Jesuits would never allow anyone to join them on the spur of the moment. So after taking the risk of being seen by doing some necessary shopping which, for Oscar, included books, he and More Adey caught the night boat to Dieppe. More Adey, a literary figure himself, was sure that Oscar had been recognized while browsing in Hatchard's, where he had been unable to resist the pleasure of being surrounded once again by beautiful books. But they arrived safely in Dieppe where Robbie Ross and Reggie Turner, who had raised money for Oscar's immediate needs, were waiting.

Though I was never to see him again, it seemed that Oscar had shed much of his surplus fat and was looking much fitter than when he had been sentenced. The prison governor had even allowed him to grow his hair and have it waved for the great occasion. I know that it sounds ridiculous, but his re-entry into freedom was not unlike my first entry into the society of the Domino Room. Both were a release from a kind of solitary confinement, and both of us were limited in our concourse with our fellow human beings, I by my affliction, Oscar by the shunning disgust he knew he would experience from many, if not most, people. I therefore felt particular sympathy and joy when the news rang round the Domino Room: 'Oscar's out!' I also wondered whether, in those long hours alone, he had come to know himself thoroughly, as he had said he would like to do.

While Ross remained in France More Adey and Reggie Turner returned to London, and I heard both of them telling Max Beerbohm and other friends how Wilde was faring. At that stage he clearly hoped to regenerate his creative faculties, for in *De Profundis*, the extracts of his long letter to Bosie, penned in prison and published after his death, he had written, 'If ever I lie in the cool grass at night-time it will be to write sonnets to the moon.' From the first he was aware that he would never be forgiven by society. 'I have come not from obscurity into the momentary notoriety of crime, but from a sort of eternity of fame to a sort of eternity of infamy,' he wrote. Only

Bernard Shaw, among literary men, had kept his professional reputation alive by mentioning him in articles and reviews. Either
through lack of courage or genuine disgust the rest had behaved as
though he were already dead.

Reggie Turner revealed that in the hope that his notoriety might
be forgotten he had changed his name to Sebastian Melmoth, after
the central figure in *Melmoth the Wanderer*, a variation of the Faust
theme by his great-uncle, Charles Maturin. Melmoth, taken from the
name of a demon, had been a wanderer on the face of the earth, and
Oscar chose Sebastian because that was the name of the saint who had
been pierced with arrows, as he felt he had been. Reggie had known
about this change of name in advance and, in his usual kind and
generous way, had sent Oscar an expensive dressing-case marked
with the initials S.M.

Wilde took up residence through the help of a few loyal friends at
the Hôtel de la Plage in Berneval, a small resort about five miles from
Dieppe. He was visited there by several of our mutual Domino Room
friends including the artists Charles Conder and Will Rothenstein
who brought back the news. And the news was good. Oscar was full
of ideas for writing projects, including more biblical plays like
Salome. Frank Harris was so pleased that he did all he could to
encourage him, advising that, 'Constant creation is the first condition of art, as it is the first condition of life.' This was excellent
advice, for absorbing work is an excellent remedy to anyone with
troubles, as I had found myself, and Oscar acted on it with commendable speed. He drafted his splendid 'Ballad of Reading Gaol', in my
opinion his finest effort at poetry.

W. B. Yeats, the tousle-haired, bespectacled Irishman, best
known for his poem 'The Lake Isle of Innisfree' (though he came to
hate being reminded of it), even brought back news of an effort by one
of Oscar's friends to turn him back to sexual normality.

'Ernest Dowson, who is living near Dieppe, talked him into going
to a brothel in the hope that he might enjoy the experience so much
that he would stay away from the boys,' Yeats told Aubrey Beardsley.
'It was a disaster. Oscar, who was slightly tipsy, slouched out looking
bitter and dejected. "The first time in ten years and the last!" he told
Dowson, who was waiting for him along with a crowd of locals, who
had cheered as Oscar went in, "It was like dining on cold mutton."'
The remark reminded me of Crowley's observation after his easy
conquest of an actress who had attracted him — 'It was like waving a
flag in space.'

It seems, however, that Oscar hoped to derive some advantage from his experience. 'Tell them back in England,' he shouted to the crowd. 'It will restore my character.' It would not have done so. When Arthur Symons wrote an article about Oscar early in 1900 every editor rejected it.

Dowson, who had told Yeats the story at a meeting of the Rhymers' Club, which met in the Cheshire Cheese in Fleet Street, had meant well, but the incident hastened Oscar's return to his old habits. Prison had not reduced his homosexual requirements, and experience seems to prove that punishment for that offence has no result in that direction. But then what chance had he in the company of life-long homosexuals like Ross and Turner? Once in the freedom of France Oscar began to advertise his peculiarity, using women's make-up, dyeing his hair, wearing enormous cork-soled shoes and developing a voice which became increasingly affected and effeminate. There were several incidents in which old acquaintances spotted him, with dismay, especially after he moved to Paris. Of these the most extraordinary involved Sir Edward Carson, the barrister who had made such a terrible impact on his life. It seems that while Carson was walking alone in Paris on a wet day the driver of a *fiacre* so nearly ran him down that he had to spring back on to the pavement. As he did so he collided with a heavy man and knocked him into the gutter. He bent down to help him up and apologize, and turned away as he saw the painted face of Oscar Wilde. I can understand Carson's embarrassment and, as I have already recorded, he had made some effort to prevent the criminal prosecution of Oscar, but I often wonder whether lawyers who have destroyed people in pursuit of their livelihood — for, let us face it, they do it for money — can still sleep at night. And what of those who secure by some technical legal trick or by the sheer power of their oratory the acquittal of a dangerous criminal they know to be guilty? Do they sleep soundly when the criminal strikes at some other victim?

The other bad news that reached us was Oscar's decision to join forces again with Bosie Douglas, with whom, he told himself, he was still 'in love', even though the relationship had ruined him. If it could be described as 'love', then it must rank as one of the most romantic, as well as tragic, love affairs in history. That news was brought back by Vincent O'Sullivan, an American who lived in Paris. He said that he had paid Oscar's fare to Naples, where Bosie had rented a villa. Perhaps it was just the sunshine that attracted Oscar, for he had always claimed to 'sing best in the sun', especially on a pea-soup, foggy day in London. Anyway sing he did, by finishing 'The Ballad', but it was to be a swansong. Prison had eaten too deeply into the creative faculty, which depends not only on inspiration but on application – the ability to keep at the task. Lord Alfred Douglas never ceased to recount to his friends, in later years in the Domino Room, how he had done everything to help Oscar to recover his powers, giving him money when he could, and how, when his mother insisted that the relationship must be ended he had left Wilde at the villa with £200 to tide him over.

Oscar could not bear being there on his own – after prison he hated loneliness more than ever – and he moved to Paris, which could have been a fertile place to work but turned out to be a trap for someone who so loved the fleshpots and had been denied them.

Convinced that he had been wronged by society because he was 'one of those made for exceptions, not for laws', he believed that the world in general, and his friends in particular, owed him a living. He became lazy, a scrounger playing one friend off against the other if he thought it would bring him money. Thus, while Harris, who sold the *Fortnightly Review* at the end of 1898 and bought a hotel in Monte Carlo with the proceeds, helped him financially, so that Oscar wrote thanking him for his generosity, he told others that Frank was only a promise-maker whom he loathed. In fact there can be no doubt from independent witnesses that Harris helped Oscar a great deal, not only with occasional cash, but with the entertainment he so enjoyed. When in Paris he delighted in taking Oscar to a restaurant called Durand's because diplomats from the British Embassy, who all shunned Wilde, ate there and he liked cocking a snook at them.

Oscar also complained to others that even though Bosie was living in Paris, in the fashionable Avenue Kléber, he rarely gave him anything. Bosie was later able to prove this to be quite untrue by publishing a bank statement listing cheques he had given to Oscar.

I have often wondered whether this sad decline in Wilde's honesty had anything to do with the fact that during his two years in prison he was forced into contact with common criminals. Whatever the cause, his behaviour does not detract from the quality of 'The Ballad', and I believe that when Oscar wrote: 'If I can produce only one beautiful work of art I shall be able to rob malice of its venom and cowardice of its sneer,' he achieved the work, though, sadly, not its hoped for consequences. This was true not just of beneficial effects on his embitterment, but also of the financial reward. 'The Ballad of Reading Gaol', published in January 1898 over the signature 'C.3.3.', the number of his prison cell, ran through many editions in England and America but Oscar made little money out of it.

Oscar was reduced to living in the little Hôtel d'Alsace in the Rue des Beaux-Arts on the Left Bank of the River Seine, and spent most of his time reliving his Domino Room days in the Café de la Régence, where there was a corner with a marble-topped table. He pretended to write as he lounged there and in other cafés of the boulevards, like the Café de la Paix and the Café Procope, where he met his old acquaintance, the poet Paul Verlaine, but was really more interested in the 'boulevard boys', the young male prostitutes who operated there quite openly. For this, the writer Ford Madox Ford told us, he was tormented by hordes of students who followed him from café to café, cat-calling and ragging him without mercy, stealing his walking-stick and threatening to beat him with it.

He justified his idleness to himself by claiming that to be a great talker was every bit as admirable as being a great writer. 'Christ wrote nothing down but only spoke,' he explained to those who remonstrated with him for dissipating his talent (yet another association of himself with Our Lord). It is easier, of course, to talk well than to write well, for the speaker has the added advantage of gesture, nuance of voice tone and facial expression. The great conversationalists of my experience, like Wilde and Frank Harris, whose words never seemed quite so scintillating on paper, were convincing actors. In this resides the author's difficulty, for a rich soufflé of highly flavoured talk can fall flat and insipid in type.

Wilde had an enormous capacity for both drink and food. I remember hearing Bosie say to another friend, while they were waiting for Wilde, 'I'll back Oscar to eat the head off a brewer's drayman three times a day!' He attributed this appetite to gluttony, but I have often wondered since whether it was not the result of anxiety, perhaps even of deep dread. Some people turn not only to drink to dispel their fears, but to food as well.

Though Oscar never seemed much the worse for wear so far as his gait was concerned, alcohol made him even more loquacious and more reckless in his conversation. To explain the drunkenness which became a hallmark, Oscar claimed that he could only talk well under the influence of absinthe, which he drank in far larger quantities than he had in the Domino Room, once more proving my observation over the years that willpower, like a woman's resistance, is soluble in alcohol. He was deluded about the quality of his conversation at that stage of his life, a common enough consequence of alcohol, as it is of dreams, for the artist Augustus John was very disappointed when he met Wilde in Paris after seeking him out there while on a visit with his fellow painter, Charles Conder, another man who was to drink himself to death. John, too, was destined to become an habitual drunkard but then, being only twenty-one, he had both less to drink and less to say. Later I heard him describe Oscar as 'amiable but a great man of inaction', but at least he had been willing to sit with him and listen. Not everyone was like John in that respect. Englishmen who recognized Wilde would leave their tables or ask the *patron* to have him removed. Even former associates, as near to him as Beardsley had been, cut him.

Still, as Frank Harris put it, 'Everyone gets tired of holding up an empty sack. Oscar's disgrace would have been a challenge had his character not been so weak. Strong men are made by opposition. Like kites they go up in the wind.' What gift of poetry and prose might we have inherited if Oscar had taken Harris's original advice and avoided the poison of two years' hard labour! Even with that handicap, the man who had written *De Profundis* and 'The Ballad of Reading Gaol' after the shock of his downfall might still have produced something really great had he not drowned his talent as well as his sorrow in drink.

Oscar seemed to go out of his way also to capitalize on another social sin, blasphemy, even identifying himself with Christ. 'I want to imitate my Maker and like him I want nothing but praise,' I once heard him say. He was forever weaving fables about himself and the Saviour. Two such, of which I made notes as he told them, are worth retelling in this context:

'When Jesus was minded to return to Nazareth, it had so changed that He no longer recognized His own city which was filled with laughter and song. Christ went out of His house, and behold in the street He saw a woman whose face and raiment were painted and whose feet were shod with pearls, and behind her walked a man who wore a cloak of two colours and whose eyes were bright with lust.

'And Christ went up to the man and laid His hand on his shoulder and said to him, "Tell me, why art thou following this woman, and why dost thou look at her in such wise?"

'The man turned round, recognized Him and said, "I was blind; Thou didst heal me; what else should I do with my sight."'

Some found the second 'parable' even more shocking, which no doubt it was intended to be.

'When Joseph of Arimathea came down in the evening from Mount Calvary he saw on a white stone a young man seated weeping.

'Joseph said, "I understand how great thy grief must be, for certainly that Man was a just Man."

The young man answered, "Oh it is not for that I am weeping. I am weeping because I too have wrought miracles. I also have given sight to the blind, I have healed the palsied and I have raised the dead; I too have caused the barren fig tree to wither away and I have turned water into wine . . . and yet they have not crucified me."'

I seem to recollect, though I admit that I made no note of it, that I wondered then whether Oscar would end up being crucified and whether, like Christ, he would make it inevitable. If so, it was through his blatant disregard of what people might think about his homosexuality that he achieved his, perhaps subconscious, objective.

That Wilde had no fear of admitting his homosexual tendencies to his friends I can testify from numerous instances which I have witnessed. On one occasion, while having a drink with an actress, he had remarked, 'If only you were a boy, how I would adore you.' I have even heard him make a blasphemous joke about homosexuality by remarking, 'Never mind, trust in God. *She*'ll help you.'

This not only shocked but surprised me, because it was not up to Oscar's usual standard of wittiness, and I can only assume that he was rather the worse for wear when he said it. Normally nothing coarse or obscene passed his lips. Contrary to many, I might say most, in the Domino Room he never used profanities, regarding them as evidence of inability to make proper use of the language he loved.

In the context of the classics — for both he and Bosie professed to be pagans — Oscar was forever recalling the ancient Greek love of young boys and masculine beauty. 'Pagan love was guiltless and I am a pagan,' he would declaim, in a tone suggesting that homosexuality was something to glory in. The force of the homosexual drive certainly seems to have a compulsive power which fewer heterosexual men experience. The drive seems to be stronger and leads those subject to it to take inordinate risks.

As Oscar's intake of alcohol increased, so his health declined. Though one could never be sure when Oscar was joking, he seemed to know that he would soon be gone, for he remarked to his sister-in-law, 'I am dying, as I have lived, beyond my means.' News of his death on 30 November 1900 was received with sorrow by many in the Domino Room, though some of his former friends who knew of his circumstances pronounced it 'a happy release'.

There was immediate controversy about the cause of his death, for he was only forty-six. Some put it down to drink, but others 'knew' it was suicide, recalling Oscar's remark: 'Suicide is the greatest compliment one can pay to society', and even saying that, like the boy poet Chatterton, Oscar had poisoned himself. I have to admit that my old haunt was always a hot-bed of wild rumour but, though Oscar had loved life so much, suicide had been occasionally in his mind. 'There is only one way into this life, but fortunately there are several exits,' I heard him say, and it can be argued that any death from long-sustained over-drinking against doctors' warnings is suicidal in some degree. Oscar must have heard of the death of Ernest Dowson, in February of that year, from tuberculosis, hastened by drink, an event which did not surprise me after I had seen him in earnest prayer at the Requiem Mass for Aubrey Beardsley in the Farm Street Jesuit Church.

There was also a story about a fall in Reading Gaol which had led to a brain infection, but I inclined to the opinion that, after his health began to fail through over-drinking, Oscar simply lost the will to live. His world had vanished — as mine now has — so it was not unreasonable that he should go with it. The contrast between his old life in London, successful and lionized, and his life in Paris, a failure and shunned, must have been shattering. 'I went down the primrose path to the sound of flutes,' he had written about his former years. When the flutes ceased to play, life held nothing for him. Perhaps he was being prophetic in *De Profundis*, though we did not know that at the time, since it was not published until 1905: 'Many men on their release carry their prison about with them into the air, and hide it as a secret disgrace in their hearts, and at length, like poor poisoned things, creep into some hole and die.'

Then, some months later, the riddle seemed solved for me when I heard Robert Ross, Oscar's most loyal friend, make a staggering revelation. Ross, along with Reggie Turner, had been with Oscar when he had died and seen him through most of the previous weeks. 'Oscar died of tertiary syphilis of the brain,' I heard him tell Beerbohm. 'Of that I am sure. Very few people knew it, and I would never have told anybody in his lifetime, but Oscar admitted to me that he had contracted syphilis from some dreadful old tart called "Old Jess" while he had been an undergraduate at Oxford. He had been treated with mercury, which was why he had those black teeth and was always at such pains to hide them.'

Good God! I thought, where does that leave you, Robbie? You had your homosexual affair with Oscar after that, and venereal disease can be contracted that way. Still, perhaps the mercury treatment had cured him. To my astonishment, however, Ross then disclosed that the treatment had failed.

'Oscar told me that he had taken the precaution of a medical check before his marriage and had been pronounced clear, but a couple of years later he found out that the disease was still active.'

'But his children seem quite normal,' said Beerbohm.

'They are. So was his wife, so far as we know, though the operation from which she died was to relieve her creeping paralysis. Maybe he was no longer in the infective stage, but the disease was still in his system and finally affected his brain.'

This, then, could explain why Oscar had told Harris he had 'softening of the brain'. It might also explain why he took to homosexual habits soon after his second son was born. Knowing that he might be infective, would he not cease sexual relations with his wife in the hope that she had escaped that far? Ross then mentioned some further evidence for syphilis which Frank Harris also knew about. For a few months before he died Oscar had severe rashes on his chest and back, though Ross said Wilde believed these had been caused by eating shellfish.

Of course, I only have Ross's word for all this, but it was not the kind of statement he would make unless he believed it. And he would not have believed it without good cause. How often have I noticed that some situation which we believe we understand suddenly becomes quite different in the light of new facts! Yet such facts need professional appraisal and, as it did with most things in time, the Café Royal provided it.

A famous ear specialist called Terence Cawthorne had taken an interest in Wilde's last illness, and I heard him one day discussing some article he intended to write about it with Lord Horder, a most eminent general practitioner. Cawthorne was convinced that, while

Oscar may well have suffered from syphilis, he had died from the brain infection called cerebral meningitis. As with any serious infection, Oscar's heavy drinking, against which his French doctors had warned him repeatedly, fatally lowered his resistance to the invading germs.

Many of us were gratified to learn that Oscar had not died alone. Robert Ross and Reggie Turner had been with him at the end in his dingy room at the Hôtel d'Alsace and had washed him and laid him out. Bosie had been in Scotland, grouse shooting, but on receiving a telegram from Ross rushed to Paris in time to be at the funeral where he claimed he was 'chief mourner'. He also declared that Oscar was received into the Catholic Church on his deathbed by a Franciscan friar sent for by Ross. It would not have been out of character, for I had heard Oscar in the past extolling the Roman Catholic faith by saying, 'It is the only Church to die in', but I am not prepared to take anything Douglas said on absolute trust.

I was to learn later, through overhearing another conversation between Robert Ross and Beerbohm, that Ross, as Oscar's official literary executor, had suggested after the funeral that they should go through any manuscripts to see if any might be sold to help educate the two Wilde boys. Douglas petulantly refused, which was a grave error on his part because Ross would surely have told him about *De Profundis*, concerning which Douglas was then totally in ignorance, though it had been addressed to him as a long letter.

The extraordinary story of this document, as told to me by Ross (inadvertently of course), was as follows: Originally entitled *Epistola in Carcere et Vinculis* – Letter in Prison and Chains – it had been given by Wilde to Ross, who changed its name to *De Profundis*. Douglas was told nothing about it, though it blackened his character, until Ross published an expurgated version of it five years after its author's death. Ross then presented the manuscript to the British Museum on the understanding that nobody would be allowed to read it until 1960, when Douglas would be dead.

In the event, the expurgated parts were produced in a court action brought by Douglas against a young author called Arthur Ransome and they lost the case for Bosie who, as it were, was defeated by Oscar testifying from the grave. Stupidly, Douglas continued to claim that the document must be his because it was in the form of a letter addressed to him, but in fact it had never been delivered and the copyright clearly belonged to Wilde's literary executor, Robert Ross.

Queensberry's spiteful satisfaction had been short-lived. He died even before poor Oscar in January of the same year, and I remember noting his departure in *The Times* without regret. I do not know whether there was a post-mortem examination of his vile body but, had there been one, it might well have been found that he died from a hardened heart. Douglas used to claim that he had been fully reconciled with his father before death separated them but this could have been wishful thinking, for Bosie, who became a regular attender again in the Domino Room, particularly in the company of Willie Crosland, became progressively deluded by arrogance, vanity and self-pity.

Now for my theory about Oscar's ruination and death. I have pointed out numerous ways in which Wilde identified himself with Christ. I suspect that this became a delusion – Oscar was riddled with self-deception – and he saw himself as a Christ-like figure who would inexorably bring about his own martyrdom, at least in the professional sense. Like Jesus, Wilde was a spellbinder with a superb turn of memorable phrase. He tended to speak in epigrams and parables and attracted to himself a group of 'disciples'. His friends denied him and in Douglas he saw his Judas, referring to him, I believe, in a refrain from 'The Ballad of Reading Gaol':

> *Yet each man kills the thing he loves,*
> *By each let this be heard,*
> *Some do it with a bitter look,*
> *Some with a flattering word,*
> *The coward does it with a kiss,*
> *The brave man with a sword!*

I heard Frank Harris say that Wilde had called Bosie 'my Judas' during a conversation he had with him in prison. He must also have been referring to Douglas when he wrote, 'Every great man has his disciples, and it is usually Judas who writes the biography.' Wilde's public disgrace was his scourging and his imprisonment his crucifixion. If I am right, he may have deliberately pursued the Queensberry action, knowing in his heart what would happen. Like Christ, he could have escaped had he wanted to – but needed to stand to be taken before the 'high priests' of righteousness. W. B. Yeats reported to us in the Domino Room that Wilde's brother Willie had told him while Oscar was on bail: 'He is resolved to face the music *like Christ*.'

Surely Oscar was referring to all this when he wrote in *De Profundis*, 'The great tragedies of the world are all final and complete.

Socrates could not escape death though Crito opened the prison door for him. I could not avoid prison. We are fated to suffer as an example to humanity – "an echo and a light unto eternity".' During his long introspection in prison, Wilde may have developed his delusions into thinking that he would achieve his own redemption through his suffering. There was a brief period after his release when he believed he might be cleansed this way, and during it he wrote 'The Ballad' but, perhaps because he thought that society was continuing to crucify him, he hastened his early death with drink. I suspect he foresaw this continuing harassment by society when he wrote in 'The Ballad':

> *For he who lives more lives than one*
> *More deaths than one must die.*

Fleetingly, on occasions, he seems to have believed that a literary 'resurrection' might be possible, as when he pleaded with Douglas to '. . . remake my ruined life for me'. But I believe there was a strong factor of deliberateness about the brevity of his life after his release. As Frank Harris said, 'No one sinks to the dregs but by his own weight.' Perhaps when he realized that the effort to recover his writing ability, and the necessary application, was failing beyond recall, his death wish was fortified and he turned to it, through drink, for release. 'Each man kills the thing he loves. . . .' Above all things, Oscar loved himself.

Perhaps if his rise to fame had been more difficult, as it is with most writers, he could have fought through the problems he faced. After all, as the great success of 'The Ballad of Reading Gaol' and the resurrection of his plays have proved, the world would have been prepared to recognize his genius again, with acclaim, after a few years. Perhaps one day there may even be an official plaque to his memory either at the St James's Theatre or over his old home in Tite Street. * The world is certainly not finished with Oscar Wilde. He was one of those extraordinary people with whom the world is never finished.

* *Editor's footnote*: The London County Council commemorated the centenary of Oscar Wilde's birth by placing a plaque on his home in Tite Street in 1954.

12

SOULS OF INDISCRETION

In my early days at the Café Royal ladies were forbidden to enter the portals alone, even if waiting for a perfectly respectable friend. This was a precaution against the entry of prostitutes into the Domino Room and entrance hall, where they might ply their trade in the hope of being taken up to one of the private rooms. It was always a rather futile ban because prostitutes could circumvent it by coming in with their pimps, and there were often several to be seen at the far end of the Domino Room. Further, it greatly inconvenienced reputable ladies, especially those who believed they had as much right as a man to enjoy a quiet aperitif, as, of course, they could on the Continent. One such was Miss Margot Tennant, the forceful daughter of a rich Scottish landowner, who solved the problem on occasion by bringing in her cab-driver to sit with her while the horse munched at its nosebag outside. To her credit she never ceased to object to the rule, which was eventually withdrawn.

I always enjoyed listening in to Miss Tennant's conversations. Apart from being a leading socialite, she was a member of a literary gossip group of mainly titled men and women called the Souls, about which I learned a lot through her talk with other members like George Wyndham, a very handsome young MP and poet who was a distant relative of Bosie Douglas, as I believe Margot was herself.

Slightly built and only a little over five feet in height, Miss Tennant was nevertheless a very formidable lady and the waiters went in fear of her tongue. Her chief love in life at that stage seemed to be hunting foxes, in which she was joined by Daisy Brooke. Both were fearless riders and I once heard them talking together in the Domino Room about their recent exploits, since they hunted with different packs. Both had suffered heavy falls and I was eventually to hear Margot boast that she had broken '. . . both collar bones, several ribs, my kneecap, my skull and my nose'. The break in her nose was certainly evident, and it did nothing to improve her rather plain though pleasant features. Nevertheless that did not stop her, when she was thirty, from making an impressive marriage to Herbert Henry Asquith, who was known affectionately as 'Squiffy' and was later to become leader of the Liberal Party and Prime Minister.

Even before she became Margot Asquith (later to be Lady Oxford when her husband was elevated to the Lords), she knew almost every politician. Indeed some of them, like Arthur Balfour, who was a Greek scholar as well as a politician, Lord Curzon and Lord Pembroke – Margot was a great name-dropper – considered themselves to be members of the Souls when they met at London dinner parties or in great country houses at weekends (though I should point out that the word 'weekend' was not used in the nineties or before the motor car made it a national institution: we had to refer to 'Saturday to Monday').

Margot was very straightforward in her speech – even perhaps as reckless as she seemed to have been with her riding – and I heard her say quite openly that she had married Asquith for his intellect rather than for any other quality. When she was young she also dressed rather differently from other girls of her age, and she delighted in telling a story about how she had first met the Prince of Wales while wearing a white muslin evening dress which looked rather like a nightgown.

'The other rather grandly dressed ladies were furious when the Prince came straight up to me and told me I was to sit next to him at supper. They had been making catty remarks saying that I was deliberately advertising myself as an intellectual! Well, the Prince could not have been kinder. I told him that some of the other ladies felt I had insulted them by coming in my nightgown but he said he liked the frock very much because it looked like an old picture.

'"You see, my dear," he said, "you need not be afraid of me, and when you meet my mother don't be afraid of her either – though everybody is, with the exception of John Brown."'

I pricked up my ears at this remark, because John Brown was the rough Scottish ghillie suspected by many of being the widowed Queen's 'fancy man'. He took such liberties with her in front of other people that there was much wonder about those he might take when they were alone, especially when it became known that his apartments were always near hers and that she had put up statues to him in the grounds at Balmoral.

Though Margot was obviously flattered by the attentions which the Prince had paid her she seemed an unlikely companion for him, not only because she was rather plain, but because Bertie hated anyone with a pretence to being intellectual. It was well known that he would always rather play cards than converse, which was one of the reasons why he would never have long drinking sessions with the men after the ladies had left a dinner table. So I was not surprised a few weeks later to hear Margot Tennant criticizing him as 'just a professional love-maker' and 'a man who hates listening'. The truth, I suppose, is that he was bored by her, as he was by the rest of the Souls, for at that time of his life he was interested in talking only about racing, shooting and clothes, especially uniforms, of which he had a huge collection.

Like so many young people do, Margot began to conform with custom once she assumed the responsibilities of a married woman, who inherited five stepchildren from Asquith's first marriage and was to have five of her own. My last recollection of her is seeing her in the street near Westminster wearing a dress down to the ankles, with a high, buttoned-up collar, long gloves and a hat with a lot of trailing feathers.

I never discovered whether Oscar had been regarded as a member of the Souls or not. He certainly knew Margot well, and from his and her conversations it was clear that they often met at the same country house gatherings, where, no doubt, he held forth in his inimitable way. He would certainly have used the name a lot, for there was no word that Oscar enjoyed rolling around his tongue more than 'soul'. The whole concept of the soul had enormous appeal for him.

Still, in conversation with other members of the Decadents, his own group of which he was Master, the rest being Disciples, he was often scathing about the Souls, considering them far too serious for conversation, which should always be fun. 'The trouble is that we are born in an age when only the dull are taken seriously,' he remarked, after describing one of his weekends with some of the Souls.

It was a remark I was to hear echoed by Bernard Shaw. 'It took me nearly thirty years of studied self-restraint to make myself dull enough to be accepted as a serious person by the British public.'

Does anyone ever say anything truly original? To misquote the American writer Emerson, I would say, from my long experience, that nothing is so rare in a writer as a statement of his own! Even Shakespeare plagiarized his plots – as I have mine.

13

THE DISHONOURABLE MEMBER

It was no surprise to me when the Hansard Union, the company Horatio Bottomley and Frank Harris had once discussed over lunch and which became known as 'Bottomley's Swindle', eventually went bankrupt. It was such an obvious fraud that its perpetrator was inevitably prosecuted.

I attended the trial, which opened on 30 January 1893, queuing from early morning to make sure of securing a seat in the public gallery at the High Court of Justice. Such was Bottomley's growing reputation as a public figure that the court was packed with people expecting fireworks. They were not to be disappointed for his opponent, the chief prosecutor, was none other than the Attorney General himself, Sir Charles Russell, one of the finest advocates of his day.

I spotted Frank Harris and he was vastly impressed, as I was, for Bottomley conducted his own defence against evidence that he had fraudulently pocketed money — evidence which seemed so strong that, in equity, he should have gone down. Horatio's habit of defending himself had arisen at the instigation of another Café Royal habitué, Mr (later Sir) Edward Marshall Hall, the distinguished advocate, who also became a Member of Parliament, a common practice in those days for lawyers who wanted titles and preferment through service as law officers in Parliament.

I had witnessed that occasion for, as Bottomley always preferred to do his business over champagne, he had invited his counsel to the Domino Room to discuss a previous case in which he was being sued for using his newspaper, *The Sun*, to raise cash by what was obviously an illegal lottery. Suddenly, on being appraised of the facts, Marshall Hall, a tall, fine-looking man, liked by many but described by one I overheard as '. . . a combination of Henry Irving at his worst and Serjeant Buzfuz at his best', had said: 'There's only one counsel in England who'll do justice to this case.'

'Who's that?' Bottomley asked. 'Let's have his name.'

'Yourself.'

While I 'listened', Marshall Hall then explained how this would carry great advantages. First, Bottomley would have the licence usually granted to those laymen conducting their own defence, while Marshall Hall, who was appearing for the publisher, also being sued by the Crown, would be on hand with his experience to advise if need be. Hall's suggestion proved very wise for Bottomley acquitted himself excellently, both then and in the numerous court appearances they made together thereafter, the professional advocate usually following the amateur and addressing the jury with the quip, 'Following as I do after my unlearned leader. . . .'

Bottomley's performance in the Hansard Union case, delivered in a fine voice, was so outstanding that he quickly had the judge and jury on his side and the damning facts became irrelevant. I should point out that Mr Justice Hawkins, previously the hammer of all evil-doers and known as a 'hanging judge', was seventy-five and should have long since been retired. My shorthand notes record that Bottomley cast himself in heartrending terms, as the innocent man of enterprise who had served Hansard so selflessly that he had gone bankrupt in the process. 'Though not of an advanced age, I am supposed to have committed twenty-one pages of crimes,' he protested. 'I ask the jury to say that I have remained true to my post and done my duty to the company, which has been wrecked by others and whose assets have been recklessly dissipated.

'I am the first to admit there has been gigantic fraud, but you have not got the right man before you. I would be the last to attack absent men, but circumstances force me to speak. I am not going to plead for sympathy. I assure you that no criminal intention ever passed my mind and I ask with confidence for your verdict.'

He had cunningly twisted the facts to make it appear that he was the victim of a conspiracy organized by the villainous Official Receiver, who, he claimed, had repeatedly lied to the court. His speech, unsoundly based though it was, brought loud applause as he sat down and the judge summed up so much in Bottomley's favour, and so much against the Official Receiver, that the verdict was a foregone conclusion. The twelve good men and true returned 'Not Guilty' after only twenty-five minutes, and I saw the judge whisper, 'That makes thirteen of us.'

Though it was a gross miscarriage of justice, I was delighted with the verdict, the case having been simply a game in which my Domino Room companion had so impressively taken the laurels. The triumph established Bottomley's reputation as an advocate and orator, and it did nothing to curb his vanity when the judge later presented him with the wig and gown he had worn during the case and urged him to leave the world of finance to study for the Bar. His success with judge and jury – and the audience – also fortified his belief that, such were his powers of persuasion, he could safely exploit the emotions of ordinary people with crooked money-making schemes because, even if he was brought to court, he would always escape conviction.

Through his long experience as an official shorthand writer at the Law Courts, and aided by his prodigious memory, he seemed to know all the law books to consult. He had also noted the advantage of maintaining good humour throughout a trial, however much he was attacked, and never lost his temper. He did, in fact, become perhaps the greatest lay lawyer of modern times, and never enjoyed it so much as when the odds were so heavily stacked against him that conviction seemed inevitable. To what extent he was ever deluded into believing in his own innocence will never be known, but his behaviour continually reminded me of a saying by the redoubtable Dr Johnson, which I came across in my omnivorous reading: 'There is an art of sophistry by which men have deluded their own consciences by persuading themselves that what would be criminal in others is virtuous in them.'

Of course, Bottomley could never have qualified as a barrister – not because he lacked the intelligence, but because he would never have stuck at his studies long enough. He was a hand-to-mouth man, a gambler who needed quick results. As I heard Harris say, with his usual insight into character, 'Bottomley is sustained by the belief that tomorrow's winnings will always liquidate today's losses.' I am sure that is true of most compulsive gamblers, but as I observed Bottomley's rise and fall over the years I realized that he was particularly eloquent proof of the belief that all inveterate gamblers work towards their own ruin.

I overheard so many private discussions between Bottomley and his cronies about their money-raising schemes that I soon knew he was the worst kind of crook, for he took money from the poor – little people whom he was claiming to champion. I felt that his whole attitude to life was summed up in the advice I heard him offer to Harris on that first day I had seen them together, and with which I believe Harris had agreed: 'I'd rather be thought a rogue than a fool, and I'd rather trust a rogue than a fool. You know what a rogue will do, but you can never say that about a fool.' In spite of such a cynical outlook I could not help liking him; neither could most of those he swindled. He, of all people, became the epitome of fair play! One of the likeable things about him was that he knew people thought he was a rogue and never took offence at it. When a new Archbishop of Canterbury was being enthroned, F. E. Smith, later Lord Birkenhead, said to Bottomley: 'You ought to go along there, Horatio. He needs a crook.'

Bottomley laughed uproariously. His attitude to honesty was further displayed in a story I heard him relate about an office boy who had been hauled before him for stealing stamps and petty cash.

'The cashier wanted me to sack him,' Bottomley explained to a friend, 'but I told him to give the lad another chance. Remember, I told him, that we all started in a small way!'

Perhaps it was because he was by nature so dishonourable that he loved being called the Honourable Member for South Hackney, which he eventually became. Nevertheless, mass confidence trickster that he was, he had a generous streak, especially when he was flush. When one of the railway train attendants who used to cash cheques for him was arrested he ordered his aide, Tommy Cox, to send his wife some money.

'But he is in prison for bigamy,' Cox explained.

'What a hero!' Bottomley exclaimed. 'Send both his wives some money.'

Looking back over the great array of talent which displayed itself in the Domino Room over the years, the running tragedy which I perceive is the extent to which so many of those gifted with it chose to squander it. Nobody exemplifies this truth more than Bottomley, who, I think, could have done anything had he only applied himself with honesty and foresight.

His great strength resided in his unparallelled popularity with ordinary working-class people. Part of his appeal, I suppose, lay in the fact that he was so obviously one of them, but I believe that his main attraction stemmed from his way of life. With his lavish spending, his horse-racing, his women, he lived the kind of life most working-class men of that time would have liked to live themselves. While they knew he was a rogue, they believed that he would not betray them, which was just what he did, time and again.

He was probably the first really great exponent of what have come to be known in recent times as public relations. His ability to sell himself was quite extraordinary. One way in which he did this was by cashing in on his rabble-rousing speaking ability: he would speak on any subject anywhere if the fee was high enough, and referred to himself as an 'oratorical courtesan', a polite name for a prostitute. It was usually possible for me to tell what kind of an audience he was going to address by his clothes, if he chanced to drop into the Café Royal for a drink or a meal prior to catching the train. For a working-class audience he dressed in an ordinary dark grey suit, black tie, black boots and bowler hat. For a more distinguished audience of politically-minded people or financiers he would wear a frock-coat, grey spats, an overcoat with a fur collar and, of course, a top hat.

'You must identify yourself with the audience,' I heard him say to Harris when explaining his working-class garb.

I attended several of his meetings and lectures and was always carried away by his apparent sincerity. 'Take it from me,' he repeatedly told his audience when he was giving them some inside information, which he may well have fabricated, 'If Bottomley says so, it *is* so.'

Such was the reputation of this arch-twister for fairness – of all things – that pantomime jingles were even composed about him, though it is not impossible that he paid to have them included, having written them himself. One I remember well went like this, *John Bull* being the magazine he founded:

> *A wire I'll send to a gentleman friend,*
> *I'll call him Horatio B.*
> *He's noted today for seeing fair play,*
> *In a country that claims to be free.*
> *If you feel in a plight, to his journal you write*
> *And get reparation in full.*
> *So you'll say with me, 'Good luck to H.B.*
> *And continued success to* John Bull'.

He was always so confident of getting money by some means or another that he and his cronies would set off for a speaking engagement without a penny in their pockets, writing IOUs and dud cheques for anyone who would part with cash. I have heard them discussing their ideas for raising what Bottomley called the 'getting-away money' before setting off for some meeting or other. There would be argument about whether the sleeper attendant on the train could be induced to cash a post-dated cheque, or whether this device should first be tried out in some restaurant or hotel. The 'getting-back money' was easier to obtain, since there would be income from the visit, Bottomley being one who charged high rates and always demanded payment in guineas.

The aide with whom he was seen most frequently in the Domino Room was called Tommy Cox; he was the chief organizer and even arranged to have claques primed to ask the right questions, lead the clapping and cheering, and silence over-persistent hecklers. I attended several of Bottomley's election meetings, at which some of the questions to the platform had obviously been thought out by him in advance, along with the answers. Thus when one of his claque asked, 'Is the candidate in favour of mixed bathing for the unemployed?' Bottomley immediately responded, 'I am unable to consider the possibility of their being unemployed under such conditions.' I remember Bottomley saying that the going rate for the people hired into his claques was three shillings an hour — high pay in those days — so they were well rewarded for their work, which in fact they seemed thoroughly to enjoy.

Bottomley's income was enormous and he claimed that he needed £1000 a week to live on, a colossal sum then, but not to Horatio, who always took the sanguine view that there was plenty more where that came from. As a result he was often so short of cash-in-hand that his creditors found it hard to get their money. Yet there he was talking in millions and offering financial advice to everyone including the government. I remember seeing a huge poster, at a time when he was in debt to the Café Royal, proclaiming: 'Mr Bottomley's advice to the Chancellor of the Exchequer. How to raise £50 millions sterling. . . .' With great laughter Bottomley told Tommy Cox in the Domino Room how this poster had induced a sharp-witted solicitor to send him a note saying, 'I see you are about to raise £50 millions for the Exchequer. In the magnitude of your financial operations it may have escaped your memory that you still owe my client £50, for which I shall be glad to receive a cheque forthwith.'

The tears rolled down Bottomley's fat cheeks as he read the letter, shaking with laughter. 'Send him a cheque for £50, Tommy, with the bald statement: "Dear Sir, Your argument is irresistible."'

Bottomley pioneered the Fleet Street 'stunt' in his first big journalistic venture, *The Sun*. One effort, which kept London laughing for a week, was to bring out the paper with a banner headline: 'Has anybody seen our cat?' followed by a description of the animal which, if it existed at all, was said to be missing. In the hope of reward, his readers went cat-hunting and all manner of strays were taken to the newspaper office.

The Sun eventually collapsed but, always bursting with ideas, Bottomley started the magazine *John Bull*, which first appeared on 12 May 1906 and was to be a sensational success. The firm of Odhams Brothers were the publishers and Bottomley was to be editor for life. I still have a copy of that first issue, which was widely discussed in the Domino Room. Bottomley owed a great deal to Frank Harris, who helped him with the layout of the magazine, but he soon generated a stream of brilliant ideas of his own, especially new competitions, like 'Bullets', which required an entrance fee and so brought in huge sums from gullible readers. Bottomley's impudence knew no bounds, and while he was defrauding people right, left and centre *John Bull* would come out with placards announcing: 'Another Ramp Exposed!'

He had a rooted objection to paying any bills, except gambling debts, though he always did so eventually at the Café Royal, so he was forever beset with bailiffs and duns. He had a further problem with cast-off women trying to corner him; the offices at *John Bull* were designed so that he could always pretend to be out or, if that ruse failed, make his escape. A special door with a brass plate marked 'Mr Bottomley' led to a small room which was always empty, his sumptuously furnished office being reached through a locked door with no markings whatever. From the office a long corridor led to the back entrance of the building and out to the street via a locked door, to which he always had a key at the ready. He had regular need of it, and because of his great weight he often arrived in the street perspiring and breathless, mopping his face with a silk handkerchief. I was never inside his office, but I have heard those who were describe how the walls were lined with black deed boxes lettered with gold, containing the records of his numerous court cases, which he almost always won.

Bottomley had been elected MP for South Hackney in 1906 when he was forty-six and quickly made his mark with his maiden speech, which I went to hear in the public gallery. He was unusual in that, almost instinctively, he knew how to curb his speech to suit the peculiar nature of the House of Commons, for many men who are highly effective at the hustings fail there. The highest compliment he received in this connection was from his fellow MP F. E. Smith, who said that his parliamentary style was almost ideal, 'Self-possessed, quiet, irresistibly witty and distinguished equally by common sense and tolerance.' What a tribute! And what a pity that Bottomley was unable because of his other characteristics to make proper use of such a gift.

Though his way of life was common knowledge he was re-elected in 1910 but, as was inevitable, he was eventually made a bankrupt; though this did nothing to reduce his style of living, because money continued to pour in through his swindles, it did mean that he had to resign his seat in Parliament in 1912. He wanted desperately to recover his platform and his prestige as an MP, but owing to his gambling and other stupid excesses he had the greatest difficulty in winning back to solvency.

Horse-racing made a major contribution to his downfall, as it did to that of so many other men of ability. As I heard him say himself, the horses he bought were always 'no better than cats' meat', but he could not resist the vanity of running them in his own colours – red, white and black. These also happened to be the colours of the German Emperor William, so when war broke out in 1914 he was advised to change. 'That's not necessary,' he replied. 'Like my horses, the German Emperor will never win!'

I heard him complain repeatedly how his horses, which he usually called 'gee-gees', 'ate their heads off', but it was the enormous bets he placed on other people's which kept him bankrupt. The consistently unlucky gambler not only backs the wrong horses but fails to back the right ones, and I remember listening to Bottomley tell a story, which he then believed was a credit to his good judgement, but in fact was to deny him a fortune. He was explaining to Frank Harris how he had been approached by a well-known comedian called W. S. Penley to back a new farce.

'He must have thought I was a fool or a soft touch,' Bottomley told Harris. 'I said, "Penley, is there a good part in this farce for you?"'

'"Yes," Penley replied. "It's the best part of my life." I told him that in that case I wouldn't put up a penny.'

'Why not?' Harris asked. 'Penley's an excellent comic.'

'I know,' Bottomley replied, 'but I couldn't resist saying, "Because, my dear Penley, if any of the other actors were to get one laugh you'd wreck the show!"'

Penley took his offer elsewhere. The farce, which opened in 1892, was called *Charley's Aunt* and became one of the biggest money-spinners of all time.

As one of the biggest gamblers on the turf Bottomley was understandably very popular indeed with the bookies in the Domino Room. He always believed that by 'the laws of chance', whatever they might be, his luck just had to turn, and he made it a point of honour never to be prepared for further adversity, claiming that this made

life more exciting. His luck never did turn, but such was Bottomley's
optimism that I heard him telling Frank Harris that he could become
Chancellor of the Exchequer if he could only get back into Parliament.

'You have no chance at all!' Harris thundered. 'How could they
appoint someone who had bankrupted himself to run the nation's
finances?'

It was a good question, but knowing Bottomley's charm and
powers of persuasion I do not think that the idea was so far-fetched.
Indeed, Bottomley continued to believe that the call to take up the
Chancellorship would come, perhaps through his elevation to a
peerage. And he did eventually get back into Parliament again in
1918 as MP for South Hackney, securing his discharge only hours
before applications by candidates closed.

In addition to his horse-racing, his drinking and the great style of
his country home at Upper Dicker in Sussex, where his wife, Eliza,
was kept out of London, Bottomley continued to spend lavishly on
women. The lasting love of his life was a chorus girl called Peggy
Primrose, a chocolate-box blonde who was more intelligent than she
looked, as I quickly learned through hearing them converse on their
many visits together to the Café Royal. Bottomley had lured her away
from her husband, a certain Aubrey Lowe, who took some revenge by
beating up his wife's seducer in public. Peggy was the only one of the
'fancy women' who stuck to him during and after his disgrace.

Bottomley was a master showman and he also secured an immense
following through 'ghost-written' articles in the *Sunday Pictorial*, for
which he was paid the then lordly sum of £100 each. The result,
which I could not resist reading, was often quite appalling, but
Bottomley understood the mass mind and believed in going down to
its level by producing what he knew ill-educated people wanted to
read. Indeed, his formula was so successful that he became the most
widely read journalist in Britain, as well as the most popular speaker.

The peak of Bottomley's popularity occurred during the 1914–18
War when he stomped the country raising recruits and money for the
war effort, but pocketing plenty for himself in the process. Hundreds
flocked to see and hear him and cheered him to the echo. I heard the
scoundrel myself at a great rally he organized in April 1915 at the
Albert Hall. The place was packed with people who clearly held him
in the highest regard. He had various celebrities on the platform,
including the music-hall star Charles Coburn, who had made his
name with the song 'The Man who Broke the Bank at Monte Carlo'

and was a Domino Room regular. That night Coburn sang a song which he had written himself about what, so Bottomley said, Britain was going to give the Kaiser – 'Two Lovely Black Eyes'.

Through wartime journalism and speeches Bottomley set himself up as the Great Patriot, which I believe he genuinely was at heart. He realized that one way of keeping the war effort going was to drum up hatred of the German enemy in any way. Once when he saw Lord Morley drinking hock, a German wine, he remonstrated with him, saying, 'Surely that is an unpatriotic beverage? Why don't you drink champagne, the wine of our allies?'

Morley was quick with his response: 'It's all right, Bottomley. I'm only interning it!'

Sadly, though Horatio certainly secured thousands of volunteers and raised the soldiers' morale by visiting them in the trenches, his main attitude to the Great War to End Wars was the same as his general approach to life: 'What can I get out of it?'

Had Bottomley stuck to *John Bull* he might well have become a venerable public figure, but he found that the money he took from the paper, which was huge, was not half enough for his needs. So on the side he indulged in swindles, which in retrospect were so blatant that it is astonishing how he remained unsuspected for so long.

These were usually some kind of sweepstake, but most of the winning tickets were never issued: he kept them back for friends or nominees acting for him, and pocketed almost the lot. In those days the law governing sweepstakes and lotteries was not so tight as it is now, and Bottomley exploited that situation to the full. He got away with it for so long that he became more and more reckless and started the completely crooked bond prize clubs, which I heard him planning with Cox and other cronies. Those who realized the truth turned against Bottomley; his former friend Harris declared that: 'This scoundrel must not be allowed to pollute the soil of Britain,' but those two would have ended up hating each other anyway, being too alike in too many ways.

Laughing until the tears literally trickled down his cheeks, Harris told a story of how he had tricked Bottomley into paying some money which, he said, was owing to him.

'I was passing Bottomley's office when I saw a famous person, who I will not name, leaving furtively. Remembering that Bottomley had been attacking this fellow in *John Bull*, and was probably holding back much worse in reserve, I put two and two together and marched into his office.

'Rapping my cane on his desk I said: "Right, Bottomley, I want £500 of that hush-money you've just been paid or I'll blow the whole affair in the newspapers."

'Bottomley blanched, then went to his safe, counted out £500 and handed it to me like a lamb. "How did you know about it?" he asked as I pocketed the cash.

'"I didn't," I replied, making for the door.'

Willie Crosland, too, had the measure of the man. He stood outside the Café Royal, asking every portly man who went in or out, 'Excuse me, sir, are you Mr Horatio Bottomley?' As each person denied the charge, some vehemently, Crosland shouted, 'Thank God,' seized him by the hand and offered his most profound congratulations.

Most reprehensible of all Bottomley's schemes was the Victory Bond Club, which he launched in 1919 to raise money to buy war bonds and so assist in Britain's recovery from the war, which had drained away so much treasure. Having raised huge sums from well-meaning members of the public, who also expected to see their investment grow, and hoped to win money in a draw, Bottomley siphoned off money to buy newspapers and champagne, pay his debts, and keep his horses in the style to which they had become accustomed. He had tried to confuse the evidence by merging the Victory Bond Club with a Thrift Prize Bond Club based in Paris, so that all the books were sent there. Understandably, when the bondholders began to demand their money back not much of it was forthcoming, and one hundred thousand creditors, of whom, because of my inside knowledge, I was not one, lost their investment.

The Victory Bond Club was a most scandalous fraud, but I do not think Bottomley would ever have been brought to book over it had he not commited the same mistake as Oscar Wilde – he decided to prosecute a former colleague who had issued a pamphlet calling him a swindler. The pamphlet, of which I still possess a copy, pulled no punches: 'The British government has allowed one of the greatest crooks ever born of woman to issue £1 shares, nearly one million pieces of blue paper,' it read. 'Horatio Bottomley became the possessor of nearly one million pounds of the poorer people's money with no trustees to watch the interests of the widows and the demobbed soldiers. . . .'

He could have laughed it off – God knows he was thick-skinned enough – and all his cronies urged him to do just that, but he insisted on going ahead with prosecuting the man, called Reuben Bigland, for criminal libel. Bigland came up for preliminary trial before magistrates at Bow Street, accused not only of criminal libel but of attempting to blackmail Bottomley. Some of the charges were dismissed, and Bottomley was castigated by the magistrate as a liar under oath. The immediate result was that Bottomley was sacked as the editor of *John Bull*, though with £25,000 compensation. Bigland was tried at the Old Bailey on 23 January 1922 on the charge of publishing the libellous pamphlet; Bottomley was represented by Sir Edward Marshall Hall. The trial never got off the ground, and I and others who had queued for seats were intensely disappointed. Marshall Hall refused to offer any evidence against Bigland, who was acquitted with costs against Bottomley.

The parallel with Oscar Wilde's libel action then became even closer. Bottomley was viciously attacked in *The Times* and urged to clear his name or to clear out of public life. Bottomley replied with a weak letter to *The Times* and an even weaker article in the *Sunday Illustrated* entitled 'The Secret History of the Bigland Case'. As Bigland still had to face some more charges in another court, the article was judged to be a contempt of court and cost Bottomley and his publisher a £1000 fine.

Many in the Domino Room were betting that Bottomley would soon be finding himself in the dock once more. I believed that he would still manage to wriggle out of his predicament, but I was wrong. On 19 May 1922, Bottomley appeared at the Old Bailey before Mr Justice Salter to defend himself against accusations of defrauding the public. The trial was to be every bit as sensational as Oscar Wilde's. Inevitably Bottomley, entering the dock with a plea of 'Most decidedly not guilty', chose to defend himself, and I am sure that it was his complete confidence in his skill to outwit any professional barrister that had originally induced him to go ahead. It proved to be a fatal error. For one thing, he was up against a most formidable opponent, Mr Travers Humphreys, who had appeared as a junior in the Wilde case and had the special gift of being able to deal with complex financial deals and make issues clear to a jury. Up until that time Bottomley had always made the evidence as complicated as possible and cleverly exploited its effect on a lay jury, who would tend to acquit on evidence they could not understand. Second, Mr Justice Salter – known as 'Drysalter' – was not the type of man to be carried away with admiration for Bottomley's brilliance in court.

Bottomley pursued his usual tack of being 'victimized', claiming that such a patriot and splendid citizen as himself could never stoop to the behaviour of which he had been accused. He claimed that to help him with the schemes he had engaged a hundred ex-soldiers – an absolute lie. Typical of his appeal to the jury was this note I took at the trial: 'You have got to find that Horatio Bottomley, editor of *John Bull*, the man who wrote and spoke throughout the war with the sole object of inspiring the troops and keeping up the morale of the country, went out to the front to do his best to cheer up the lads – you have got to find that that man intended to steal their money. God forbid!' He put on a most moving theatrical act, resorting to tears to say: 'There are times in the silent hours of the night when I think of all I have endeavoured to do to wipe out my sordid past and to justify the confidence of the fighting man. I hope to satisfy you, if they were the last words to pass my lips, that I am incapable of robbing an ex-soldier.' Sadly for his friends, of which I still considered myself one, the court was not moved at all. Travers Humphreys was on masterly form and riddled Bottomley's defences.

Every day during the trial, while he was on bail, he came to the Café Royal; clearly he appreciated that he might go down, for on one occasion I heard him say to Peggy Primrose, while they were drinking the usual champagne, 'Let's have another bottle; I may not be able to get any soon.'

Even my sympathy for one of the nation's most remarkable men at bay began to wane as Bottomley told one terrible lie after another. When asked if he had been paid for his patriotic speeches during the war Bottomley replied: 'Never a farthing for my recruiting meetings but, later on, as a lecturer, I got certain remuneration, nearly every penny of which, if you force me to say it, I gave away to wounded soldiers in the towns I went to.' I had too often heard him discussing with Tommy Cox how much they could get from the lectures to spend on themselves to be able to suppress a wry smile at this answer. I could sense that Bottomley was destroyed when Travers Humphreys produced a letter which the defendant had sent to his bank seeking a loan, and claiming that he was earning up to £400 from his lectures!

In his final impassioned plea to the jury on the seventh day of the trial Bottomley tried every gambit, including a passage from Shakespeare:

My honour and my life are one,
Take honour from me and my life is done.

Then he added: 'If things go wrong it would be the most appalling error of justice the world has ever known. The jury is not yet born who will convict me of these charges. It is unthinkable!'

He worked on the jury's emotions for an hour and a half but, unluckily for him, the weekend elapsed before the judge's summing up, at which time the jurymen could take a more detached view; so they based their verdict on the evidence and the now too obvious fact that Bottomley was a consummate liar and inveterate rogue. During that weekend Bottomley went to a big prize-fight between Bombardier Billy Wells and Frank Goddard and, after visiting his wife in the country, had dinner with Peggy Primrose in the Café Royal on the Sunday evening. Few stopped by his table, but those who did were told that he was confident of being acquitted. 'I put my trust in British justice,' he said brightly.

When the jury returned I watched Bottomley's face as closely as I could in the crowded little court as the foreman announced that he was guilty on all counts except one. It flushed as Mr Justice Salter said: 'Horatio Bottomley, you have been rightly convicted by the jury of this long series of heartless frauds. These poor people trusted you and you robbed them. . . . The crime is aggravated by your high position, by the number and poverty of your victims, by the trust which they reposed in you and which you abused. It is aggravated by the magnitude of your frauds, and by the callous effrontery with which your frauds were committed and sought to be defended. I can see no mitigation whatsoever.'

The judge sentenced him to seven years and, though this was a terrible blow to all his hopes, financial, political and journalistic, Bottomley soon recovered his sense of humour in prison, where he was popular with the other criminals, though not with the warders who had to help to dress and undress him because he was so fat.

One day in Wormwood Scrubs prison he saw one of his racing friends, who had been convicted of a fraud on bookmakers, hard at work mowing the prison lawns. 'Still on the turf, I see,' Bottomley remarked. On another occasion, after he had been moved to Maidstone, a prison visitor saw him sitting in his broad-arrow convict's suit sewing mailbags, and remarked, 'Ah — sewing, I see.' 'No, reaping,' Bottomley replied.

With full remission for good conduct Bottomley was released after serving five years and two months, and really thought he could take up the threads of his old life again. What he had failed to appreciate was that, while the public could forgive him for being a crook, they were not likely to forget the fact that he had been in prison. This was the stigma in those days – the fact that he had 'been inside', as I suppose it still is.

Even the Domino Room, normally a forgiving place, would not really accept him. He returned as bold as brass, though much thinner, but few of his former acquaintances were prepared to speak to him because of the appalling way he had exploited the war to line his pockets. He could still turn on the charm as he explained, 'I was monstrously misjudged but I bear no grudge. It's water over the dam. . . .'

Turning first to journalism, Bottomley wrote his story for the *Weekly Dispatch* which serialized it under the title 'I have paid but . . .', to which the common response quickly became '. . . but not twenty shillings in the pound!' Still the vain optimist, Bottomley, who had of course lost *John Bull*, which continued successfully, produced a rival paper called *John Blunt*. It was quite a good title but only one issue ever appeared. As usual, Bottomley blamed everybody but himself for its failure, for even after his long experience in prison he did not learn to be honest with himself and could never bring himself to admit he might have been wrong.

He gradually went downhill, and at seventy-two was so hard up that he was forced into trying an entertainment act at the Windmill Theatre, just round the corner from Piccadilly. I went to see it out of curiosity, but it was a pitiful failure and I felt deeply sorry for my old friend. Had I ever met him I would have liked to take him back to the Domino Room for a square meal in the surroundings he had so long enjoyed. I would love to have asked him if he had any regrets, though I fear his answer would have been, 'Only about being found out.' His old girlfriend Peggy Primrose, who looked after him to the last, expressed this most eloquently when she said, 'Bottomley's trouble was that he fancied he was walking on a red carpet that stretched to infinity.'

Bottomley died in February 1933 and such old Café Royal colleagues as remembered him seemed grieved. Given the opportunity, I suspect that he would have done it all again. He must have been highly intelligent and simply chose to fulfil himself in an extremely dangerous way. I remember his saying to one of his friends, some time in 1920 or so, 'I've been sitting on a barrel of gunpowder for thirty years and it might go up at any moment.'

14

PRIDE OF PARISIAN LIONS

The sheer Frenchness of the Domino Room and the Café Royal as a whole made it a magnet for Frenchmen pining for their beloved Paris. Many were domiciled in London, others were visiting, while some were in exile for political or personal reasons. Among the exiles none interested me more than Henri Rochefort, a wiry, wild-eyed radical with a mane of white hair, beard and moustache. He was really a *marquis* but, as a staunch Republican, had dropped the title and was believed to be plotting against whatever French government was in power.

Among the exiles in the nineties were scores of French Anarchists, who wanted no government at all, and seemed to spend their time conspiring in Soho and making bombs. They were led by a man called Georges Pilotelle, who hated Rochefort. I knew them because they both used the Domino Room and I was not alone in believing that when they appeared there with strangers it was to further some dark conspiracy. When Rochefort arrived he was often followed in by Fleet Street reporters, who played up the 'plots' in their stories, and any French man or woman he might speak to was sure to be a courier from Paris or a spy.

Rochefort bore it patiently until one day an over-zealous reporter found an empty table next to his and began to note down everything he did. After paying the bill Rochefort, who had been eating on his own, suddenly whipped out a big black cigar and pointed it with malevolent concentration at the reporter who, in the terror of the moment, mistook it for a pistol. We had the joy of seeing Rochefort backing the reporter out into Regent Street and then returning, to cheers and applause, to enjoy a smoke in peace.

Pilotelle, a professional caricaturist, could not resist making his hatred of Rochefort obvious when they chanced to be in together, especially when the arch-Anarchist was drunk. He also detested the owners of the Café for decorating it with symbols of the Imperial Bonapartist régime; this was not old Nicols's fault, for he had been tricked into it by his son-in-law, the mountainous Georges Pigache, who gave him to understand that the 'N' was for Nicols. The old man had been furious when he saw that each 'N' was surrounded by a laurel wreath and topped by the French Imperial crown, but grudgingly accepted that it was good for business.

Another French exile who chose London as a temporary refuge was that literary lion Monsieur Emile Zola. I had never read any of his works, but had heard plenty about him because he was often mentioned in the literary reviews and Domino Room conversations, and I knew there was fear that some of his books might not be publishable in England for a long time because they were regarded as too openly sexual for British morals. Nevertheless I had seen him, for he had visited England in the autumn of 1893 at the invitation of the Institute of Journalists.

A great fuss had been made when he arrived at Victoria Station, named after our Queen. The newspapers were full of reports about the dinners and receptions given to him, and when I learned that the Lord Mayor was to put on a banquet for him at the Guildhall I took the horse-bus in that direction to see the procession as it entered, always a colourful sight. I was astonished at the size of the crowd which had gathered to see Zola and, being small, had to elbow my way through to make sure of seeing anything at all. I thought he looked very French but otherwise unimpressive, with his greying beard, pale face, pince-nez spectacles on a thick nose and his half-bald head, which was visible as he raised his top-hat to the crowd. He seemed to me to be really revelling in all the publicity, which some authors affect to despise, and it was publicity generated by his intervention in the Dreyfus case, of which more in a moment, which was to bring him more general fame than his works.

Naturally, I was hoping that he would be brought to the Café Royal by some of the people in the Domino Room who knew him well, like George Moore or Robert Sherard. There was much talk about him there and it was inevitable that someone would make a feeble quip about Gorgon-Zola. Still, I was surprised when the perpetrator turned out to be the usually subtle Oscar. He had, of course, a score to settle, though personally I thought he had already done that – with interest. Previously, when Oscar had been addressing a banquet in Paris Zola, who disliked him, had ended a toast to him by saying, in French, 'Unfortunately Monsieur Wilde will be obliged to reply in his own barbarous tongue.' Oscar had risen with the memorable riposte: 'As Monsieur Zola has said, I am condemned to speak the language of Shakespeare.' I never saw Zola in the Café, but one of the waiters in the Restaurant said he had been there for a quiet lunch with a British publisher interested in his works.

I would have been even more keen to see him on his next visit, when he chose England for his place of temporary exile in 1898. He had left Paris to avoid imprisonment for libel over his insistence that Captain Alfred Dreyfus, a Jewish officer who had been sent to Devil's Island for spying, had been falsely convicted by an anti-Semitic court martial. On this visit, however, Zola's whereabouts were kept secret, and though he was here for almost a year nobody ever found him, save for those few who were in the conspiracy of silence – details of which were eventually disclosed in the *Evening News* by the friend of Zola mainly responsible for it, who happened, of all things, to be a journalist! It would have been impossible for him to visit the Café Royal, because so many would have recognized him. In any case his conversation would have been of scant interest to me, for I gather that he could speak hardly a word of English.

In that same autumn, London received another French literary giant, the poet Paul Verlaine, who had been invited to make a lecture tour on the initiative of the artist Will Rothenstein, who was only twenty-one but had already made drawings of Verlaine in Paris.

I could understand Will's artistic interest when the poet stumped into the room in the company of Ernest Dowson and Arthur Symons, the poet who edited literary magazines and pronounced his name 'Simmons', on a late November evening. He was certainly paint-worthy, as the artists used to say. I had often heard Verlaine discussed by other poets and knew that he was ugly, but the strange little man in the overcoat that was too big for him, with a shoddy old muffler round his neck and what seemed like just the stump of a pipe in his small mouth, was ugly beyond belief. His face was flat, his eyes oblique, his chin weak, his skull bald and knobbly, his moustache and beard limp and straggly.

The newspapers assured us that 'the convict poet', as they called him, was only forty-nine, but with the yellowness of his skin and his lameness due to leg ulcers, he looked twenty years older. He had indeed been a convict, for he had been sent to prison for wounding his young lover, the poet Arthur Rimbaud, with a revolver. Yes, he was a homosexual, or bisexual I should say, for he also had a wife and mistress, but how anybody of either sex could fancy him I cannot understand: he looked unclean. From all accounts he *was* unclean, and that evening looked reasonably dressed only because Symons had rustled up some clothes for him. In Paris, Symons had reported, he was inclined to live in filth, partly through poverty but mainly because he was drunk so much of the time on absinthe – Oscar's 'green fairy'.

I should at this point make it clear that there was nothing homosexual about Arthur Symons, who was to remain almost as faithful to the Café Royal as myself. I had entertained doubts about him when I saw him on his first visit to the Domino Room when he was young and handsome with blue eyes, rosy cheeks and light brown hair, for he was in the company of an elderly writer of similar-sounding name, John Addington Symonds, who was well known to be homosexual. I had thought the worst when the two of them took off, after a long conversation about poetry, to the Empire, a music-hall in Leicester Square which belonged to the Café Royal company. However, my fears concerning young Arthur evaporated as soon as I saw him in the company of Dr Havelock Ellis, that magnificently set up personality in both body and mind, who was writer, poet, doctor, scientist and daring pioneer in the study of sex problems, including homosexuality, but entirely normal himself, though he did seem to be obsessed with visions of women urinating!

I had to take the word of people like Ernest Dowson, who spoke French fluently, that Verlaine was a great poet, with an enormous output and the unusual distinction of being accepted as among France's greatest during his own day. In fact Dowson said that Verlaine thought in verse more easily than in prose. Symons, who had lived in Paris, also spoke French, so that I was unable to hear what they were saying as they conversed in that language with much gesturing, though Verlaine knew English. So, as I watched, my mind recalled Oscar's aphorism: 'It is better to be beautiful than good, but it is better to be good than ugly.' Verlaine from all accounts was not good, and was to die from his excesses less than three years later, another genius who had the self-destructive streak and chose to commit suicide slowly rather than at a single stroke.

This visit, which included lectures in Oxford and Manchester, was not Verlaine's first, either to England or to the Domino Room. He had been in England in the early seventies in the company of his mop-haired boyfriend, Rimbaud, and they were well remembered by some of the older waiters for their violent quarrels, though they had not fought with knives as they had in France. Later Verlaine had taught French at schools in England, including one in Bournemouth, when Max Beerbohm had cartooned him with his battered umbrella in charge of a crocodile of top-hatted, booted and Eton-collared schoolboys. Fancy a homosexual being in charge of small boys! But then Verlaine was not addicted to children.

Another equally famous Frenchman, whose appearance was even more memorable for its peculiarity, and who was also to kill himself with drink, showed up in the Domino Room on the two occasions when he visited London. This was the painter Henri de Toulouse-Lautrec. The sight of this little man stumping down the aisle towards the centre of the room had everyone staring, a breach of manners to which he must have been accustomed and to which he responded with a most pleasant smile. His head and body seemed normal enough but his arms and legs were much too small for it, due, I learned later, to some mishap in childhood. He was bearded in the French style with pince-nez glasses on a rather prominent nose, the paleness of his face contrasting with the redness of his full lips. He wore a check suit and elastic-sided boots and his head was topped by a flat bowler with the tiniest rim I had ever seen – aptly called in France, I believe, a melon hat.

He was escorted to a table by his host, the artist Charles Conder, then living in Paris but an occasional visitor to the Domino Room and eventually to become almost a fixture. The lanky Conder made the Frenchman look smaller still until they sat down when he seemed to be of normal size. They were soon joined by Arthur Symons.

Toulouse-Lautrec, who had met both of them in Paris, quickly showed himself capable of pacing even the bibulous Conder for drink. He had visited Whistler's studio in Chelsea that morning and been so enraptured by the American painter, who was not much taller, that he had borrowed brushes and palette and painted with him.

'I have never seen anyone paint like that before,' he said in good English. 'Whistler stands way back from his canvas and goes through the motions of painting in the air with his brush. Then he leaps across to the easel and puts little dabs of colour on very, very slowly.'

'They must be little dabs,' Conder replied, from the cloud of cigarette smoke which permanently enveloped him, 'because I gather that he never wears a smock but paints in those white drill suits of his which never have a mark on them.'

'That's right,' Toulouse-Lautrec agreed. 'He's the cleanest painter I've ever seen. Very fussy, but his pictures aren't.'

'Yes, that's the surprising thing,' Symons said, 'because Whistler's whole nature is very fussy. Everything has to be just so.'

Symons was knowledgeable about painting as well as being a growing authority on literature and music.

From the general hubbub and laughter, the Frenchman was obviously an excellent table companion, though they did keep lapsing into his language. Whistler must have been equally taken with him because a couple of evenings later he put on a special dinner for him at the Café Royal, being convinced that, since he was the heir to a count, he would expect the best. For some reason the meal was a culinary disaster; Whistler was so furious that he called the chef to the table and, fixing him with his monocled stare, gave him a dressing-down that rivalled any performance by Frank Harris.

Toulouse-Lautrec took it extremely well and did what he could to help the poor chef. 'You shouldn't have bothered to arrange French food for me,' he said. 'I always believe in eating what the natives eat.'

'In that case I'll take you to an English restaurant tomorrow,' Whistler responded. 'There are some good ones, you know.'

'I'm sure there are,' the artist said. 'But do me the honour of being my guest.'

I was sorry to see my beloved Café Royal being spurned, but I learned that they had gone to the Criterion next day and enjoyed an excellent meal centred on roast beef and Yorkshire pudding.

I was to have the pleasure of Toulouse-Lautrec's company again the following year, though in sadder circumstances. He was back in London with Conder, spending his time going from bar to bar, including the Domino Room and the music-halls, the nearest things to his beloved Moulin Rouge, which provided the subjects for so many of his paintings.

Toulouse-Lautrec was appalled at the way the public was treating Wilde and was most anxious to see him. Conder discovered that Oscar, then on bail, was in Oakley Street and took the artist there, hoping that Wilde would pose for a drawing. He declined to pose, but allowed the Frenchman to make some quick sketches. Back in France the little man, whose work I have never rated very highly, converted the sketches to a portrait, which in the reproductions I have seen made Wilde look not only effeminate but more dissipated and arrogant than he was. I never heard whether Oscar had remarked on it but, after hearing his comments on far less cruel caricatures by Beardsley and Beerbohm, he could not have liked it.

It was a case of the pot calling the kettle black because Toulouse-Lautrec, crippled in mind as well as body, was even more drink-sodden and every bit as debauched. Admittedly he was interested only in women, but these were prostitutes in the cheaper brothels of Paris. Such were his excesses that they were to kill him in 1901 before he was thirty-seven.

Toulouse-Lautrec! Verlaine! Pilotelle! Rochefort! This quartet strengthened my suspicion that all foreigners are rum, to say the least. They are certainly proof that Victorian England had no monopoly on eccentrics. Au contraire!

15

LEFT TURN FOR THE COUNTESS

I have mentioned that Bertie's affair with Daisy Brooke had faded before his appearance with Lillie at the St James's Theatre. No doubt this upset her, but she soon had a replacement love – two in fact. One was a dashing young soldier called Captain Laycock; the other, of far greater importance, was a life-long affair with Socialism, which for many of her friends was the most scandalous aspect of her behaviour since it made her a traitor to her class and to the system which sustained it.

The way this had come about was the result of an event held far away from my prying eyes, in Warwick Castle, but once again a Domino Room visitor was to give me first-hand information about it. He was a man called Robert Blatchford, a former soldier who had managed to make himself into a journalist and had founded the *Clarion*, the most widely read left-wing journal of its day. He had also published a simply written satirical pamphlet called *Merrie England*, which converted thousands to Socialism by describing the true plight of working people in vivid terms that they could understand.

Daisy had already become interested in improving the lot of the poor, particularly the agricultural poor, on her huge estate at Easton Lodge near Dunmow in Essex, which she had inherited before she married Lord Brooke. In this work she had been influenced by another Fleet Street journalist, William Stead, a powerfully built, heavily bearded bore who edited the *Review of Reviews* and was a puritanical reformer, seething with self-righteous indignation. With his backing she had set up needlework schools and other charitable units for providing work. Once she had become Countess of Warwick, when her husband succeeded his father in 1893, she intended to expand these activities, which cost her quite a considerable amount of money, and one of the vehicles for doing this was a huge celebration ball at Warwick Castle. This had not been permissible until a year of mourning for the late earl was completed, but in the meantime Daisy had been heavily engaged in preparations for it.

Her excuse for spending so much on the festivities was that they provided work for many people who would otherwise be unemployed, and when one read the accounts of the lavish ball in the London papers it was clear that the costs had indeed been enormous.

Stead sided with Daisy in her argument, but Blatchford, a much more genuine crusader and a deeper thinker, I believe, did not. In the 17 February issue of the *Clarion* he attacked her Ladyship with forthright ferocity: 'Thousands of pounds spent on a few hours' silly masquerade; men and women strutting before each other's envious eyes in mad rivalry of wanton dissipation. Other men and women and children huddling, the while, in rugged hovels, without food, without fire, shuddering, shivering   '

Daisy's fury when she read it was so uncontrollable that she left her guests and immediately entrained for London. This is what happened according to Blatchford's account, given to another Socialist friend over a modest meal in the Domino Room:

'I was sitting quietly at my desk in my office round about midday correcting some proofs when this woman, dolled up to the nines, burst in unannounced and asked, "Are you the editor of the *Clarion*?" When I admitted it she pushed a heavily marked page of the paper under my nose and I realized she must either be the Countess of Warwick or some friend acting on her behalf.

'"How could you be so unfair and so unjust?" she said angrily. "Our ball has given work to half the county and to dozens of dressmakers in London."

'"Are you the Countess of Warwick?" I asked.

'When she said that indeed she was, I asked her to sit down and I would then explain why my attack on her had been perfectly justified.

'By that time it had become clear that she had raced down from Warwick that morning to confront me, probably in a special train. In the simplest terms I pointed out the difference between productive labour and unproductive labour. I think I convinced her that the effort spent by all those seamstresses and labourers was no more productive than if she had asked them to dig holes and fill them up again.'

As I listened I thought that Blatchford was being unkind. Daisy's intentions had obviously been good, and intentions do matter. Surely it is always better to encourage people to earn money, however trivial the purpose, rather than dole it out as charity, which most people loathe. It was by no means uncommon in those days for landed gentry who wished to provide work to build follies – deliberate ruins to improve a view. Such people were more praiseworthy than those who sat back with their wealth and did nothing, or squandered it on the gambling tables.

It seems the Blatchford sermon had continued for a couple of hours.

'I was so warmed to my subject and the lady seemed so interested that we both forgot about lunch.'

'Did she accept the argument?' Blatchford was asked.

'Hard to tell. She seemed a bit punch-drunk when she left the office. But she had a copy of *Merrie England* in her hand.'

As the world was soon to learn – her friends with horror – Blatchford had converted Daisy into a life-long Socialist and, as with religion, there is nothing like a convert for zeal.

She saw Blatchford again only occasionally, but she strengthened her political relationship with Stead, whom she introduced to Bertie in an effort to convert the future King to her cause of bettering society. As could be expected, he refused to accept the argument that society could quickly be levelled up by any political action. 'Society grows, my dear Daisy, it is not made,' was his response. Looking back, I have to agree with him.

Poor Stead! He did not live long enough to see the catastrophe of the first Labour Government. He was drowned when the unsinkable liner *Titanic* struck an iceberg on its maiden voyage to America.

The redoubtable Daisy pressed on, to the dismay of her friends and of her family who saw the vast riches she had inherited frittered away in schemes to assist the Labour Party and the trades unions. These schemes came to nothing, but they so impoverished Daisy that, in an effort to pay her creditors, at the age of fifty-three she embarked on the most scandalous conduct of her whole life. In April 1914 she began what can only be described as an attempt to blackmail the Royal Family, then headed by King George V.

Having lost so much in her various charitable and political

schemes, she turned to what she had regarded as a nest egg – her many letters from the late King Edward VII who, it seems, had a habit of addressing her not only as 'My Darling Daisy' but as 'My own adored little Daisy wife'.

Once again, an old habitué of the Domino Room was to be the central figure in this sordid business – Frank Harris, to whom Daisy wrote, reminding him that Bertie had once introduced them and saying that she would like to consult him about '. . . a matter of great interest regarding certain letters. . . .' Her idea was that Harris should write or 'ghost' a book about her life, bringing in many of the letters, which were likely to give the book extensive sales. Harris, who was then in the South of France, was as hard up as she was; he responded with great enthusiasm and, since he could not visit England because of a pending bankruptcy case, she went to see him.

Daisy justified her action by telling Harris that one of the main reasons she was so heavily in debt was because of the cost of entertaining Bertie and his retinue over so many years. No doubt this had been expensive, but it was her crackpot schemes and her entertainment of hordes of fleshpot-loving Socialists which had really ruined her. Harris assured her that he could sell the letters alone in the United States for £100,000, which would have cleared her debts completely, and she signed a contract with him promising to pay him £5000 for editing her memoirs. In addition he was to receive a percentage of the money realized by the sales. Later, Daisy was to justify her action to her friends by arguing that the social disgrace of publishing the letters would be no worse than that of the bankruptcy, which it might forestall. Such are the terrible ways in which money can warp human behaviour.

It was not long before the Royal Family and their advisers heard of the proposition, and when she knew this Daisy changed her tactics. She let it be known that she would be prepared to abandon the memoirs provided a substantial sum was paid for the letters. This of course was sheer blackmail, and Daisy should have realized that King George would be the last man to submit to it, especially when his mother, Queen Alexandra, to whom the letters would have been very hurtful, was still alive. The King's advisers took immediate steps to thwart Daisy and yet make sure that the letters would never be published. Late in June they secured an injunction claiming copyright on all the late King's letters, which meant that any attempt at publication was prohibited until further order by the court.

Harris was naturally as disappointed as Daisy. Though he had said he would never return to Britain, which had treated him so badly, he had to get out of France when war was declared against Germany: he was not popular there because he had espoused the German cause. Instead of going to London, where the bankruptcy officials would have been interested in him, he joined Daisy at Easton Lodge in Essex. Under a pseudonym he stayed there with his wife and began to write Daisy's life from information she gave him each morning. Half-way through, Daisy became so frightened that she abandoned her project, and Harris took off for America.

Eventually, after a legal action, she handed over the letters with bad grace and never made a penny out of them. Indeed, when in 1929 she came to publish her memoirs under the title *Life's Ebb and Flow* she made no mention of the letters. She did not mention Frank Harris either. But the book was full of photographs of her late husband!

16

A CLUTCH OF ULTRA-ECCENTRICS

Of all the denizens of the Domino Room, the man who pushed to the furthest limits the belief that a 'man of genius' is entitled to do precisely what he likes, whatever the consequences to others, was Aleister Crowley, alias the 'Beast'. Crowley deliberately set out to secure for himself the reputation of being the Most Evil Man in the World, his motto being: 'Evil be thou my good.'

I first noticed him enter the Domino Room in 1897, soon after he had left Cambridge University without taking a degree. He was then calling himself Count Vladimir Svareff but this was only one of many pretentious poses, for which he always dressed the part extravagantly, having been left with large private means. Even his name of Aleister was false, for he had been baptized Edward Alexander.

How much he was a deliberate fraud and how much self-deluded nobody will ever know, but he appeared to believe that he was the reincarnation of 'Count' Cagliostro, the eighteenth-century Italian adventurer and *poseur* who claimed all sorts of magical abilities, such as the power to change base metals into gold. He also claimed to be the reincarnation of Pope Alexander Borgia and other villains. Most of the people in the Domino Room considered him to be patently fraudulent, but I suppose this happened in the past with many self-deluded cranks who are now dignified by the name of 'mystic' and have even in some cases been made into saints.

In pursuit of magical powers, in which he at least genuinely seemed to believe, he had set himself up in a flat in Chancery Lane, off Fleet Street; in those days when people made more use of their legs it was a relatively short walk from the Café Royal, which he quickly realized was an excellent venue for drawing attention to himself. I heard someone who had visited his flat describing it as being equipped with two 'Magical Temples':

'One temple was white, the walls being lined with six huge mirrors to throw back the evil forces. The other temple was a black-lined cupboard containing an altar supported by the figure of a negro standing on his hands. The presiding genius was a human skeleton which Crowley fed from time to time with blood, small birds, mammals and beef tea in the hope of restoring it to life.'

Crowley, who claimed he was the 'Beast' foretold in the Bible, regaled his visitor with tales of terrible cruelties he had committed. Apparently at the age of fourteen, having been assured that a cat has nine lives, he set out to disprove it scientifically. He caught a cat, poisoned it with arsenic, chloroformed it, gassed it, stabbed it, cut its throat, burned it, stove its skull in and then threw it out of the window.

'I was quite sorry for the animal,' Crowley had explained. 'I simply had to carry out the experiment in the interests of science.' He offered no such explanation for his habit of crucifying toads and other small animals, however; that was all part of his 'magical' rituals.

How could one tolerate such a creature? the reader may ask. In spite of his sadism and other peculiarities he was a man of considerable ability, a prolific poet who could afford to pay to have all his works published, a brilliant chess player, a daring mountaineer who climbed some of the most dangerous peaks in the Himalayas, then a very uncommon achievement, walked across vast tracts of China and was a practitioner of Yoga.

While some in the Domino Room considered him a bore, I found him most interesting as a character study as he sat there puffing at a huge pipe filled with perique soaked in rum. I was not alone. Arnold Bennett and G. K. Chesterton both rated him a good poet, and he was friendly with several people who were to become famous in their fields, like the portrait painter Gerald Kelly and a young army officer called Fuller, who was to become a major-general and a highly respected strategist.

Deciding that Chancery Lane was too noisy for magic, he bought an estate on Loch Ness with a mansion called Boleskine House, where he continued his magical studies in earnest. This gave him the excuse to wear the garb of a Scottish chieftain and he frequently appeared in the Domino Room as the Laird of Boleskine, though I was told he owned only two acres; still this, at least, was nearer the truth than some of his other titles, such as the Earl of Middlesex, Frater Perdurabo, Count von Zonaref and the Comte de Fénix!

Whatever uniform he was wearing he made himself look as evil as possible, staring with his eyes and eventually shaving his head to make himself appear more menacing, his evil mien being enhanced by a remaining lock of hair which he trained to look like a horn. In this quest he also filed his canine teeth so that he could give specially honoured ladies what he called 'the Serpent's Kiss'. I saw him on one occasion seize the arm of a lady companion – the heiress Nancy Cunard, with whom he was friendly – and bite her wrist, drawing blood and a cry of pain.

He advertised his bestiality by wearing what he called the Mark of the Beast, a medallion consisting of the sun in the arms of the moon within the seven-pointed star of Babylon, and bearing the number 666. Much of his poetry was erotic, and even his monogram of his initials, A.C., was in the form of an erect penis and a testicle pouch. He was forever chasing women, who seemed to succumb and become his disciples; this eventually entailed bearing his illegitimate children.

He founded a religion called 'Crowleyanity', to replace Christianity, which had only one law: 'Do what thou wilt.' Naturally with such a belief he was outraged by the treatment meted out to Oscar Wilde. 'Nobody has any right to say what anyone else shall or shall not do with his or her body,' I heard him declare. 'Establish this principle of respect for others and the whole nightmare of sex is dispelled.'

That, of course, was outrageous thinking for that era and to most people still is, but I have a feeling that within a few more decades the majority of people will be agreeing with him. I already see signs that 'Do what thou wilt be the whole of the law' has more appeal for many young people today than the disciplinary demands of Christianity.

Of course I could not go along with his beliefs, but I owe him a debt for the entertainment he provided, for nobody could deny that he had a sense of humour. On one occasion when he had ventured south in his Highland costume I heard him telling Gerald Kelly about a letter he had written to some society which concerned itself with the suppression of vice. On headed notepaper from Boleskine, Crowley had complained that prostitution was most 'unpleasantly conspicuous' around the shores of Loch Ness, and that something should be done about it.

'The damned idiots sent an observer poste haste to come to grips with the problem, and of course could find no trace of it. I received a communication to this effect, whereupon I replied, "I meant that prostitution was unpleasantly conspicuous *by its absence*, you fools!"'

There were numerous occasions when some incorrigible wag like Willie Crosland or Horace Cole would shout 'Ah, Frater Perdurabo!' as Crowley entered the Domino Room. Crowley would invariably respond with a venomous stare and then gesture some terrible curse, at which the wag would subside in his seat with a gurgling death rattle. His entry in his Highland costume usually touched off a mass rendering of a Harry Lauder song. I shall have more to say about this outraordinary man, who lived to a considerable age — he died in 1947 — never retracted any of his beliefs, and was never punished for them by the law.

Most of the other habitués of the Domino Room laughed at Crowley's firm belief in the existence of the Devil as a real force exercising evil throughout the world, just as most of them scoffed at the existence of God. But one man who could not have been more dissimilar in many other respects agreed with him wholeheartedly about the Devil. This was the journalist and author Gilbert Keith Chesterton, who frequently strayed from his favourite pubs in Fleet Street to patronize the Domino Room.

Chesterton, like Crowley a minor poet of distinction, shared with him another characteristic. He was an incorrigible showman who, a little later in his life, dressed most eccentrically in order to draw attention to himself, sporting a battered slouch hat and a black cloak which made his bulk look ever grosser and the whole impression more open to caricature. In my view one was as vain as the other, and there were those who said that both were deluded about religion. I frequently noticed, for instance, that whenever Chesterton lit one of the black cheroots he smoked incessantly he would make the sign of the cross with it or with the match.

There were many Christian hypocrites in the Domino Room, people who professed a Christian belief and would argue strongly in its favour, while at the same time being un-Christian in their behaviour towards others – as, for example, most of them were towards Oscar Wilde in his extremity. For that reason I had some private admiration for Crowley, who stated his views about Christianity openly and with no qualifications. I once heard him argue that he was obviously right to worship evil, because if there was a Devil then clearly he ruled on earth, as it was the villains who prospered while the good received little justice.

Unfortunately Crowley was really evil by nature as well as by conscious intent, whereas Chesterton was in every sense a good man who cared for the welfare of others. Crowley had few friends – indeed most people shunned him either as a charlatan or because they feared that his claim to be in league with Satan could be justified – but Chesterton was surrounded by friends wherever he went. His most frequent companions in the Café Royal were Bernard Shaw, Maurice Baring, a half-mad but talented member of the rich banking family, who had written poems for the *Yellow Book* and was a member of the Souls group which I have already mentioned, and Hilaire Belloc, a writer and short-time Member of Parliament, who had great gifts but whose behaviour sometimes went beyond the bounds of eccentricity. In the hottest weather Belloc would enter the Domino Room clad in souwester and sea boots. On one occasion, before settling himself at Chesterton's table in this garb, he seized G.K.'s glass, pointed to me and shouted: 'Let us all drink to that brave and gallant man. You may not know who he is, and who am I to breach his silent modesty, but I can tell you that he is a hero, a man of action, a man of courage whose deeds have done service to us all. God bless you, sir!'

He raised his glass as I looked away in some confusion, though most of those in the Domino Room realized – just by looking at me – that Belloc must have been pulling their legs.

'Who is he?' G.K. whispered as Belloc sat down.

'I haven't the foggiest idea,' Belloc replied, summoning the waiter. 'And I have no wish to find out.'

Chesterton and Belloc were to be so bound together by the Roman Catholic faith that Shaw referred to them as a two-headed monster called the Chesterbelloc. Both could not stop writing: Chesterton because he was a compulsive scribbler, even using his shirt cuffs if no paper happened to be handy; Belloc because he needed the money, his view being that 'The whole art is to write and write and then offer it for sale like butter'.

'I'm tired of love and still more tired of rhyme, but money gives me pleasure all the time,' he used to jest.

I remember the first time I saw Chesterton, Belloc and Baring together in the Domino Room. They were all heavy drinkers of wine and beer, and became noisier and noisier as their intake progressed. Belloc, burly and pugnacious with a bullet head and close-cropped hair, had arrived wearing his oilskin and souwester while Chesterton, six-foot-two, was recognizable to all with his droopy moustache, long, wavy hair and pince-nez spectacles on a black ribbon round his neck. Baring, who had a long, bald head and a moustache, and chain-smoked cigarettes, was slouched with his wine glass balanced on top of his head; he took it down at intervals to sip from it and replaced it without spilling a drop, even when nodding agreement with the incessant arguments of the other two. He had been a war correspondent, and was a remarkable linguist and a great authority on horse-racing, being capable of reciting the name of every Derby winner since the first race in 1780, a feat he performed with the smallest inducement.

Belloc, who was half-French, as the pronunciation of his r's betrayed, was bemoaning his poverty in a foghorn voice, firmly believing that he was 'entitled' to enough income on which to live comfortably without worry and to pursue his peculiar interests; these included taking off suddenly to walk over the Pyrenees or to Rome, buying what he needed on the way and, as he put it, 'taking advantage of no wheeled thing'. He was talking about himself as usual. Though the subject under discussion was of no consequence – even the most brilliant habitués tended at times to talk more air than sense – Chesterton was extremely animated about it, occasionally forcing home his points by waving the swordstick from which he would never be parted, firmly believing that one day he might have to use it in defence of himself or others and regarding it too as a badge of the freedman, compared with the slave.

Belloc, whose ruddy complexion was more like a farmer's than a writer's, preferred a stout blackthorn, which he called 'my great staff' and always kept by his side; however it was not for use as a weapon, only as a companion in case he suddenly decided to stride off into the night.

'Waiter, bring me a bowl of *moules marinière*,' he bawled, pulling from his capacious pocket a hunk of the bread he always seemed to carry.

Chesterton was jumping up and down in his seat like a small boy as the second bottle of claret arrived, chanting from one of his own poems: 'Noah said to his wife when he sat down to dine, "I don't care where the water goes if it doesn't get into the wine".'

'The trouble with Shaw is that his wine is all water,' Belloc boomed, referring to the inevitable bottle of Apollinaris which Shaw had ordered when he had joined them.

'Nothing nauseates me more than the sight of friends who have to get drunk in order to endure one another's company,' said Shaw, who was almost as tall as Chesterton but proud of weighing only ten and a half stones. 'You'll regret it later. All three of you,' he added, pointing a bony finger. 'Your stomach would be much happier on a simple diet.'

'Nonsense,' Chesterton replied. 'There is more simplicity in the man who eats caviare on impulse than in the man who eats grape nuts on principle.'

'What *moules* these fortals be!' Belloc remarked as the steaming bowl of mussels arrived. 'I don't know how you pursue our filthy trade without the stimulus of alcohol, Shaw. It releases the inhibitions. Have you never been tempted to try it?'

'I have no inhibitions,' Shaw answered loftily. 'And it so happens that the things that are bad for me do not tempt me.'

'I'm full of inhibitions,' Chesterton confessed. 'Any really civilized man has to be. But I still don't quite agree with you,' he said to Belloc. 'Wine should not be imbibed as a deliberate aid to creative production, yet one may find that increased power of creation sometimes follows in its wake.'

'What's the vintage?' the urbane Baring asked.

'Who cares?' Belloc said, gulping a glassful. 'It's all alcohol to me.' This remark, I suspect, was purely to stimulate Shaw, for the waiters had assured me in the past that Belloc was a considerable connoisseur.

'Do you think there is ever a time, day or night, that your brain is not under the influence of alcohol?' the astringent Shaw inquired. 'Even when you believe you have slept it off?'

'I sincerely hope not,' Chesterton replied affably. In the end, however, excessive alcohol was to kill him, for whereas Belloc could consume enormous quantities apparently without harm, Chesterton could not and soon showed the effects, presumably owing to some difference in the efficiency of their livers.

Shaw shook his head. 'I have a feeling that my best creations will come late in life, so I have to be fit and healthy then, not pickled in spirits. I suppose it's all right for you – you are content with being a journalist. I consider myself made for efforts of greater permanence. You will be the master of language who left no masterpiece.'

'I take your point,' answered Chesterton. He had not yet written *The Napoleon of Notting Hill*, his first major book. 'I am a journalist at heart. I like the short burst of effort. I like to see my words in print next day, or even the same day, if possible. And in journalism we can use the same ideas over and over and get paid each time.'

'I agree,' said Belloc, who was a prodigious producer of words but was forever moaning that he had too little income. 'We have to sell the same article more than once. Otherwise we are drudges facing a sea of endless endeavour, just to make a living.'

Shaw had recently given up dramatic criticism for full-time play-writing, welcoming Max Beerbohm as his successor on the *Saturday Review* with the remark: 'The younger generation is knocking on the door, and as I open it there steps in sprightly the incomparable Max.' Now he pointed an accusing finger at Chesterton and Belloc, declaring, 'You are both wasting your prodigious gifts in the service of Fleet Street. And of the Pope.'

'Oh, let's not get on to religion,' Baring, a Catholic convert himself, said wearily. 'It will only end up in a quarrel and you know how Belloc loves that.'

'My only objection to a quarrel is that it interrupts the argument,' Chesterton said. For him interminable argument was an obsessive requirement.

Chesterton looked at his watch and remarked, without any sign of preparing to go, 'I should now be addressing a meeting in Balham.'

'How late are you?' Baring asked.

'Thirty minutes.'

'Oh, then you've time to share another bottle,' Belloc said, summoning the waiter.

Shaw, who among his other virtues was very punctual, clearly thought Chesterton's behaviour appalling. 'Do you mean to say that an audience has been waiting half an hour for you and you don't care?'

'I care very much,' Chesterton protested. 'I care so much that I shall shortly take a cab all the way to Balham. They always seem to applaud, even when I am late.'

'To hell with Balham,' Belloc said, rapping the table with the knob of his 'great staff'. 'Let's get a boat to France, walk to the Pyrenees and drink wine with the muleteers.'

What was extraordinary about this apparently ridiculous remark was that Belloc meant it. Had Chesterton agreed, he would have marched out with him, and with no luggage at all set out for the mountains of the Franco–Spanish border without telling a soul, though his wife would eventually have received a letter.

'The wine appeals,' Chesterton said. 'But you know what I think about walking. A great deal more instruction, to say nothing of pleasure, is to be got out of the nearest haystack or hedgerow taken quietly, then trotting over two or three counties to see "the view".'

'For once I agree with you,' Shaw remarked, rubbing his hands vigorously – one of his habits. 'Why does an oak grow taller and live longer than a man? Because it does not waste its energy moving from one spot to another that is no better. The greatest men, like Christ, Buddha, Mahomet, Shakespeare, Beethoven and Rembrandt, did not travel out of the country in which they were born.'

'There's something in what you say,' said Baring, who was a greatly travelled man, but accomplished little considering that he was so talented. 'There is truth in that old saying about rolling stones.'

'Ah,' said Chesterton, who could never resist a play on words. 'But the stone that gathers most moss is the gravestone.'

As was his wont, Belloc began to sing quietly one of his favourite ditties – he would sometimes sing right through lunch:

> *Anne Boleyn had no breeches to wear,*
> *So the King got a sheepskin and cut her a pair,*
> *Skin side out and woolly side in,*
> *It was warm in the summer for Anne Boleyn.*

He then gnawed at the customary hunk of bread kept in his pocket to sustain him on his peremptory travels.

Shaw looked across at Aleister Crowley, who was sitting alone and scowling in a cloud of dense smoke.

'Do you think he has brimstone in that mixture?' he asked.

'He is certainly in league with the Devil,' Belloc said. 'But then you don't believe in the Devil, do you, Shaw? I'll give you proof of the Devil's existence,' he said, banging the table with his great fist. 'A perfectly foul woman often has a lovely voice. That shows how powerful the Devil is.'

Chesterton refilled his glass, gulped it and prepared to move. 'I shouldn't be more than an hour and a half late, provided I can get a cab outside.'

'Are you going like that?' Baring asked, as Chesterton picked up his battered hat.

'Like what?'

'You are wearing two ties.'

It is possible that Chesterton did not know that he did indeed have two ties round his neck. If so his immediate retort was excellent:

'People say I pay too little attention to my dress. I'm proving that, on the contrary, I pay too much.'

As he shambled out of the Domino Room towards Regent Street, muttering another line from one of his poems: 'The night we went to Birmingham by way of Beachy Head', Shaw remarked, 'There goes my favourite foe. An incorrigible optimist. He fixes his eyes on the silver linings and just ignores the clouds.'

'What better way of running your life?' Belloc asked, thrusting out his jaw combatively. 'As G.K. puts it: "There is one thing that gives radiance to everything – the idea of something round the corner." And he has respect for mankind, while you have only contempt for it.'

'I wouldn't say for all mankind; only for the English. Being French, that shouldn't upset you.'

While Shaw smiled through his red beard, Baring slowly removed the wine glass from his cranium, quaffed its contents, bowed and followed the Irishman to the foyer. There were no signs that he was intoxicated and he almost certainly was not, but before asking for his coat he sat in the fountain there, immersing himself to the maximum degree until, rising from it and shaking himself, he put on his coat and strolled out to call a hansom.

Shaw, who had gone to the foyer to buy the *Irish Times* – most overseas papers were available there – was so astonished at the sight of Baring sitting happily in the water that he remarked on it when he returned to the table.

Belloc did not think it peculiar and simply remarked, 'Well, it is hot in here.'

'He approves of total immersion, does he?' Shaw asked.

'Yes, and preferably in full evening dress,' Belloc replied, as though it were a custom common enough.

I asked myself on that occasion, as I did on so many others, where does eccentricity end and certifiable behaviour begin? Had Baring not been of good family and a gentleman, might he not have been locked up for his own safety?

17

A RIOTOUS CELEBRATION

As with so many campaigns by its invincible army, the British public felt sure that war with the Boers in South Africa, being of course a 'righteous' war with God on our side, would be over within a few weeks. They were soon to learn that the Boer farmers were not only resolute fighters but accurate sharp-shooters, and three colonial towns, Ladysmith, Kimberley and Mafeking, were soon being besieged. The first two were relieved once a stronger force, under Lord Roberts, had been dispatched to the battle zone, but the Boers continued to threaten Mafeking. The spirited defence of that little town by Colonel Baden-Powell, later to become immortal for founding the Boy Scout movement, captured the public imagination, and when British troops relieved the garrison on 18 May 1900 the public reaction was so phenomenal that it put a new word into the language – 'mafficking', meaning riotous celebration.

As the news came through on the late evening-paper placards there was a spontaneous upsurge of patriotic fervour such as had never been seen. People began to cheer and dance in the street as though the metropolis itself had been relieved from imminent occupation, rather than a far-away, corrugated iron settlement of which few had heard before the seven months siege. The mob enthusiasm was extraordinarily contagious. Plays and music-halls were interrupted by announcements from the stage: 'Ladies and gentlemen, Mafeking has been relieved.' And from then on there was so much cheering and back-slapping that the entertainment came to an end. It spilled into the Domino Room from the streets where the noise was deafening, and even those 'intellectuals' who were against the Boer War, some even siding with the enemy, seemed infected by it, joining in the loud rendering of 'Goodbye Dolly I must leave you'.

For others it was just another excuse for getting drunk, and prominent among these was Charles Conder, who had moved to London from Paris. His great friend Aubrey Beardsley had died of tuberculosis two years previously, aged only twenty-five, and Conder was sitting with a group of young artists whose names I never heard. He had become noticeably ill with a shuffling gait, and it was rumoured that his persistent cough was due to something more than cigarettes. He was in fact in the grip of tuberculosis himself, yet was gaily undermining his hope of recovery by an enormous intake of alcohol.

Thanks to friends like Will Rothenstein, who helped him to exhibit his work, Conder was developing a substantial reputation as an artist in both oil and watercolour, but mainly for his beautiful paintings on silk fans. That night he was punishing the Pernod bottle while the admiring art students listened to his romantic ramblings about life with the great artists in Paris.

Every few minutes he would have to push back the long honey-coloured hair which promptly fell back over his eyes and prominent cheekbones. Actually, I believe I heard more of Conder's conversations than any of his close-by companions, for the waiters told me that his speech was usually so inaudible that they had difficulty in hearing his orders, but I could always see what he was saying. When his talk subsided he would keep the company amused, as he did that night, by his favourite trick of baring his arms and knees and thrusting pins deep into them without a wince. Maybe his sense of pain had been obliterated by alcohol.

At that time Conder's sartorial appearance had improved, because he had married a nice Canadian girl called Stella, who came to the Café with him once or twice. She could not stop him drinking but at least she smartened up his appearance, and his suits were pressed and his shirts and collars clean.

It was rumoured in the Domino Room that even Queen Victoria, who in the darkest days of the Boer War had said, 'We are not interested in the possibility of defeat', threw her little bonnet in the air when she heard the good news. But she was not to live to celebrate the final victory, for the Boers continued to wage skilful guerilla war, about which, years later, I was to hear a first-hand account from the lips of Edgar Wallace, the thriller-writer, then a war correspondent. Edgar secured a scoop on the Peace Treaty by bribing a sentry guarding the British and Boer leaders to wave a white handkerchief when the Treaty was about to be signed. That was in 1902 but before then, on 22 January 1901, we learned that Queen Victoria had passed away at the age of eighty-one while resting at Osborne House on the Isle of Wight. After a reign of nearly sixty-four years it was literally the end of an era and most of us were subdued by the news, but

Aleister Crowley was delighted by it and threw his hat in the air.

'She was like a thick fog that blanketed every artist,' he cried. 'Thank God it's been dispersed at last.'

I suspect that other poets and artists in the Domino Room agreed with him.

Queen Victoria had become such an institution, not just in Britain but throughout the Empire, that most of us felt not only a sense of loss but, perhaps, some fear of the unknown days that lay ahead. I suppose, looking back on it, that the Victorian Age had ended before her death, partly because of a public requirement for change, partly because the Prince of Wales had given the lead to a new Edwardian Age. For all her greatness it must be admitted that she had reigned too long. Nevertheless the public grief at her funeral, where I and many thousands of others watched kings, maharajahs and other potentates paying their respects, was deeply sincere. It seemed extraordinary that this fat little woman should have been able to preside for so long over what was to prove to have been the peak of Britain's power.

There are always legends about the last words of a monarch, and Victoria's was said to be just 'Bertie!' Whether this was yet another admonition, a gasp of affection or fear of what he might do when unrestrained is anybody's guess. There were of course those who said that the dying word was 'Brown', and Bertie certainly lost no time in removing every trace of John Brown's existence from Balmoral and every other royal residence.

As I shall be happy to relate, Bertie was to prove himself an excellent King, a man of ideas and of outstanding diplomatic skills.

18

ADULATION OF A MASTER

Early in the spring of 1902 Frank Harris, who had sold the *Fortnightly Review* for at least £20,000, entered the Domino Room with a man who was a complete stranger to me, and from the way he gazed around him was clearly making his first visit there. Even the knowledgeable Jules could not help me at first, though he quickly confirmed my decision that the new visitor was a Frenchman. Unfortunately I do not understand French, but after Jules had made a few inquiries he told me that it seemed as though he might be some sculptor, because Harris was promising to take him to the British Museum to see the Elgin Marbles, the figures from the Parthenon in Athens, which had been saved from destruction by the heathen Turk through the splendid action of Lord Elgin.

The hugely bearded and moustached figure turned out to be Auguste Rodin, who was to become world-famous through his sculptures like *The Thinker*, *The Burghers of Calais* and, no doubt, many other works of which I have never heard. He was then about sixty years old, I would guess, for his beard and hair were white. Harris had apparently met him during a previous visit to London in 1881 and been greatly impressed by Rodin's views on art in general.

The sculptor could not speak or understand English, which made it impossible for me to decipher what they were saying. But one of the other French waiters – Alphonse, I believe it was – told Jules the time of the forthcoming visit to the British Museum, and I decided to be there myself as I had never seen the famous Marbles. Indeed, though I passed the Museum twice a day on my way to and from the Domino Room, I had never entered its portals.

Harris and Rodin were late, so I had plenty of time to take a good look at the Marbles before they arrived. I was never so disappointed by a work of art. No doubt they are unique and their age, some 2300 years, if I remember rightly, makes them interesting, but the faces and torsos of the human figures and the horses and other animals are, for the most part, so disfigured by weather and rough treatment as to be almost meaningless. The only memorable feature of the Marbles for me was their revelation that the Ancient Greeks, brilliantly intelligent as they are supposed to have been, did not seem to have had the wit to invent either the stirrup or the bridle, but rode bareback, holding the horse by the mane! I nevertheless enjoyed the visit, for I have found that sight-seeing is so much more pleasurable, and the sights more memorable, when done for a purpose.

Rodin was obviously entranced by the Marbles, his rugged features being repeatedly illuminated with the widest of smiles, and Harris, who claimed he had seen them several times before, seemed to be equally enthralled. As I approached rather closely to them to get a better look at Rodin I thought I detected a hint of recognition from Harris, who must have seen me scores of times, but if it was there it quickly vanished. It was possible that he could not see me plainly because he was short-sighted, as was apparent when he was examining the Marbles, being too vain to wear spectacles.

Again I could not understand what they were saying but their gestures were eloquent, Rodin using his hands most expressively to follow the graceful curves of the figures, and later I was to hear Harris's version of the conversation, for he invariably retailed his encounters with any famous person, being what has now become known as a name-dropper.

On the occasion in question he was having a drink in the Domino Room with T. W. H. 'Willie' Crosland, a tall, lugubrious-looking Yorkshireman with a large nose, big chin, sunken cheeks, and dark hair straying lankly over his huge and wrinkled forehead. He had taken up residence in the Domino Room, where he vied with Harris for the title of 'rudest customer', and was so perennially hard-up that he would write anything on any subject for money, which he always called 'boodle', and could do so with astonishing speed and skill. He had been so poor when he had arrived to try his luck in Fleet Street in 1890 that he had slept rough in Green Park. He carried a visiting card, one of which is before me now, a little tatty, in conformity with Crosland's appearance. It says: 'T. W. H. Crosland, Jobbing poet. Editors' own material made up. Distance no object. Satisfaction guaranteed. Neatness, promptitude and despatch. Cashiers waited upon in their own apartments. Funerals attended.'

Poor Willie! He was in fact an outstanding poet and wrote many excellent sonnets. He was also a fine writer of satirical prose, and having just given up his poorly paid editorship of a little magazine called *The Outlook* to start one of his own, *The Tiger*, was churning out books, including one which was to be a sensation, *The Unspeakable Scot*. 'Churning out' is no exaggeration. As with some other Domino Room literati, writing was a compulsion. Just as some people cannot stop nodding their heads or shaking their hands, Crosland could be said to have had 'St Vitus dance of the fingers'. I believe that in wordage he outwrote G. K. Chesterton, who never seemed to stop scribbling.

Like Harris, he believed himself to be a genius, and expressed this belief in a parody of the poem 'Invictus' by W. E. Henley:

> Out of the cloud that covers me
> And blots the stars and seldom lifts,
> I thank whatever gods may be
> For my indubitable gifts.

As for the funerals, perhaps Willie had his own in mind, for he was plagued by poor health and did nothing to assist it, smoking like a chimney and imbibing any drink on offer. He was incredibly hard-nosed about free drink. I heard his Fleet Street colleague, Hannen Swaffer, telling how Crosland had been asked by a footman if he would like a cup of tea while reporting some fête being given by Lady Londonderry. 'No tea! Bring me a whisky,' he commanded. The footman brought him a bottle and a glass on a silver tray, whereupon Crosland poured himself a huge drink, seized the bottle, pencilled his name on it and hid it for his further use that afternoon.

On the occasion I am recalling, when he had told Harris he would like a whisky he had been asked, 'What kind of whisky would you like?' – meaning which brand. 'A big one,' Crosland replied. Having imbibed their 'sneck-lifters', as Crosland called the opening drinks, they were sharing a bottle of hock when I recorded the following notes of the visit to the British Museum.

Harris began: 'Rodin, whom I have spent hours watching at work in France, said to me, "Your Lord Elgin is to be congratulated on saving what remains of these splendid works by Pheidias", and I had to explain that his lordship had been dead these many years. I also had to explain to the old boy that Pheidias was only the master-sculptor on the Parthenon for a few years and that most of the work he was seeing must be by the hands of other men.'

It was typical of the boastful Harris to suggest that he knew more than the professional sculptor, but he had an explanation for this.

'Whereas I had been to Athens to acquire the spirit of Greek art and literature, Rodin told me that, while he had always longed to travel widely in Greece, he had been too poor ever to afford it. He knew enough, however, to agree with me that if the Marbles had been left to the Greeks, God and Providence there would have been nothing left of them.

'"I particularly admire the female figures," Rodin said. "They are so sensuous, as sensuous as any figures in plastic art." I agreed and pointed out that it was the dress that made them sensuous. One could see that the women had nothing else on underneath. The dress would cling to the body in the heat of Athens, revealing all – at least to a virile imagination.'

Harris, who rarely had sex out of his imagination, made the curvaceous shape of the female figure to Crosland with his hands.

'I know nothing about plastic art, but I'm prepared to write an article about these Marbles if anybody wants to print it,' Crosland said in a broad Leeds accent.

'Even though you know nothing about them?' Harris asked.

'That gives me greater scope for my imagination. I agree it would be piffle, but very well-written and very readable piffle.'

'Rodin and I also discussed the interesting fact that none of the Greek men and women in the Parthenon sculptures look like any Greek you'll see today in Soho or in Greece itself,' Harris said. 'What on earth happened to all those straight noses and noble brows? Where did they go?'

'Ah, I could write an interesting thesis on that,' Crosland offered, making it clear that his glass was empty. 'I can think of all sorts of possibilities.'

'No doubt,' Harris replied dryly, for he clearly had no intention of commissioning anything from the 'jobbing poet' on that subject, though they were to co-operate five years later when Crosland joined Harris's magazine *Vanity Fair*.

'I asked the old boy if he thought my mug was sensuous,' Harris continued. 'But he just laughed and said, "It has a certain life and energy."'

'We would all agree with that,' Crosland said. 'Is he going to make you immortal by sculpting it?'

'No, but what you should do, Crosland, is to invest in Rodin's sculptures if you can get your hands on them. That's what I intend to do. They are bound to rise in value if you just hang on to them for a few years.'

Crosland, who had never had any money, laughed at the idea.

Later I was to wonder whether Harris's grandiose suggestion had been in his mind when, not far from death, Crosland was taken by friends into the Domino Room for the last time and wrote his epitaph there:

> If men should say aught of me
> After I die,
> Say there were many things he might have bought,
> And did not buy.
> Unhonoured by his fellows, he grew old,
> And trod the path to Hell,
> But there were many things he might have sold,
> And did not sell.

Happily that sad day was well in the future and I shall have some more stories of Crosland to retail, including a barbed riposte to that little poem. Harris was to take his own advice and later acquire some Rodin bronzes for a shop he proposed to set up in London, one of his many money-making schemes which came to nothing. Rodin charged him through the nose for the sculptures he received.

I was soon to discover why Rodin had been in London at all: it was in order to be present at the unveiling of a copy of his statue of *St John the Baptist* which he had made specially for the Victoria and Albert Museum. Once I had learned this I could not, of course, resist going to the V and A to see the *St John*. I thought that, like Harris's 'mug', it had life and energy.

To celebrate the occasion of Rodin's visit his English admirers organized a banquet in his honour, and where else could they hold it but at the Café Royal? Of course it was in one of the banqueting rooms upstairs and, with the subscriptions at two guineas a head and the list limited anyway, I could not possibly be present; however, through Jules and Alphonse, who had become rather proud of their famed compatriot, though having no interest themselves in sculpture, I was given some information about the laudatory speeches.

One of these was delivered by George Wyndham, the Tory MP for Dover who was then Chief Secretary for Ireland and a member of the Souls. Another came from the lips of Sir Charles Dilke, the Liberal politician who might, but for gross misfortune, have one day become Prime Minister.

I was fascinated to see Dilke, a handsome, bearded figure with slightly receding hair, as I stood watching the celebrities as they left the dinner. The scandal which had ruined his political life was sixteen years old by that time, but few had forgotten it and his enemies were determined that none should. This was the man who had been accused in open court, in such titillating detail, not only of seducing another man's wife but of demanding sexual trimmings of a sordid nature.

Dilke and the other chief guests, who included the French ambassador, were followed down the Café Royal stairs by a number of art students from the Slade School and the Royal College of Art, who had been invited free to join the banquet after the meal so that they could meet Rodin and hear the speeches, which was a splendid idea, for I like to see the young encouraged in any creative way. They had been given plenty of champagne to drink and made the most of it with an uproarious result, which I witnessed: the mental picture of it remains in my memory as freshly as though it had happened only yesterday.

The students made their way down to the lobby which was already packed with others from the Slade who had not managed to get into the banqueting room. Though it was raining slightly there was also a great press outside on the pavement and surrounding the four-wheel cab which, as the young artists had learned from the cabby, was waiting to take Rodin to the Arts Club in Hanover Square.

There was tremendous cheering as Rodin came down the stairs and elbowed his way towards the door. By that time the cabby had been removed forcibly from his box and students were unharnessing the horses. Sensing what was about to happen and apparently not in the least nervous, as the whole atmosphere was so good-humoured, Rodin allowed himself to be helped into the carriage. Then, with a great shout, a dozen of the strongest lads seized the shafts. The painter John Singer Sargent, who had been at the banquet, jumped on to the cabby's box and with a loud 'Gee up' and a crack of his whip the equipage set off through Piccadilly Circus. I raced down Swallow Street and watched them recede along Piccadilly shouting, 'Rodin! Rodin! Rodin!' It must have been a marvellous experience for the Frenchman for, though the majority of passers-by had no idea who Rodin was, they took up the cheering and waved their hats and umbrellas in salute.

19

'DISGUSTUS' JOHN

One of the men who witnessed with me the extraordinary episode of Rodin's adulation by the crowd, but took no active part, was a former student of the Slade School, perhaps its most gifted; he was one of the most striking personalities ever to frequent the Domino Room, which he did for many years. Augustus John, at that time only in his early twenties, had, at the even earlier age of eighteen, been hailed by Sargent as 'the greatest draughtsman since the Renaissance'. Such was his reputation in the art world that when he entered the Domino Room, or the Brasserie as it later became, Slade students would stand in deep respect while young model girls were set 'all of a flutter' by his fine physique and appearance.

With his protuberant eyes, flaming red beard, unkempt hair half hidden by a battered, black, Bohemian-style hat, the black silk scarf worn round his neck to show his contempt for those who wore collar and tie, and the gold ear-ring he affected because of his love for gypsies, he was flamboyant in the extreme. He was, in fact, without question an exhibitionist drawing attention to himself just as deliberately as did the dandies he affected to despise.

I have to say that from the beginning I did not like John or at least that part of his character he chose to expose, for I sensed that there was something sinister about him. He had his favourite corner in the café, happily not far from my table, and would sit there for hours on end, drinking and smoking his pipe, with one or two cronies like Walter Sickert, William Orpen, James Pryde, Charles Conder, the young Epstein and, of course, his favourite model of the day, who was almost invariably his mistress. It was in the area served by Alphonse and usually John had a bottle of brandy, which was gradually demolished, but he also drank a mixture of hock and seltzer or crème de menthe, well iced and sucked through a straw. Occasionally he let us down by being picked up by the police drunk and disorderly but, as a rule, while others became the worse for wear, John only became exuberant, and it was said that it was John who had the drinks while his friends got the headaches. Perhaps they deserved them, for I noticed over the many years I watched Augustus John and his friends that it was he who was usually left with the bill and paid it.

He began to be a regular attender in the Domino Room in 1902 and it literally became his home from home, where he could escape from his growing brood of children. I suppose that he replaced Wilde as the dominant personality there, Harris perhaps excepted, just as Oscar had replaced Whistler. Surprisingly, though he revelled in the company of other artists and models, he rarely talked about painting in the Domino Room, whereas writers were forever talking about their work. Most often John seemed to like to talk about women, about whom he had ideas which could only be regarded as brutal. His mistress-models were legion, but among those I recall with affection were Esther, Alick, Euphemia, Chiquita, Mavis, Eileen and Dorelia, the last being incomparably the most important in his life.

Dorelia was not her real name: she had been born in Camberwell in 1881 and christened Dorothy McNeill. Though somewhat dumpy, she had a haunting beauty, which is now preserved in galleries in many parts of the world, for John drew and painted her for many, many years, rather as Rembrandt painted his wife Saskia, who has thus been immortalized. I have seen him sketch her at the table, so besotted was he with her features. And of course it was not only that merit which attracted him. John was a veritable ram and set up such a *ménage à trois* with his lawful wife, herself a gifted pupil of Whistler, that he had them both pregnant at the same time. In the respect of begetting children John was irresponsible in the extreme, saying to his wife, 'I love you and always will, so long as we are not hand-cuffed.' What he meant was that he found matrimony convenient so long as he could do exactly as he liked, admitting, as I heard him say in a voice I understand was soft and rather musical, 'I am aware of my brutalities and will continue as God made me. I have never pretended to be an exponent of the faithful dog business.'

I felt very sorry for his wife, Ida, a delightful-looking girl, very dark and sensuous, who had been a student with him at the Slade. It was his treatment of her and women in general which earned him the nickname 'Disgustus' John, with which I came to agree. It is hard to believe it, but I heard him say that when his wife died in Paris in 1907 as a result of giving birth to another of his children, he was overjoyed at being relieved of her. 'I could have embraced any passer-by,' he confessed. 'It was strange but, after leaving her poor dead body, I had nothing but a kind of bank-holiday feeling.' He showed this by failing to turn up for the funeral when she was cremated, though I noticed that, as long as I knew him, he continued to wear his wedding ring.

John was a horrible man in my view, eaten up with self-interest, forever needing to draw attention to himself and believing to a degree as outrageous as Oscar's that it was permissible for 'artists' to do whatever they liked to anybody. Genius, even real genius, does not excuse such appalling behaviour. John encouraged the story that he had become a genius after diving into shallow water and hitting his head on a rock when he was young. He certainly had hit his head on a rock, but I do not believe he was a genius. He was a very competent artist, no doubt, but hardly a genius in the mould of Rembrandt, Raphael or Leonardo da Vinci. I would rate him as one of those overblown 'personalities', found in all professions, whose shadow loomed much larger than his substance. More people are likely to remember him for the eccentricity of his behaviour than for his output. It was also widely believed that after seeing Gounod's Faust at the age of fifteen Augustus had modelled himself on Mephistopheles. If that is true, he succeeded only too well.

20

'LORD LEAVE-A-HOLE'

In 1920 Augustus John was at the centre of a rare old rumpus which was the subject of much controversy in the Domino Room and in the newspapers. He was by then in great demand as a portrait painter and among the famous who commissioned him was Lord Leverhulme, the clever Lancashire man who had made a huge fortune out of Sunlight Soap, which was in every household, and out of margarine, which was bought by the poor for themselves and by the rich for their servants. He came down to London and sat, impatiently according to John, in the famous Chelsea studio. John told his friends that the picture was a great success, not only artistically but as a likeness. Leverhulme, however, who had wanted a more flattering portrait, as so many sitters do, hated it.

'He told me it was "humiliating",' John said. 'So I offered him my palette and told him to get on with painting it to his own satisfaction.'

Reluctantly Leverhulme paid John's fee; when the picture finally arrived at his home he opened the packing case himself and found he loathed it so much that nobody should ever see it. Taking a pair of scissors, he cut out the head and locked it in his safe, leaving the rest of the picture in the packing case. One of his servants mistakenly sent the packing case back to John, who exploded when he saw what had happened to his master-work. He immediately wrote to Leverhulme, demanding an explanation for what he called 'the grossest insult I have ever received'.

After his anger had subsided, John showed the headless portrait to several of his friends, calling it 'Lord Leverhulme's Watch-chain', and when I heard this retailed in the Café to Horace Cole, the professional prankster, I knew that it would not be long before the newspapers got wind of the story. There is nothing Fleet Street likes better than a row between two famous figures. Sure enough, on 8 October 1920 the *Daily Express* ran an account of the saga on its front page. Leverhulme blamed John for the publicity and was quoted as saying that, as he had bought the picture, he could do what he liked with it. John argued that the purchaser of a work of art merely pays for the right of custody and that the artist still has moral rights concerning what happens to it. As can be imagined, this gave rise to lively discussion in the Domino Room, most of the artists siding with John.

Needled by Leverhulme's complaint that, 'While Mr John seems to be able to get his advertising free, the poor soapmaker has to pay a high rate for a much poorer position in the newspaper', Augustus handed over the letters between himself and Leverhulme to the *Express*. This enabled the paper to keep the story running and provoked demonstrations by art students against Leverhulme and his descriptions of what was, no doubt, a fine painting, though none of those making the noise – mainly art students – had set eyes on it.

The biggest demonstration which I went to watch, hoping that Augustus might appear and perhaps be chaired in the procession, was organized by art students from the various colleges. They marched through the streets to Hyde Park, chanting their indignation and carrying a headless torso to represent the soap magnate's vile body. I watched with much amusement as the torso, bearing the witty title 'Lord Leave-a-Hole', was solemnly burned to the cheers of hundreds of people, most of whom did not give a damn about art but who, I suspect, took some envious delight in seeing a man who had raised himself from their position by hard work and brains publicly downgraded. From Hyde Park the procession then wound its way towards Trafalgar Square, where there were to be more speeches in front of the National Gallery. By that time I was weary of the protest and wended my own way back to Regent Street, but others were about to take it up.

Because the two men concerned were international figures, and because art is international, the foreign press had followed up the story. I found that the French papers in the Domino Room were reporting wild scenes in Paris, while in Italy the reaction was even stronger. All Italians involved in the art 'industry', including the models, were being urged to stage a day's strike in protest – which they did. In Florence another headless effigy, aptly made of soap and fat, was carried into the main square. There, near the spot where the monk Savonarola had been burned to death for heresy, they set fire to 'His Margarine Majesty'. To complete the allusion, the students then marched to one of the churches where there was an altar dedicated to St John! Some saint! I thought, but I had heard the comparison often enough before. Because of Augustus's unkempt appearance Crosland used to call him John the Baptist; no doubt the Baptist was unkempt, but it is unlikely that he had red hair.

To the disappointment of the students and myself, 'St John' had not appeared for the Hyde Park procession and, realizing that the commotion might be bad for future business, had taken refuge outside London. Astute reporters tracked him down and he assured them that he had never sought all the publicity. That, I knew, was a lie – but then I have found that artists make a point of blurring the boundaries between reality and imagination. Augustus, in particular, always blamed fate or other people for problems he had created himself.

He was urged by some of the newspapers to take the issue to court to get a ruling about the ownership of the copyright of a painting which has been sold outright. They recalled the famous case when Whistler had taken Ruskin to court on a matter of principle. Remembering how this action had ruined Whistler, through the greed of the lawyers involved, with their 'refreshers' and other outrageous demands, he ignored the call.

A typical suggestion by Horace Cole was to defuse the issue: 'Why not put "Lord Leverhulme's Watch-chain" on public exhibition, Gus?'

'A splendid idea,' John replied, his face relishing the prospect of turning what had become a serious embarrassment into a farce.

The ruse worked and the story faded away, as most stories do when newspaper editors themselves have become bored with them and are looking for something new.

21

'DO WHAT THOU WILT'

Any day when I made a new friend, a new entry to the Domino Room community who was eventually to establish a name for himself, was a Golden Day for me and my diary. The rare occasions when I made two or more such friends might be called my Diamond Days.

One such Diamond Day occurred in the summer of 1905, when the painter Will Rothenstein arrived, accompanied by a youngish man I had not seen before, and seated himself at the plush banquette of the table usually reserved for Augustus John. The way he sat the newcomer in the chair on his right, leaving the other banquette seat free, suggested to me that another guest, probably Augustus himself, was expected, for that irascible artist felt deeply aggrieved should he arrive, even after days of absence, to find that someone had usurped his throne.

Rothenstein's guest was a shortish, dapperly dressed man sporting an almost white billycock bowler, a bright yellow waistcoat, a bow tie and a check suit which made him look like one of the bookies who usually occupied the tables at the Glasshouse Street end. His most striking natural features were a protruding lower jaw with a crumpled chin, teeth which made full closure of his moustached mouth difficult for him, and an obviously carefully cultivated quiff of hair like a cock's comb, which remained upstanding as he carefully removed his bowler. If this man was an artist, and Rothenstein rarely consorted with anyone who was not, using 'artist' to include writers and similarly creative people, then surely here was another vain enough to take pains to draw attention to himself by striking an attitude as different as possible from the accepted image of an arty man.

I was soon to discover when Rothenstein's other guests arrived that his name was Arnold Bennett, that he was a journalist and novelist from the Potteries, and was making a name for himself with novels about the Five Towns which constitute that part of Staffordshire. I experienced some difficulty in understanding what he was saying until I realized that he stammered and sometimes had to struggle to get his words out.

My guess about Augustus John had been correct and he arrived with a most unprepossessing little man, obviously Jewish like Rothenstein himself, and whose scruffiness, even by the Bohemian standards of the Domino Room, contrasted sharply with the studied tidiness of Bennett. While John, complete with black Parisian wide-brimmed hat, which he always kept on his head in the Domino Room – as did many other men – ordered his usual hock and seltzer from the waiter, Alphonse, his companion staggered all the waiters by ordering a glass of milk, a situation later exploited by the cartoonist H. M. Bateman in a drawing showing the hilarity of the waiters and habitués at the expense of the customer who asked for a glass of milk at the Café Royal.

The milk-drinker was introduced by John as Jacob Epstein, a New York Jew who was living very frugally, being supported by a Jewish charity while trying to establish himself in London as a sculptor. He was also something of a painter, though that was a secondary interest. When Bennett was introduced as the author of *Anna of the Five Towns*, *Grand Babylon Hotel* and *A Great Man* as well as being a friend of Joseph Conrad and of H. G. Wells, who both on rare occasions patronized the Domino Room, he tilted back on his chair, stuck his thumbs into the armholes of his waistcoat and smiled happily, a habit I was to notice many times when he was praised. After a few minutes' conversation, however, I could see that Bennett and Epstein would not hit it off as friends. Apart from the temperamental gulf, they both liked to blow their own trumpets.

I was fascinated to notice that as soon as Bennett had sat down he had produced a large, leather-backed notebook from his jacket pocket and was making occasional jottings. For some time I feared that he might have the same idea as myself. Indeed he did keep a journal, which was later published, but most of the time he was just collecting local colour and making notes about the Café Royal to use in his novels about the way of life in big hotels. Over the years the ebb and flow of life through the Domino Room was to fascinate him almost as much as it did me.

Suddenly there was a clatter, a great guffaw from Augustus John and some ironic clapping from other habitués. Bennett had tilted his chair too far backwards while explaining how he had become a writer about the Potteries after staring in a tiny shop window, in a dowdy Burslem back street, which sold sweets and vegetables and also carried a notice: 'Well-aired beds to let.'

'I decided there and then that I would put it all down for posterity,' he declaimed, waving his arms so violently that his balance was destroyed and he crashed to the ground.

I could have imagined what Wilde would have said had he been present. Oscar hated stories about squalor and believed that an artist's purpose was to romanticize about life and make it more acceptable, while Bennett was an early exponent of the school dedicated to recording life as truthfully as he could, kitchen sink and all.

Bennett picked himself up with considerable embarrassment, and whatever he wanted to say by way of explanation was stifled in his stammer. But it did not cure him of the habit of balancing himself on two legs of his chair, and I was to see him turn turtle in the Domino Room at least twice more in later years. Recovering his composure, Bennett walked out with a jaunty, quarter-deck swagger after putting on his bowler with care, so as not to disturb his quiff, and carrying the cane which always accompanied him on what he called his 'thinking walks', during which he sorted out his ideas so that they would be clearly in place when he returned to his writing desk.

'What a pompous ass,' John declared as he watched him depart.

'He's compensating for his sense of social inferiority,' Rothenstein said perceptively.

'Why the hell would he have to do that with us, especially with Jacob here?' John queried.

'I've noticed it with a lot of people from the North when they come to London,' Rothenstein said. 'I agree he is pompous, but he is certainly no ass. He not only has the ability to write a great book one day, but the application. He sets himself a target of so many words a month and achieves it.'

'That's the trouble with success. There's too much bloody application,' John remarked scathingly.

Rothenstein smiled. 'Application is certainly not your forte, Gus.'

He had a point but, when John did decide to paint, his models said that he went at it with a fury, just as he went at them when the mood took him, forcing them to the studio couch with grunts and snorts and not even bothering to remove his paint-stained smock.

He gave one of his grunts at Rothenstein's remark and, in his usual manner of ending a conversation with which he was bored, stood up and announced, 'Come on, Will, let's go.'

Bennett certainly was pompous, especially when speaking about the art of writing, on which he considered himself an authority in all its forms, especially journalism. But Rothenstein was right. Bennett was to write at least one classic – *The Old Wives' Tale*.

I was pleased to see Bennett establish his interest in the Domino Room by arriving with a guest of his own the following day – none other than Aleister Crowley, the Beast himself. They made an ill-assorted couple to look at: Bennett dandified and this time in a waistcoat so red that the Cockney children could be guaranteed to shout the music-hall song 'Cock Cock Robin' had he ventured into their areas, and Crowley, less extravagant than usual but wearing a long-sleeved silk shirt, a very floppy bow tie, several enormous rings and a bright red waistcoat that was also heavily jewelled. The two had met previously in Paris and, while Bennett genuinely admired Crowley's poems, I suspect that in his quest for characters for his novels he cultivated eccentrics, as I am sure a novelist should, for who wants to read about ordinary people?

Having ordered drinks, Crowley began what became an animated conversation with the apocalyptic statement: 'Christianity has collapsed. It can no longer serve humanity – if ever it did. A new eon for mankind has commenced. My Holy Guardian Angel, Aiwass, has appeared before me to dictate a new Book of the Law.'

Crowley was deadly serious, but Bennett had difficulty in keeping a straight face.

'You must give me the details when your angel has finished his task,' he remarked.

'That I will certainly do, but already I can tell you the basis of the New Law. There shall be no law beyond "Do what thou wilt". The word Sin is a restriction. On no account live within your own skin. . . .'

Bennett's mouth, which was always half open, gaped wider as the Beast continued, his narrowed eyes making him look more Mongolian than ever.

'Dress ye in fine apparel, Aiwass commanded. Eat rich foods and drink sweet wines and wines that foam!'

'Ah, that's good,' Bennett remarked, glad of the opportunity to smile without offending his guest. 'He recommends champagne,does he?'

Crowley professed not to hear. 'Take your fill and will of love as ye will when, where and with whom ye will.'

'I say, isn't that more a recipe for lust rather than love?' Bennett asked.

'They are two aspects of the same to me. "Bind nobody to you," Aiwass said. "There shall be no property in human flesh."'

'The world would not revolve very steadily if everybody took that view,' Bennett commented.

Crowley shook his cannonball head slowly. 'I totally disagree. There is far too much interference in the private lives of individuals, not only by the State but by other people. My mission is to bring every man to the realization and enjoyment of his own kingship, and my apparent interference with him amounts to no more than advice to him not to suffer interference. Do what thou wilt shall be the whole of the Law! I intend to found a society where all people behave as they want to; in any way they want to.'

'Here in London?' Bennett asked incredulously.

'London will be the most difficult capital to convert. There is greater interference here by other people – by so-called society – than anywhere else. Look at the treatment meted out to poor Oscar Wilde.'

'Yes, but he asked for it,' Bennett said.

'Perhaps Wilde deserved to be savaged by society,' Crowley conceded. 'He was such a snob himself. He denied his true nature in the pursuit of social ambition; he adopted affectations as a sign of superiority.'

Bennett nodded his agreement with that.

'Anyway, he did well to get out of England,' Crowley continued. 'London is not a stimulant to a poet of my calibre. The air here is damp and depressing. It suggests the consciousness of sin. Whether one has a suite at the Savoy or an attic in Hoxton, the same spiritual atmosphere weighs upon the soul. In London one cannot even go to the National Gallery or the British Museum with a pure heart, as one goes to the Louvre or the Prado. One cannot get away from the sense that one is performing an act of piety.'

'London stimulates me,' Bennett argued. 'But I agree that for the act of writing itself one needs to get out of it. Where do you propose to go?'

'Right out of England. The English poet must make a successful exile or die of a broken heart. I think I shall go to Italy and found an abbey there, which I shall call the Abbey of Thalema. I speak so many languages that almost anywhere is possible. But first I must attain the Magical rank of Master of the Temple. I must find the abode of the Secret Chiefs and become one of them.'

'But all this crazy ritual. . .' Bennett protested. 'Your conical hats, your cloaks – I've even heard that in some of your orgiastic rites you sacrifice children!'

'Perhaps, but at least they have always been beautiful and of noble lineage.'

I could sense that Bennett, who was no respecter of persons, was on the point of bursting into laughter, but he managed to stifle his amusement with another question. 'But aren't you wasting time fiddling with magic when you could be devoting it to your poetry. . . ?'

'There is a crucial link between poetry and magic, which most people, including yourself, fail to grasp. Any work of art justifies itself only by its direct magical effect on the observer. Shakespeare believed in magic. Otherwise how could he have written *A Midsummer Night's Dream* or *The Tempest*? It is a strange coincidence that the small county of Warwickshire should have given England her two greatest poets!'

Before Bennett could ask the name of the other one, Crowley supplied it. 'I was born in Leamington, you know.'

Bennett and I could see that Crowley's vanity was such that he was deadly serious. Bennett might think highly of the Beast's poetry, much of which was published at Crowley's own expense, but to equate himself with Shakespeare. . . . I did not think I should ever witness such vanity: but there was more to come.

'As regards my withdrawal into the great world of Magic, I cannot understand why people imagine that those who retire from the world are lazy. It is far easier to swim with the stream. I learned that at Cambridge. You know, like Byron, Shelley, Swinburne and Tennyson I left the university without taking a degree.'

'Ah, I'm sure you lost nothing there,' said Bennett, who had received no higher education. 'The sooner one enters the University of Life the better. . . .'

'Of course,' Crowley concurred. 'The first thing it taught me was that any form of self-denial is a romantic folly. Particularly when this is applied to women. Four is probably the ideal number. With two women you have to explain each to the other; with three, two compare notes while you're with the third; but four make a crowd and so can be neglected. Actually, the more sides a man has to his nature the more women he needs to satisfy it. One side can be satisfied only by seeking out the most degraded and disgusting specimens of women that exist.'

'Is that why you call yourself the Beast, Aleister?' Bennett asked flippantly.

'The "Great Beast",' Crowley corrected without taking offence. 'My mother called me the "Beast" because she hated me. But my full title is the "Great Beast 666".'

Bennett did not seem to understand, but from my reading of the Book of Revelation by St John the Divine, from whom, readers may remember, I took my new Christian name, I knew he was referring to the terrifying beast which rose up out of the sea and had the mystical number 'six hundred three score and six'.

'Were your parents interested in magic?'

Crowley, who was the son of a brewer, threw back his head and laughed. 'I suppose they were in their way. They were fanatical Plymouth Brethren. They fed me on a solid diet of the Bible.'

This explained to me, presumably as it did to Bennett, several things about Crowley's strange personality. First, it must have been the incessant Bible-punching which turned Crowley against Christianity as a child, but also interested him in the prophecies and fantastic concepts in the Book of Revelation. Second, it was probably his hatred of his mother which was responsible for his dreadful attitude to women in general. 'They should be brought round to the back door with the milk,' was one way I heard him express it.

In this regard, however, I should in fairness record that, in explaining why he usually had several women in his home, he said, 'I fail to understand why it should be considered excusable to seduce a woman and leave her to shift for herself, while if one receives her as a permanent friend and cares for her well-being long after the liaison has lapsed one should be considered a scoundrel.'

Such an argument was hard to counter but, of course, with Crowley it was probably no more than lip-service. He seems to have treated his women abominably, and most of them seem to have thoroughly enjoyed it. The revulsion to Christianity brought about by his parents' religious fanaticism seems the likeliest cause of his decision to worship the Devil, though I have heard him argue that it was logical thought which led him to Satanism.

'If there is a choice between worshipping God or the Devil then the latter offers the safer bet for, if it should be God who turns out to be in command, then he may forgive you, but if the reverse is true, the Devil will never forgive but take his revenge.' Crowley's disciples were urged to offer their souls to the Devil '. . . to have at least somebody on their side'.

I can make no pretence at knowing much about theology, for few divines ever entered the portals of the Domino Room, which, for most of them at that time, was probably the mouth of Hell, especially after the Wilde scandal. But after listening to people like Chesterton and Belloc it became obvious that, if God exists, then so must the Devil. A just God cannot be held responsible for all the evil in the world. It is as simple as that – at least to my mind.

As to Crowley's general interest in magic, I deduced from his conversations that what he was really after was finding some means of making himself immortal, in some form or another. To become Magus, an expert in the secret magical arts, he experimented with dangerous drugs like opium and cocaine, and their effect soon began to show in his face and of course in his behaviour. Apart from the eccentricities I have already described, he also had the habit of depositing his excrement on the carpet, believing it to be sacred and therefore of inestimable value. Happily he never did that in the Domino Room, and when I heard of this habit I often wondered what he did when he used the toilets there. Did he wrap it up and take it away? There was certainly a very peculiar smell about him, but I understood that this was due to his 'sex-appeal ointment' with which he smeared himself. The habitué who really was odorous was Epstein – 'He stank like a polecat,' to quote Augustus John.

It was of course my own fascination with mysticism and fantasy which stimulated my interest in Crowley when most others, eventually including Bennett, considered him a complete charlatan, apart from his output of passable poetry. Sadly, it is not possible to draw a line between insanity and mystic insight. Both seem to be attended by hallucinations, which for the madman are regarded as complete delusions, while for the accredited mystic they are 'miraculous visitations' or at least 'supernatural phenomena'.

On the occasion I have already mentioned, when Crowley walked slowly through the Domino Room wearing the star-encrusted conical hat and black cloak bearing zodiacal symbols, I am satisfied that he really believed that he was invisible because of his magic cloak. Nobody could convince him that everybody in the room had seen him. His question, 'Then why did nobody speak to me?' was asked in all sincerity. I believe that though, like so many students of the occult, he cashed in on his knowledge by confidence trickery on the credulous, he did make genuine efforts to explore the Unconscious, and his use of rituals and stimulants, which have been used down the centuries in many civilizations, were part of this.

Of one thing my close observation of people over so many years has convinced me – that we are all of us deluded to some extent, and all indulge in fantasy to some degree. Indeed, both self-delusion and fantasy would seem to be essential to the creative process.

22

DEMON ANGEL AND DEMON MAN

It had not been possible for me to be present at the funeral of dear Oscar. At that time, in December 1900, I had never been out of England (and very little out of London) but I had heard descriptions of the event from Lord Alfred Douglas and others who attended the interment.

From the Hôtel d'Alsace the funeral had processed to the church of the artists' quarter in Paris, called St Germain-des-Prés, on a cold, wet and windy day. Thence, after a Catholic Requiem Mass, by which Douglas seemed to set great store when he spoke of it, the few mourners of this great soul then followed the hearse to the distant cemetery of Bagneux, the only place where Ross could secure a plot.

Fewer still mourned him then in England, where for many years he remained the subject of ribald schoolboy jokes and rhymes, some of which I heard retailed by bookmakers like Dick Dunn, acknowledged as the most fluent curser of all time, winning every swearing match he entered; Kennedy Knight, who struck down slow-paying clients with anything handy; and those other coarser members of the Domino Room community.

Bosie, who, as he matured, tended to require to be addressed by his full title, made some amends with a sonnet called 'The Dead Poet', which contained the rather splendid lines:

> *I mourned the loss of unrecorded words,*
> *Forgotten tales and mysteries half said,*
> *Wonders that might have been articulate*
> *And voiceless thoughts like murdered singing birds*
> *And so I woke and knew that he was dead.*

But while Wilde's plays and poems continued to make money for others after his death, his name was not mentioned in polite society. He was not even allowed to rest in peace at Bagneux, though I heard Ross say that it had never been the intention to leave him there. After nine years, at Ross's behest, his remains were transferred to the more famous Parisian cemetery of Père Lachaise, where at least he could repose in the company of other famous men, though at that stage his resting place was covered only by a plain stone slab.

Over the years I often heard friends who still loved him, like Ross and Adey, speak of the need for a memorial worthy of a man whose name was clearly destined to become world-famous again one day. Finally in 1911 Ross and a few friends met to take some firm action on the matter. They had raised the money to pay for a substantial memorial and decided that the man to design and produce it was Jacob Epstein, the Domino Room habitué whose name had quickly become a household word. His instructions were to produce not just a memorial, but a tomb fitting to Oscar's character.

I had visited Epstein's Chelsea studio, which like others was open to the public on Sundays, on one of my morning walks. The sculptures of this strange man who liked to call himself 'the best-hated artist' were hardly popular, indeed they were severely censured – rightly in my humble opinion, for his work was uncouth, like himself – and I heard him say that he was so surprised to be given the Wilde commission that at first he thought it must be a joke by one of the numerous Café Royal hoaxers. He particularly suspected Horace Cole, who hated him.

For some time it was something of a running joke among the Domino Room habitués to sketch likely memorials and some, drawn on scraps of paper and described to me by Jules, were frankly pornographic. In the result Epstein, who at that stage was heavily influenced by a fine artisan stone-carver called Eric Gill, produced a very fitting monument.

Having settled on what Wilde's friends called 'a splendidly majestic design', Epstein travelled up to a quarry in Derbyshire where he bought a twenty-ton stone block. Naturally this took some time to be delivered to his studio at 72 Cheyne Walk, but he set to work on it with his hammers and chisels as soon as it arrived and in the following year, 1912, it was finished. The memorial had by that time achieved so much newspaper publicity that it was agreed that it should go on exhibition in his studio for a month and, with hundreds of others, I went to see it.

Used as I was to seeing Epstein in the Domino Room, dishevelled, his shoes scuffed and his clothes stinking, I was still astonished at his appearance at the public showing of what was then his most important work. His trousers and jacket were filthy where he had wiped clay on them while modelling other works. His fingernails were black, and he looked more like some half-demented anarchist than a serious artist. I suppose it was another way of drawing attention to himself, an inverted display of vanity, the reverse of dandyism and a way of demonstrating his unconcern for convention.

He gave no hint of recognizing me as I walked round the memorial several times, though such an observant person must surely have seen me in the Domino Room. Nevertheless I had to admit that he had done an excellent job, even by my old-fashioned standards. The front of the large sarcophagus was carved like a Greek Sphinx. Epstein himself told us it was a 'flying demon angel representing the dead poet as a messenger', but unlike the mystical Sphinx this one was unmistakably male, a feature which was later to turn what should have been a solemn set of circumstances into a farce. The face of the 'demon angel' had an inscrutable expression, very reminiscent of Oscar in his pensive pose, with the symbol of Fame, complete with trumpet, carved on the forehead. Above the head were figures which, the sculptor explained, represented two further relevant characteristics, Intellectual Pride and Luxury. The arms of the symbolic figure were stretched backwards, furthering the impression of flight through space, and on the back of the tomb was carved the inscription from Oscar's 'Ballad of Reading Gaol':

> *And alien tears shall fill for him*
> *Pity's long-broken urn,*
> *For his mourners will be outcast men*
> *And outcasts always mourn.*

Surprisingly, in view of the public attitude to Wilde's memory
and to Epstein's previous statues, the British newspaper response to
the sculpture was very favourable. Certainly nobody thought that the
fact that the genitals were exposed, as they are in most ancient
sculpture, made the tomb unacceptable. Yet in France, the legendary
home of artistic and sexual licence, it produced a most extraordinary
reaction. When Epstein went to Paris in 1912 to assist in putting the
tomb in place he was astonished to find that the offending portion of
the flying figure had been covered with a huge lump of plaster. A girl
artist called Nina Hamnett, about whom I shall have more to report,
was with Epstein in Paris and later, in the Domino Room, which she
loved, she described what had happened.

Epstein had promptly chiselled off the plaster, but when he arrived
to continue the work next day he found that the whole tomb had been
covered with a huge tarpaulin and his way was barred to it by a
policeman, stationed there at the request of the Prefect of the Seine.

'The tomb is banned,' the policeman declared. 'Indecency! You are
forbidden to work on it.'

Unable to believe his ears, Epstein brought a group of prominent
French artists to show them what had happened. They were outraged
to see the guard and the tarpaulin still there. There were immediate
protests in the French and British press against this infringement of
artistic liberty, Shaw, Wells, Lavery and others lending their names
to the indignant protests. As you can imagine, the insult was hotly
discussed in the Domino Room.

'It's because he was a homosexual,' Harris argued. 'Private parts of
a person which had been used normally would never have caused
affront, particularly in France. It's where these particular parts have
been that's upsetting the authorities.'

The French reacted by asking Epstein to modify the tomb, presumably meaning that he should remove the offending organs. He
refused. The alternative was that the tarpaulin should remain and any
official unveiling of the tomb would be postponed indefinitely, so,
with Robert Ross's agreement, a bronze plaque was cast to cover the
offending portion.

Naturally I was entranced by all this to-ing and fro-ing when I
heard it in the Domino Room, and it drove me to take a decision
which, for me, was monumental. I would go to see the tomb myself
in Paris, making my way there by ferry and railway! It would be the
first time I was to travel overseas and, as it turned out, my last.
During the four years of the Great War, which was soon to follow, I

could not have travelled anyway, except as a combatant from which I was barred owing to my deafness. In any case, my brief trip to Paris convinced me that foreigners had nothing to offer me in their own lands. It was much easier, and cheaper, to let them come to me in the Café Royal, as so many of them did, including, of course, people I would never have been able to meet abroad. Having taken this decision to visit Paris one evening on my way back to my lodgings, all that remained was to select the most interesting time to make the journey.

The question had arisen of finding some poet or artist to unveil the monument in a formal ceremony, but because of the odium still attached to Oscar's reputation – twelve years after his death – nobody of eminence was forthcoming. There were several who said they would like to do it, but made various excuses because of the tainting effect on their own reputations. Augustus John was the only one who gave a really honest answer, quoting Oscar by saying that regrettably he had a subsequent engagement. *Faute de mieux*, as I understand the French say, the task fell to the extraordinary Aleister Crowley.

As was his wont, and as I witnessed so often in the Domino Room, Crowley sought the guidance of what he called the 'Yi King' by casting a bundle of short sticks on to the table and carefully studying the pattern in which they fell. Convinced that Yi King was urging him to accept, he not only embraced the opportunity of being publicly associated with someone as 'evil' as Wilde, but genuinely believed that he was well fitted for the honour.

The opportunity appealed not only to Crowley's colossal vanity but to his undoubted sense of humour – expressed later in the Domino Room in an incredible incident I will presently describe – and he set it out in the following manner. First, at his own expense, for he still had considerable private means, he wrote a manifesto called *In the Name of the Liberty of Art* and had it printed and widely distributed in Paris. Then he urged all who were prepared to protest against the tyranny of authority to present themselves on the due date at Père Lachaise cemetery. It was by overhearing Crowley's plans discussed in the Domino Room with Betty May, one of Epstein's former models, that I knew when to set off for Paris, and being unable to speak the language I decided that I might as well stay in the cheap hotel where Oscar Wilde had died, the Hôtel d'Alsace in the Rue des Beaux-Arts. Betty May, incidentally, had previously distinguished herself in the Café Royal in a most peculiar way. Hoping to catch the attention of artists like Epstein, who might engage her, she adorned her cheap dress with brightly coloured patches of cloth and painted her shoes. Sadly the latter stuck together when she crossed her ankles and the only way she could stand up was by removing them!

I had long wished to see Oscar's 'deathplace' (isn't it odd that, while birthplace is common, nobody speaks of deathplace?) and fortunately there was room there. Perhaps the Hôtel d'Alsace also suffered from the taint of Wilde for, while it was generally believed in the Domino Room that the fuss over Oscar had made Britain a laughing stock in Europe, the French authorities appeared to take a similar puritanical view. I discovered that the same family, called Dupoirier, were still running the hotel, but when I mentioned the name Wilde to the landlady she appeared or pretended not to understand. I then tried 'Melmoth', and at this she nodded affably, though it was with some reluctance that she let me peep into the room where my friend had breathed his last. We mounted a curving stairway to the first floor, and there was what we would call a bed-sitting room looking out on to a small backyard. The furniture looked worn and, not understanding French, I was unable to ask whether the flowered wallpaper was the one to which Oscar had remarked: 'One of us will have to go.'

The landlady motioned that we should have to leave because somebody was occupying the room and was expected back, which, of course, explained her reluctance to show it to me. I found it fascinating, even if slightly creepy, to sleep under the same roof where poor Oscar had died 'beyond his means'. Later, back in London, I was to hear the artist Nina Hamnett telling some friend how she had gone to a hotel where Wilde had lived and that the old proprietor could only remember him as 'the man in room fifteen' (rather as I might be remembered as 'the man at table ten').

I also took the opportunity of visiting Père Lachaise cemetery on the day before the unveiling ceremony by Crowley, which was an experience in itself. On that day Crowley and a young American friend were in the cemetery, though not when I was there. They hid themselves until the gates were closed and, having half cut through the ropes attached to the tarpaulin, attached some fine steel wires to it and led them to a tree many yards away. Their idea was to unveil the monument even if the police placed a guard round it, though it was unlikely that they would fail to notice the wires.

This precaution proved unnecessary, for there was no guard when our rather small procession marched to the tomb next day in November drizzle and fog. Fortunately I had brought my umbrella and this helped to conceal me from the few who might have noticed me. None did, and I spoke to nobody who was there that day. Conspicuous by his absence was Bosie, Lord Alfred Douglas. Was it any feeling of guilt that kept him away? Could he have felt that, but for him, Oscar might still be alive? I doubt it. In fact I suspect that he always believed that he was the injured party. Otherwise how can we explain his verse: 'O thrice betrayed and seven times crucified, is there no issue from unhappy ways, no peace, no hope, no loving arms at last?'

This persecution mania showed itself at the end of 1913 when Epstein left Douglas a letter at the Café Royal warning him about derogatory remarks he had made about the Wilde tomb. The message threatened that, if the warning was disregarded, Epstein would '. . . spoil the remains of your beauty double quick'. Instead of ignoring the note, and in spite of Oscar's experience in court, Douglas brought an action against the sculptor for 'using threats against him'. Epstein, who had undoubtedly been provoked, was bound over and the judge did not grant Douglas his costs.

Many thoughts crossed my mind, as I stood there looking at the tomb. 'If I do live again I would like it to be as a flower, no soul but perfectly beautiful,' Oscar had said. I wondered if any part of him was present in the few flowers visible in the cemetery. Of one other declaration which Oscar had made, while still a student at Oxford, before I knew him, there could be no doubt concerning its fulfilment – 'Somehow or other I'll be famous, and if not famous I'll be notorious.' Crowley pronounced a few words, then unveiled the tomb. Some of us then saw that the shape of the bronze plaque covering the offending parts was rather unfortunate: it was remarkably like a butterfly which, of course, had been the emblem of Whistler, the American artist who had fallen out with Wilde.

In spite of the solemnity of the occasion I have to admit that I was hoping that the *gendarmes* might appear because Crowley, who looked strong, might well have put up a fight and been arrested, but they had made themselves scarce. Nevertheless the ceremony achieved a lot of publicity in the British and French press and served to tell the world that at least a few stalwarts had been prepared to take considerable pains to honour the dead writer.

A few days later when I was back in London after an uneventful crossing, though I was rather seasick, I was sitting at my table in the Domino Room, which was pretty full of the usual habitués, when in walked Crowley. One never knew what garb he might be wearing, and this time he was in full evening dress. His great shaven head held high, his eyes ablaze, he walked into the room and saw Epstein sitting at a table with the model Betty May.

As Crowley stood before Epstein, Betty May suddenly pointed in the direction of Crowley's private parts and burst into laughter. She had observed that his dress had a peculiar addition to the orders and decorations he so often affected. Depending from a cord, so that it covered his loins, was the bronze plaque which had disgraced the tomb of Wilde! He bowed and presented it to Epstein who, I regret to record, did not seem at all amused, though the rest of the room showed its approval of his gesture.

I think that Epstein simply resented the interference of the Magus, who always seemed to be seeking publicity. A few days later the sculptor's lack of enthusiasm was justified: the tarpaulin was back on the tomb. And there it remained until the war broke out in 1914 when, with more pressing matters to concern them, the authorities took the tarpaulin away, perhaps wanting it for another purpose. Since then the tomb has apparently remained unmolested and, save for a few visitors, unremarked.

No memorial to Oscar has ever been erected in Britain,* and most assuredly his name will never appear in Westminster Abbey among the poets and writers recorded there, yet the lasting value of his work has more than compensated for his social crimes. As Oscar so rightly said: 'The emotions of man are stirred more quickly than man's intelligence.'

23

ROYAL SNUB TO A 'QUEEN'

My diary shows that Oscar Wilde was not the only one of my Domino Room friends to be treated shabbily in 1911. It was in that year that the Royal Family first recognized the music-hall by agreeing to a Command Performance of music-hall stars. Unbelievably, the great-

* *Editor's footnote*: See note on page 134.

est of them all, Marie Lloyd, was omitted from the list, no doubt because her songs were too risqué.

This omission caused caustic comment among Marie's many admirers in the Domino Room, especially from Willie Crosland. There could be no denying, however, that the way she sang her songs was very suggestive. The words of most of them seemed innocuous enough but her face, framed in a mass of golden curls, her winks and her hands were so expressive when she sang Cockney songs like 'I always 'old with 'avin' it if you fancy it . . . 'cos a little of what you fancy does you good', or 'They've given me half a crown to run away and play — hi-ti-iddly hi-ti-iddly hi-ti-iddly-ay!' that the audience was left in no doubt as to what she meant. She would raise her dress to show her petticoat when she ran about 'winking the other eye'.

Then there was the notorious story of her song about a girl sitting in a kitchen garden, with the line, 'She sits among the cabbages and peas'. When an official objection was raised against this line, while she was singing at the Tivoli, she promised to change it and brought the expectant house down with the line, 'She sits among the cabbages and leeks.' Eventually Marie had to appear before the 'Watch Committee', composed of elderly gentlemen who were supposed to be guardians of morals for the London stage. She sang all her songs in a straightforward way, and they had to admit that they contained nothing objectionable whatever. Then when they had passed them all she sang the drawing-room ballad 'Come Into the Garden, Maud', but with such gestures and leering innuendo that the Watch Committee retired in great embarrassment. I only wish that I had witnessed that performance. I was, however, witness to the conversation which led Crosland and a few cronies to visit Marie in her dressing-room at the Pavilion, not far from the Palace where the Command Performance was to be staged. She must have taken their advice because bills were quickly printed naming Marie Lloyd as 'The Queen of Comediennes', with a broad slip pasted across the billboards declaring: 'Every performance given by Marie Lloyd is a Command Performance — by Order of the British Public!'

Good old Marie! When she let rip she could swear like a soldier and she taught me one or two words I had never heard. I saw her many times in the Domino Room, usually with stage people, like Dan Leno, the Irish comedian and clog dancer who always looked so sad, and died young. Fortunately she could cheer up anybody on or off the stage with both stories and wit. On one occasion, when the waiter brought her some soup far below the usual standard, she called him over confidingly and said, 'Unless you're keeping it a dead secret what sort of soup is this?'

'Pea soup, madam.'

'I'll give you a tip. Next time you make pea soup be really reckless. Use three peas and damn the expense!'

On another occasion a fellow actress was assuring Marie that she never suffered from stage fright. 'I don't know what nerves are, Marie,' she said. 'Why should I? I know the curtain's bound to come down some time.'

'I fancy that's what the poor bloody audience feel while you're on,' Marie replied.

She was a big spender – lavish, I would say – but she could afford it. Before she was twenty she was earning £100 a week, a huge sum then in 1886, and ended up drawing in £10,000 a year! She would bring several friends and scroungers with her into the Domino Room or the Grill Room, and I was there one night when she caused a rare rumpus by objecting to being charged forty-four shillings for twenty-two measures of brandy which she and her friends had consumed. The head waiter, Greguglia, refused to reduce the bill so, after letting out a mouthful of the foulest language, she pulled two hatpins from her hat and chased him round the tables, determined to stick him if she could. The waiter escaped and soon the owner, then Monsieur Daniel Pigache, who knew her well, came to remonstrate. Before he could say a word she flung her arms around his neck and rained kisses on his face. He was so mollified that he solved the situation by giving her and her six guests another brandy on the house.

Dear Marie, I can see her now, rather dainty and doll-like, with prominent white teeth with rather wide spaces between them. She gave so much pleasure but did not reap much herself; both her marriages were unhappy. One of her husbands was a man called Dillon, whom, I suspect, knocked her about, since he was feared in the Domino Room for his violence when in drink. I was glad to see him barred after he ended an argument by hitting his friend on the head with a soda siphon so viciously that the police had to be called.

Marie was, I think, one of those who showed only part of her nature to the world and managed to hide the rest. But what am I saying? Surely we all do that. I am only too aware that, even with the inside knowledge I was able to acquire, my concept of any other person can be no more than an impression.

On 7 October 1922 the rumble of conversation in the Domino

Room was hushed, as it were by a wave of silence spreading from the Regent Street entrance, after a man had entered with an evening paper, which he showed in dismay to the waiters as he walked slowly and sadly to his table. I wondered if King George had dropped dead, but it was in fact a Queen whose death was announced – the Queen of Comediennes, my beloved Marie Lloyd.

It is commonplace for journalists to exaggerate a nation's grief by writing that it was 'stunned' by the news of the death of some prominent figure. But, so far as Londoners were concerned, this was literally true. The Domino Room conversation remained at a low level for many minutes, and when the volume increased it was because so many people were recalling the pleasure that Marie had given them. I was told that outside in Piccadilly and in Leicester Square, where Marie had so often appeared, the quiet was noticeable. In Hoxton, where she had been born, and in many other North and East End areas of London, thousands were in tears.

It turned out that, unknown to anyone but her closest friends, Marie had been seriously ill for many months, with a complaint which remained unnamed, but had continued to fulfil her engagements and take on new ones until she could no longer stand. I had known she was not well because Willie Crosland, whom she admired for his 'Man in the Street' column in the *Daily Sketch*, had been to see her in her dressing-room at the Alhambra only a few days previously. He had returned with the news that she looked drawn and tired, but nobody realized she was at death's door. She died in harness at the age of fifty-two while playing in East Ham. Her last song had been her most famous, and appallingly apt in the circumstances: 'I'm one of the ruins that Cromwell knocked abaht a bit'. As she had lurched about the stage in imitation of a drunken old Cockney woman she really had been staggering, through weakness, and had to be carried home.

It is another banality to say that someone who dies is irreplaceable. Again, in her case this was true. There had been many imitators of Marie Lloyd, and there would be many more, but none could approach her in the sheer force of personality, which had made her capable of rousing the most dispirited audience within minutes of her appearance. Most of us sat there, intellectuals, 'toffs', bookmakers, waiters, tarts and working folk alike, mulling over the pleasure she had given us in her thirty-six years of stardom. To use yet another overworked phrase, it was the end of an epoch, because the old-time music-hall had come to the end of its days, and Marie, who started there, was the last great link with it.

Marie had died in her sister's arms at her fine home in Golders Green in North London, and as soon as the details of the funeral were made public I felt that I must attend. I am glad that I did, not just to pay my sincere respects but because the occasion provided memorable proof that the affection for Marie had indeed been deep and wide. There must have been fifty thousand people following or trying to follow the cortège with its car-loads of wreaths and posies. There was every kind of conveyance from Rolls Royces to costers' carts, but most of her devotees were on foot and many of the poorest had walked the whole way from the East End. There were famous names from the theatre and from journalism. There were old entertainers who had never made the top but had played at the same theatres or simply admired her talent. There were cabbies, flower-sellers, waiters, jockeys and the hundreds of ordinary people whom Marie had befriended and were the main reason why, after earning perhaps a quarter of a million pounds, she left only one thousand.

As I watched the fantastic throng I was reminded of poor Oscar's funeral in that bleak cemetery in Paris, with no more than a handful of mourners and the rest of his former admirers unmoved by news of his death. Marie, at least, had ended her days at the height of her acclaim, sometimes earning the then phenomenal figure of £600 a week, while Oscar had died in near-poverty and disgrace.

Of course I could get nowhere near the church in such a crush, but I waited to file past the grave. It was a long wait and over the next few days it was reported that more than a hundred thousand people made the same pilgrimage.

I gave much thought, as I shuffled in that long winding queue, as to why so many people, many of whom were weeping openly, men as well as women, had put themselves out, giving up a day's work perhaps, to say farewell to a woman whose tiny coffin showed how physically small she had been. There were, of course, many personal friends and many more acquaintances, including the army of scroungers who battened not only on Marie's generosity but on her susceptibility to flattery. The great mass of the throng, however, had never met Marie, except across the footlights, so they must have been paying their tribute to someone who had entertained them so well, not just by her performances, but by her catchy numbers, which they were able to sing or whistle down the years. Above all, she had helped them to forget their troubles and often their poverty by making them laugh. It seems to me that those with the gift of being able to make others laugh can write their own tickets.

24

'THE WICKEDEST MAN IN THE WORLD'

In 1921 the Great Beast assumed the further titles of Magus and then Ipsissimus, the highest magical grade of all. By that time the prediction I had heard him make to Arnold Bennett that he would end up in Italy with a 'Whore Hell, a secret place of the quenchless fire of lust and eternal torment of Love', had been fulfilled and he had established his Abbey of Thelema near the small town of Cefalù in Sicily. Those who went there reported back to the Domino Room that the Abbey was something of a disappointment. It was in fact no more than a little farmhouse in which he had established several 'disciples', who were mainly his mistresses. They had to put up with rather extraordinary names like Whore of the Stars, the Scarlet Woman, the Ape, and the Snake, and to bear and rear Crowley's illegitimate children. They also had to endure the now painful version of the Serpent's Kiss, a bite on the neck so deep that it drew blood, the Beast evidently fancying himself as a vampire too.

His 'Do what thou wilt be the whole of the Law' had enabled him to indulge in sexual excesses of all kinds associated with magical and orgiastic rites, and the walls of the 'Temple' and other rooms were covered with Crowley's paintings of sexual acts in every kind of position. 'Sex magic' remained his name not only for fornication but for sodomy, which he practised both as the active and passive partner with other men, his women sometimes serving in the revolting capacity of hand-maidens.

It might well be asked why women were attracted to such a man and put up with his demands. The sad truth was that he was a drug peddler and he converted his disciples into fellow addicts so that, like himself, they were hooked for life. By that time, at the age of forty-five, Ipsissimus had gone through most of his fortune, and some of the addicts had money which he confiscated for the Abbey.

One of these addicts was a lady to whom I have already referred, Epstein's former model Betty May, who had been such a regular character in the Domino Room, with her habit, much deprecated by the wine waiters, of spooning sugar into her extra-dry champagne. She had met Crowley there while he was wearing his Highlander outfit before he left for Sicily, and was making money out of old ladies by demonstrating devil-worship to them in a temple in Fulham. She was scared of him and refused to meet him again until Fate intervened in the curious way that it chose to affect so many habitués of the Domino Room.

Betty May fell in love with a clever young history graduate of St John's College, Oxford, called Raoul Loveday. He had become interested in studying the occult and inevitably met Crowley, through whom he quickly became addicted to heroin. When Betty May and Raoul were married Crowley was in America but sought out the couple on his return. Betty May, a cured addict striving to keep her husband away from drugs, realized the necessity also of keeping the Beast at a distance, but without success. Even though Epstein and his wife, who continued to bring Betty May to the Domino Room, accompanied her to Crowley's temple, then in Holland Park, to plead with him, Loveday refused to part from the magician. Instead he followed Crowley out to Cefalù, taking his wife with him, because Crowley wanted Loveday to succeed him as head of the Abbey and, presumably, as the Wickedest Man in the World.

Soon after their arrival, when Betty May was moping for her Soho friends, Crowley sacrificed a cat in front of her on the Abbey altar. He then threatened that she too would be sacrificed unless she agreed to obey him in all things and to take part in the rites, in which Crowley worked himself into a frenzy, dancing and chanting in apparent ecstasy, a condition usually followed by 'sex magic' in the various outrageous forms depicted on the walls.

They had not been there many months when Loveday fell ill and died. Crowley claimed that he had contracted Mediterranean fever and died of 'heart paralysis', but Betty May believed his death had been hastened by the evil practices of the Abbey, including the drinking of cats' blood. No post-mortem was carried out because the Magus conducted the burial service himself, 'according to the rites of the Order'.

He also claimed that Betty May was content to remain with him, but in fact she returned to England and told the newspapers a sensational story of her husband's death and Crowley's extraordinary behaviour. On 25 February 1923 the Domino Room was agog with gossip about an article which had appeared that day in the *Sunday Express*, which had attacked Crowley before. It was a lurid interview with Betty May and described the orgies, sacrifices and other diabolical rites being practised at the Abbey, making Crowley what he had always claimed, the Wickedest Man in the World.

I remember the big black headline: 'New Sinister Revelations of Aleister Crowley', which followed up articles the previous year when the paper had attacked the Beast following publication of his novel *Diary of a Drug Fiend*. With such titles Crowley certainly asked for trouble, and he got it. The *Sunday Express* demand for action against the perpetrator of 'bestial orgies' was quickly followed by articles in *John Bull*, which revived Bottomley's hatred of Crowley – though the former editor was in jail -- with headlines like 'The Man we'd like to Hang!', 'A Cannibal at Large!' and 'The King of Depravity!'. Out of curiosity I read *Diary of a Drug Fiend*, which was not very good but had been given tremendous publicity. James Douglas, the well-known campaigning journalist who had written the attacks, had called for the enforced withdrawal of the book, and there has never been anything like the threat of a ban on any written work to make people want to read it.

Later I was to hear Crowley telling H. G. Wells, whom he had met through Arnold Bennett, that the instigator of these vicious attacks was none other than Lord Beaverbrook, the proprietor of the *Sunday Express*, whom I knew from his regular visits to the Café Royal, though he patronized the Restaurant, rather than the Domino Room. He claimed he was going to write to the 'little Canadian adventurer', as George V called him, and I believe that he did so but without effect.

Crowley encountered a more implacable opponent than Beaverbrook when Mussolini, the Italian dictator, issued a decree forbidding foreign mystics to practise on Italian soil as all secret societies were to be outlawed. The Beast moved with what remained of his retinue to France, but he was expelled again and reluctantly came back to England, which could not deny him re-entry.

I was present on the day when he suddenly appeared in the Domino Room. Never since Queensberry came in looking for Wilde had there been such sudden and sustained silence, made all the more noticeable by the sudden resumption of the usual conversational buzz as the Beast sat down and ordered a brandy. After all the newspaper attacks and the scandal of Loveday's death few had expected to see him there again, but he had real brass nerve and lived up to his claim: 'I have always been utterly contemptuous of the criticism of people whom I do not respect' – implying that he respected few but himself. He had

put on his Highland dress to mark his return, and eventually the
silence was broken by derisory shouts of, 'It's a braw, bricht, moon-
licht, nicht the nicht', and other snatches from Sir Harry Lauder's
music-hall repertoire. Responding with the evil eye, he sat down and
began writing furiously. I noticed that his strong face was haggard
through the effects of the massive doses of heroin he was taking – said
to be four or five grains a day – though he was doing his best to hide it
with make-up and powder, which I had never known him use before.

I was delighted to see him back because too many of the Domino
Room eccentrics had disappeared but, instead of leading an apparently normal life until the fuss of Loveday's death had died down, he
was soon up to his tricks of peddling drugs, alleged sexual rejuven-
ation courses and an Elixir of life said to contain fragments of his own
body, including his own semen. Though warned that the police were
watching him – to which he replied, 'Good, then I won't be burgled'
– he proceeded to write a very large volume entitled *The Confessions*,
dedicated to Augustus John among others, reducing the chances that
any bookseller would stock it by insisting on having a most demonic
self-portrait on the cover. He also continued his feud with Beaverbrook, presumably hoping for some financial settlement, but he had
picked on a character as eccentric as himself, if that word means
'different from other people'.

Eventually in April 1934 he appeared in court in the King's Bench
in what became known as 'The Black Magic Case', a libel suit which
he had brought against the authoress of a book who was none other
than Nina Hamnett, the artist who was a former friend of Crowley,
and of so many other Domino Room regulars. By that time Nina was
looking rather worn, and many years had passed since the occasion
when she had been so proud of her figure that another habitué of the
Domino Room, a witty little Cockney known as 'The Virgin', had
challenged her to a show-down by stripping off all her clothes, to
loud cheers from the assembled men. Like so many of the Café
Royalites Nina had turned to writing (has any other group of people
written so many books?) and her effort was called *Laughing Torso*,
presumably after the torso of Nina made by the sculptor Gaudier-
Brzeska. I borrowed it from the London Library and could not see
why Crowley was so upset, when he had gone out of his way to make
himself seem wicked. Once again, as with Oscar Wilde and Horatio
Bottomley, the case demonstrated the danger of bringing libel
actions when the character of the aggrieved person is known to be
disreputable. Crowley's counsel made the cardinal error of trying to

establish his client's high moral character, and this gave the defence a field day.

Betty May, who was a friend of Nina, described the goings-on in the Abbey and the case quickly turned into a trial of Crowley himself. Crowley made the mistake of trying to establish a difference between Black Magic and White Magic. He was then asked to make himself invisible in the court to prove that he was no impostor, and of course he declined to try. Not only did he lose but the judge, Mr Justice Swift, castigated him as 'dreadful, horrible, blasphemous and abominable', the newspapers giving this verdict the widest publicity. Poor Crowley's costs were so heavy that, as with Oscar, his creditors made him bankrupt. What a tragedy it is that most of us fail to learn from other people's blunders! It almost seems as though there is some destructive impulse demanding that we make them ourselves.

We all wondered how Crowley would continue to survive. He did continue, for such was his attraction for certain women that a whole succession of them became the Whore of the Stars and helped not only to keep him with money, but to produce yet more illegitimate children. I imagine that some of these ladies were sex-starved, as the saying is, and, no doubt Crowley offered all manner of possible delights. I remember how in 1937 one quite elderly lady, who should have known better but was foreign and rich, was set up by Crowley to buy a pot of his so-called Celebrated Magical Sex-Appeal Ointment for the enormous sum of £2000. Exactly what she planned to do with it I leave my readers to guess, but in the hope of a quick sale Crowley, who was actually sixty-two, put on a party for his sixtieth birthday in a large private room at the Café Royal. As he failed to sell the ointment the huge bill for more than twenty guests was placed in front of the lady, who had already been given the resounding title of First Concubine. The head waiter did not know her so he refused to accept her cheque at first but, seeing that nothing whatever was forthcoming from Crowley, he took it, and I was told later that it was duly honoured.

At Crowley's next party, however, the Café Royal did not fare so well. He invited his oldest friends and ordered a most sumptuous repast with the best wines and brandies, the occasion allegedly being yet another important birthday. Draining his brandy balloon, he asked to be excused for what his guests assumed to be the usual reason. He slowly walked down the stairs, took his hat and coat from the cloakroom, tipping the attendant half a crown, a good tip in those days, and hailed a taxi. Thus departed, to my everlasting regret, one of the most colourful characters of the old Café Royal, for he never returned. The bill had been more than £100 but for old times' sake, as Crowley had been an excellent customer in his day, the management did not sue him. Or perhaps they assumed that they would be flogging a dead horse, because the great Magus was completely broke.

He must have acquired some money, however, for he lived on for a further ten years in dull and straitened circumstances, first in lodgings in Jermyn Street, where I sometimes saw him on my perambulations. I heard an intriguing story about him through the newspaper columnist Tom Driberg, who had somehow acquired one of Crowley's diaries, a red leather book encased in beautifully embossed silver, which he brought into the Domino Room. Driberg had been dining with Crowley who had drawn a five-pointed star – a so-called pentacle – and told him to stare into it and describe what he saw. Driberg then proceeded to describe the diary, which Crowley had lost years before. The Magus was staggered, urging his guest: 'Go on, go on. . . .' Perhaps this was his first encounter with real 'magic'.

He ended up in a boarding house in Hastings, where he died in 1947. Like others, equally vain, he had written his own epitaph:

> *Bury me in a nameless grave!*
> *I came from God the world to save.*
> *I brought them wisdom from above.*
> *Worship, liberty and love.*
> *They slew me for I did disparage*
> *Therefore, Religion, Law and Marriage.*
> *So be my grave without a name*
> *That earth may swallow up my shame.*

Here again, as with Oscar, Bottomley and others, was the ultimate vanity – comparison with Jesus Christ. There was, however, no grave or memorial for poor Aleister. He was cremated.

25

GLUTTONS FOR FOOD, DRINK AND POWER

I have mentioned a number of men with enormous appetites, and will have more to name, but in the spring of 1905 I set eyes for the first time on a world-famous Italian who could out-eat them all. His name was Enrico Caruso and he was already on his way to becoming perhaps the greatest and most popular operatic tenor of all time, though of course I was never in a position to appreciate his talents except at the table.

I discovered that he had been in the Restaurant during previous visits to the Covent Garden Opera House but 1905, I think, was his first appearance in the Domino Room. He was with two other famous musical Italians, Antonio Scotti, the baritone, and Ciccio Tosti, the composer, known, even to those who had never heard the song, for 'Tosti's Goodbye'. Caruso, who was already fat and stockily built with a very short neck, not only ate a five-course dinner but in between the normal courses demolished three different kinds of spaghetti! He was fortunate that evening to escape a mass rendering of a music-hall song, with which other massive eaters had been regaled:

> Carve a little bit off the top for me, for me,
> Just a little bit off the top for me, for me,
> Saw me off a yard or two, I'll tell you when to stop,
> For all I want is a little bit off the top!

I was also surprised to see that Caruso was almost a chain smoker, and I often wondered whether this habit had anything to do with the chest complaint which finally killed him when he was only forty-eight. When taxed about these excesses he had a ready answer – 'I was the eighteenth child of my parents and all the previous seventeen died in infancy. So I must have a constitution like a horse – a Neapolitan horse!'

Caruso should have felt at home in the Domino Room, because by nature he was a practical joker and thoroughly enjoyed ribbing his friends. He was also quite a clever caricaturist and would make lightning sketches on menu cards, which he would often sign and give to the waiters. My waiter friends in the Restaurant upstairs were sometimes even given a free recital, for Caruso would sing quietly into the ear of the wife of his friend Otto Gutekunst, an art dealer, when he was there with both of them.

While rather cockily self-assured as he walked, he was a most pleasant-looking fellow with his smart suits and the carefully upturned moustache he sported during his early visits to London. Unfortunately he tended more and more to use the Restaurant on his later visits, by which time he was richer, fatter and clean-shaven. But on the odd occasions when he did grace us with his unmistakable presence, the Room would rise almost to a man and raise their glasses to him, such was the respect in which he was held throughout the civilized world.

My diary records only one further entry of interest about Caruso apart from his death in 1921. In 1911 the tax collectors discovered that he had a house in Maida Vale and, though he never stayed in England longer than about ten weeks, for the Covent Garden season, they proposed to tax him on his earnings. Furious, in garrulous Italian style, Caruso refused to pay, closed down his house and gave the furniture and effects away to his friends.

In the summer of 1905 Willie Crosland told his Domino Room friends that his doctor had given him six weeks to live because of severe diabetes. This had not been helped by his heavy intake of alcohol, particularly of strong liquors like brandy, which he would drink in gulps while dictating copy in a hurry. The doctor had suggested that to ease his last days he should raise what money he had and spend them at a German spa, pointing out that if he took the waters and lived abstemiously, he might add a few more months to his life.

Crosland took off for Germany and, acting on impulse, did everything there which the doctors had forbidden. Willie had displayed this impulsiveness all his life, so much so that, on being invited to a party at a house in Camberwell in 1892, he had vowed that he would marry the first girl he met there if she had any appeal for him. He did just that, and they remained wed until his death. Fortunately his wife was not with him to see that he carried out the doctor's orders, for after his alcoholic holiday he returned to the Domino Room looking like a new man!

'A hair of the dog – in fact a complete pelt – is the best treatment for diabetes,' he announced. 'I've proved it.'

In his case 'Kill or cure' had worked, and it was tuberculosis, not diabetes, which was to end his life nineteen years later. But some of his equally bibulous literary friends, whose livers were in a sorry state, took his advice and their ends were hastened. The truth was that, in body as well as in mind, Crosland was an exceptional person.

His recovery heralded a meeting with Lord Alfred Douglas, Bosie himself, then thirty-six; it was to be a lasting relationship, though interrupted by violent quarrels accompanied by scathing public criticism of each other's behaviour. Though both Crosland and Douglas were known to resort to fisticuffs, they seemed to prefer to batter each other with words, especially in rhyme. Nobody benefited from both the friendship and the quarrels more than I did, because they made the Domino Room their regular meeting place, patronized the table near mine, which Crosland had always used, and so provided me with entertainment and education for many years. Further, their relationship was to result in one of the most sensational criminal libel actions of all time, an action which was to resurrect so much of the dirt about poor old Oscar.

The two first met through that other tempestuous character, Frank Harris, after Crosland had been invited to contribute to yet another of Harris's magazines called *The Candid Friend*. Crosland called at Harris's office in Covent Garden, and who should be with him but Lord Alfred. As both were convinced that poetry was the highest form of art and 'the highest demonstration of the human intellect', they had much in common, especially when Crosland praised Bosie's so highly. Over the years Crosland, through his various papers and magazines, was able to print some of Douglas's best poetry, including the sonnet originally entitled 'In memoriam O. W.', which was later changed, after Bosie's hatred for Oscar had intensified, to 'The Dead Poet'.

The older he got, the more convinced did Douglas become that Oscar had ruined him and his whole family, and was forever saying so to Crosland or to anybody else who would listen. In my view they ruined each other but, whereas Oscar could do nothing about his fate, Bosie, who lived until he was seventy-four, had plenty of time to come to terms with the hatred which, as Oscar had warned him, poisoned his whole character. He never did.

Shortly after Crosland met Douglas he fell out with Frank Harris because he found out that Frank was literally eating the profits of

Vanity Fair, for which Crosland was working. Instead of taking the revenue for advertisements placed by various restaurants he was having meals or, in the case of furriers, taking fur coats for his wife. Crosland's anger at this, particularly when funds at the magazine were low, may have been intensified by Frank Harris's behaviour on the first occasion they dined together at the Café Royal. As usual Harris sent back course after course with a cry of: 'A plague on both your houses', so that Crosland sat there starving. Not at all amused by this behaviour, Crosland took a big chop with him next time he came to dine with Harris at the Café Royal and plonked it down, wrapped in greaseproof paper, on the plate in front of him.

'My dear man, what in the name of Chatterton, the sleepless boy, have you got there?' Harris inquired, peering down at the plate.

'My dinner,' Crosland answered, unwrapping the chop.

Willie always had some answer to those who crossed him, a characteristic he had shown from his boyhood, as a story I heard him tell many times illustrates. Before he came to London he secured a temporary job as a scene-shifter at the old theatre in Leeds. Beer had been supplied for the stage hands but, as Crosland was new, the manager drank his share. A few nights later, during one of the intervals, Crosland spotted the manager in between the folds of the curtain kissing and groping round one of the chorus girls. He immediately raised the curtain and exposed them before they could disengage. It brought the house down – and Willie the sack.

I was present in the Domino Room, in 1907, when Douglas, dandily dressed in a tightly fitting suit, invited Crosland, who always looked as though he had slept in his clothes and usually wore a napless bowler, to join him on *The Academy*. This was a high-level magazine which had been bought by one of Bosie's relatives, Eddy Tennant, later Lord Glenconner, and Margot Asquith's brother (how the Domino Room habitués dominate the literary history of the time!). Tennant had acquired it so that he could make Bosie the editor and give him some way of using his undoubted talent. Crosland accepted with delight.

'In another couple of years this paper will be making at least £10,000 a year,' he told Bosie confidently. 'You will hear people in the streets whispering, "Who is that fair youth?" And the reply will be, "That is the wealthy Lord Alfred Douglas, who owns *The Academy*."'

As Bosie preened himself at this prospect, his companion added,

'Then they will ask "And who is that dazzling object by his side?"
"That's Crosland," will be the reply.'

As Crosland knew, he was capable of dazzling with his wit, both in
conversation and in print, but the idea that anyone would describe his
person as 'dazzling' was utterly ludicrous.

In various journals to which Crosland contributed, apart from *The
Academy*, he ran a campaign to clean up the Fleet Street newspapers
which had become progressively 'yellow', trivial and sensational in
the struggle for circulation.

'It is neither seemly nor desirable that the great body of Englishmen and Englishwomen should be completely under the dominance
of a venal, trivial and degraded press,' he clamoured. Then quoting
Oscar Wilde, for he had a prodigious memory, he said, 'In centuries
before ours the public nailed the ears of intruding journalists to the
village pump. In this century journalists have nailed their own ears to
the keyhole.'

His main target was Lord Northcliffe, the former Alfred Harmsworth, who had once been employed as a sub-editor by Horatio
Bottomley, but had branched out on his own with phenomenal
success, first with his magazines and then with his newspapers.
Crosland called him: 'That little, ineffectual Alfred Harmsworth,
chief proprietor of *Answers*, *Forget-me-Not*, *Ha'penny Chips*, *Slimy
Chunks* and the *Daily Mail*.' He claimed that he had inflicted greater
harm on the English people than any other living man. 'It is better
never to see the stars at all than to insist on pretending to discover
their reflections in cesspools,' he said.

Already, by that time, Northcliffe was beginning to show early
signs of the dementia which was to cloud his life. I once remember
Hannen Swaffer telling how Northcliffe had suddenly appeared one
evening in the *Daily Mail* office and noticed a grey-haired man
sub-editing in a corner, where he had worked reliably and efficiently
for years.

'Who is that man?' Northcliffe asked of the editor, who was
showing him round.

'That's Brown, sir.'

'Then sack him. Journalism is a young man's game.'

The poor man was duly sacked, and thereafter it became a canon in
Fleet Street that it was safer to be bald than grey, for a young man
could be bald.

Crosland's anger when he heard this story had to be overheard to be
believed. 'That man has touched nothing which he has not degraded,'

he raged. 'He has degraded journalism; he has degraded journalists.' He demanded that the editor should resign in protest, but few in Fleet Street had the integrity of Willie Crosland.

Northcliffe, who forgot nothing, waited for his revenge. This came in 1916 when Crosland, who was hard up as usual, induced Hannen Swaffer, then the editor of the *Weekly Dispatch*, to allow him to contribute poems about the war at £10 a time – good payment in those days. The poems were published anonymously under the symbol 'X', and they were so good that Northcliffe eventually asked Swaffer who 'X' was. I heard Swaffer, 'Swaff' as his Domino Room friends called him, and who had a slight stammer, tell the story:

'The p . . . p . . . poems are all by T. H. W. Crosland, sir.'

'Are they indeed?' Northcliffe answered. 'Then they must be discontinued.' They were.

Swaffer was something of a poet himself, having written successful lyrics for Florrie (the Old Bull and Bush) Forde and other music-hall stars. It was usually dreadful, heartrending stuff about poor crippled boys in garrets, but because of his versifying ability and the long hair, wide black stock and other peculiarities Swaffer affected, Northcliffe addressed him as 'Poet'.

On the occasion I am recalling 'Poet' mentioned that there were growing fears for the 'Chief's' health. 'His doctors have told him that he's working far too hard and that he'll crack up if he doesn't take a rest. He was told that eight years ago, but he just can't leave the papers alone. Between you and me I suspect he's having brainstorms. If they were just due to overwork, all his staff would be having them.'

I shall have more to say about Northcliffe as well as about Crosland and Swaffer, who were both irascible, especially when in drink. Crosland would send a waiter's tray flying, drinks and all, if he dared to interrupt him with anything so trivial as the bill while he was making some telling point. The cadaverous Swaffer, whose guiding principle was, 'Never prolong a quarrel: clear the decks for the next one!' was a regular drunkard, insulting anyone in sight as he staggered back to the office, his battered, black homburg hat askew. Both had cigarettes perpetually hanging from their lips and seemed able to smoke them down to the smallest butt without ever touching them. The result, especially in Swaffer's case, was that the ash fell continually on to his lapels, which never seemed to be brushed. On one occasion when Swaffer entered the Domino Room he was greeted with the comment, 'Ah, Swaff, I see that you are wearing Gold Flake tonight.'

Like most things that Douglas tried, *The Academy* did not last long. Though he paid nothing for contributions it lost so much money that, in the words of Fleet Street, 'it folded'. As usual, Douglas blamed Crosland and anybody else who was handy for the failure of this vehicle for his genius. He tried to borrow from some of his rich friends to keep the magazine going, but without success. Later he was to say: 'It has always seemed to me a scandalous and discreditable thing that there was not one solitary rich man in the country who would back us.' To his dying day Douglas believed that the world owed him a living.

26

WARRIORS OF THE WORD

If Willie Crosland hated Bottomley, the man he detested even more was Oscar Wilde, whom he had never met and who had been dead for a dozen years before his loathing developed. Crosland had a hatred of unnatural vice, which was why his disgust spilled over to Wilde's most staunch surviving friend, Robbie Ross. But no doubt his dislike was fired by his own association with Bosie and with a particular event arising out of that on-and-off relationship.

What happened was that a young writer called Arthur Ransome, who was later to achieve fame as an author of children's books, had published in 1912 a work called *Oscar Wilde, a Critical Study*. It did not mention Douglas by name but there were obvious implications, and Bosie decided to bring one of the libel actions which he never seemed able to resist. By this time he had decided that he was a brilliant witness and, as one who saw him in action on several occasions, I can say that there were times when he put on a creditable show. But going to law is always a risky business because a litigant never knows just how powerful the ammunition may be which the opponent has in reserve, even if this happens to be no more than money. In the Ransome case it was very much more, for the young author had made the acquaintance of Robert Ross, who had shown him the unexpurgated manuscript of *De Profundis*.

It sounds almost incredible but at that time, fifteen years after Wilde's release from prison, Douglas still had no idea that *De Profundis* had, in fact, been a very long letter addressed to him in person, and that only parts of it had been published. Nor did he know that the unpublished parts were extremely damaging to him. To Douglas's consternation, long excerpts from this unexpurgated document were read out at the trial and there was no way that he could possibly win. He was being condemned by Oscar's own words, uttered, as it were, from the grave in France.

The Times Book Club, which had published Ransome's work, was represented by the ubiquitous F. E. Smith, who, I was glad to hear, took the opportunity of paying a moving tribute to Oscar: 'We have heard much of the vices of Oscar Wilde. We have heard little of the suffering with which he paid for those vices, the long-drawn out months of imprisonment and the squalid agony of his lonely death. It would be wrong if, twenty years after, no word was spoken in this case save one of revilement.' It was well and beautifully said.

The heavy costs bankrupted Douglas after he had borrowed from money-lenders and was then unable to repay, in spite of having sold letters from Oscar Wilde and some books signed by him. Understandably, Douglas was appalled by what had happened, especially when he discovered that the full manuscript had been deposited in the British Museum by Ross, for use later by students of the Wilde affair. From then on his venom was concentrated on Ross and he did everything he could to bring about his downfall.

As I have already indicated, Ross was an easy target. He was without doubt a practising homosexual, who corrupted others, and was almost certainly the man who had introduced Oscar to whatever pleasure it is that sodomy holds. Douglas set about libelling Ross in the hope that he would be sued for criminal libel and so get his enemy into the witness box. In print he called Ross 'an unspeakable skunk', 'the high priest of the sodomites', and 'a filthy bugger and corrupter of young boys'. Though part of Bosie's purpose may have been to rehabilitate himself in the public mind by lambasting Ross in this way, what he wrote was all true. I myself saw Ross haunting the urinals round Piccadilly, which I occasionally needed to patronize for other purposes. They seethed with young boys using the most blatant means of indicating their 'charms' to prospective customers.

To strengthen his attack Bosie sought the help of Willie Crosland, and it was willingly given after that master of invective had read the full manuscript of *De Profundis* for himself. I can hear him fuming in the Domino Room now at what he thought was a monstrous betrayal of a man whom Wilde had professed to love. Crosland's first strike was a small book called *The First Stone*, which he published in 1912. He had always claimed that 'It is the bludgeon that hits the mark and the rapier that misses', and in this long, blank-verse poem, which was a reply to *De Profundis*, he swung the bludgeon savagely at the corpse of poor Oscar:

> *Thou, The complete mountebank, The scented posturer. . . .*
> *Who went down the primrose path, to the thin sound of flutes,*
> *And down the Old Bailey stairs. . . .*

Crosland alleged that 'a blacker, fiercer, falser, craftier, more grovelling or more abominable piece of writing never fell from mortal pen' than *De Profundis*.

Willie then turned his pen on Ross, accusing him of foisting Wilde on the public as a penitent figure when he had actually gone from bad to worse. The time came when Ross could take no more without response, and Crosland was charged with libelling him. This time Willie, who was in and out of Charing Cross Hospital with various complaints, was fit enough to appear and acquitted himself magnificently. Once again his opponent was F. E. Smith, and Crosland set about him with vigour.

'Have you taken it upon yourself to regulate the life of Mr Ross?' asked Smith.

'Oh, no,' Crosland replied. 'I don't object to Mr Ross making a pig of himself, but what I do mind is him making a sty of the world.'

When Smith commented, 'Never mind the jury, Mr Crosland, the jury can take care of themselves,' Willie replied, 'Yes, but I want them to take care of me.'

After an eight-day trial at the Old Bailey Crosland was acquitted, to the dismay of Ross and the whole homosexual fraternity. We in the Domino Room soon knew that Willie had won, for he arrived from the court, having imbibed several drinks on the way, with bunches of flowers for the two ladies behind the bar, as was his custom when he was in a particularly good humour. Ross, however, was by no means finished.

Bosie, as was his wont, had stayed out of England, in France, once Crosland was arrested but thought it safe to return after his friend had been acquitted. He was very surprised to find himself arrested for criminal libel against Ross, though once he had recovered from the shock he welcomed the challenge. He was, however, shattered to find himself committed to Brixton prison for five days, while on remand, because bail had been refused, and so experienced a mild taste of Oscar's medicine.

His trial took place in November 1914, after war had broken out, and he was able to call fourteen witnesses to testify to Ross's homosexual habits. The most damaging of these was Inspector West of Scotland Yard, and previously of Vine Street, who told the court that he knew Ross to be a regular procurer of male prostitutes and an habitual associate of sodomites. Out of the jury of twelve only one was opposed to a verdict against Ross, even though men as eminent as H. G. Wells had given evidence on his behalf. Because a verdict had to be unanimous, the case was abandoned pending a new trial with a new judge and jury. The other eleven felt so strongly about this that a delegation, including the foreman, waited outside the court to apologize to Bosie. On advice from his lawyers, Ross decided to withdraw his charge and abandon the proceedings. Douglas agreed only after Ross paid all his expenses, which was a damning admission of guilt and a public triumph for Bosie.

Though their mutual enemy had been defeated, the trial caused another bitter break between Douglas and Crosland, and in this case all my sympathies were with Bosie, as I heard him describe Willie's unforgivable behaviour.

'I asked Crosland to appear as a witness and give evidence for me because there were many things he knew which he had not been able to use in his own trial. What do you think he said? First he bluntly refused to help, then said he would give evidence if I would pay him £50! I told him to go to hell. I would rather have gone to prison than give money to that knave, who is the reincarnation of Ancient Pistol and basely deserted me when he thought there were no more pickings.'

In the usual manner of their fall-outs Bosie attacked Crosland with a poem, which was written in answer to the epitaph Willie had written for himself, beginning:

> *If I should be in England's thought,*
> *After I die. . . .*

and which I have already recorded. Douglas's clever reply ran as follows:

> *What was there, tell me, that you might have sold*
> *And did not sell?*
> *What secret was there that you might have told*
> *And did not tell?*
> *And did you smooth with NO convenient gold*
> *Your path to Hell?*

It was well said, but of course it was not to be the end of the feud. Crosland retaliated in a subtle way by publishing a book entirely devoted to the sonnet and how to write it, with examples from England's greatest sonneteers. Though I know that he regarded Douglas as an outstanding exponent of that particular form of poetry, and had published some of his best works in his literary magazines, he avoided mentioning any of them. And, as usual when they quarrelled Crosland fell back on the fact that Douglas was a Scotsman, for he affected to hate all that was Scottish. 'Where the carcase is, there the vulture will be; and where there is a soft job, of obvious pickings, there you will find a Scotch man. . . .'

What a pair they were! Even after that monumental breakdown of their friendship they were to make it up and collaborate yet again, but their relationship had suffered irreparable damage. My observations have taught me that old friendships are rather like old houses. When the dilapidations become too great they are beyond sensible restoration.

After the collapse of the trial Ross, who had been given an officially paid position by Asquith, the Prime Minister, as assessor of picture valuations – he ran a small art gallery in Bury Street at the time – had to resign the post. But many of his friends, including Asquith's wife, Margot, stood by him and raised a subscription and a 'testimonial' for him; several famous literary figures, such as Shaw and H. G. Wells, were associated with it. In spite of his disgrace Ross was even allowed to continue as a member of the Reform Club, which duly received this verse from Bosie, which I first heard read out in the Domino Room:

> *The question finds the Wilde clique at a loss,*
> *The controversy's raising quite a storm.*
> *Is the Reform reforming Robert Ross?*
> *Or Robert Ross reforming the Reform?*

I must say, for me to hear Bosie referring to the 'Wilde clique', of which he had once been the central figure, was to hear a quite astonishing expression of self-delusion. But by that time Bosie was referring to the former friend he had idolized as 'that filthy beast'.

Ross continued in his peculiar ways, occasionally putting in an appearance in the Domino Room, since his picture gallery was so close by, and looking more and more vicious as he aged, but he did not last long. In October 1918 he was found dead, aged fifty, in Half Moon Street, not far from Shepherd Market, which has always been a haunt of homosexuals and prostitutes, as it is to this day.

Poor Robbie! He did some good things, the best being to take his responsibility as Wilde's literary executor so seriously that he rescued the estate from bankruptcy, paying off all the creditors, with interest, from the continuing royalties on Oscar's works. And what a dreadful way to end: 'Found dead'. I can think of no coroner's verdict more poignant. It usually marks the death of a very lonely man. Now I have fears that this will be my fate, as I wait in what Crosland called, as he beat his bronchitic chest with his fist, 'the dark ante-room of death', as indeed it could have been at any time, for while I numbered my friends by the dozen none of them, apart from Jules and my landlady Mrs Moffat, who have long been dead, knew me.

27

JOKER IN A PECULIAR PACK

It was always fascinating to watch a new coterie developing in the Domino Room. Usually it formed around one commanding personality, as the Decadents had formed around Oscar Wilde, and the Bohemians around Augustus John. The Bloomsburyites, who congealed in 1908 or thereabouts, were the first to form around a family – two sisters and a brother with the surname Stephen.

The elder girl, Vanessa, who was the prettier by my standards, was apparently a competent painter, though I cannot recall seeing her work. She married a man called Clive Bell and the two became rather notorious, even in Café Royal society, for the freedom they allowed each other to enjoy sexual affairs. (Curiously, though such an arrangement was regarded as being permissible for the aristocracy it was not so for the middle class, to which the Stephens belonged.) The younger sister, who had gaunt, though arresting, features recalling the women in pictures by the artist Sir Edward Burne-Jones, himself a Café Royal 'regular', was named Virginia. A few years later, in 1912, she was to marry Leonard Woolf, and become world-renowned as a novelist. The brother, Adrian, stood out in any crowd because he must be six feet five inches in height (I think he is still alive as I write). I remember seeing him in the Domino Room first with Horace de Vere Cole, the arch practical joker, and it may have been he who first brought the sisters there. Adrian was very argumentative and witty in a sardonic and often hurtful way.

I believe the Bloomsbury set originally derived its name from the house in Gordon Square in Bloomsbury where the Stephens lived and entertained their friends for evenings of argument about literature, art, women's suffrage and sex, almost making a profession of being 'intellectuals'. Happily they spilled over quite frequently into the Domino Room and provided me with many absorbing occasions. I always felt that the group was rather pretentious, even though talented, but in time several of them became really famous.

In addition to Virginia Woolf and her husband Leonard there were Lytton Strachey, with his books like *Eminent Victorians*, Roger Fry, a moderate painter but distinguished as an art critic, and regarded in the Domino Room as the leader of the Bloomsbury group, Duncan Grant, a more successful painter, Desmond MacCarthy, who talked big about what he was to achieve as a novelist but was to be limited to literary criticism, and the more productive writer E. M. Forster. There was also something of an odd man out, who was to achieve historic distinction and riches as an economist – Maynard Keynes, whose name I thought at first was Canes, for that was how he pronounced it.

Horace de Vere Cole, a good-looking Irishman of private means and a matchless flow of profanity, was never a member of the Bloomsbury set, but he did involve some of them in his most audacious hoax that was to become a classic for all time. I was one of the very few people who could have forestalled it, because I overheard the chief conspirators plotting it in the Domino Room, but it was too good a jape to prevent, though I gave them no hope of success.

One cold January day in 1910 Cole, an old Etonian who claimed descent from Old King Cole, and who had his regular table rather distant from the ones near the centre of the room patronized by the Bloomsbury set, was in whispered conversation with Adrian Stephen and another man whom I had never seen before, called Tudor something-or-other. Their initial conversation reminded me that Cole had carried off a splendid gag while he was at Cambridge University, some years earlier, when he had disguised himself as a senior member of the family of the Sultan of Zanzibar, paying a ceremonial visit to Cambridge. With a few friends, also in disguise, he had brilliantly organized the hoax so that they were received in style by the Mayor at the Guildhall, were then shown round some of the colleges and finally seen off in splendour at the railway station. I remembered the details because the newspapers carried full accounts at the time. Normally the perpetrators of such a successful hoax keep the joke to themselves, if only to avoid repercussions, but to the extraordinary Cole full publicity was part of the fun, and he had told the *Daily Mail* about it.

That day in the Domino Room I learned that Adrian Stephen had been one of the Zanzibar hoaxers and was keen to be involved in the new conspiracy.

'I'm sick of hearing these damned admirals boasting about their new battleship,' Cole said. 'It's time they were brought down to size.'

'What do you propose?' Adrian asked. 'Sink her?'

'Something a little more refined. We should repeat the Zanzibar coup. I suggest that if we can get another half dozen trusties to form a retinue we could hoax the admirals into receiving us with full honours and then be shown all over the ship.'

'Not from Zanzibar again?' Tudor asked.

'No, from Abyssinia. It's got to be some country where no Navy man is likely to know the lingo. One of us will be the Emperor of Abyssinia, "The conquering Lion of Judah" himself.'

'It can't be me, I'm too tall,' Adrian said.

'No. I have Anthony Buxton in mind.'

'Yes, he could carry it off. But if it has to be HMS *Dreadnought* I don't see how I can come at all.'

'Why not?' Cole snapped.

'Because the commanding officer, Willer Fisher, is my cousin.'

'Oh God! Then you certainly can't come.'

By this time Adrian was smiling broadly. 'Willie's a silly old sod. I'm sure I could get away with it. I find the prospect even more entrancing.'

Cole did not seem keen, but had already done so much planning that he was loath to abandon the project.

'What part are you going to play?' Tudor asked him.

'I shall be the man from the Foreign Office, making sure that protocol is observed and the Emperor is properly received. With luck we might get a twenty-one-gun salute.'

'Yes, and you might be in front of the guns if they rumble you,' Tudor warned. 'The least they would do would be to throw you overboard, and that puts me out because I can't swim a stroke.'

'You don't have to be there, Tudor,' Cole said. 'All I want you to do is to send a telegram from the Foreign Office to the Commander-in-Chief Home Fleet. I'll draft it in a way that will sound official.'

Tudor shrugged resignedly, as though happy to be relieved of the risk of a ducking or worse.

'What date have you in mind?' Adrian asked.

'The Navy will have to make the final decision, but it must be early in February because they'll be told the Emperor is only in England for a fortnight.'

I could not help but admire their courage, for I knew Cole well enough to be sure that the jape would be given the widest publicity if it succeeded and then the sparks would fly. Making a fool of the Mayor of Cambridge was one thing. Making a fool of the Royal Navy was quite another.

I heard no more of the plot until 11 February, when the *Daily Mirror* and the *Daily Express* were full of the story of how Cole and his cronies had completely bamboozled the Admirals and secured access to the most secret parts of HMS *Dreadnought*. There were pictures of Cole in his Foreign Office top hat and winged collar. There was the heavily bearded 'Emperor' in robes hired from a theatrical costumier, three other turbaned figures with blackened faces, and the lanky Adrian, falsely bearded and in bowler hat, acting the part of Foreign Office interpreter.

The reports revealed that the 'Emperor' and his party had been met by naval officers at Weymouth railway station and conducted through waiting spectators, including press photographers, to a steam launch which ferried them to the great warship. There the 'Emperor' inspected a guard of honour, was shown all over the ship and then escorted back to the station. A twenty-one-gun salute had been offered but the 'Emperor' had declined it. The news that William Fisher, the flag officer, had been introduced to his own

cousin, Adrian, without recognizing him while he spoke the gibber-
ish which had passed for Abyssinian was bad enough. But it turned
out that the smallest of the turbaned and bearded figures was a
woman – none other than Virginia Stephen, who had stood in for a
man who had been unable to take part. Claiming to be 'Ras Mandax',
she too had shaken hands with her cousin without being recognized.

The Stephens claimed to be horrified when they read the newspaper accounts, for it had been agreed that there should be no
publicity which would reveal the hoax. But, as I had anticipated,
Cole had been unable to resist gilding the gingerbread even if he had
ever had any intention of keeping quiet. The public and press
reaction varied from hilarity to fury. The papers kept the story going
for days with demands for the fullest inquiries into naval security.
Then MPs, always anxious to get their names into print, asked
questions in Parliament, which embarrassed the First Lord of the
Admiralty, the Sea Lords and the government.

When it was realized that no official action against the culprits was
in prospect because it would have prolonged the publicity, the Navy
decided to take its own revenge. A group of young officers were
detailed to kidnap the hoaxers and chastise them with a cane. They
would have been very foolish to try to seize Cole, who was as quick
with his fists as any man I ever saw, and the only one they were able to
abduct was Duncan Grant, the painter, who had been one of the
'Abyssinians'. It seems that they took him to Hampstead Heath,
but as he was a pacifist he offered no resistance, so they let him
go.

This was to be by no means the last of Horace Cole's hoaxes, as my
readers will see. But I never saw him again in the company of the
Bloomsbury set. He made no pretence at being an intellectual and his
brash, loud manner seemed to irritate Virginia, whom I once heard
being extremely rude to him. Of course Virginia could be rude to
anybody, especially if she happened to be approaching one of her
periods of mental instability, which some of her friends called frank
insanity, when she would be highly excitable and wild-eyed. During
these sad periods, when she would be absent from the Café for months
on end, and would later refer to openly as 'the last time I was off my
head', her friends and relations would talk to each other about the
grave danger that she might take her own life. From them I learned
that when quite young she had made a half-hearted attempt to
commit suicide and her long-suffering husband, Leonard, endured
agonies of anxiety about the danger of a further effort.

As I heard him say many times, he believed that Virginia was a genius – again that overworked word. But during the time of which I am now writing, 1910 and before, while she was still Virginia Stephen, she had done little more than write short articles and reviews. Her full-lipped and sensuous-looking sister Vanessa was the one who was talked about – as the centre of licentiousness attached to the name of the Bloomsbury set. This, I have little doubt, was exaggerated, but was not helped when a couple of years later she and Virginia went to some ball with so little on that they were described as 'almost naked'. I heard Cole claim that Vanessa was prepared to copulate in public at parties to demonstrate her belief in sexual freedom, her favourite partner for this highly popular performance being Maynard Keynes, who was later to urge the Liberal Party to make sexual liberty part of its election programme. I could never find out if this was true or not but Keynes, with his dark moustache, thick lips and receding hair somehow looked lecherous enough, a bit like one of those Greek satyrs, I used to think.

It was often said that Keynes was, in fact, bisexual and that Duncan Grant had been one of his lovers – against fierce competition from Lytton Strachey! Grant, I believe, was totally homosexual, and I used to see him in the Domino Room with many different men with whom he was on such affectionate terms that they would sometimes kiss him in public. Still, it was rumoured that he had managed to sire a daughter by Vanessa Bell.

Having listened to people like Sir Ray Lankester and Julian Huxley, Aldous's elder brother, discussing such matters I suspect that we are all bisexual to some extent. All men have some female characteristics and all women some male. In people like Keynes, the female inclinations may be exaggerated, the reverse situation being the case in lesbians like Virginia Woolf, who had several 'affairs' with women, including one which became notorious with a woman called Vita Sackville-West. What is not in doubt is that sexually the Bloomsbury set were a deviant lot. I have already mentioned some of the homosexuals of whom Lytton Strachey, he of the straggly beard and the ear-rings, was the most blatant. There was also E. M. Forster, though he was more secret about his peculiarity. Virginia openly admitted her lesbian tendencies, being as much 'in love' with other women as Oscar was with Bosie. Roger Fry – Rogier de la Friture, as he was known in the Domino Room – who was normal enough, had a long affair with Vanessa while she was still married to Clive Bell, who had a succession of mistresses.

If Horace Cole was excluded from the Bloomsbury set, which he probably detested, he was compensated by a firm and lasting friendship with Augustus John, though, as might be expected with two such fiery characters, there were quarrels and occasional punch-ups. I think they first became acquainted in the Domino Room, and when they were both drunk in a taxi had gone through the ritual of making themselves blood brothers. Cole had made a small incision in his palm, but Augustus had stabbed his leg deeply with the knife, producing so much blood that the cabby was furious when he saw the mess. I noticed that John walked with a limp for some time, and he explained that the blood ritual had been the reason.

John was vastly amused, as we all were, by the occasion when Cole had gone to great trouble to discover the addresses of a number of people whose name ended in 'bottom' and invited them to a banquet, sadly not at the Café Royal. When their host failed to appear, they were driven to introduce themselves and their wives to each other: 'My name is Winterbottom. . . .' 'Happy to meet you, mine is Ramsbottom. . . .' and so on through Shufflebottom, Higginbottom, Sidebottom, Rowbottom . . . it was said that Cole had even discovered a Jellibottom! Though Cole was unable to witness the scene, he must have been waiting in lonely glee for the moment when dinner was finally served and his guests discovered that the only dish was rump steak. Presumably he thought the bill cheap at the price.

Augustus was far from amused, however, at another prank by Cole, who had surreptitiously taken some of John's sketches from his studio and then set them up for sale outside the National Gallery in Trafalgar Square. He sat by them all day, though regrettably not disguised as John, and managed to sell only one or two for a few pennies. He handed the money over to John, claiming that it must be the 'true market value' of his work.

It was just as well that Cole managed to retain John's friendship, because he came to be shunned by most other people in the Domino Room. He was regarded not only as a bore but as too ready with his fists, taking any remark as justification for a punch on the nose. There were rare occasions, however, when the opportunity for a joke overcame his belligerence. The most vivid of these occurred after Cole's hair, which he had allowed to grow into something of a mane, had turned white, along with his upswept moustache. He had been trying to provoke by personal remarks an artist he did not like, and eventually the poor man was taunted into quoting from Shakespeare: 'How ill white hairs become a fool and jester!'

I was waiting for the thump or worse, for Cole had developed the habit of flashing a Corsican dagger, which I always feared he might use, so ungovernable was his temper. Instead he thought for a moment, bowed, as though admitting defeat, and left the building. About an hour later he strode up to the artist with all eyes on him. He had dyed his hair and moustache brilliant vermilion.

'Better?' he asked. Then he sat down at his table and ordered a drink.

Horace Cole was not certifiably mad, but Augustus John's other crony at this time definitely was. This was Arthur Symons, the versifier who talked obsessively about sex but, unlike John, did not seem to do much about it. He had gone mad while living in Italy and had to reside in an asylum when he returned to England. John believed that Symons had only a short time to live, so he did all he could to make the rest of his life bearable by securing permission for him to visit his studio two or three times a week. The visit to the studio was only a blind, though, for the cab picked up John and the two of them then came to the Domino Room, where they would sit drinking absinthe for two or three hours of an evening.

Some time before he went mad Symons had brought off a major literary coup by discovering some of the missing memoirs of Casanova and several thousand of his letters, some in Venice, the rest in a castle in Bohemia. Augustus delighted in talking about the great lover, being made in similar mould. As an artist he was fascinated by Casanova's looks as demonstrating fashion changes in masculine beauty. Casanova had a sharply sloping forehead and somewhat receding chin – to which features I can lay some claim – and while these were considered handsome and aristocratic then, now they are regarded as merely 'weak'.

When I saw Symons after his sojourn in Italy I was convinced that his time must indeed be short. His hair, always sparse, was an unhealthy-looking grey, and the skin was tightly stretched over his high forehead and sharp-edged, aquiline nose. But the absinthe treatment succeeded where the doctors had failed. He recovered his sanity, lived a further thirty-six years, and was to write a splendid essay called 'The Café Royal', containing a poem in which he remembered 'the hot nights and the heated noons' and 'those rare and radiant conversations'.

Augustus John was the right age to have belonged to the Bloomsbury group, but their pretentious conversations would not have appealed to him. There was, however, a link with them through a strange person who insinuated herself into the lives of many of the Domino Room habitués – Lady Ottoline Morrell. This formidable lady, a close relative of the Duke of Portland, was rich in her own right, and presumably her husband, Philip Morrell, a Liberal MP, also had money. Apart from a large house in Bloomsbury (Bedford Square and, later, Gower Street) they had a beautiful manor house in Oxfordshire and both places seem to have been open houses for intellectuals and self-styled intellectuals. I suppose she was trying to re-establish the old days of the *salons*, which figure so much in literature.

The entire Bloomsbury set were among her frequent guests, and as a result I saw her several times in the Domino Room in the company of people like Roger Fry, Lytton Strachey and Vanessa Bell. Apart from her stature and distinctive walk she attracted attention through her bizarre dress. Sometimes she appeared in the attire of a Cossack or looking like some oriental princess, but the garb most certain to set the street urchins shouting after her was what I called her 'Bo Peep' outfit, which included a large floppy hat and yellow stockings with black cross-garters. She was very tall and angular with an over-prominent nose and heavy lower jaw, the overall appearance reminding me of a giraffe. She also had mahogany-red hair, accentuated by her white make-up and reminding me of one of Frank Harris's coarser axioms – 'There's always something doing with a red-haired woman.' Certainly the voracious Augustus John found this to be so, though in his case it seems she did the chasing. As usual they had their quarrels, but she remained one of his mistresses, on and off, for many years. She also had other lovers, including the philosopher Bertrand Russell and the painter Henry Lamb, whose wife Euphemia became one of Augustus's mistress-models. Talk about musical beds!

As my readers will see, I was to hear much about Lady Ottoline from the lips of her many friends, some of it scandalous, and it was a pity that she so rarely came into the Domino Room for she was cast in the mould of its great eccentrics with her theatrical dress, her loud, snorting laugh and her general behaviour – though perhaps she was one of those who tried too hard to be a 'character'. She befriended many a young writer such as D. H. Lawrence and Aldous Huxley, but they tended to ridicule her behind her back, calling her 'The Ott', and to satirize her in their books. There is little gratitude in this life and I suppose one should not expect it. We all dislike being beholden to anyone else.

In November of 1910 we Café Royalites enjoyed some comic relief by visiting the so-called Post-Impressionist Exhibition staged by one of our comrades-in-conversation, Roger Fry, the painter and art critic, then in his early forties. With what turned out to be considerable courage he staged an exhibition of paintings by an avant-garde group of French artists whom he called the Post-Impressionists. There was so much excited talk about it in advance in the Domino Room, after Fry had been to Paris to select the pictures, that I decided to go and see it on the day it opened at the Grafton Galleries in Bond Street.

The exhibits were all by artists of whom I had never heard — Gauguin, Cézanne, Signac, Van Gogh, who didn't sound French, Matisse and Picasso. They were referred to in the catalogue as paintings, but to me they were appalling daubs of the kind which could have been done by a child, and a backward child at that. One picture by Cézanne showed a group of bathers who looked like monstrous Stone Age people, while another, by Van Gogh, was of a wild, half-witted yokel with a flower instead of a straw in his mouth. I quickly found that I was not alone in my opinion that this was another example of artists 'throwing a pot of paint at the public's face'. Most of the visitors were highly amused by them, a few in uncontrollable fits of laughter as they moved from canvas to canvas. But many were angry, brandishing their canes at the canvases, and claiming that the exhibition was a swindle and a waste of their time.

The weirdest of all the paintings were by the man Van Gogh, who turned out to be a Dutchman. There was one large so-called painting of chrysanthemums in which the paint stood out from the canvas in great ridges. One of the guides explained that it had been applied not with a brush but with a knife. Fancy painting with a knife! What next? I wasn't surprised when I heard later that this artist had cut off his ear and sent it wrapped up to some girl who had remarked on it. Then there was a man called Seurat whose pictures were made up of countless thousands of tiny dots of paint, alleged to give the picture 'luminosity'. As for Gauguin and Matisse, they had no concept of perspective whatever. Their figures were flat, crude and out of all proportion.

Fry, who was in charge, sat at a table in rough tweeds, looking on imperturbably through small-lensed glasses, his dry, staring hair parted in the middle, accepting the censures with a wide-mouthed smile. He tried to explain that these men were 'primitives' and had to be judged in that light, but it seemed to me to be just an excuse for lack of craftsmanship. Considering the hostility of the reception, Fry remained remarkably composed, but it was not just the general public who considered his exhibition to be a bad joke. Accepted authorities like Professor Henry Tonks of the Slade School, who thereafter called supporters of the Post-Impressionists 'the Roger Fry rabble', loathed it. So did artists as advanced as Epstein. Augustus John had a different reason for concern: his own exhibition at the Chenil Gallery was overshadowed by the row centred on the Grafton. As for the newspapers, they said that the artists concerned must be wrong in the head. Writing in the *Morning Post*, Robert Ross called them lunatics, but I noticed that some of the art critics kept their options open, avoiding committing themselves in the cowardly way they adopt when they think that time might prove them wrong if they give a firm opinion.

I cannot remember any art exhibition ever causing such public reaction, and inevitably hundreds flocked to it if only for a laugh. It was very much a case of bad publicity being better than no publicity at all, and when it was over I heard Roger say that he was very well satisfied as he had put these new painters on the English map, even though it had made him the most hated man in the art world for 'undermining values'. He was even more satisfied a few years later when the National Gallery, the Tate and others began to buy Post-Impressionist paintings. Now, of course, works by Cézanne, Gauguin and even Van Gogh command huge prices. I still can't understand why. As for Picasso, he must surely get a belly laugh every time some fool pays good money for one of his insane dissections of the human body.

Naturally, Roger, who stayed in our company on and off until his death in 1934, pointed out that his judgement had been right all along, and it came to be accepted that he had changed the trend of art appreciation in England. He wrote a great deal, and as a result was widely used by millionaires to vet pictures they wanted to buy. In this context I heard him tell an engaging human story to his friend Logan Pearsall-Smith, a very interesting man in his own right. Fry had gone to Vienna to advise a Count who needed to sell off some of his inherited paintings to pay debts.

'As the Count took me round the masterpieces I could see that, almost without exception, they were copies or outright fakes. His face got longer and longer as I took him through the list. Then, with wonderful old-world charm, he told me that he had always suspected that the paintings were not genuine and thanked me for confirming his judgement.'

Poor Roger – he needed some luck for his private life had been tragic. Soon after his marriage in 1896 his wife had become insane and, while he did everything he could for her, she eventually had to go back to the asylum. As I was to observe, he found much-needed solace with Vanessa Bell, for Roger's poor, mad wife was to outlive him.

28

TYRANNY BY SELF-TORTURE

It was in the autumn of 1911 that I first clapped eyes on a young man who was to become a fairly regular attender of the Domino Room, and was without question the most tortured person I have ever encountered. His name was John Middleton Murry and he would eventually make a considerable reputation as a 'man of letters'. On that day, however, when he had been invited to lunch by Frank Harris, he had little to say for himself, being obviously captivated by the older man whom he had met the day before in a bookshop off St Martin's Lane run by another Domino Room customer, Dan Rider.

Though he could not be more than twenty-two Murry had a face which looked as though it had been saddened by all the cares in the world, as it was destined to be. His chin seemed strong enough but his large eyes stared as though they looked in on him instead of out into the world, his nose was slightly curved on one side, and his dry-looking hair was already thinning. He had a large mouth which smiled widely but half-heartedly, 'like a split in a custard', said Willie Crosland, who disliked him on sight. Murry was editing a little magazine called *Rhythm*, so Harris was immediately interested, especially as some promising new writers were contributing to it.

I watched with fascination as Harris went out of his way to impress this pale and frail young man in his ill-fitting suit, going through the whole gamut of name-dropping, and hailing well-known personages in between being rude to the waiters and calling imperiously for the manager. He ended his act by paying the bill with a slip of paper and getting three crisp, white fivers as change, an event which seemed to impress Murry beyond anything the great talker had said.

'Between us we could build *Rhythm* into a rival for the *English Review*,' Harris averred.

The conversation then passed to Murry's financial circumstances, which were very poor. He also needed help for an emotional problem which was interfering with his attempts to work.

'I had a long and very serious love affair with a French girl in Paris – serious for me,' Murry explained with a pained expression. 'I had to come back to England and I'm still sick – and I mean physically sick – with love for her.'

'And you have no intention of returning to her?' Harris asked.

'I can't while I am editing *Rhythm*.'

'Then the solution is very simple. You are much too young to have known Ernest Dowson, but you must have read his poem about Cynara, the one based on a quotation from one of Horace's Odes?'

'I have heard of it, but I have not read it.'

'Then you should, young man, you should. I was the first to hear parts of it when Dowson recited them to me in this very room:

> *I cried for madder music and for stronger wine,*
> *But when the feast is finished and the lamps expire*
> *Then falls thy shadow, Cynara. The night is thine.*
> *Yea, hungry for the lips of my desire:*
> *I have been faithful to thee, Cynara, in my fashion.*

'Marvellous lines and they contain the solution to your problem. You break the spell of the girl in Paris by going to bed with another woman – to get her out of your system. I've done it myself many times. It almost always works.'

Whether the wide-eyed and rather horrified Murry took any further advice I do not know, but shortly afterwards when he visited the Café Royal he limited himself to soft drinks. He had done what Harris said and caught the clap for his pains!

Later that year he appeared in the Domino Room with a girl I had seen before at the table of A. R. Orage, the editor of the magazine *New Age*, which attracted some very able writers, including her. Her name was Katherine Mansfield, but Murry called her 'Wig' while she called him 'Bogey'. Their frequent conversations over two cups of coffee, which they literally took hours to drink, being unable to afford more, fascinated me, for I never saw a couple so much in love yet so intent on destroying each other.

Katherine, whose maiden name had been Beauchamp, was separated from her husband who refused to divorce her, so she and Murry were living together. She was attractive in a most unusual way. She was quite small and slim with a face like a Meissen mask behind which, one sensed, there lurked violent passion, though when she spoke it was very quietly and with minimum movement of the mask. She had bobbed her dark hair before that style became fashionable, and combed her fringe very neatly down her forehead. Unlike so many of the Domino Room literary ladies, she was altogether neat in her appearance, wearing unfashionably short skirts which showed off her rather good legs and, perhaps, demonstrated her pro-feminist feelings. Both Murry and Katherine seemed incapable of saying anything without dissecting it for hidden meanings and significances, which may not have been there.

'Do you ever feel you have been yourself?' she would ask intensely.

'Never. I think there's no way I could communicate with myself.'

As a result of such mind-searchings Murry was always looking for the 'real Katherine' and she was looking for the 'real Jack'. While utterly convinced that they were deeply in love, they were forever 'reacting away from each other' so that she would leave him or he would leave her. Then the one who was left in London would come into the Domino Room with some friend bewailing the situation, the 'desolation', the 'futility of life' and what they called the 'human predicament', occasioned by man's uniqueness in being the only creature to realize he must die and to experience doubt about his purpose. They talked as though most people go through life in a state of fear, yet my observations suggest that the human animal is very difficult to frighten, compared with any other. The Murrys, as they were known, talked too much and did too little. If only they had taken note of Bernard Shaw's wise dictum, as I did, that '. . . the secret of being miserable is to have time to bother about whether you are happy or not'.

They would wail about feeling rootless but never stay long enough in one place to put any down. I remember one particular occasion early in 1915 when, war or no war, Katherine had managed to get a permit to go to Paris to live with some Frenchman and was being quite open about it. She was wildly excited about leaving Murry, but in no time she was wanting to come back, and Murry was 'analysing' whether it was the 'real Katherine' who would be returning and, if not, should he tell her to stay where she was. Even in the rare intervals when things went right for them she was always looking for what she called 'the snail under the leaf', while his world was always 'falling to pieces'. I suppose the truth was that she was looking for a real man and Murry wasn't one. He let her wear the trousers when maybe she yearned for a master.

Frankly I soon became bored with their tortured performance, for they seemed to be forever sensing the overwhelming significance of things which seemed self-evident and would be taken by mentally healthy people in their stride. I sensed that all the self-analysis signified nothing save disaster and they were indeed headed for tragedy, though they were eventually to enjoy a few years of marriage, if, in fact, they truly enjoyed anything.

If their behaviour was an expression of true love, then I thank God that I have been preserved from it. I have been lonely, at nights, but solitude has advantages. One of them was neatly expressed by my Domino Room friend, Bill Davies the 'Supertramp':

> *Death can play one game with me*
> *If I do live alone;*
> *He cannot strike me a foul blow*
> *Through a beloved one.*

Among the earliest friends of the Murrys in the Café Royal was another self-tortured character, the egomaniac D. H. Lawrence, with various members of his small circle. Lawrence, who was forever having appalling quarrels with his wife and fell out with one friend after another, accusing them of treachery unless their devotion to him was full-time, was another man who seemed to spend his conversational life being quite staggered by glimpses of the obvious, as though such things had never been realized by anyone before. Such people were extreme examples, but they highlighted what to me is the artificiality and half-world nature of so much of the literary and artistic life. Books and talk about books are not life; they are only guides to life.

Meanwhile, having already mentioned Orage, I should at this juncture say a little more about him, for he and some of his coterie remained loyal to the Domino Room for many years. Orage, whose Christian name was Alfred but, like Wells, was always known by his initials, A. R., was a tough-looking and tough-speaking Yorkshireman. He did not look a bit like an 'intellectual', yet there were many, including Katherine Mansfield, who were grateful to him for the constructive help he was able to give them about the craft of writing. Bernard Shaw, who with others had helped him to buy *New Age* as a platform for Socialist ideas, thought him a quite outstanding editor and he certainly had the capacity to draw talent towards him. When he shambled towards his special table – his walk reminded me of Oscar's – it was to join young men like Richard Aldington, Herbert Read, Ezra Pound and T. E. Hulme, who were all to make their mark. Tall, dark and slim in those days, he usually wore a bright red tie to advertise his extreme beliefs.

'Eliminate private property and you will abolish poverty,' was the kind of maxim which he would fire off to generate a political discussion with friends like Cecil Chesterton and his brother G. K. who, with Belloc, would argue that Orage's idea of Socialism spelled tyranny over rich and poor alike. How I longed, sometimes, to give them my view, reinforced by my observations over so many years, that most people, however poor, become conservatives as soon as they have something to conserve!

Orage would have such violent arguments with T. E. Hulme that strangers on nearby tables felt sure it must end in a fight, though it never did. Hulme, a big, Teutonic-looking man, with greying fair hair, was a mathematician who had turned his sharp mind to the problems of philosophy and also wrote poetry. He was an admirer and friend of the elegant Ezra Pound and they were often together, either at Hulme's table or at Orage's. Hulme was a man of many parts, but his strangest characteristic was the suddenness with which he would require sexual relief and his openness about it. On one occasion he interrupted a serious philosophical discussion by pulling out his watch and declaring, 'I have a pressing engagement.' He then walked out of the Domino Room, to return about twenty minutes later, mopping his brow.

'I've never copulated in a more uncomfortable place,' he said as he sat down.

'Than where?' Pound asked, in his strong Philadelphia accent.

'Than on the steel emergency stairs at Piccadilly Tube Station.'

He would make such remarks even in front of women, and two were present when he told a story of how he had been apprehended by a policeman while urinating in the street in Soho.

'I looked at the copper disdainfully and said "Do you realize that you are addressing a member of the middle class?"'

'"Beg pardon, sir," the constable replied, touching his hat as he walked away.'

For a few years there was usually one woman at Orage's table – a woman I greatly disliked. This was his mistress Beatrice Hastings, who also wrote articles for *New Age*. He was fortunate that he never married her, but it would have been fitting in one respect: her name would have become Orage which, I am told, means 'thunderstorm' in French. She was certainly tempestuous, almost to the point of madness, I would say. I had a feeling that she hated men and would rather have indulged in a lesbian affair with Katherine Mansfield.

Beatrice was physically attractive, but her ideas, which Orage allowed her to expound in *New Age*, were obscene. She regarded the bearing of children as an imposition forced on women by men, and wanted the Government to give them legal protection against it! I suppose that this created controversy and was good for sales, but it did not make much sense. It was no surprise to me to learn that, after moving to Paris, where she lived with various artists, Beatrice became a hopeless alcoholic and eventually committed suicide.

What sorry people so many of these 'intellectuals' were! In my experience intellectualism seems to hold more hazards to health than any other profession! How much more fortunate were those who could place their art in reasonable perspective in the ranging landscape of life, as Shakespeare did, a down-to-earth situation expressed in the Domino Room, only half in jest, as 'Art for art's sake! Money for God's sake!'

Orage was not a heavy drinker, but he suffered from another character weakness from which highly intelligent people ought to be immune. This was gullibility. He was always searching for 'the meaning of life' and, as a result, came under the sway of various charlatans who claimed to have found it and may even have believed that they had. Orage was extremely susceptible to meaningless ideas like 'the psychology of the world process', 'the quest of the Absolute', the 'Cosmic' this and the 'Universal' that. Though I honestly do not count myself an intellectual, I do believe that I had a stronger defence against being deluded by words which, on analysis, often mean nothing. What still surprises me most about highly intelligent people is their belief that any proposition should be accepted until it can be disproved. Surely the proper approach is to avoid wasting time on ideas until there is some worthwhile evidence for them. It was because so many, like Orage, took the other view that they were so susceptible to buying 'gold bricks' in the form of ideas which really made no sense. Over the years I have trained myself to ask what words really mean because I have learned that they can be so deceptive, exerting their own tyranny over the mind susceptible to them. To be able to give something a name, say a few words about it or quote someone else's words, as self-styled intellectuals are fond of doing, does not mean that one *knows* something about it. All this seems obvious, yet I can testify that intelligence is no sure defence against the persuasive con-man, whether in the world of money or ideas.

I labour this point in connection with Orage because it led him to abandon *New Age* after fifteen years to become a disciple of a Greek Armenian from Russia called Gurdjieff. This extraordinary-looking creature, whose photograph I have seen, had an 'Institute' near Paris and somehow attracted money to send 'disciples' like Orage to America and elsewhere to preach his fatuous 'gospel'. Not only did this take Orage and his interesting circle away from the Domino Room – he did not return to England until 1930, by which time he had realized the fallacy of Gurdjieff's ideas – but it also hastened the death of Katherine Mansfield, as I shall record.

29

A LEAVENING OF YOUNG LADIES

Among the young ladies who saved the Domino Room from becoming like another male-dominated club none was more lively or more charming than the young artist Nina Hamnett, who seemed to be popular with other artists of all ages. I think I had seen her in the Café somewhat earlier with Aleister Crowley, with whom she was eventually to have a sensational legal wrangle, but my diary first notes her late in 1912 in the company of a sculptor called Henri Gaudier-Brzeska. I had heard John Middleton Murry, a friend of his until they fell out viciously, point out that his real name was plain Henri Gaudier, and that he was French and had changed it for a reason I was to learn later from Epstein, who also knew him.

Henri, who was very young, and slight of build with a feeble, downy moustache and a couple of wisps of hair on his chin, looked half-starved and very shabby with frayed collars and cracked boots but, for all I knew then, this could have been part of his peculiar act, for he loudly referred to anybody who was decently dressed as 'bloody bourgeois'. In fact, it soon became apparent that he was as poor as Nina, and I recall many occasions when they sat the whole evening in most animated conversation over a couple of cups of coffee, unable to afford the crème de menthe frappé which was their favourite drink when in funds. She seemed not to care about money, and affected strange garb which she no doubt regarded as 'Bohemian' – a gaudy skirt, check coat, white stockings, men's dancing pumps and a round hat like a parson's of that day. For his part Henri regarded poverty as a virtue for an artist, believing with Jesus that wealth spoiled men of talent, and that the cold, comfortless garret with a hard chair was the most productive environment for painters and writers – not that he thought any other contemporary artist was any good!

From their early conversations I suspected that Nina Hamnett was in love with Henri, unwashed as he was, though I knew from his previous visits that he was tied up with a much older Polish lady called Sophie, whom he passed off as his sister. Henri and Sophie always seemed to be on the point of exploding and occasionally they did, even in public, screaming, cursing and shouting obscenities in Polish, French and English. From the unduly affectionate way they would subside in laughter and make up their quarrel I suspected that they were more than brother and sister, and I was right. Though she was twenty years older than Henri, and looked it with her high Slavic cheek bones, staring eyes, hair pinned tightly back and dumpy figure, they were living together and had both changed their names, hers to Brzeska, to further the pretence. For three years they were frequent visitors to the Domino Room and they will reappear in my narrative.

For her part Nina Hamnett, with her plainish looks, short hair, long legs and the trousers she sometimes wore – uncommon behaviour for women in those days, and even considered indecent – looked boyish, but there was nothing lesbian about her. I once heard her relate in detail to another man how she had gone about losing her virginity, because she felt it would help to 'liberate' her, and after that she had numerous affairs both in London and in Paris where she seemed to spend most of her time.

She loved talking about the wild parties she attended, one of which followed an evening when I remember seeing her in the company of a young man dressed most unusually for the Domino Room in white tie and tails, complete with topper which he insisted on keeping on his head. I suspect he had already been rather drunk when he had arrived with a strikingly beautiful girl, whose blonde hair contrasted with a vivid purple evening dress. Nina later related to Henri how she had gone back to the young man's splendid home in Holland Park where, after more drinks, the blonde then ordered him to take off his clothes.

'He was one of those weird masochists who get sexual gratification out of being insulted and abused in public,' Nina explained. 'Eventually he was standing in front of us with nothing on and the girl found a heavy stick and chased him round the room, thrashing him with it. I imagine she had done it before and was something of a sadist herself.'

Crosland used to say, in his Yorkshire accent, 'There's nowt so queer as folk!' I already knew that a need for flagellation was not confined to young men with more money than sense. Swinburne was addicted to it, spent a lot of money to induce people to beat him, and wasted much talent writing verses about it. Frank Harris had it right when he said, 'Every great man reveals himself in his sexual abnormalities.'

Various artists of note with whom Nina appeared in the Domino Room from time to time, like Epstein, Augustus John, Adrian Allinson, Lucien Pissarro and particularly Walter Sickert, rated her line drawings highly. But she may best be remembered for her body. Gaudier-Brzeska fashioned a nude torso of her which is now in the Victoria and Albert Museum. I have been to see it and, if it is a fair representation, I can understand why so many men were keen to see the original. Nina also posed as a nude model for artists of the Bloomsbury set.

Her band of cronies included Horace Cole, who by then had achieved lasting notoriety with what will be, perhaps, his best-remembered practical joke. With a couple of friends Cole had set up a small hut labelled LCC for London County Council, and surrounded it with poles and red warning lanterns. Near the hut he had deposited a heap of sand and a few tools including a wheelbarrow, buckets, picks, shovels and a brazier. After lighting the brazier Cole and his friends took turns digging a small hole, but most of the time they spent sitting round the brazier frying sausages and bacon and eggs. Meanwhile the traffic was so badly held up that a policeman – a real one – was directing it. The cabbies, who began to stop and jeer at Foreman Cole for doing so little and taking so long over it, intensified the traffic snarl, for Cole always responded heatedly in a Cockney voice. The knot of people leaning on the rails watching the 'workmen' devouring their enormous meals did not help either. It included Augustus John, who had been let into the secret, and myself who had overheard Cole telling him about it. John was in such fits of laughter that I feared he might give the game away, but the policeman and the other onlookers ignored him as just another crank 'Bohemian'.

For the three days that Cole was in the middle of Pall Mall nobody asked to see his credentials. Had he and his mates been more energetic they could have excavated an enormous cavern. The only reason he eventually packed up and departed, leaving the hole guarded by lanterns, was because he had become bored with the escapade. Of course Cole made sure that there was plenty of publicity, realizing that no officials were going to prosecute him, because it would make them look so slack and stupid.

The LCC brought in regulations to prevent a repeat of their embarrassment and this, I think, was the only public service ever rendered by Cole in his long, eccentric life, though the Tory Party may have rated another of his efforts in that category. This was the occasion when his resemblance to Ramsay MacDonald, the Labour Prime Minister, touched off a cry of 'Good old Ramsay!' from navvies digging up the pavement in Regent Street. According to the Café Royal commissionaire, Cole stuck his fingers in the armholes of his waistcoat, as was MacDonald's habit, and made a rousing political speech.

In a passable Scottish accent he announced: 'As I have to be honest with men like you, who are the salt of the earth, I must now confess that you made an unfortunate mistake in voting Labour. Sadly, and you can guess how hard it is for me to say it, the Labour Party is not yet ready for office. We need more experience, more administrative talent in the House of Commons. That will come. Have no doubt. But for the moment the task of good government is beyond us and in the interests of the nation, and of you who voted us in, I have to admit that the safest thing you can do at the next election is to vote us out.' Then, as perhaps some in the crowd were becoming suspicious, he called for a taxi-cab in a loud voice and shouted: 'Number 10 Downing Street and hurry!'

As usual, Cole made sure that as many people as possible heard of the escapade, and these included MacDonald himself. As Cole afterwards told his friends, he was invited to dine at No. 10 and told the Prime Minister the story. MacDonald took it well, laughed and remarked, 'No wonder I am so unpopular with certain sections of my party!'

What was Cole's motive in perpetrating these pranks, which were often expensive? Perhaps it was his expression of the yearning for some kind of immortality, or at least remembrance, which seems to be in all of us, or should I say in all the people who assembled in the Café Royal? Who knows? He may have achieved it.

Having always been subject to the delusion that, while others might die young my lifespan stretched ahead limitlessly, I was especially interested in any new coterie of young people who might keep me entertained over many years. Such a group formed itself in 1912 around a painter called Chris Nevinson from the Slade School of Art in Gower Street. An odd but pleasant-looking fellow with a bulging forehead, flattish nose and dark, crinkly hair – all of which earned him the nickname 'Bucknigger' – he was the son of the famous writer and journalist H. W. Nevinson.

Young Nevinson already dressed the Bohemian part, with the customary floppy velour hat and flowing bow tie, when he arrived with two other Slade students who were to become fixtures. They were Mark Gertler, an intense mop-haired East End Jew, of delicate build, who was possibly the most talented of the group, and Adrian Allinson, who was to paint a famous picture of the Domino Room. Allinson had the doubtful distinction of having been expelled from a good public school for preaching atheism. Gertler, on the other hand, painted rabbis and other aspects of Jewish life in Whitechapel – Jack the Ripper territory – where he lived in poor circumstances with his immigrant parents.

The three were joined a few weeks later by another artist, who was certainly talented but had an air of repressed violence behind his dark good looks as he talked of revolution. This was John Currie, who spoke in such a broad Lancastrian accent that I could detect that he was from the North. I often spotted him slipping a Café Royal knife or spoon into his pocket and nearly warned Jules about it, but did not want to cause trouble or to break up the promising group.

Naturally these boys attracted girls, two of whom were Slade students, Dora Carrington and the Hon. Dorothy Brett. The other, who was Currie's girl, and jealously guarded, though he was already married, was Dolly O'Henry, a fashion model from a nearby shop in Regent Street. Mark was obviously in love with Dora who, because of the Slade tradition, was called by her surname, as was Dorothy.

Carrington was not really in love with him, mainly I suspect because she was a tomboy, probably with lesbian tendencies. This pair reminded me of the Murrys, being incapable of giving each other happiness yet unable to part and so, perhaps, destined for tragedy.

At a nearby table towards the end of 1912 and throughout most of the following year Frank Harris was often to be seen in the company of a striking young girl who was destined to make a fine reputation for herself as a novelist and playwright. She was Miss Enid Bagnold, a colonel's daughter and obviously, from her bearing, of good stock. While Harris's friends – and his enemies – were always interested in the women he moved around with, most thought that such a nice young lady should be warned about the wiles of this arch-seducer before it was too late for, with the possible exception of his wife, Nellie, Harris held women in contempt. As it happened, it would have done little good. The lady was quite bowled over by Harris, whom she described aptly to her friends as 'like Lord Kitchener cut off at the legs'. She was later to admit that his ugliness and his wicked reputation, which she quickly realized had been well earned, capti-vated her.

At that time Harris, then in his mid-fifties, was running a rather low-standard magazine called *Hearth and Home* and Miss Bagnold wanted a job there to learn the art and craft of journalism. Ever with his eye to one particular chance, he was soon impressing her with lunches in the Café Royal Restaurant and the Savoy, sending the food back as usual, and name-dropping all over the place. I was privy to what might be called the overture to the seduction when Harris, who had sensed or discovered that the lady was a virgin, tried to convince her that until she had experienced sex she would never make a writer of any kind.

'Sex is the gateway to life,' he pronounced. 'There is no other key.'

I immediately recalled some advice I had heard him dispense to some younger man – 'Always take "No" from a woman as consent and push on after a refusal. A woman is often at her weakest then.'

It seems that in Miss Bagnold's case he did not have to 'push on' very long. She seemed so taken with his ability and experience that she believed his ploy about 'the gateway'.

Though the old *salons privés* had been shut down, Harris, being Harris, managed to secure a private room for his lunch, his only guest being Miss Bagnold. When I was told about the assignation I was in no doubt that Miss Bagnold had gone 'through the gateway' and I have little doubt that, had Harris been around when she became so successful as a writer, he would have claimed the credit for it!

Presumably the intimacy was repeated, because she stayed with him after he left *Hearth and Home* in 1913 to run a a rather tawdry journal called *Modern Society*. Most of the writing was done by Miss Bagnold and a young fellow called Hugh Lunn, who became well known in literary circles after he had changed his name to Hugh Kingsmill. As the offices were near Covent Garden, Harris and his lady-love were often in the Domino Room for a cheap meal or a drink. I vividly remember one occasion when they came into the Domino Room and Bosie Douglas, who was already there, deliberately pushed his marble-topped table on to Harris's legs. While Harris retaliated with his fists, Miss Bagnold was escorted from the fray by a waiter.

The Harris-Douglas relationship had been simmering and I had guessed it would boil over when, some while previously, Bosie had greeted his old friend with: 'Ah, Ancient Pistol!' as he passed his table. Harris had won that round with an immediate: 'Well roared, Bottom!' This encounter culminated in a fisticuff fight in the lobby, which Harris should have won, but those who saw it said that Bosie did not observe the Queensberry Rules. Still, I never thought I would live to see the ferocious Harris afraid of Bosie but, according to Gaudier-Brzeska, this was the case and it followed a further event I had watched with great amusement.

Harris had taken a fancy to Gaudier and had brought him into the Café Royal, realizing that he might provide some drawings cheaply for *Modern Society*, for Henri was, in my view, a better artist than sculptor.

'I like to help young artists and writers,' Harris said with some truth. 'Some manage to vault on to the saddle of success, but others need a stirrup. I shall be doing another long article on Oscar Wilde, and I should like you to do me a caricature of Lord Alfred Douglas to go with it.'

'Fine, but where can I see him?'

'Oh, he's here most evenings. But for Gawd's sake don't let him see you doing it. He's very touchy these days.'

The next evening Henri came in with a friend I did not recognize and sat himself at a table as close as he could get to Bosie, who for some reason was wearing a most peculiar hat. It was common practice in those days for customers to keep their hats on in drinking places and, no doubt to draw attention to himself, his lordship, as he liked to be called by then, was sporting a straw hat with a high conical crown and narrow brim. The friend opened a newspaper and held it in front of him to hide Henri while he made his sketches. I could not help laughing as I watched the eager, rather cocky face of the artist popping out from the cover of the newspaper, comparing the effort to the surreptitious way I had been required to operate for years. The sketches completed, Henri and his chum disappeared, no doubt to complete the caricature for Harris.

Unfortunately I was never to see it, but I heard Enid Bagnold tell what happened to it. Henri had made the drawing so unflattering that Harris was too scared to use it, fearing another assault from Bosie or maybe even a writ from his lordship, who remained very litigious in spite of his experiences in the courts.

I was to see further evidence of this change in Harris's nature on an occasion when he gave drinks in the Domino Room to Henri and the man who had held the newspaper, whose name I then learned was Brodzky, for Harris preferred to use surnames, except for those with whom he was on really intimate terms. Harris, who was always anti-Semitic, launched into an attack on the Jews, though he must have realized that, from his name, Brodzky might be of that race. Brodzky took it very well but eventually said, 'But why all these insults? I'm a Jew.'

In former days Harris would have responded aggressively with some remark like: 'Well, what do you propose to do about it?' Instead all he said was: 'So was Jesus', which calmed the conversation down.

In public, though, the effect of advancing years on Harris was to make him both louder and ruder, and he once asked a Dean, at a large formal party, 'Tell me, Dean, did Jesus Christ wear gaiters?' He met his match, however, in Mr Justice Horridge, before whom he had to appear in February 1914 for contempt of court, concerning remarks he had made in *Modern Society*'s scandal column about a society divorce case. It was F. E. Smith who asked for him to be committed for contempt, but the judge would probably have let him go with a warning had not Harris been stupid enough to roar some insult at him, whereupon he felt the touch of the tipstaff and was escorted to Brixton Prison to cool off and purge his contempt.

The effect of this on the magazine was catastrophic. Poor Miss Bagnold found herself in sole charge with empty pages to fill and no editor to guide her. I heard her explain her predicament to Robbie Ross while drinking with him in the Domino Room.

'I wrote off to Shaw, James Pryde and other so-called friends of

Frank's for some quick items to save the day. Anything would have done, but only dear old Max Beerbohm was prepared to help. Shaw and Pryde made excuses but Max, who happened to be in London for a month or two, visiting from Italy, came up with a marvellous cartoon showing him sitting at a table sharing a bottle of wine with Harris, who was declaiming away in his usual style, pulling the stars out of the sky. It was a wonderful compliment to Frank, for Max had inscribed it: "The Best Talker in London with one of his best listeners", but he made one condition – the drawing mustn't be used on the cover or made into an advertising poster.'

'I'll wager that Frank didn't think much of that when you told him,' Ross said.

'He certainly did not, but after I visited him in jail and told him I had given my word to Max he accepted the situation.'

Ross smiled as he lit a cigarette, in that effeminate way he had, then said, 'And then, no doubt, knowing dear Frank, he immediately broke his promise.'

'That's exactly what he did. He went behind my back and instructed the advertising girl to have the posters printed. "Damnation take those fancy promises," he told her. That's the trouble with Frank, Robbie. Like I say, he can pull the stars out of the sky but then he flushes them down the drain.'

'I couldn't have put it better myself, Enid!'

'When I found out I was so furious that I went round right away to Max Beerbohm's to tell him.'

'And what was dear Max's reaction? Pretty frosty, I should think.'

'That's about it,' Miss Bagnold replied. 'Angry but very cool. Anyway, he didn't blame me. I waited while he dressed and we went to the office together where he picked up the entire roll of posters. Then we went off to the printers, who parted with the block without a murmur. Max then directed the cab to the Thames at the back of the Savoy, and after he had given me one poster as a souvenir, I helped him to throw the roll and the plate into the river.'

'Oh, what fun! Wouldn't Frank's face have been a picture if he could have seen it!'

'Too bloody true,' said Miss Bagnold, who on occasion could swear like a trooper. 'Max is going to give me the original drawing, but only on condition I never let Frank get his hands on it.'

Harris, who, with typical panache, had arranged to have meals sent in by the Café Royal served in his cell, emerged from prison shortly afterwards looking very chastened, though not of course for long. His bombast quickly returned, along with his huge appetite for food, wine and women, in spite of his admonition to others about over-indulgence — 'When will we lovers learn that the most highly powered engines require the strongest brakes?'

I never saw him with Miss Bagnold again, and he didn't stay long with *Modern Society*, which was just as well because there were ugly rumours that he was copying Bottomley by virtually blackmailing people who paid to keep their names out of the magazine when he had juicy tit-bits about them. I had heard him challenged about this and he had simply laughed, as was his wont when caught out, saying, 'You must be confusing me with that Renaissance rascal, Aretino. He lived in great style, you know, by warning vulnerable princes and cardinals, "I am thinking of writing a few verses. . . ." The money was round in a flash.'

Unhappily for the Café Royal, for Harris had provided us with rare entertainment for many years, he went abroad, mainly to escape his creditors but partly because, as he put it so modestly, 'In Britain the man of genius is feared and hated in exact proportion to his originality.'

I did see the delightful Miss Bagnold again — in the company of H. G. Wells, another practised seducer — but I gather he had no luck in that direction, though at one stage he seemed to be making steady progress. She also looked in occasionally with Hugh Kingsmill, with Gaudier-Brzeska, who sculpted a head of her, which seemed grotesquely unflattering, from a photograph I once saw of it, and with W. H. (William Henry) Davies, the poet who called himself the Supertramp in the autobiography which has become a classic.

Bill Davies was rugged, broad-shouldered and with the dark features and prominent nose which have helped to perpetuate the myth that the Celtic Welsh are one of the lost tribes of Israel. He was also easily recognizable by his wooden peg-leg, as he had suffered an amputation below the right knee while trying to jump on to a train in America along with another hobo, as I believe tramps are called there. In spite of this disability he walked hundreds of miles round England from one workhouse or dosshouse to the next, composing his poems as he stumped along in destitution. It was not until 1908 that he was recognized as a poet of standing, after the newspapers had publicized his story and after Domino Room men like George R. Sims, Arthur Symons and Bernard Shaw had helped him. Once established, he was lionized by hostesses like Lady Cunard and accepted by leading writers and artists of the day, but he is generally remembered for just two lines of poetry which are not only wise but of special and secret significance for me:

> *What is this life if, full of care,*
> *We have no time to stand and stare.*

Admittedly I have spent more time sitting than standing, but I have never stopped staring!

30

'COME ON AND DIE!'

In the autumn of 1912 there entered the Domino Room the first young man I had seen who could compare in looks with Bosie, when I had first set eyes on him. Like Lord Alfred, he was blond with a complexion so fair and clear as to be almost effeminate, but he was somewhat taller and more robustly built and had a definite air of virility about him. I judged his age to be in the mid-twenties, which turned out to be accurate, and from his conversation with the two friends who came in with him his passionate interest was poetry. When he undid his jacket he was seen to be wearing the most extraordinary shirt – purple with green stripes. I had seen nothing like it before but somehow it suited him and, as I was to see, brightly coloured shirts and enormous ties were his trademark, or perhaps I should say, more respectfully, his hallmark, for I was to discover later that his name was Rupert Brooke. Like so many, I had never heard of him, though that year, apparently, he had made his name in the literary world with his first book of poems; but within three years, for the saddest of reasons, his name was to be on everybody's lips as the embodiment of all that was fine about the young men of England.

That night – it was quite late – the three young men, one of whom, Wilfrid Gibson, was also to become a poet of distinction, had been watching a huge fire which had devastated the woodyard at King's Cross. They had seen the glare from Brooke's lodgings in Gray's Inn, which, incidentally, were not far from my own in Guilford Street. As they drank their beer and ate their sandwiches they could talk of little else, for the crowd had been enormous, with the firemen and police making heroic efforts to keep them away from the danger; but their conversation soon turned to the merits of various poets. I had never heard of most of them, though I recalled three – Swinburne, who used to visit the Domino Room in the old days and had been dead some three years, W. B. Yeats, whom I had seen there with Aleister Crowley and was to see again quite frequently, and Ernest Dowson, who had died in 1900. I knew that Dowson was becoming highly regarded but Brooke said, in a joking way, 'Ernest Dowson is one of the seven geniuses of this age. I am the other six.'

It seemed that Brooke also admired another friend of mine, Hilaire Belloc, and I was sorry that he was not in the Domino Room to keep the three young men there longer for I found myself fascinated by Brooke's appearance. If he was gifted as a poet, it seemed to me that evening that nature was unfair in giving him such physical attributes as well, while some of us have fared so poorly in the share-out. Experience was to teach me, however, never to begrudge any man his luck. As Oscar's experience had shown, and Brooke's soon would, one never knows what misfortune Fate has stacked up round the corner.

From his conversation Brooke, though so young, seemed to be moving in refined, indeed exalted, circles, for he mentioned Winston Churchill, with whom he seemed to be on very friendly terms, and Lady Ottoline Morrell. He was in the Domino Room occasionally with Bill Davies, John Drinkwater and others who had banded together to publish their work under the title *Georgian Poetry*, an anthology to be edited by Edward Marsh, and meaning the era of King George V. Then in 1913 I was pleased to see him enraptured by a very striking young lady who turned out to be a promising actress called Cathleen Nesbitt. He had taken her to the London Hippodrome to see a show which was the rage of the town and was the first introduction of jazz into the lives of the many thousands who saw it during its long run. I saw it myself and thought it rather raucous, especially the American-style singing, but there were marvellous numbers like 'Alexander's Ragtime Band' and 'Waiting for the Robert E. Lee' which were destined to become almost immortal, in the sense that generation after generation would sing or whistle them. I was surprised to hear that Brooke, who seemed so sensitive, should have liked the show so much that he had already seen it several times. It soon became quite clear that the two young people, who were probably the handsomest couple ever to enter the Café Royal, were in love.

'If you don't know that you are the most beautiful thing in the world either you're imbecile or something's wrong with your mirror,' Brooke said.

He seemed to be quite unselfconscious about paying such compliments. I have never had occasion to be in such a situation but my observations convince me that many people, perhaps most, find it extremely embarrassing to praise anyone else lavishly to their faces. It is strange that this should be, and on occasions, I imagine, sad. How often has some comment, which might have changed a whole relationship, been suppressed because of the inability to utter it, even though the thought and the words were present in the mind? Anyway, Brooke had no such inhibitions, not even when the compliment could be interpreted as slightly barbed. 'It is a good thing that your nose has that ripple in the middle,' he told his lady. 'If you had a straight, unindividual nose you might merely have been a goddess.'

'Go on, you are drunk with your own words,' Miss Nesbitt replied.

'That's a thing no lady should say to a gentleman. I am entirely sober. Anyway, I refuse to be bullied by your knowledge of mankind.'

As on so many other occasions. I felt it was wrong to go on intruding on such an intimate conversation, but I found 'listening in' irresistible.

My diary tells me that in my mind I always called the young poet 'Brooke', because I did not know him long enough or well enough to use his Christian name. It also reveals that the next time I saw him was in June of the fateful year of 1914, when he lunched with the then rather notorious writer D. H. Lawrence and his German wife Frieda, a blonde Brunnhilde type.

I had seen the red-bearded Lawrence in the Domino Room before, when he only had a rather full moustache. He had come in with John Middleton Murry and Katherine Mansfield, with whom he had what can only be described as a love–hate relationship. They would argue heatedly about the Russian writer Dostoevsky, as though nothing else in the world mattered, and Lawrence would usually vent his anger on his wife, with whom he had the most fearful rows in public, sometimes muttering under his breath that he would 'slit her bloody throat'. It has always astonished me that couples like the Lawrences, the Murrys and the Gaudier-Brzeskas could stay together after such slanging matches. What people say is often so much more hurtful than what they do. Many men and women who would be incapable of hurting one another physically are verbal sadists. Their shafts of wit are well-named, for they often go right to the heart.

While Lawrence was to make use of the Café Royal in his book *Women in Love*, calling it the Café Pompadour, I always thought that this slim, restless figure, who looked evil-tempered and was, seemed uneasily out of place there, as though wishing he was somewhere else. For some years, however, he was to be a fairly frequent attender and I shall have more to say about him. On the day in question the last thing that Lawrence wanted to talk about was the rumour of war, but Rupert Brooke had time for little else.

'Winston Churchill tells me he is certain that there will be a war with Germany before the year is out,' he said. 'He has offered to help me to get a commission.'

'But Rupert, you won't have to fight,' said Lawrence's wife, who was Germanically aggressive. 'The soldiers will do that.'

'We shall all have to fight,' Brooke replied.

Lawrence said nothing on that score, and he did not look to me like a man who would do much fighting.

'I don't want us to fight Germany,' Brooke said. 'I want Germany to attack Russia and smash her to fragments.'

'Whatever for?' Lawrence asked.

'Because when Germany was weak from the fight France could then break her. France and England are the only two countries which should have any power. The danger is that Germany will smash France and then be wiped out by Russia. Then we could have a Slav empire, world-wide, despotic and insane.'

Brooke did not get his commission so easily and was still a civilian when war was declared. I remember him looking at a late-night edition of one of the newspapers while his two companions, Ashley Dukes, a drama critic, and T. E. Hulme were playing chess. They were all awaiting the arrival of Walter Sickert who had also grown a beard, which surprised me for it not only made him look older but masked his strikingly good features.

'Why can't I just go and fight?' Brooke asked. 'They won't admit volunteers yet, and if I join the Territorials I shall get some dull posting after six months' training. Why can't I just go and fight?'

Hulme simply gave him a despairing stare because he was so sure in his mind that he was not going to fight somebody else's war that, when the writer Richard Aldington eventually volunteered for the Army and was rejected, he called him a 'bloody fool who did not deserve such good luck'. On a later occasion, just before Brooke secured a commission in one of the naval battalions, he was in the Domino Room when he saw his friend Henri Gaudier-Brzeska.

'Come on and die,' Brooke shouted to him.

It was a sadly prophetic remark, as was the poem Brooke had written called 'The Soldier' (originally 'The Recruit'), which began:

> If I should die, think only this of me:
> That there's some corner of a foreign field
> That is for ever England. . . .

When one 'character' left us he was soon replaced, and in those early months of 1914 the Domino Room became the haunt of a number of strange young men and women who behaved as though determined to get the most out of life before the holocaust which was to end life for many of them and change it for all.

Among this 'wild bunch' nobody impressed my memory more than a tall, slim, fair-haired young girl who affected chalk-white make-up, heavy rouge and long cigarette holders. She could not have been more than eighteen, and her name was Nancy Cunard. The daughter of a rich American mother and a father who was a baronet, she seemed to rebel against everything regarded as 'proper'. Having escaped from home into a flat somewhere off Tottenham Court Road, she regularly appeared in the Domino Room with two other girls of similar age and class – Lady Diana Manners, daughter of the Duke of Rutland, who was to become a Society beauty as famous in her way as Lillie Langtry, though not notorious, and Iris Tree, the attractive daughter of Sir Herbert Beerbohm Tree who later took up with the artist Mark Gertler after his great love, Carrington, had gone to live with Lytton Strachey of all people! These girls and the young men they attracted, like Duff Cooper and Michael Arlen, became known to us as the Young Souls as distinguished from the Souls of the previous generation.

The girls were notable for their lavish use of cosmetics and were pioneers in that respect, for at that time powder and paint on that scale were the deliberate mark of the prostitute. When there were hundreds of whores on the streets of London, they had to be instantly recognizable for what they were, just as a taxi-cab has to look different from a private car if any man is to hail it.

This use of make-up, soon to be followed by other Society women, did not put off the numerous young men with whom the Cunard group kept company, or the older ones like Augustus John and

Horace Cole, who of course were unshockable, as I have to confess I had become myself after a few years in the Domino Room.

It certainly did not put off a good-looking young South American, Alvaro Guevara, who had come to London from Chile and was studying at the Slade School. 'Chile', as he was soon called after being introduced to the Domino Room by Augustus John, was a fine amateur heavyweight boxer, which of course immediately endeared him to Augustus's crony Horace Cole, and the three were often together. It looked at one stage as though Chile and Nancy might make a match of it, especially as Lady Cunard approved, since Chile had some money and good 'background'. But, sizing up the two of them, I was pleased when their affair petered out. Chile was bisexual; Nancy was anything where sex was involved.

Of all the Young Souls and those associated with them, the weirdest was a wealthy young man called Ronald Firbank, who dedicated his life to writing novels peopled with characters as odd as himself. Few read them except for a small following he developed in America. I had taken note of him in the Domino Room in previous years occasionally with Oscar's son, Vyvyan Holland, though he was usually in the company of known homosexuals like Bosie Douglas, Reggie Turner and Robert Ross. He did not become a regular attender, however, until shortly before the war, when he became almost as much a fixture as myself except when he was abroad, for he had private means. Mostly he would sit alone at the same table near the centre of the room from mid-day to midnight, a spare, effeminate figure with a long, thin face and curved, Roman nose. From time to time he would giggle nervously to himself as he made notes of ideas which had occurred to him. He would writhe about restlessly, running his hands through his hair like a woman, and had a strange habit of grasping his left shoulder with his right hand as though cuddling himself.

When I passed his table I noticed that he would smell of incense to a degree which reminded me of a Catholic church. He may have been in the habit of burning it at home or it may have been some perfume because he certainly used make-up, and before leaving the Café would rub his cheeks with one of those tissues impregnated with powder which women carry in their handbags. Why he rouged his cheeks I do not understand, for they already had the flush of the consumptive. Perhaps he was deliberately exaggerating this feature, as do so many people who have some peculiarity.

I saw Firbank lunch with a guest occasionally in the Café but he rarely ate anything. He was said to have a throat affliction which made it difficult for him to swallow and I used to watch with fascination as he toyed with course after course, cutting up the food but conveying none to his mouth. I heard him say that as a special gesture to one favoured host he swallowed one pea!

The throat affliction was, I believe, a cover for his lack of appetite, occasioned partly by his illness but also by his intake of alcohol. His waiter, George (one of the few old hands still alive as I write), kept his glass topped up with brandy, without request, so Firbank often consumed more than a bottle a day. It was usually impossible to tell whether he was intoxicated or not, because his behaviour and conversation were crazy at any time.

Sometimes he would be racked by coughing fits, and I used to wonder if the brandy was responsible. I have often noticed that if I drink more than my wont I develop a cough and, as I have never smoked, I am convinced that there is such a thing as a 'drinker's cough'. Maybe some of us have lungs which are specially sensitive to alcohol.

Occasionally Firbank was drunk, but usually he looked no worse for wear as he donned his velour hat, picked up his gloves and hat and minced out in his doeskin shoes.

My diary records that his most favourite companion in the Domino Room was another precious young gentleman called Evan Morgan, son and heir of Lord Tredegar, who first attracted Firbank because he thought he looked like Rameses, the great Pharaoh. Morgan was a close friend of Nancy Cunard and he brought Firbank into her circle, where he met Chile Guevara, who painted a devastatingly honest portrait of him.

One of the older men with whom Nancy appeared on occasion in the Domino Room was George Moore, the Irish author of *Esther Waters* and other novels regarded as classics. The sight of the old bachelor with his drooping moustache, sloping shoulders, unpressed suit and brown buttoned boots talking animatedly with this slip of a girl was incongruous, to say the least. He was certainly very fond of her, though, for I even saw him pay for the drinks they had, and he was notoriously mean and so given to disputing small items on his bills that he was hounded out of Boodles Club. He was petty, even childish, in other ways. I heard his fellow countryman, W. B. Yeats, recounting how Moore had a vendetta with a woman neighbour when living in Dublin. He would go out after midnight and rattle his stick along her railings to make her dogs bark. What a display for a 'genius'! Inevitably the woman retaliated by hiring organ-grinders to play under his window when he was trying to write. Oscar, who was a shrewd judge of character, summed him up by saying, 'I know Moore so well that I haven't spoken to him for ten years.' Still, there's no accounting for taste. Being an aspiring poet, Nancy may have been in love with Moore's mind, but I once heard her offer a different explanation in confidence: 'I believe that George Moore may be my father.' Moore, who had previously remarked to Oscar Wilde during their brief friendship, 'I am too interested in other men's wives to think of getting one of my own', apparently did have a long love affair with Lady Emerald Cunard before she took up with the musician Thomas Beecham.

Nancy made no bones about her own sexual promiscuity. 'My mother is having an affair with Thomas Beecham so I can do as I please,' she said in a voice described by Jules as high-pitched and somewhat breathless; and please herself she did, discussing with men – with no words barred – the ideas put forward by Professor Havelock Ellis, who often visited us, in his *Psychology of Sex*, and once being apprehended by the police for swimming in the Serpentine in her underwear after some all-night party. The simple truth was that young Nancy enjoyed shocking people and, whilst most girls tire of that pleasure as they mature, she never did, as I shall have to relate with some regret.

Most of the young people who frequented the Domino Room were poor. Those who were rich like George Baird and Nancy Cunard were ruined by their money so far as their characters were concerned. Both were excellent examples of what Jesus meant in his parable about the rich man. Of course not all rich people are spoiled by money. Some make creative use of it, and I recall Bernard Shaw saying that the parable of the rich man was '. . . palpable nonsense: as Jesus never had any property and left all the business of his ministry to Judas, he simply did not know what he was talking about'. Another blasphemy? Not so, Shaw would have argued. Only the true believer can really blaspheme.

31

AND DIE THEY DID!

The murder of Archduke Francis Ferdinand at Sarajevo in June 1914 is supposed to have been the fuse that set off the Great War, but it meant little to us in the Domino Room and still less, I suspect, to the general public outside. There had in fact been talk of an inevitable war with Kaiser Wilhelm's Germany for several years. As the politics, in which none of us had any say, moved to a climax, it was known that Asquith's cabinet was split on the issue of whether Britain should be involved or remain neutral. Winston Churchill, ever a fire-eater, was all for war, while Lloyd George and several others opposed him.

The crisis came when German troops marched into Belgium and the British government felt driven to issue an ultimatum demanding their withdrawal. By this time hysteria had gripped the public and large crowds were collecting outside Buckingham Palace singing 'God Save the King' and cheering as though wanting a declaration of war. Many of those making most noise were to die in the mud of Flanders, and somebody in the Domino Room, I forget who, wisely recalled Robert Walpole's remark: 'Now they are ringing the bells; in a few weeks they will be wringing their hands.'

On the next day, when the ultimatum had expired without result, I was among the packed crowd in Downing Street when war was formally declared. Again there was wild cheering, echoed throughout the streets, as I walked back to the Domino Room feeling for some reason I cannot explain a degree of elation myself, perhaps simply because the uncertainty was over. Like most people I felt sure that the war would be short and would probably be over by Christmas.

That night the Domino Room was packed with customers in a mood of celebration, as was most of the Café Royal. Most of the regulars were there: Augustus John and his group; Hermann Finck and Arthur Wimperis, who were to produce recruiting songs like 'On Sunday I Walk Out with a Soldier'; and a number of other theatricals including, later in the evening, C. B. 'Cocky' Cochran, the impresario, the French actress Alice Delysia, formerly of the Moulin Rouge, who had recently become a London star overnight in a show called *Odds and Ends* and was then appearing in the highly successful *Passing Show* at the Palace. I remember seeing Edgar Wallace, then editing a racy racing journal called *Town Topics* printed on pink paper and as renowned for its improper jokes as for its tips.

There was quite a sprinkling of khaki already, several regular soldiers and Territorials being present, while John and some other artists were in uniform, having volunteered for home defence. Their training ground was aptly enough the courtyard of Burlington House, home of the Royal Academy, so they did not have far to come to slake their thirsts.

The most interesting behaviour that night was that of those Germans present: there were always some, for there were a few German waiters and quite a number of German prostitutes. The waiters, who must have been quite frightened, tried to demonstrate their loyalty by joining the French waiters in singing the 'Marseillaise', surely the most rousing call to arms ever written. Sensing the atmosphere of resentment, the German tarts, who were mainly Teutonic blondes, quietly disappeared and, after a few days, returned with their hair dyed black in the hope that they might be taken for French whores.

Regrettably, both London and the country as a whole were quickly gripped by anti-German fever, stirred up to the limit in *Town Topics* by Wallace, who was over military age and was barred from being a war correspondent again by the vindictive Lord Kitchener because he had circumvented the censor twelve years previously in securing a scoop on the Boer War Peace Treaty. The windows of German pork butchers who had lived in London for generations were smashed in. I even saw dachshunds kicked in the streets by English dog-lovers! The German waiters and the tarts were rounded up and interned, which was just as well for their safety because, in short order, every German was branded as a spy. How glad I was that Jules, Alphonse and Adolphe, among my waiter friends, were French. I did not have their company for long, however. Those who were young enough – happily, Jules was not – volunteered for the French Army.

The first memorable result of the war so far as Domino Room life was concerned was the arrival of Belgian refugees. Naturally, as they spoke French, some of them gravitated to the Café Royal and were made welcome. We were soon to find, however, as did the public as a whole, that their welcome was short-lived. Whatever one did for the Belgians, they expected and demanded more, almost as though we had been responsible for their plight. They even picked fights with occasional Swiss customers in the Café Royal because they happened to be German-speaking. War is supposed to bring out the best in everybody. I am afraid that in some instances it brings out the worst — at least the most primitive.

The Café Royal management, then under Auguste Judah, behaved splendidly towards its staff, promising every volunteer that he would be sure of having his job back when the war was over, however long it lasted. I remember when the first of the French waiters returned home on leave. His name was Villaret, and as soon as he was seen he was grabbed by the customers and chaired round the Café, a rowdy compliment also paid to returning battle-seasoned customers.

One might have thought that, after the violence of the front line, these homing warriors would be seeking peace and quiet. Not a bit of it! Once in the Domino Room with a few drinks inside them their object seemed to be to wreck the place, and trying to keep them in order took years off poor Judah's life.

For some reason just being in officer's uniform, or perhaps just being a young officer, seems to trigger off hooligan behaviour. I remember how, shortly before the war, when there had been no excuse about being on leave, a group of Guards officers had been giving a pre-wedding party to one of their number in a private room upstairs, and behaved so outrageously that the management had to call in the police who marched them away. They broke up the furniture, threw champagne bottles into the street, wrecked the grand piano, and were about to push it out of the window with the head waiter, Fumigali, crouched on top of it!

In an effort to reduce the friction which might start a fight the management removed the dominoes 'for the duration'. Betting on the results of the game had always been prohibited but was impossible to prevent, and I had seen wads of notes changing hands — as much as £100 on an 'odd or even?' throw of one domino! Inevitably the bookies, and others determined to gamble as they sat with their drinks, came up with an alternative. Each sat with a sugar lump in front of him, and the man whose lump attracted the first fly was the winner. Various methods of doctoring the cube to improve its attractiveness, some unmentionable, were quickly devised.

The most serious consequence of the war for me was the management's decision that they would have to close the premises every night at 10.30. This followed the raids by German Zeppelins, after one bomb had fallen too near Piccadilly for comfort. I remember rushing out with almost everyone else to see the first Zeppelin over London. The searchlights had the great silver cigar firmly in their beams but the anti-aircraft shells were bursting far below it, as the Zeppelin commander clearly knew. It was not until a gallant British flying officer shot one down that the invulnerability of the Zeppelins ceased, but they had shown that Britain, the island fortress, was no longer invulnerable either.

Judah's idea in closing the Café early was to forestall a major disaster from a bomb which might fall on the crowded building, but all that most of the habitués did was to go elsewhere in Soho and such places. For myself I felt this was rather disloyal, and once the Domino Room had closed I usually went home and worked on my diaries.

Early in 1915 we in the Domino Room and the nation as a whole were immensely saddened by the news of Rupert Brooke's death from blood poisoning while aboard a ship which was part of an expeditionary force to the Dardanelles. The Dardanelles action against the Turks was Winston Churchill's idea, and it was a poignant coincidence that Brooke and Churchill had been such friends. In June of the same year news reached us that Henri Gaudier-Brzeska had been killed in action with the French forces, where he had proved extremely brave and had risen to sergeant. It was T. E. Hulme, the man who had said he would not fight but finally went to the trenches with his chess companion Ashley Dukes, who brought the news into the Domino Room while home on leave with the rank of captain. Even those who had not cared for Henri were saddened as the information passed from table to table. The young sculptor who, according to Epstein and Augustus John, had shown fine promise, had been only twenty-three. The general sorrow was even greater when news of Hulme's own death came through, for by common accord he represented, like Brooke, the finest of his generation. I am not given to profanities, but what a bloody waste!

32

MIXED-UP MINOR MASTERS

In 1915 I noticed Nina Hamnett, the Bohemian artist, in the company of a striking young man, tall, with fair hair and a somewhat derisive smile, who would then be in his early twenties. From the cut of his clothes and the lavishness with which he bought rounds of drinks he seemed to have private means, and looked out of place among the down-at-heel artists with whom he consorted – though, as I was to witness on many occasions, he was as eccentric and exhibitionist as any of them. His name, I discovered, was Philip Heseltine, and by profession he was a musician who was to make a formidable reputation, though mostly posthumous, under the pseudonym Peter Warlock.

Heseltine, who liked to say that he had been born on the Embankment, like some tramp, when he had in fact been born in the Savoy Hotel there, lived in Chelsea, finally moving to Oscar's old habitat, Tite Street. He was a great supporter of a then little-known musician called Delius, and wrote musical criticisms in various journals, making a number of enemies in the process. He was also rather good at writing doggerel verse and limericks, and loved to shock any nearby audience by reciting some of his cruder efforts, for he seemed fascinated by sex, being a keen follower of Dr Havelock Ellis.

As was later revealed, he was a gifted composer himself, mainly of songs and chamber music, and probably chose to publish them under the name of Warlock because he wanted to fool those critics who would otherwise automatically attack him. I suspect, however, that the name Warlock also appealed because it meant a demon, and during the few years I was to see him he became demonic, especially when in drink.

His favourite expression of such activity was to dance on one of the tables or in the aisles, leaping about with great agility as though driven to do so by some compelling force, recalling the biblical phrase 'possessed of a devil'. He would then fall fast asleep, to awake refreshed and ready for further drink and conversation. I welcomed him because the Domino Room was becoming a bit short on such eccentrics, but I never liked him because he seemed excessively cynical and derisive about other people. I used to think that his loud and flamboyant behaviour was, as is usually the case, a means of drawing attention to himself. But, as he was later to prove when he took his own life, it may have been a cover for deep-seated insecurity or feelings of inferiority.

He may even have suffered from what has come to be called a split personality, Heseltine being one character and Warlock the other. In what was probably his Warlock phase, he grew a beard and became a mighty drinker, claiming to start the day with a glass of Eno's fruit salts laced with gin – a 'cocktail' which I once saw him mix in the Domino Room for his closest friend, Cecil Gray, a Scottish professional critic of art and music. He left the distinctive Eno's bottle on the table to puzzle the waiters and habitués nearby, but I suspect that they were so used to odd occurrences in the Café that it caused less surprise than he would have wished. We were, however, perturbed when he began to get so drunk that he had to be picked up out of the gutter and then bailed out next day, as the young Augustus John had been. I, for one, felt he was letting the 'Club' down.

Later Heseltine also edited a musical journal called *The Sackbut*, which I believe to be an ancient name for the trombone, and appeared to do much of his editing in the Domino Room, assisted by a couple of young and attractive girls who would march in with him carrying documents and musical scores. *The Sackbut*, which was too esoteric for my taste, also published occasional poetry, including some by a remarkable South African who drifted into the Domino Room called Roy Campbell. I liked him because he had written a book of poems called *The Flaming Terrapin*, and that was the nickname by which his friend Augustus John called him, though to most of us he was known as 'Zulu'.

Heseltine also wrote an anthology of poems on drink and drinkers which he called *Rab Noolas*, which was Saloon Bar spelled backwards. Most of the literary people in the Domino Room found him unbearable, however, because he could not resist making puns of the worst kind and coarse jokes based on *double entendre* or other plays on words. One such, I recall, of which he seemed rather proud, asked the question: 'What is the difference between a bald-headed lunatic and a maid taking her master's breakfast to bed?' Heseltine's answer was:

'One is bald on the head and mad as a hatter, of course, while the other is hauled on the bed and had as a matter of course.'

Though some of the Fleet Street critics praised Warlock's work they turned against it when they found it was really Heseltine; one in particular who disliked him and his set was Edwin Evans, the critic of the *Daily Mail*. One evening Evans was having a quiet drink alone in the Domino Room shortly after he had written a scathing account of a concert which Heseltine and his friend Gray had mounted to promote the 'avant-garde' music of Bernard van Dieren, a Dutch composer and friend of Epstein. Heseltine moved over to Evans's table and, sitting down uninvited, insulted the critic in the derisory terms of which he was a master. Evans, normally a quiet and rather sedate Welshman, who always wore a frock-coat and silk topper, took the insults as any critic should whose business is handing them out, but Heseltine really needled him by announcing another concert. This time he was to promote the works of Bela Bartok, the then little-known composer from Hungary, which was an ally of the hated Hun. Evans pointed a quivering finger at him and said, 'If you perform the music of this enemy or any other I will recruit a group of the toughest Australian soldiers I can muster. I will stoke them up with strong liquor in El Vino's at my expense and under my command they will wreck the hall.'

Realizing that he meant what he said, Heseltine jumped up and punched him on the face, not having the knobkerrie with which he had crowned a previous critic of van Dieren. Evans swiftly retaliated and Gray attempted to join in. Others at nearby tables, who had overheard the later part of the row, began to take sides, and soon a sizeable part of the Domino Room looked like one of those Wild West saloon bars where everybody is hitting anybody. The waiters were no doubt originally intent on stopping the fisticuffs, but finding themselves punched in return they too joined in, perhaps seeing the opportunity to retaliate against a few customers they disliked. Poor Evans was knocked out cold in the fray.

It was in the company of Heseltine that I first took really serious note of D. H. (for David Herbert) Lawrence. This tallish, red-haired young man, who, except when he was holding forth in what I heard described as a 'eunuchy voice reminiscent of H. G. Wells's high-pitched squeak', looked disturbingly restless and aggressive. He had been a schoolmaster, but quickly made great impact in the literary world with his writings, which were so forthright regarding sex that he called himself the 'priest of love'. To my surprise he was still married to Frieda, the tall, blonde, full-bosomed German girl with high cheek bones who had run away with him while still wed to an older man by whom she had children.

As I was quick to realize, Lawrence insisted on moulding the characters of his friends as though they were his own inventions in a novel. Naturally, anybody with a character as strong as Heseltine's rebelled and friction was inevitable, the precise cause in his case being a misunderstanding, or what writers now like to call a failure of communication.

One evening a group including the Armenian, Dikran Kouyoumdjian, about whom more anon in another guise, had a copy of a book of poems which Lawrence had just published. One of the party was reading the poems in a mocking way and, while listeners nearby joined in the fun as the laughter intensified, there was one table where the occupants were anything but amused. They were Katherine Mansfield, by then making quite a name as a writer, Mark Gertler, rising rapidly to fame, though not to fortune, and a swarthy Russian they called Kot, which was short for Koteliansky. All three were admirers of Lawrence's work, so, after a whispered conversation, Katherine stole quietly to Kouyoumdjian's table, snatched the book, and walked out of the Café with it.

Lawrence soon heard of the incident and understood that it had been Heseltine who had been parodying his work. Instead of talking to his old friend about it, he stored up his anger until he published the novel *Women in Love*, which is his best-known work next to *Lady Chatterley's Lover*. The Café Royal is clearly represented in it as the Café Pompadour, the name of one of its banqueting rooms, and Lawrence portrayed Heseltine, under the name 'Halliday', as a rather drunken and malicious character in a scene reminiscent of the poem-reading incident.

Heseltine was furious at the caricature and attempted to have the book withdrawn on the grounds of indecency by reporting it to the Purity League. When this failed he initiated libel proceedings, which were somewhat more successful: the publishers paid him £50 and promised to change the physical description of the Heseltine-like character in future editions.

Every habitué in the Café heard the story and, while Lawrence was not a popular figure there, it was felt that Heseltine had made a fool of himself.

The Domino Room was to play an important part in Heseltine's life, for he eventually married one of the prettiest of the artists' models who frequented it – a girl called Bobbie Channing. She was full of vitality but was to achieve little happiness with her temperamental husband. While Heseltine continued to put on an act with most of the world he confessed to his close friends, like Gray, that he considered himself a complete failure, and when he began to lament 'the barrenness of my life' and 'my cesspool of stagnation' I began to fear for him, for there were times when he seemed to be in the blackest pit of depression. So it was not too surprising that this young man who seemed to have everything – good looks, talent and some money – should have ended his life by gassing himself as he did, having first put out his cat, in 1930 when he was only thirty-six. Of one thing I am certain after my long study of people – one never really knows anybody else and some people never know themselves. Heseltine is said to have written his own epitaph:

> *Here lies Warlock, the composer,*
> *Who lived next door to Munn, the grocer,*
> *He died of drink and copulation*
> *A great discredit to this nation.*

D. H. Lawrence, who did not live long enough to enjoy the fortune which has since been made from his work, was so distrusted by the waiters that cash was always demanded from him. He occasionally sat alone or with his wife, but more usually with the few friends there he knew – Anna Wickham, one of the most beautiful of the Domino Room regulars and known as 'The Queen of the Café Royal', who wrote poetry and novels and was also an excellent contralto singer, and Katherine Mansfield and John Middleton Murry.

After I had heard Lawrence quoting Shelley: 'War is the statesman's game, the priest's delight, the lawyer's jest, the hired assassin's trade', I was not surprised when he decided to 'ignore' the battle in Europe, dismissing it as 'an irrelevancy'. He carried on writing in a manner which was guaranteed to provoke censure and, sure enough, his novel *The Rainbow*, published in 1915, caused a furore. The Purity League attacked him for obscenity, raucously assisted by *John Bull*. There were court proceedings and copies were ordered to be destroyed.

Naturally Lawrence was in despair at being accused of perpetrating 'an orgy of sexiness', and all he could talk about was the coming 'revolution'. When this was clearly not going to happen he thought about escaping with a few chosen disciples to some idyllic 'colony' he proposed to found in Florida, Mexico or some other place with a suitable climate. He invited Murry, Heseltine, Kouyoumdjian and Koteliansky among others to join him, but few accepted, presumably not relishing being a captive audience for Lawrence's monologues which, in political terms, were not very original.

Instead, Lawrence and his wife took off to stay with Lady Ottoline Morrell at her Oxfordshire manor house, where no doubt he absorbed some atmosphere for his even sexier novel *Lady Chatterley's Lover* which was to cause a great literary row.

There seems to be no evidence that Lady Ottoline ever patronized her gamekeeper. Her sights were usually set much higher: while the Lawrences were staying with her she was still having an affair with Bertrand Russell. I saw him once in the Café – he looked more like a terrapin than I do.

In the autumn of 1923 D. H. Lawrence and his wife returned briefly to London and to the Café Royal. I was surprised to find that they were still together, because their arguments had been so dreadful that Lawrence might well have carried out his threat to 'slit her bloody throat', and since then there had been much gossip among their friends that Frieda had taken off with John Middleton Murry.

Lawrence was one of those who believed he knew just how people should run their lives, while being unable to control his own, a delusion common among writers as well as among politicians. His belief in his powers as a leader and a prophet had become so inflated that he regarded his friends as 'disciples' and demanded their total agreement for his crackpot Communistic proposals, especially for his idea of setting up an escapist commune for which the new venue was to be in New Mexico.

In the hope of securing firm commitments for this wild venture, Lawrence went to the expense of arranging an evening meal in a private room at the Café Royal, where once again, the waiters – and later some of the participants – were to be my on-the-spot reporters. I had been given advance notice of the dinner because there had been some problem over the deposit for the expensive meal. Not being impressed by the look of Lawrence, the manager had declined to accept his cheque and had demanded cash. Lawrence had been unable to attract more than half a dozen possible recruits for what soon became known in our room below as 'The Last Supper'. Others who might have been expected to answer the summons had fallen out with him, could no longer tolerate his imperious demands, or had matured more than he had.

His guests included Middleton Murry, whose wife Katherine Mansfield had recently died and who was already in love with Lawrence's wife, and Samuel Koteliansky, the swarthy Russian translator of Tolstoy and Dostoevsky, who had once accompanied Lawrence on a walking tour. Mark Gertler, the painter, by then tuberculous through overwork, was there. So was Mary Cannan, a former actress who had been married to Sir James Barrie, the author of *Peter Pan*, and then to Gilbert Cannan, a barrister turned writer, who had produced a widely read novel called *Mendel* about a Jewish artist modelled on Gertler. Dorothy Brett, who was rather plain and deaf, was also present. I felt a bond of sympathy with Dorothy because when she appeared in the Domino Room, where there was so much background noise, she carried a hearing apparatus in a sizeable case. Like many deaf people she had a habit of turning off the device or pretending that it would not work when the conversation bored her. A couple called the Carswells, with whom the Lawrences were staying, completed the party. Catherine Carswell, who had written a biography of Robert Burns, and would write one about Lawrence, had long been a faithful friend and admirer of D.H. along with her husband, who was a barrister.

I suspect that Lawrence was intensely disappointed by the poor turn-out, but made the most of the occasion by the ill-mannered device of being late enough for all his guests to have arrived so that he could make a 'Master's' entrance.

According to the waiters, the atmosphere of the dinner was unpleasant from the start. Carswell happened to speak some Spanish, and Lawrence ignored his other guests while practising the little of that language he had picked up in Mexico. By the time Lawrence announced that they should all follow him into the wilderness of New Mexico to escape from the oppressiveness of English life some were irritated and they had all drunk what the *sommelier* described as '. . . more claret and port than I had expected'.

Pledging his allegiance, Murry seized on the resemblance to the Last Supper and ended by declaring: 'I love you, but I won't promise not to betray you.' At this Lawrence looked so disappointed that Murry kissed him on the cheek, a gesture which reinforced the idea that he would prove to be the Judas of the feast.

The lumbering Koteliansky then rose unsteadily to make a speech, insisting that Lawrence was such a great man that he had the absolute right to demand such a sacrifice from his disciples. As he paused to drink he slammed one of the glasses on to the table, breaking it. Warming to his theme, he then offended the women guests including Frieda by shouting: 'No woman, here or anywhere else, can possibly understand the greatness of Lawrence.' By the time he had finished denigrating women in general he had broken most of the glasses within reach, sweeping them off the table right and left. Mary Cannan, an attractive woman whom I had seen in the Domino Room with the Murrys, and who was memorable for the way she rolled her eyes pensively when she spoke, was the only one honest enough to tell Lawrence that, much as she liked him, she would not change her home and abandon her other friends for him. Lawrence was unable to reply because, being normally the most temperate of those present, he suddenly slumped forward, vomited on to the table and collapsed unconscious.

I was informed that the dinner was about to end and had positioned myself to watch the 'Master's' departure. I saw him carried downstairs dead drunk by Murry and Koteliansky, who may well have likened his senseless form, already emaciated through illness, to that of the dead Christ as it was carried away from the cross.

I was not alone in witnessing this spectacle. There were several others in the foyer including Hannen Swaffer who, having been severely warned by his doctors, had managed to give up drink completely. Swaff always looked as though he had a bad smell under his nose, but I shall never forget his face as he gazed down at Lawrence with contempt. Holier than holy, like any sudden convert, he was pressing for Prohibition in Britain and urging the Labour Party to incorporate this in its election manifesto.

Lawrence left London soon afterwards, never to visit the Café Royal again. Of the disciples at the 'Last Supper' only Dorothy Brett followed him, and, as even I could have predicted, she soon fell foul of the jealous and tempestuous Frieda who told her to clear off, for all her pain and devotion.

33

DUTIFUL ARTISTS AND ARTFUL DODGERS

Soon after it had become clear that the war would not be over in a few months and casualties began to mount to unprecedented levels, a number of women started the habit of stopping civilians in the street and giving them white feathers as a sign of cowardice. I myself was a recipient on more than one occasion and, being unwilling to explain why there was the strongest medical reason against my becoming a soldier, or because I knew that with my lip-reading skill I would not be believed, I simply had to take the feathers with a shrug or drop them contemptuously on the pavement. No doubt many men, including some invalided out of the Forces, were insulted this way. So were others who were natives of neutral foreign countries, like Chile Guevara. As he was young, obviously healthy and with a fine physique, he was singled out for treatment. His reaction was to offer to prove his individual courage by fighting any man the white feather ladies were prepared to nominate. A few, like G. K. Chesterton, were able to joke their way out of being white-feathered. Once, when 'G.K.' was asked by an irate woman 'Why aren't you out at the Front?', he replied good-naturedly: 'Madam, if you look at me sideways on you'll see that I am very much out at the front.'

As I have already recorded, some of the habitués quickly volunteered for active service, including artists and writers like Wyndham Lewis, Chris Nevinson and Bosie Douglas, who was perhaps rejected because of lingering concern about his homosexuality. But there were others who regarded those ardent patriots as fools and dodged going to war or tried to do so. For them, as Horace Cole remarked, 'It was war to the knife and fork', or, as Rupert Brooke put it, they were 'the sick hearts that honour could not move'.

The Bloomsbury set had a particularly poor record of war service. The homosexuals like Lytton Strachey and Duncan Grant pleaded conscientious objection to any form of violence, though E. M. Forster, who took the weird view that loyalty to one's friends, whatever their nationality, should outweigh loyalty to one's country, at least volunteered for Red Cross work. When Strachey, known as the 'arch-bugger of Bloomsbury', was asked by the tribunal how he would cope with a German who tried to rape his sister, he replied, 'I should attempt to interpose my body between them.' I have no doubt that he would have done so, but not to save his sister. He was every bit as guilty of sodomy as poor Oscar had been, probably more so.

Adrian Stephen, who had been so keen to rag the Navy, was a vocal pacifist. I heard Mark Gertler arguing that the best way he and his fellow artist could help the war effort was to paint! Leonard Woolf was not a 'conchie', as these objectors to risking their skins were contemptuously called, but he was exempted on medical grounds, which did not surprise me because for a long time I had noted that his hands trembled when he picked up a glass or cup. In his conversation I heard Maynard Keynes sympathizing with the pacifists, but his position as an economist in the Treasury ensured his exemption. Keynes, who made a fortune from shrewd financial deals, showed where his sympathies lay by putting on dinners at the Café Royal for his 'conchie' friends like Lytton Strachey, who, at one of them, was heard to cry: 'What difference would it make if the Germans *were* here?' My God! Had the real men of Britain taken that view, our country would have been the doormat of the world.

Even Clive Bell, the husband of Vanessa Stephen, who was fit and sexually normal, managed to get himself exempted as an agricultural worker, though I do not suppose he exerted himself much on the land. Others, including Mark Gertler and Aldous Huxley, joined him on Lady Ottoline Morrell's farm, her husband being one of the few pacifist MPs. Amongst them the Bloomsbury set could have collected enough white feathers to stuff a mattress.

They would certainly have deserved them. I remember hearing Middleton Murry argue that he believed it would be appalling if he were killed in the war because that would make an end to his burning desire to achieve something. What vanity! As though that did not apply to everybody in some degree or other. Murry eventually made some effort but, having suffered from pleurisy, he was given a low medical category and ended up doing censorship work in the War Office. Even there he had to be given sick leave to recuperate from 'nervous strain' – again with the ubiquitous Lady Ottoline, who kept the Bloomsbury set going as a group throughout the war, putting on hectic parties for them at her house in Bedford Square as well as in the country.

Details of one of these country weekends, circulated gleefully in the Domino Room, cast revealing light on the nature of the Prime Minister, Herbert Asquith. According to people who were there, Asquith visited the Morrells one afternoon during the Easter of 1916 and, though he had recently introduced the Conscription Bill making all unmarried men liable for military service – and was soon to extend it to married men – he spent the day consorting with Lady Ottoline's collection of pacifists. But not quite all the day: while Asquith's wife, the redoubtable Margot, was being shown round the estate by Mr Morrell, Ottoline inveigled the Prime Minister into her bedroom where they indulged in what she called 'prostitute love'! Perhaps there was something in the air there for, according to Roger Fry, everybody, except himself, was blithely at it!

The conscientious objectors pretended to be proud of their non-combatant status and I remember one of them, who would have been among the first on his knees had the Germans arrived, calling out to someone in uniform on leave from the trenches: '*We* are the civilization you are fighting for!' He was fortunate not to be ducked in the foyer fountain.

Another who did not serve was the bellicose Philip Heseltine, alias Peter Warlock. He voiced conscientious objections to spilling anybody's blood, including, of course, his own, and made no attempt to join the war effort as a stretcher bearer, which many who were not afraid for their skins did. 'They can blow themselves to bits so long as they don't touch me,' was his reaction. When he appeared before the tribunals he had been excused because of 'nervous trouble', but when called to appear again in the summer of 1917 he took off for Ireland, only returning the following year when the war was as good as won. I noticed that he then wore dark blue spectacles and a hat with a floppy brim covering his eyes. Perhaps they were badges of his shame.

I did not need to be told that Ronald Firbank had been rejected on medical grounds. Even had he not been tuberculous his obvious effeminacy would have barred him, though his friend Evan Morgan served. In any case he would have been worse than useless in any kind of action. He even pretended to be allergic to the colour of khaki, poor sensitive soul, and recoiled in horror when someone in the Domino Room introduced him to Chris Nevinson, who became an outstanding war artist and was in uniform. After the bombs started dropping on London, Firbank immediately took off for Oxford to continue with his novel *Caprice*, in which he portrayed the Café Royal, and to forget the war.

How different was the behaviour of C. E. Montague, the distinguished critic, who always expressed his highly original views so quietly and inoffensively. He dyed his grey hair black so that he would not be rejected by the Army on age. As Nevinson put it, 'He is the only man whose hair turned black overnight through courage.' Happily, Montague survived the war to entertain us with his wit for many more years, as did Ashley Dukes, who became a successful playwright and brought us an exciting new 'recruit' – his Polish wife Marie Rambert, who founded the ballet of that name.

Horace Cole, who had his own method of handing out the white feather, selected Jacob Epstein as his main target; he would insult him whenever he could, especially if the sculptor was accompanied by one of his models, such as the beautiful and notorious Dolores, who affected black veils to make herself look 'mysterious' and whom Cole would loudly describe as 'a whore'. He was particularly vicious when Epstein, who was not very articulate, was in the Café with Bill Davies, making arrangements for sculpting his head. Presumably Davies was exempted from the tirade only because of his wooden leg, which made war service impossible, but at one point I thought he might take off his leg and hit Cole over the head with it. When Cole heard that Epstein, who had accepted the hospitality of England, had applied for exemption to military service, he did all he could behind the scenes to ensure that the tribunal would reject his application, inducing other sculptors to write to the newspapers about it. The tribunal did what Cole wanted, with the curt advice: 'You have made a name for yourself as a sculptor, so we are giving you a chance to make a name for yourself as a soldier.'

The moment Epstein appeared in the Domino Room in a Tommy's uniform, reasonably clean for once with a khaki 'cheesecutter' on his balding head instead of his usual porkpie hat, Cole let out a whoop of delight, for it meant that none of Epstein's friends who were officers, as several were, should sit with him. He was therefore red with anger when Osbert Sitwell, the writer, who with his brother Sacheverell, the poet, had attached himself to the Bloomsbury set, and by now was a Grenadier Guards officer, entered the Domino Room in uniform and sat at Epstein's table to have a drink with him. Cole made sure that this breach of army discipline was reported to Sitwell's commanding officer but nothing could have been done about it because Lieutenant Sitwell continued to consort with Private Epstein.

I was only sorry that Frank Harris was not in the country to receive one of Cole's white feathers, for Frank fancied himself as a boxer and they would have been well matched but, after spending a month in prison for contempt of court, Harris was bankrupt so he had left for France. A little later Cole, who seemed bent on carrying on the feud-fighting tradition of George Baird, the Squire, harassed Epstein in front of Cecil Gray. When someone suggested that Cole should shake hands with Epstein now that he was in uniform he replied, 'I didn't know that snakes had any hands.' Gray, who heard the remark, happened to be a great admirer of Epstein's work and for once – wallop! Cole was hit on the nose before he could strike first; Gray put up a good show but Cole was more experienced and, like the Irishman he was, he loved a brawl. The two men were separated by the commissionaires and then treated in the time-honoured way laid down by Auguste Judah, the general manager. Gray was escorted to the front entrance and Cole to the back, the latter being told that he was finally barred from the Café until further notice.

I have to confess that, while Cole was a bully, my sympathies were with him so far as Epstein was concerned. The sculptor was not a nice man. In his way he could be almost as truculent himself and he never ceased blowing his own trumpet. He was also very jealous, and I believe that it was his envy of Augustus John's growing success which suspended their friendship during the war.

Though Cole's hostility was so open, Epstein chose to blame Augustus John for his call-up, and drew attention to the fact that John was sitting out the war at home. In fact I knew that John had made several efforts to get to the Front as a war artist, but was repeatedly rejected because of some knee injury. It was not until the autumn of 1917 that the War Office finally accepted him, and by then he had already taken up an offer from Sir Max Aitken, the future Lord Beaverbrook, to be a war artist for Canada. John staggered us all by appearing in the Domino Room, with his old friend Arthur Symons, in the uniform of a Canadian major – laced riding boots, spurs and all! Further, he had undergone the indignity of having his hair cut and his beard trimmed. What greater sacrifice could he have made! There were loud cheers as he went to various tables to shake hands before leaving for the Front, where, he explained, he had undertaken to do a massive painting depicting the Canadian war effort.

It turned out that John was one of only two officers in the British Forces who were allowed to wear a beard. This meant that he was often confused with the other one – King George V. He remained only a few months at the Front and, characteristically, though he did a lot of work on the painting, he never finished it. It was rumoured round the Domino Room that Augustus had been sent back in disgrace after striking a Canadian officer while drunk. I was soon to see evidence that this was more than likely. One evening, soon after his return, still in uniform, he was sitting with Chile Guevara, David Garnett, a member of the Bloomsbury set, and a few others. Though the drinking was heavy there was no angry argument, but suddenly Augustus turned to Chile and stubbed out his cigarette on his cheek. I was waiting for Guevara to shout and strike but he sat impassively, pretending not to notice the pain though the burn was visible. Either it suited him to show how tough he was or he felt that *Le Maître*, as he called John, was so privileged that he could do what he liked. The latter was certainly Augustus's view.

While some artists were away at the Front, their models remained and they greatly helped to enliven the dark days of the war. Foremost among these was a former model of Jacob Epstein's called Lillian Shelley (no relation to the poet, I am sure), who also happened to be a friend of Horace Cole, whose exile from the Café had been short-lived. The raven-haired Lillian was full of energy and fun, and was also a good singer, appearing at, or perhaps I should say in, the Cave of the Golden Calf, one of the first night clubs in London, run by an extraordinary woman called Madame Strindberg, widow of the famous Swedish writer. Madame, always wearing a fur coat whatever the weather and with a face chalk-white with make-up, occasionally looked in at the Domino Room, from which she drew some of her best customers.

Lillian also appeared along with other model—mistresses, like Euphemia Lamb and Betty May, at a rival club started by Augustus John called the Crab Tree, to which many Domino Room regulars repaired after the Café Royal closed for the night. I peeped in once, but found the atmosphere oppressive and the decor by Wyndham Lewis and others too modern for my taste. Lillian's best known numbers were 'You Made Me Love You' and 'Popsy Wopsy', which she had made a Domino Room favourite years before and was always in great demand when she was in the Café because we could join in the lines we knew. Lillian never failed to oblige, usually climbing on top of one of the marble tables to perform. In the style of Marie Lloyd, she accompanied her songs with suggestive gestures, taking out her hatpin and using it with an upward jerk, then throwing away her cartwheel hat and loosening her long blonde curls in the manner of what is now called 'strip-tease'. She would also dance as she sang, and one night she fell off the table on top of Horace Cole who, I remember, was getting the best possible view of her long, shapely legs.

Lillian was great fun and it was she, I believe, who told the story about how she was lying half-clothed on a couch with some ardent artist who, on hearing footsteps cried: 'Quick, it's my wife. Strip!' The song for which I remember her best did much to keep our spirits alive during the darkest days of the war. It was called 'Sing, Sing, Why Shouldn't We Sing', and the last lines used to bring a lump to my throat:

> *There's one thing we never should forget,*
> *Old John Bull is still alive and kicking*
> *And we haven't pulled the blinds down yet!*

Another whose songs and spirit uplifted us all was Alice Delysia, though she kept her efforts to the legitimate stage. Within the Café Royal she restricted her entertainment to her favourite toast, which became so popular and so well responded to that it was incorporated in the revue *Passing Show* – 'Let us eat, drink and be merry, for we will be a damned long time dead!'

With many artists away, and few people in the mood to buy pictures or have their portraits painted, most of the models had to find other employment. Some took the easy way, for demands in that direction had increased, but others got themselves ordinary jobs. One I recall had gone to work in a hairdresser's and, having heard that someone who had handled imported hairnets had developed leprosy, rushed into the Domino Room shouting: 'I've got leprosy! I've got leprosy!' There were a few moments of consternation in case it might be true, but a few brandies provided by her friends effected a rapid cure.

While behaviour in the Domino Room had always been extravagant, to say the least, it became more so during the war, which somehow loosened inhibitions and accentuated the trivial in conversation, seriousness being out of joint with the time. Few, therefore, took much notice when George Belcher, the very capable artist, was beaten about the head with a large lobster wielded by his lady guest, the actress Olive Richardson, or when Sir Edward Marshall Hall, the distinguished advocate, suddenly found himself dripping with red wine thrown by a woman who thought he had been eyeing her legs with lascivious thoughts.

Nor was the great scientific experiment on the precise cause of drunkenness, carried out by G. K. Chesterton and Hilaire Belloc, out of character either for them or for the Domino Room. In this carefully controlled test they met one evening and drank nothing but whisky and water, becoming drunk in the process. The next night they drank gin and water with the same effect. On the third night brandy and water also produced the frank symptoms of intoxication. After a logical summing up they concluded that, as water was the only constant factor in the experiment, it must be the cause of the symptoms. So water was to be avoided in future. Q.E.D. Both Chesterton and Belloc hated science for its inroads into religious belief and never missed an opportunity to deride it, especially when it was being championed by H. G. Wells who made a God of it.

Further comic relief from the horrors of war was provided by Lord Alfred Douglas, who conducted a campaign against the Asquiths because of Margot's friendship with Robert Ross. The trial in which Ross had sued Douglas for libel, and which Ross had effectively lost, had revealed that he had been a frequent visitor to No. 10 Downing Street during Asquith's premiership. After it had also demonstrated that Ross was an inveterate homosexual, well known to the police, Douglas wrote to Asquith insisting that he should denounce him. Instead, no doubt at Margot's behest, Asquith organized a testimonial to Ross which was signed by Shaw, Wells, J. L. Garvin, the Bishop of Birmingham, and, sure enough, Lady Ottoline Morrell. Lord Alfred was so furious that he wrote to King George urging him to proceed against Asquith for giving comfort to such 'a notorious sodomite'. He also published some vicious verses, one of which ended:

> Since here 'at home' sits Merry Margot, bound
> With Lesbian fillets, while with front of brass
> 'Old Squiffy' hands the purse to Robert Ross.

'Squiffy', of course, was Asquith's nickname, and the 'purse' was the Board of Trade appointment he had given Ross.

One of the few benefits of the war was that it brought Max Beerbohm back from Italy, where he had set up permanent home with his wife. I was delighted to see him in his old haunt, looking a little older but otherwise the same. He was living mainly by drawing caricatures and selling them at exhibitions in London, and it was remarkable that he had been able to do this from a distant villa in

Rapallo. Somehow he conjured up the mental pictures of his subjects and all he needed was a pencil, paper and a card table. Many of Max's old friends had died or deserted the Domino Room for other reasons, but there were enough to keep him in convivial company. He remained, of course, a writer of some distinction, but I had heard him explaining to Reggie Turner how much he preferred drawing.

'Literary composition is so tiresome. Words have to be carved out of stone, while for me drawing is fun. As for my days of dramatic criticism, the only theatre I have ever taken seriously was a cardboard affair given me on my fifth birthday.'

Reggie, whose guiding principle was '. . . always to say the things that please one's friends most', had replied rather lugubriously, 'I agree. Writing is an agony but it is all I shall ever be able to do. With most authors it is the first editions that are rare. With my novels it will be the second editions.' He was right, but his lack of commercial success was of no financial consequence. He was always independent and became very rich when his half brother died, leaving him much of his fortune.

Meanwhile the wretched 'war that was to end wars' ground on, killing and maiming thousands every day. Lord Kitchener was in charge, as Secretary of State for War, his heavily moustached face on hoardings everywhere telling what young men remained that their country needed them. In May 1916 he received an invitation from the Tsar of Russia to visit that country to discuss how the 'Russian steamroller', as the Tsar's huge army was called, could be used to better purpose. He left London on the night of 4 June and the public was stunned next day to hear newsboys shouting that he had been drowned at sea. It was so staggering that some newsboys, who were notorious for shouting false alarms to sell their papers, were assaulted by disbelieving customers. But it was only too true. Kitchener had been lost at sea off the Orkney Islands and there were many who suspected that he had fallen into some kind of trap, though few sided with Bosie's fantastic suggestion that it had been organized by the Jews.

Later that same month there was another sensation – the arrest of Sir Roger Casement, the Irish Nationalist politician who had deserted to Germany in October 1914 to secure assistance for an Irish revolution. After German arms had been dispatched to Ireland for the Easter Rising he returned to Ireland by U-boat, but was captured and brought to London for trial. With my Café Royal friend, F. E. Smith, prosecuting and the facts being so clear-cut the result was inevitable.

Casement was convicted of high treason and sentenced to death. He appealed, but five judges rejected his case and he was duly hanged at Pentonville, to bitter cries of protest from the Irish, to whom he was a hero. Once again we were to learn that a man of great distinction and intelligence had been a practising homosexual. Diaries recording details of his activities had fallen into the hands of the authorities and I suspect that, when the cabinet had met to consider the political repercussions if he were executed, his abnormality, which was then a crime, had sealed his fate. I understand that his diaries, the existence of which was 'leaked' by the government, revealed such extraordinary behaviour that some attempt was made to have him declared insane, but medical experts decided that he was not certifiable. How strange is the way in which sex, in its various forms, cuts clean across intellectual capacity!

Another fascinating aspect of human behaviour is the extent to which the mind can adapt to almost any circumstances and learn to live with them. As the war dragged on, those of us at home, and, I suspect, many of those in the trenches, came to regard it as just another 'way of life'. We became so punch-drunk with the appalling casualty rates that they ceased to have impact, save to those bereaved. It is now clear that in 1917 the nation was in mortal danger, with the German U-boats threatening to starve us into submission, the French almost exhausted and Russia on the brink of revolution. Yet we seemed almost unaware of our extremity and lived optimistically from day to day.

By the grace of God, and not, as widely believed, through German stupidity in sinking the liner *Lusitania* with many Americans aboard, for that had happened two years earlier, the United States entered the war in the spring of 1917 and helped to turn the tide. But there was still a long, long trail a-winding. . . .

One evening in February 1918 Augustus John, Jacob Epstein and Osbert Sitwell were enjoying a drink together in the Domino Room when a very young and very good-looking army officer approached their table and asked John for a light for his cigarette. I had never seen him before and it was obvious from the pristine condition of his uniform, especially of the greatcoat which he had unbuttoned to display its dashing scarlet lining, that he was very recently commissioned.

Perhaps because of his extreme youth – he turned out to be nineteen – Augustus not only gave him a light but invited him to sit at his table. Smiling broadly at this good fortune, which he had clearly been trying to engineer, the officer introduced himself as Beverley Nichols.

'I take it that the red lining is to prevent your troops from being dismayed by the sight of blood if you are wounded in battle,' Augustus quipped.

'Our khaki trousers are for a similar purpose,' said Epstein, who relished lavatorial jokes which, happily, were not common in the Domino Room. The ensuing conversation was not of much note, mainly because Sitwell was trying to write a poem on a menu card, but Nichols was to become very much a Café Royalite and make a considerable name for himself as a journalist, writer and composer of revues.

His success at meeting three such eminent habitués so endeared him to the Domino Room that he was hardly ever out of it during the ensuing weeks, when he managed to insinuate himself into the company of D. H. Lawrence, a number of left-wing politicians including Ramsay MacDonald, and Chile Guevara among other artists. The way Chile made his acquaintance was of some interest. I noticed him looking at Nichols and making a pencil sketch of him on the marble top of his table. This was a common enough practice, but Chile sent his waiter over to ask Nichols to join him. I noted Nichols's suprise when he looked at the drawing, and later the waiter told me that Chile had drawn him in the nude. Rather foolishly, Nichols agreed to go back to Chile's studio, and later I heard him regretting it. As I have said, Chile, though attractive to the girls, also had homosexual desires.

I realized that Beverley, as I came to call him, must have some post in London and I saw him whisper, when pressed, that he was attached to the Secret Service. Frankly I rather doubted this myself, but it turned out to be true, though not for long. Somehow word reached his superiors, who must have sent agents into the Domino Room to spy on him, for I heard him explain afterwards that he had been thrown out of the Secret Service for suspicious behaviour. The espion- age authorities did not want a young man who consorted with dangerous people like artists, especially anyone as unstable as Guevara, or who talked to pacifists as subversive as Ramsay Mac- Donald. Fancy being thrown out of the Secret Service for conversing with a man who was soon to be elected Prime Minister and would be responsible for it!

Later that year, in November, the Germans and their allies finally collapsed. Our first news of this was a salvo of guns fired at 11 a.m. on

11 November. I am looking, as I write, at a yellowing copy of the London *Evening Standard* for that date. 'END OF THE WAR,' the banner headline proclaims, followed by: 'Germany signs our terms and fighting stopped at 11 o'clock today.'

Armistice Day was one of the most memorable in my long life, not just for the relief that the slaughter was ended but for the celebrations in the Domino Room, which were repeated in towns and villages throughout the land. Outside, the streets were packed with carts, drays, cabs and masses of jubilant men and women, singing, slapping each other on the back, hugging and kissing. There were long queues outside the shops and stalls to buy Union Jacks, which had miraculously appeared. (We had all learned to queue in patience.) It looked as though there had been a snowstorm, with everyone knee-deep in torn-up paper thrown from buildings. The day, in fact, was fine but chilly and most were wearing overcoats – soldiers, sailors, civilians and girl munition workers linking arms and singing 'It's a Long Way to Tipperary' and the other war songs which had such rousing tunes that they will never be forgotten. One such was a nonsense refrain, but when it had been sung by the boys in the trenches it had made sense to them: 'We're 'ere because we're 'ere because we're 'ere because we're 'ere. . . .' As I heard it sung in Piccadilly Circus that night I fancied it welling up from serried graves in Flanders – 'We're 'ere because we're 'ere because. . . .' There seemed to be no other reason to account for the absence of so many of 'the lads of the village' from Piccadilly and Leicester Square. Outside Buckingham Palace, which I could not possibly have reached, people were cheering and shouting for the King.

The Domino Room began to fill around mid-day, when I was already safe in my seat. For some reason all the habitués seemed to have made a point of being there, save for those who had lost their lives and the pacifists who wisely kept away, though Duncan Grant had the brass nerve to look in. The hubbub that lasted through the day made it impossible for me to record any conversation of interest, not that I was in the mood to do so. Everybody let themselves go in singing, flag-waving and dancing on the tables, the coteries forgetting their allegiances in the relief of spontaneous celebration.

There were, of course, several officers in uniform with juster cause to celebrate their survival than any of us mere civilians. One of them who had drunk more than the others, or could take less, was wandering round from table to table with a bottle and a glass trying to secure enough silence for a toast he was determined to propose. He seemed to be remarkably patient as table after table refused to be subdued, but finally he climbed unsteadily on to one of them and, with a great shout which commanded momentary attention, he raised his full glass. 'I give you a toast,' he slurred, 'To the dear old Kaiser!' For a moment I thought he might be bombarded with bottles, but the crowd saw the humour of it, for there seemed to be little doubt that 'Kaiser Bill', who had gone down in total defeat, would soon be hanged. Everyone stood, raised their glasses and there was a mighty shout of: 'The dear old Kaiser!' with additions like 'God rot him'. Emptied glasses were smashed on to the floor, hats thrown into the air, waiters' trays thumped up to the ceiling, crockery and all, as we all said 'Good riddance' to the rotten war, as we then believed, forever.

34

THE SECRET LIFE OF THE CAFE ROYAL ARAB

Augustus John's reputation continued to soar to the extent that there was a song with which he was often greeted in the Domino Room and ran: 'Oh, John, how you have got on . . .', while someone invented a rhyme recording that:

> *When Augustus John*
> *Really slaps it on*
> *His price is within fourpence*
> *Of Orpen's.*

So it surprised nobody when, in the spring of 1919, the Prime Minister, Lloyd George, invited him to attend the Peace Conference in Versailles with a view to an artistic record of some of its personalities. There John met the legendary T. E. (for Thomas Edward) Lawrence, 'Lawrence of Arabia', one of the strangest and most exciting personalities ever to visit the Domino Room.

He came there first with John in 1919 after having his portrait painted in Arab dress. When I learned who he was I was disappointed by his appearance which in 'mufti', as we used to call ordinary civilian dress in those days, was not that of a man who had been made Prince of Mecca and recommended for the Victoria Cross for his exploits against the Turks. Lawrence was only about my size, five feet five or so, but stocky, with an over-size head, unsmiling looks and a hard jaw that could be described as brutal, though he could turn on the charm.

It soon became clear from his conversation that he was peculiar, for I heard him tell John that he could not understand why he should want to draw the female body when the male was so much better proportioned. On that first occasion, and during subsequent visits, John was joined by one of his mistress-models, and it was plain to see that Lawrence was uneasy in the company of a young and pretty woman.

John was trying to discover what Lawrence, whom his friends and relations called 'Ned', proposed to do in the future, and though we now know that he had begun to write his famous book, *Seven Pillars of Wisdom*, he never mentioned it but kept fobbing John off with his bitter theme about the way Lloyd George's government had reneged on its promises to the Arabs.

Later I heard Lawrence going on about this to Will Rothenstein, another artist who drew his portrait. On Lawrence's word Prince Feisal had been assured that he would be King of Syria, but behind his back the Foreign Office had assured the French that they could have Syria as their share of a carve-up of the Middle East. It became clear to me from his talk with Rothenstein, and on a later occasion with Eric Kennington, another war artist, that Lawrence loathed the French. 'The French will make a mess of it,' he said. 'They are the wrong people to deal with Arabs. They will always be resented. With Feisal as King we could exert our influence there.'

It seemed incredible that this little man with the perpetual smile and high-pitched giggle, who so recently had captured the port of Akaba from the Turks and inflicted many other defeats in brilliant guerilla actions, should be only in his early thirties. He was understandably bitter, for shortly before the Armistice he had been landed with the job of telling Feisal that he could not have Syria and would have to put up with being King of Irak.

It was clear that, in addition to being angry about his diplomatic defeat by the French, for which he blamed Lloyd George, Lawrence was deeply concerned about his own historical standing. Maybe I misjudge him, but I got the impression that he was a vain man. Nevertheless, I had to admire the way he had refused honours from King George when I heard the American poet Ezra Pound, who was a friend, telling the story to the artist Wyndham Lewis.

'Ned was turned down for the Victoria Cross because the rules require that some British officer has to witness the deed,' Pound explained. 'They wouldn't take the word of any of the Arabs. So, as he already had the DSO, it was decided that he would have to make do with being a Commander of the Bath, whatever that may be.'

'Damn nonsense!' exclaimed Lewis, whose swarthy looks contrasted with Pound's red-gold hair and beard.

'The King called Ned to a private audience and had the decorations ready, but Ned told him he wouldn't accept them until the government honoured its pledges to the Arabs.'

'Good for him,' Lewis said. 'How did the King take it?'

'He was very crusty because Ned had underlined his anger with a few profanities.'

'Well, the King's pretty useful with lower-deck language himself, I gather.'

'Maybe,' Pound said. 'But he's also very grand. Anyway, he had no alternative but to excuse Ned from accepting the medals.'

'But what will it achieve?' Lewis asked rhetorically. 'It won't move the government.'

Lewis had been right, and Lawrence became increasingly embittered. But I wondered what he would have done had the coveted VC been on offer? I doubt whether any man would refuse such a magnificent distinction.

Incidentally, I noticed another similarity between Lawrence and myself in addition to lack of height – he was withdrawn, through some peculiarity, as I was by my deafness. Whoever he was with in the Café – and he came often enough to become known as the Café Royal Arab – he always seemed to be itching to get away.

Immediately after the war there was not all that much public interest in Lawrence. The legend arose later because of the efforts of an American journalist called Lowell Thomas who realized its potential. He gave a series of lectures in London and elsewhere, illustrated by lantern slides, and I attended one of them at the Albert Hall. The place was packed, for Thomas was a fine lecturer, with that deep American voice which somehow imparts authority, and had some excellent photographs of the desert campaigns which he had made into slides. He certainly fired my imagination and eventually made himself into a millionaire by promoting the Lawrence of Arabia legend. Lawrence himself was supposed to have deplored his efforts, but I have doubts about that. I heard Augustus John say that Lawrence had attended one of the lectures 'incognito'. What a sensation there would have been had he been detected in the audience!

In 1921, when he was acting as adviser on Arab affairs to Winston Churchill, he came into the Domino Room with Kennington and I heard him say that he wanted to get away somewhere 'to write in peace'. Shortly after that he disappeared from the public scene, and there were rumours that he had returned to the desert again as a secret agent. Then, suddenly, on the day after Boxing Day in 1922, we knew the truth. 'Famous War Hero Becomes Private,' the *Daily Express* headline blared. The Prince of Mecca had joined the Royal Air Force in the lowest possible rank, under the name of John Ross!

Immediately there was a theory that this was a new cover for spying activities, being established with government approval and now ruined by the exposure. But I think Augustus John had it right when he remarked: 'He couldn't join the Foreign Legion so he joined the RAF'. It transpired that an RAF officer had 'shopped' him to the *Express* for £30, though I suspect that sum was a Fleet Street figment relating to the thirty pieces of silver for which Judas betrayed Jesus. Augustus John had been assured that Lawrence could have remained in the RAF if he had been prepared to accept a commission, but he refused. Why? I think that his strange, secret life offers the answer.

While Lawrence never appeared in the Domino Room while in the RAF or during his brief stay in the Tank Corps, which he joined under the name of Shaw, there was much gossip about him there by certain unpleasant people, a Chelsea set with peculiar habits, dominated by a creature who called himself Bluebeard. They alleged that, while in the desert, Lawrence had become a peculiar type of homosexual who could achieve satisfaction only by being beaten on his bare backside with a cane or birch. For this service, which had to be administered by a man – unlike Swinburne who had required a woman flagellator – he was prepared to travel long distances and to pay.

What I have gathered from listening to Scotland Yard detectives discussing such cases suggests that, with the passing of the years, such a beating has to be more and more severe to produce the desired effect. In Scotland Yard's 'Black Museum', they said, there are flagellation sticks with barbed wire wrapped around them to inflict such dreadful wounds that the recipients require hospital treatment. I do not know that Lawrence ever reached this terrible stage, and whatever people do privately should be their own affair, but if the Chelsea gossip was true it explained why Lawrence joined the RAF, then the Army, insisting on the lowest rank. He was one of those weird men who needed humiliation. They are far from being uncommon, for I have heard Domino Room tarts describing how some of their clients required no intercourse but only to be abused verbally or to have strange missiles thrown at them while they stand naked. One of these women, amid gusts of laughter from the others, described a cultured man whose weekly requirement was to be ridden like a horse while the lady rider dug deep into his flesh with sharp spurs, which he provided!

As I was never to see Lawrence again I may as well dispose of him now, so far as this book is concerned. After he finally left the RAF early in 1935 he went to live in seclusion on Salisbury Plain, and again there were romantic rumours that he had been released in readiness to visit Hitler to sound out his intentions. Then, only a few weeks later, in May, he was severely injured in a motor-cycle accident and died within a few days. Murder by agents of a foreign power was quickly suspected, especially when a mysterious black car was said to have been near the scene. There were many who refused to believe that anything had happened to Lawrence at all: the 'accident' had been staged to free him for other duties in the Middle East, news-papers suggested. Time and again during the Second World War there were 'eye-witness' reports that he was active in the desert. For my part I have no doubt that when Eric Kennington and the other pall-bearers carried the coffin into the church near Bovington Camp it contained the mortal remains of Lawrence of Arabia.

Another Domino Room character who had attended the Peace Conference at Versailles and whose advice was rejected was John Maynard Keynes. He was convinced that the Germans were in such a weak financial condition after their defeat that they could not poss-ibly pay for the reparations being demanded. As chief Treasury representative at the conference he warned that, if they were forced to do so, there could be grave political consequences in the years ahead. He eventually published his fears in 1919 in an important book called *The Economic Consequences of the Peace*, and was to live to see not only the collapse of the German democracy and the rise of Hitler, but all the horrors of the Second World War, which he traced to the missed opportunities of Versailles.

I do not pretend to understand the so-called science of economics (the 'laws' never seem to work), but Keynes was regarded as an important innovator in that field and one of his books, *The General Theory of Employment, Interest and Money*, caused a tremendous stir. Whether his theories were sound or not he made a big fortune for himself through financial manipulations, and after being enobled to Lord he died of heart trouble in 1946, aged only sixty-three.

I have already mentioned how some of the habitués who had absented themselves in safe retreats during the war returned when it was over. They were soon joined by Ezra Pound and Ronald Firbank, who was back in his old banquette seat being plied with brandy by George, his waiter, and pursuing his crackpot conversation. For some time this centred on a proposed libel action against Osbert Sitwell, whom he accused of spreading a rumour that the Firbank family fortunes had been founded on the manufacture of boot buttons. In fact, as Firbank never tired of pointing out, his grandfather had 'made beautiful railways'. But what did it matter, especially when he pretended to be ashamed that his father had once been a Member of Parliament?

Firbank in the witness box was a prospect to which we all looked forward, but he dropped the idea of an action. Instead he made a public fool of himself in another way, which for a few days was the talk of the Café. Grant Richards, the publisher, decided to give a banquet at the Café Royal in honour of Chris Nevinson, who was leaving for a one-man art show in New York. His fellow artist Walter Sickert was in the chair, and after making an impressive speech he introduced the main speaker, who was the well-known, but somewhat pompous, Irish journalist, J. L. Garvin. There were about a hundred guests who 'hear-heared' as Garvin over-sang Nevinson's talents, save for Firbank who had been invited because Richards was his publisher. Firbank began to guffaw at each paean of praise, and his laughter became so uncontrollable that even when he stuffed a handkerchief into his mouth it had little effect. Finally he had to be escorted out in hysterics by Chile Guevara. Garvin and Sickert were understandably furious, though Nevinson himself shrugged off the embarrassment as being 'typically Firbank'.

35

GREEN HAT AND RED TOQUE

The great inventor, Thomas Edison, said: 'Genius is one per cent inspiration and ninety-nine per cent perspiration', and I would guess, from my own modest efforts, that this applies to literary work. If that is true, it implies that most people could write at least reasonably well and successfully if they are determined to make the effort. Such a character, whom I have already mentioned by name and who was so determined, appeared in the Domino Room in 1920 in the shape of a slight, dark and very oriental-looking young man with a large nose, sloping forehead, large ears and the unpronounceable Armenian name of Dikran Kouyoumdjian, whom the waiters were soon calling 'Kumjy Jumjy'. He had a flat in Shepherd Market, which was quite near Regent Street, so he was often in the Café Royal, though he was then quite poor.

The first time I saw Kumjy he was having a drink with Nancy Cunard, the heiress who was continuing to shock conventional society with her openly promiscuous sexual behaviour and would do so throughout her life. Nancy was the first woman I observed to approach sex like a man. She was prepared to take the initiative, and had that other masculine feature I have previously alluded to of being indiscreet about it, either because she did not care who knew about her private life, or perhaps because she gained additional satisfaction through the public knowledge of it.

The two looked an unlikely couple, as they sat close together at a table fortunately near mine, because Nancy was strikingly good-looking while, to me, Kumjy was strikingly the reverse. Their interest could of course have been purely literary, but I did not think so. Her taste in men was already catholic and eventually, because of her open love affairs with negroes, she was to break with her mother, Lady Cunard, who had kept her in luxury, for black—white relationships were deplored in those days far more than they are now.

'I am determined to be rich and famous,' I heard Kumjy say. 'And I intend to do both with my pen.'

'You won't do it as a poet,' said Nancy, whose interest lay in verse, which she had been writing from her early teens, and was, so she said, the only aspect of her behaviour of which her mother approved.

'Short stories are my *métier*,' Kumjy said confidently. 'Short stories and then novels.'

'There are a lot of poverty-stricken novelists,' Nancy warned, lighting yet another cigarette from the butt in her long telescopic holder, which she joked that she used because her mother had told her to 'stay away from cigarettes'.

'Mine will sell!'

'Why are you so sure?' Nancy asked. 'What are they going to be about?'

'People like you,' Kumjy said with a smile. 'And like the other interesting characters here,' he added, embracing the tables with an airy wave of both hands.

Naturally, I was not pleased to hear that someone else, obviously more expensively educated than I was, intended to write about the people of the Domino Room. But he had said 'novels', and he had already missed so many of the characters who I had observed and whose conversation and habits were safely crystallized in my notes at home.

'Well, I wish you luck, Dick,' Nancy said, using the anglicized form of his first name. 'Writing is an overcrowded profession. . . .'

'I shall edge my way in,' Kumjy replied.

As one who prefers to hear a man boast when taking the saddle off, not when putting it on, I wondered whether his dreams would be realized as they walked out together – she swaying her hips provocatively in a tight, almost tube-like, ankle-length dress, her short blonde hair covered by a red toque and seeming to tower over the diminutive Kumjy.

Armenians are known to be tireless workers and inveterate money-makers and Kumjy's dreams did materialize, though not before he had changed his name to something readers could say more easily and remember – Michael Arlen. After publishing a modestly successful collection of short stories he wrote his first novel, called *Piracy*, which was of great interest to me when I read it because, as I had guessed she might be, the heroine was modelled on Nancy and much of the plot was about her relationship with her mother, thinly and amusingly disguised as Lady Carnal! Arlen had been able to give graphic descriptions from life because, shortly after I had seen them in the Domino Room together, they had gone off to live together in

France, whence various visitors like Chile Guevara, the painter, also captivated by Nancy, and Iris Tree, brought back the gossip about their affair.

Two years later in 1924 Arlen, as I shall now call him, published one of the big bestsellers of this century, *The Green Hat*. It was a trashy story about a woman like Nancy, who went from bed to bed for fun and not for love, and hated herself for it. Arlen laced the narrative, which was greatly daring for the time, with descriptions of almost unmentionable subjects like promiscuity, miscarriages and even venereal disease. I had heard on the Domino Room 'bush telegraph', some time in 1920, that Nancy had deliberately had her womb removed in Paris so that she would be unable to conceive and would therefore have complete freedom in her sex life. She seemed to have such a self-destructive streak that such a drastic step was by no means out of character, but later it was rumoured that the operation had become necessary because she had contracted venereal disease, a likely eventuality in her style of life. Whatever the truth, Iris March, the 'heroine' of *The Green Hat*, if that description for such a character is permissible, underwent a similar operation.

It was therefore with particular interest that I observed their conversation when next I saw Nancy and Kumjy together in the Domino Room after *The Green Hat* had been published. I imagined that Nancy might be angry, because it must have been obvious to all her friends — and to her mother — that she was the model for Iris March. Not a bit of it! All she did was to accuse Arlen, whom she was now calling 'Baron' for some reason, of writing trash.

'You are a great worker and I think you have real talent, so why don't you write something serious like D. H. Lawrence does.'

Arlen, by then expensively and ostentatiously dressed, gave her a sly smile, which seemed to make him look more oriental than ever, and said, 'It wouldn't sell, would it?'

'So money is your main interest?' asked Nancy, whose first volume of poems, entitled *Outlaws*, had been quite well received by serious critics.

'Never having had much, unlike you, I have to confess that it is,' he said, fingering his pearl and platinum watch-chain.

In London at that time the relief from war was expressing itself, especially among those known as the Bright Young Things, in a mania for dancing, particularly in night clubs, which had sprung up to satisfy the need. The young Prince of Wales, briefly to be Edward VIII, was at the Embassy Club in Bond Street 'living it up' night after night with friends like the Mountbattens, so all Society liked to be there in the hope of being photographed in the company, for the Bright Young Things would do anything for publicity. Arlen cleverly parodied this way of life, not only in *The Green Hat*, which was turned into a play and ran in America, but in more bestsellers. As he had predicted, he did become rich, because his novels happened to strike the right note at the right time, as did those of Aldous Huxley and Evelyn Waugh, both known to me through the Domino Room. Though clever, Arlen's work was not so well written as Huxley's or Waugh's and, literary fashion being as fickle as it is, his popularity was not long-lived – after moving to the United States he passed out of our knowledge.

Before he left us, however, Arlen made a generous gesture to a struggling young Domino Room visitor who, perhaps as a result, soared to far more scintillating and lasting fame. This was the twenty-four-year-old Noel Coward who had completed a play called *The Vortex* and wanted to stage it with himself in the leading part. During lunch with Arlen, in which they discussed their ambitions, Coward happened to mention his cash problem. With no hesitation Arlen wrote him a cheque and *The Vortex* attracted such publicity that Coward became a theatrical personality overnight.

It could be said that Kumjy had been lucky, compared with so many less successful writers. Nevertheless he had made the effort and disciplined himself to work hard, so I never begrudged him his triumph as did some of the Domino Room writers who knew they were better. Sadly, in this life one is judged by results: as I have remarked elsewhere, there are few rewards for a worthwhile try.

The next literary figure to fall under Nancy's spell was Aldous Huxley, younger brother of Julian, the zoologist. He had met her on occasion in the Domino Room, which he frequented with literary friends like D. H. Lawrence and Osbert Sitwell. Iris Tree was a mutual friend and, I believe, was the first to introduce them. Probably for the simple reason that Nancy, usually a temptress, did not set her cap at him, he took little notice of her and married a Belgian girl. But some time in 1922, by which time he was twenty-eight and had a baby son, Aldous became so infatuated with Nancy that he would gladly have run away with her. On the odd occasions I saw them together in the Domino Room he would ogle her, wrapping and unwrapping his long, thin legs like some lovesick schoolboy. She was never in love with him, not even fleetingly, I imagine, and had intercourse with him only out of curiosity. His performance did not suit her.

'Aldous repels me physically,' she said. 'Going to bed with him is like being crawled over by slugs.'

He could hardly be described as handsome, with his intense, serious features and thick-lensed spectacles, but her harsh attitude hurt him deeply. For him the experience had been something very special; his friends described him as being in a state of 'sexual ecstasy', whatever that may mean. Ecstasy for him or not, Nancy was not prepared to repeat the experience and Huxley attempted to exorcise her dreadful influence by writing a novel called *Antic Hay* in which she was presented, very obviously, as an unpleasantly destructive woman delighting in enslaving men and then discarding them. Huxley's wife declared that the exorcism of Nancy was complete, but in fact his friends reported that his infatuation continued and that he made a further attempt to induce Nancy to live with him. By that time, however, the fluttering 'butterfly of steel', as Chile Guevara called her, was being attracted by other blooms – in France.

36

A BREATH OF FRESH AIR

In January 1923 we were all saddened by the news of Katherine Mansfield's death from tuberculosis. Orage, the man she had called her literary 'master', had unwittingly been responsible for it, so Murry said. Katherine had been in desperate straits and Orage put her in touch with one of those self-styled 'mystics', who always seem to be charlatans to me, called Gurdjieff. She went to his 'Institute' in Paris in the autumn of 1922 believing she would be cured, but the mystic clap-trap treatment only served to accelerate her death. It seems that one only has to devise a totally unfounded theory, surround it with some ritual and call oneself a mystic, to attract disciples by the score. The human mind can be extremely gullible, especially when beset with the fear of death.

Murry, to whom Katherine had remained married while she continued to write up to the end, remarried within the year. Surely he must have believed that he was cursed by Fate when this new wife contracted tuberculosis and died of it. He married yet again, and I hear has lived very comfortably, not only by his own pen, but on the royalties from Katherine's works which came to him as next of kin, for her last short stories were so good that she was being hailed as 'the female Maupassant'. I only read one of them, called 'The Fly'. Though clever, it was not to my taste. Neither were her novels, which had no plot and could never hold my interest. Old-fashioned I may be, but I like a beginning, an end and some meat in the middle.

Murry's critics say that too many of his books and articles have been deliberately written to promote Katherine's reputation so that he could continue to benefit from her royalties. He is still alive, as I write. I wonder if anybody came to like him. Nobody in the Domino Room did, and among the Bloomsbury set he was hated. Frank Harris summed up his character succinctly soon after meeting him — and in characteristic style — 'Murry has no balls, so he will never command respect from men or women.' Nobody could say that about Frank!

Death was also to overtake poor Ronald Firbank, whose health was rapidly deteriorating when he returned from Italy and rejoined us in the Café Royal in 1923. He was more bitter than ever about the lack of recognition of his novels, from which he said he had never earned a penny, though his own behaviour may have been partly to blame. I heard it said that when someone had taken the trouble to introduce him to a Hollywood film-maker he had recoiled in horror with the remark, 'Oh, no . . . he is far too ugly.' Shades of Oscar! He was drowning his sorrow even more deeply in brandy and boys, and could only be described as a drunkard, though no doubt he would now be dignified by the term 'alcoholic', and sometimes had difficulty finding his lips with his glass. Though I did not witness it, he was said to have been so disorientated as to spread caviare over his nose instead of on a piece of toast.

I felt very sorry for him because I suspected that it was fear which had driven him to drunkenness. This was confirmed one Saturday night in 1925, when I saw a dreadful demonstration of man's inhumanity to man. Either Firbank had been told by his doctors, or he had guessed, that he had not much longer to live. He was sitting alone at his table, when suddenly he screamed: 'I don't want to die! I don't want to die!'

The ordinary habitués would have taken no notice, but that evening there were some rough bookies in the Café and one of them, seeing Firbank's powdered face and tinted fingernails, said, 'Don't cry, lady. 'Ere – , 'ave a tanner.'

Not hearing him at all, Firbank repeated, 'I don't want to die! I don't want to die!' as tears streamed down his face.

'Oh, come on, kiss me, fancy boy,' one of the bookies' women cried in a Cockney voice. 'What a shame! He doesn't want to die. Who the 'ell does?'

The bookies and those like them began to jeer, and I was wondering what might be done to help when Nevinson, whom Firbank had once almost rejected because he had been wearing khaki, went over to Firbank's table accompanied by his wife. They took him by the arms and conducted him unsteadily from the room. In the hope that a warmer climate might help his cough Firbank went back to Italy, but died in Rome in the spring of 1926.

At the risk of repeating myself, it was truly remarkable how when one character disappeared he tended to be replaced by another, as though the Café was incapable of attracting anyone who was dull. Firbank's table was taken over by a man who could not have been more dissimilar – short, with a pugnacious jaw and little hair on his egg-shaped head, which seemed to join his chunky little body without benefit of neck. His name was James Agate, and he had come from Manchester to London to work on the *Saturday Review*, after which he had become drama critic for *The Sunday Times*. Agate, who was also to review books for the *Daily Express* and films for the *Tatler*, not only used the Domino Room for correcting proofs and for relaxation but, when he became widely known, held court there as so many had before him. He was pontifical, fancying himself as 'Johnsonian', and always called the waiters, however old, by shouting 'Boy!' in the northern accent he never lost. They did not like it, but did not object to '*Garçon!*', which means the same.

He was fully in the Domino Room tradition, affecting a characteristic dress – loud check overcoat, black bowler, gloves and stick and a monocle, which he would position to scrutinize any new arrival at his table. He set great store by his 'turnout', as he did that of the Hackney horses he owned and showed, and I heard him have a fearful row with some budding poet because he was dirty and dishevelled. But Agate's greatest vanity lay in his pride in his output. He counted the number of words he wrote each week, as Arnold Bennett did, and not only claimed to have outwritten that novelist in that respect but even to have beaten Dickens! He so enjoyed good living that he was permanently in debt, so he had to churn out the words.

He was very much a personality in his own right and he gave me many good laughs, but my main interest in him was in the celebrities he collected round him. Because of his wide professional interests – he was also an authority on classical music – he was on terms of close friendship with theatre people like C. B. Cochran, literary giants like H. G. Wells, with whom he was frequently in the Café, fellow critics like Dilys Powell, and musicians like Mark Hambourg, the pianist who used to strike the keys so hard that his rivals called him the 'piano-tympanist'.

Sometimes actors and actresses whom Agate had slated in his reviews would assail him verbally in the Café, but more often one of them, or some budding writer, would be hoping to curry favour, which I am glad to say rarely materialized unless Agate sensed genuine talent, when he was inclined to be very helpful, as he was to the young Noel Coward. He had, however, a particular dislike of the Bloomsbury set and of anyone purporting to belong to it, regarding them as spurious intellectuals. In this regard I remember his telling a story, which he may well have concocted, about a Bloomsbury 'disciple' who had told him that he was 'blaze with the theatre'.

'I'm delighted to find that one of our young intellectuals is on fire about the theatre,' Agate had responded.

'I said "I'm blaze", the Bloomsburyite explained. 'You know, French for "fed-up".'

After the maunderings of the mystics and romantics Jimmy Agate was like a breath of fresh air.

In the flaming June of 1923 – I remember that the temperature was in the nineties – the Café Royal was agog with gossip about one of Agate's Domino Room friends, H. G. Wells, who seemed about to be embroiled in a most damaging scandal. After a charmed life he faced the exposure of his sexual sins through one of the women he had enjoyed, then spurned. She was a young Austrian journalist called Frau Gatternigg, who had managed to get into Wells's flat in Whitehall Court, where she cut her throat with a razor. Newspapers soon got wind of this intriguing situation, and the *Star* printed a report suggesting that there would be further revelations. Fortunately for H.G. the girl did not die, so he avoided a coroner's inquest. The newspapers knew the background, but against his denials of any sexual involvement they lacked the courage to print the truth which could have injured Wells's reputation – and his sales.

Meanwhile in the Café Royal events of far greater significance to me were unfolding fast. In November 1922 the owners of the Café Royal had devastated us with the announcement that the whole place was to be pulled down and rebuilt. The people really responsible for this outrage were, as usual, the County Council planners sitting in some wretched office miles away, taking decisions about the lives of people for whom they appeared to have no real concern. The regulars who had drifted away from their favourite haunt immediately came back for what they thought might be a last look and their 'Last Supper'. Augustus John was loud in his condemnation. Willie Crosland voiced all our feelings when he said: 'They might as well have told us that the British Empire was to be pulled down and redecorated.' Such was the affection which the old place had generated over the half century of its existence.

Personally I thought my life was about to be totally ruined, for what would I, in my special situation, be able to do with my time? It was a question I had never had to ask myself since that day, thirty-six years previously, when I had wandered into the Domino Room. I had pitied people who had problems about 'passing the time', feeling it to be a dreadful way to look at life, which is all too short. The demolition of my beautiful room and the other splendid features of the Café was sacrilege. What was virtually my home and all my friends were to be taken from me at a stroke! I was desolated, far more than any other habitué of the Café Royal, I believe.

I spent anxious hours wondering how I could preserve my umbilical cord with what had virtually become my womb, for there was no way I could desert the Café in her extremity. Happily things turned out to be not as black as they had seemed. The old Regent Street front door was closed in August 1923 and demolition began, but the Café Royal did not close down because the rebuilding was done piecemeal in sections. We were able to use the old Domino Room for quite a while, and then moved into the new room which replaced it, a room which at first we all hated and which became known as the Brasserie — French for a beer-shop and a name I never used, for I continued to call my old haunt by its first and proper name and shall do so in this book.

The Brasserie was much larger, to create more eating accommodation, so that whole areas were denied to my eyes, and it was far more severe than the old room. We had been deprived of our beautiful mirrors and our friendly caryatids. The new room was anything but 'pure rococo', as Aubrey Beardsley had exclaimed. But the marble-topped tables and the crimson plush settees were there and, though the place could never be the same and some old habitués shunned it, we learned to live with it as one does with most of life's afflictions. A new generation of regulars developed and I was able to continue with my observations. The management made the excuse that they had taken our mirrors and caryatids away because there were not enough to cover the walls of the bigger room. At least they used them in creating the new Grill Room, which also received part of the old painted ceiling. Occasionally I was able to poke my nose inside there, and breathe in the familiar atmosphere, especially around mid-day before the lunch-time clients began to arrive. It must surely be the most beautiful restaurant room in London, maybe in the world.

It has been said that the Domino Room had had its day anyway, because the Bohemians and their like were in decline towards extinction. I disagree, profoundly. Of course the clientele would have changed, because all life is about change, as I have witnessed from my peculiar point of vantage. Indeed change, especially of people's natures, is life's only certainty, but I am convinced that those who came to patronize the Brasserie would have liked the old Domino Room much more. But then I am old myself.

One who bridged the gap between the old Domino Room and the new was Noel Coward, who leaped to fame in 1924 as the author of *The Vortex*, in which he also played the leading role of a neurotic drug addict who, like most of his type, was 'desolate', though well-endowed with wealth, good looks and almost every other attribute save the will to do anything useful. The play was criticized because of its general decadence, especially by Hannen Swaffer, who condemned it; but was a big box-office success and marked the beginning of a most spectacular career in the world of entertainment. Coward had money for the first time and became a regular figure in Café society, being seen not only in the smartest restaurants but in the Domino Room, in the turtle-necked sweaters he made so fashionable. His most regular companion, with whom he would have fearful rows, was Gertrude Lawrence, the Cockney girl with the cheeky, turned-up nose who made an equally brilliant career as an actress. But he was often in the company of C. B. 'Cocky' Cochran with whom he was working on a revue, writing the music as well as the lyrics. We certainly needed some new songs. The rage at that time was a nonsense refrain called 'Yes, We Have No Bananas'.

Another Domino Room character who was in the money in the twenties was Edgar Wallace. And how he spent it! After writing thrillers at an unprecedented rate and becoming the bestselling author of all time, he staged a highly successful play, *The Ringer*, in 1926, following it with *On the Spot*, *The Case of the Frightened Lady* and many more. His output of plays, books and journalism was so incredible that he was accused of employing ghost-writers. I knew from his anger, when he saw some critic in the Café who had suggested this, that it was not true. He offered £5000 to anyone who could show that any words appearing under his name had been written by anybody else, but nobody ever claimed it.

By dictating his tales, instead of writing them, Edgar had made himself into a literary machine capable of writing six books at once or a whole book in three days. His world sales were so vast that he became our best-known character, but he threw his money away on racehorses, Rolls Royces and living like the millionaire he could have become had he garnered his resources for a year or two. Perhaps with a presentiment that his life would be short, he said, 'If I wait until I can afford things I will never have them', which meant that, however much he earned, he was always in debt and had to drive himself to earn more. Another factor in his determination to demonstrate his success to the world may have been his illegitimacy, for which he blamed his mother, an actress who died penniless. Wallace was £140,000 in debt when he died of severe diabetes in 1932, while writing the scripts of a film called *King Kong*. Since then his words have earned the millions he craved.

Such a relentless quest for material possessions was bound to exhaust anyone, however robust. Wallace never learned, as my man-watching soon taught me, that what matters is not what you have but what you are. And it is not goods but other people, whether through your parentage or your social and educational contacts, who make you what you are.

37

OLD FRIENDS IN A NEW SETTING

The renovated Café Royal was not completed until late in 1927, and in the following January was inaugurated by a lunch for five hundred of the rich and famous, presided over by Lord Birkenhead, who, as F. E. Smith had been an old habitué, and who perhaps had made the biggest name for himself. I could not expect to be asked, but, had fidelity been the criterion, I would surely have headed the guest list!

The new seven-storey building was so much bigger that the management had to resort to cabarets and other entertainment to try to fill it, turns like Gracie Fields and Hal Swain's Band being hired to lure the customers. These moves, so much out of the Café Royal tradition, were not successful and the renovation was to prove a total catastrophe for the remnant of the Nicols family, which had started the enterprise. The bills were so greatly in excess of the original estimates that the company had to raise a large loan from the Bank of England. On reading about this in *The Times*, James Agate looked round at the sprinkling of ladies of doubtful virtue and remarked: 'A case of the oldest bank subsidizing the oldest profession!'

As the difficulties of the company intensified, various financiers were consulted in the hope that they would put up money to enable the family to remain in control. One of these, a very occasional customer, was called Clarence Hatry. He too declined to help and the whole business fell into other hands. It was just as well. Hatry was having certificates forged by an engraving firm so that they could be used as collateral for big loans. Eventually his conscience got the better of him, or he knew that ruin was inevitable. He walked into a police station and confessed all, causing a financial crash to the tune of many millions of pounds and ruining thousands of investors.

In April 1929 the Bank decided it had to foreclose on the Café Royal and appointed a receiver. The family which had begun the business was ousted and a new company was set up under new directors, one of whom, Sir George Bracewell Smith, I already knew by sight. Fortunately the Café continued to provide a home for me and many more, enabling me to keep in touch with old friends, who returned after weathering their initial shock, and to make many new ones.

Bernard Shaw was among those who never returned to enliven us, but G. K. Chesterton did and through him we heard odd items of interest about the now world-famous playwright, who had long been living in the village of Ayot St Lawrence in Hertfordshire. Chesterton, who was doing what was almost a knockabout turn with Shaw in platform debates and on the wireless, told us that Shaw had moved to Ayot because he had seen a tombstone in the churchyard there concerning some woman who had died at the age of eighty and bearing the inscription: 'Her time was short.' Being determined to reach a hundred, if he could, he thought the climate there must be conducive to longevity.

I attended one of these debates between the very thin Shaw and the very fat G.K. at the Kingsway Hall on the subject 'Do We Agree?', and of course the two disagreed on everything. What Shaw said had deeper meaning than Chesterton's words, which Max Beerbohm had likened to constant streams of lava flowing down from a volcano, but G.K. raised more laughs, for he was brilliant in repartee. I also listened to the two literary clowns on my crystal set, usually inviting my landlady Mrs Moffat into my room, though she was far more fascinated by the magic of the wireless, as I tinkered with the 'cat's whisker', than interested in what she heard.

One day I heard Chesterton tell Belloc, while shaking with laughter, how some woman in Zürich had written to Shaw suggesting, 'You have the greatest brain in the world and I have the most beautiful body, so we ought to be able to produce the most perfect child.' Shaw had replied: 'What if the child inherits my body and your brains?' This story was widely circulated and, as stories usually are, embellished. It was commonly believed – quite wrongly – for instance, that the woman was Isadora Duncan, the dancer whom I saw once in the Domino Room with Gordon Craig, Ellen Terry's son, who had continued his mother's tradition by having several illegitimate children himself, including one with Isadora. Poor Isadora! She was killed when her long scarf caught in the spokes of a sports car and throttled her!

I would bet that Shaw was delighted when he received the Swiss lady's suggestion, in spite of his reply. He was as vain as the rest and I once heard him say, 'I am proof against all illusions except illusions which flatter me.' He called this 'conceit' rather than 'vanity', but I see no difference. Surely conceit is a vain opinion of oneself. Shaw tried to argue that: 'A man is vain when he accepts the world's estimation of himself, conceited when content with his own.' This kind of argument, so beloved of literary people, was summed up for me by Oscar when he confessed: 'Between me and reality there is a mist of words. The chance of an epigram makes me desert the truth.' The same attitude, I believe, was behind the only occasion on which I ever saw Belloc refuse a drink. When the waiter moved to replenish his glass Belloc stopped him, at which the waiter protested, 'But it's just the luck of the bottle, sir; less than half a glass.'

'That may be,' Belloc barked. 'But can't you see what it does for my morale to be able to refuse it?' I sensed that Belloc had set up the situation just for the chance of making that remark.

Arnold Bennett, whose face was permanently flushed – perhaps with his success – was another who eschewed the Domino Room, feeling, I suspect, that he had become too grand. He was by that time Lord Beaverbrook's most intimate friend, having met him during the war when he served in his Ministry of Propaganda. He dined with him on occasion, in the Restaurant or in a private room, consuming more pills than food, the waiters said, but forgot all about us. The only story I heard told about him concerned his novel *Lord Raingo*, which was about a politician who kept a wife in the country and a mistress in town. At least three cabinet ministers, including Lord Birkenhead, asked discreetly, 'Am I Lord Raingo?'

Nothing was more calculated to set the Domino Room alight than a fervent literary controversy, and such was provided by the arrival in 1928 of copies of D. H. Lawrence's book *Lady Chatterley's Lover* from Italy, where the author was living and where it had been published in English. For its time his frank description of sexual intercourse between the sex-starved Lady Chatterley and her gamekeeper and his use of four-letter words were outrageous to most people. It was ironic that the most vicious attacks on the book were mounted by *John Bull*, remembering that the paper had been founded by Bottomley, but I believe it spoke for the majority when it called the book 'a landmark in evil', claiming that the sewers of French pornography would have to be dragged to find a parallel in beastliness. I eventually managed to procure a copy from one of the shops in Charing Cross Road specializing in pornographic works, along with contraceptives and aphrodisiac pills. I had read much worse, but it was obvious that the book could be suppressed under the laws forbidding the sending of indecent material through the post.

Most of the Domino Room authors who discussed the issue insisted on the right to put the full truth in any book, but others took what I regarded as a saner view! The trouble with granting licence is that there is no end to it. If frank sex could be described in a book, why not perform it on the stage? And once public morals slide in that respect, how soon before respect for other social values, like the law, follows suit? Licence is a slippery slope, and the older I get the more I am inclined to fear the relaxation of long-established rules of conduct, however stuffy they may seem to the young.

There were many who suspected that Lawrence was deliberately cocking a snook at the censor, especially when it was rumoured that he had originally intended to call the book *John Thomas and Lady Jane*. He did not appear in London while the tempest raged in Parliament, being too ill with consumption to risk the climate, even if he had wanted to, and died in the South of France in March 1930. He was forty-four.

I had not known Asquith, who died two years earlier in 1928, but I had supported him by voting Liberal, mainly through my liking for Winston Churchill. He meant well but he lived to see the number of Liberal MPs reduced from a majority to only forty. I fear they will never recover now. I have a note of a conversation of Sir Ray Lankester, the zoologist, arguing that once a species falls below a certain number it is doomed to eventual extinction, whatever efforts may be made on its behalf. That biological law may also apply to political parties.

A figure from an earlier era who died soon afterwards, early in 1929, was Lillie Langtry, or Lady de Bathe, to give her her final married name. She was seventy-five and had outlived her rival, Queen Alexandra, by nearly five years. She had also outlived her stage rival and sometime collaborator, Ellen Terry, though only by a few months. The fair Ellen had also become titled, some three years before she died: she was made a Dame. I am sure she was gratified to have the comparable honour to that bestowed on Henry Irving, but how stupid of the authorities who decide these honours to leave it so late. What is the point of an honour which is received barely in time to go on the gravestone?

I suppose it is incongruous to mention Frank Harris and honour in close connection, but we had news of the old rascal in 1928 through Beverley Nichols, after his return from New York where he had been editing a magazine. Harris had contacted him rather mysteriously and when they met had succeeded in selling Beverley a report of a conversation he claimed to have had with Wagner, way back, when they had walked by some lake in Berlin. Beverley said that he was so impressed with this first-hand material about the great composer that he paid Harris 200 dollars for it, only to find out later that it was complete fiction and had already been published before. Poor Frank! When he was hard up he would stoop to anything.

At the end of the twenties Augustus John suddenly began to age at an extraordinary rate. His great head sank into his chest and he seemed to lose height, as we all do late in life, but not so prematurely as John did. His face, with its staring, bloodshot eyes, bulbous nose and sunken cheeks, reminded me of Oscar's *Picture of Dorian Gray*. As in that case, John's past excesses seemed to have caught up with him. In addition he had begun to drink to the point where his hands trembled when he lifted a glass, and I wondered how he managed with a brush. Manage he did, however, and he still pursued the girls with success, or perhaps they pursued him. One of those on whom he had his bleary eye was Mavis Wright, a tall, willowy blonde with brown eyes and the fresh appeal of a girl of nineteen. She had been a waitress at Veeraswamy's, the Indian Restaurant across the street from the Café Royal, and had *her* eye on a higher station.

Plenty of men in the Domino Room were interested in Mavis but none so intensely as Horace Cole, who had become known as King John's Jester. One evening, sitting with Augustus, he made a beeline for her, arranged to meet her and soon proposed marriage – once he could get divorced from his existing wife. He must have been almost thirty years senior to Mavis and looked older still, because his black hair had gone snow-white and – unlike Frank Harris – he was not prepared to dye it, except temporarily for a joke, as I have described. To Mavis he represented riches – he had independent means – and entry to Society, for he was also well connected. Augustus thought he was mad, but Cole meant business and guarded Mavis as best he could, though she was determined to go on having 'fun' with other men. After a couple of years Cole secured his divorce and married her. The marriage might have lasted, but Cole lost most of his money in an ill-advised financial venture and ran off abroad, deserting Mavis in the process.

By that time we were glad to be rid of him because his practical jokes had lost all sophistication and were hardly worthy of a third-form schoolboy. With Chile Guevara he was in the habit of knocking on portentous-looking doors and demanding entry on the grounds that one or the other has seen his wife or sister being inveigled into the house for illicit purposes. Sometimes they were able to gain entry and search the bedrooms, leaving the place in disorder. In the Café Cole would pour salt in people's coffee or spit in their beer, leaving a notice to that effect. This raised few laughs and merited the black eyes he occasionally received, since he *would* fight out of his age group.

John, never one to see such an attractive creature as Mavis going spare, decided that 'out of loyalty' to his old friend he should stand in for him. Mavis was only too happy to oblige, and she became his model and his mistress. When I saw them together I thought that Augustus had turned the tables on Horace with a vengeance for his National Gallery prank. The revenge was rubbed in when Mavis gave birth to a son which, since she was still married to Cole, was christened in his name. Nobody had much doubt that the child was John's, for he was nothing if not fertile, and it seemed that Mavis thought she might induce him to marry her if she could free herself of Horace. She did manage to free herself, but she did not marry John. She married another character who affected large, arty hats and occasionally patronized the Domino Room – an archaeologist called Mortimer Wheeler. They met when Augustus took Mavis to an archaeological dig, and Wheeler fell for her just as Cole had done. Within a year were married and, though Augustus was loath to give her up, he agreed to be a witness at the wedding along with another Café Royal customer, the humorist A. P. Herbert. The wily John succeeded in 'keeping in close contact' with Mavis, and she served as his main model during the Second World War.

I have already recorded how the young Epstein staggered us all by asking for a glass of milk in the Domino Room, and how H. M. Bateman later made a cartoon about such an unlikely eventuality. In 1929 a development on a grander scale made its appearance nearby in Regent Street – competition with the Domino Room from a bar specializing in milk drinks! This was called the Meadow Milk Bar, and while the temperance protagonists must have applauded it, I am sure that it received little if any support from us. The proprietor was a young man of Italian origin called Charles Forte and, while most of us prophesied disaster for anyone hoping to sell milk drinks to Englishmen, I have to admit that he has gone from strength to strength and bids fair to emulate the success of Daniel Nicols, like him an immigrant from a foreign land.

In July of 1930 I was delighted to see Max Beerbohm, dapper as ever, walk into the Domino Room, which perhaps I should here call the Brasserie because it was his first visit to the new room. He looked around with obvious displeasure and, as his old table had disappeared, he sat at the nearest one available. The waiters did not recognize him, most of those who knew him having died, left or retired, and few of his old friends who were still alive, such as Hilaire Belloc or Arnold Bennett, still visited us.

The Silver Jubilee of King George V and Queen Mary was celebrated in 1935 with great fervour and, apart from the insults of a few Communists who managed to unfurl a nasty banner across Fleet Street, with genuine enthusiasm. The West End and Piccadilly, in particular, were thronged with revellers using the occasion to 'let their hair down', and much else besides, I don't doubt. While the King did not have the personality of his father, neither did he have his failings. He and his Queen had lived quietly and beyond reproach, which suited most of his subjects who liked to feel then that their royalty was 'up there', and unapproachable save by the favoured few. Though stern, perhaps because of his naval training, the King did have a sense of humour of which I overheard expressions from Palace servants who occasionally patronized the Domino Room. It seems that the King used to play billiards with one of his footmen called Simpson, who usually won. The stake was half a crown and the winner usually collected it on the spot. One day Simpson did not have any money on him when he lost, and the following morning as he was walking sedately past the King's bathroom a tousled head thrust itself round the door to shout: 'Simpson! Where's my bloody half-crown?'

As the King was already seventy there was no chance of a further Jubilee, but we did not realize how short the rest of his reign was going to be. In the middle of the following January we were told that the King, who was staying at Sandringham, had a 'slight cold'. But a few days later I learned from a most confidential source that his illness was really serious. Sir Bernard Spilsbury was in the Grill Room with another famous pathologist, Dr Roche Lynch, whom I remember because of his firm belief that: 'Only one poisoner in six is even suspected, much less brought to justice.' Spilsbury's usual companion in the Café Royal at that time was Lord Dawson of Penn, the King's physician, and he had heard the truth from that source. The King's health had been so weakened by a serious illness in 1928 that his chances of weathering this new infection were small.

I was therefore not so shocked as the rest of the public on 20 January 1936 when the wireless announced: 'The King's life is moving peacefully towards its close.' Great crowds assembled in the streets that evening, feeling some need to be together in time of grief, as they had during the Jubilee rejoicing. I stood with them in Piccadilly watching the electric sign which cleverly flashed the news through thousands of flickering light bulbs. Shortly after midnight the news came through. There was much weeping, and not only by women.

As I have already stated, the King had been well known personally to the Café Royal, though regrettably not to the Domino Room, first through his visits with his father, when he was Prince of Wales, and then on the occasions when he ate in the Restaurant alone or with friends. Though very popular with the staff, who liked both his manner and his manners, he invariably disappointed them by ordering the same meal – a slice of cold meat, no potatoes and a little salad, unlike his father who believed: 'Good food does nobody any harm.'

Those of us in the Domino Room on the day after his death were sad, because we knew how much he had done to refurbish the good name of the Royal Family with the British public after the inroads made by his father's poor showing as Prince of Wales. Not only had his private life been beyond reproach, but he was a dedicated naval officer, which I hope will always command respect, and he had behaved with dignity and courage throughout the Great War. His self-discipline and punctuality had become a byword. As a sportsman he was rated one of the greatest game-shots of all time, which meant little to me but more to others. It was stated in the newspapers that his last words had been 'How is the Empire?' This could have been true, I suppose, for such a man, but it did not ring true to me and I was soon to overhear one of the Palace servants, whose name I must not give because he may still be alive, telling a very different story.

It may be remembered by some of my readers that after the King's serious illness seven years previously he had been advised by his doctors to spend some time at Bognor, in Sussex, to recuperate in the sea air there. He was pictured there in a bath-chair or strolling about the promenade, and eventually, after his recovery, the town proudly took the name of Bognor Regis. According to my informant the King's doctors were doing their best to keep his spirits up as death approached. He remained conscious until near the end, and his final words were his response to a cheery remark by one of the doctors: 'It's going to be all right, Your Majesty. You'll soon be back in Bognor.'

'Bugger Bognor,' the King retorted with what venom he could muster, then said no more.

This, I think, was much more in character for a man whose lower-deck language was well known and who so enjoyed an active life that a further spell of bath-chair recuperation in any seaside town must have been a dismal prospect.

Like many thousands of loyal Londoners I queued to file past the coffin of the King on its catafalque in Westminster Hall, delaying my visit until late evening. I wished I had delayed it until midnight on the evening before the body was to be taken to Windsor, for those who did so witnessed a sight perhaps unique in British history. Throughout the time the King lay in state vigil round him was kept by soldiers, motionless with heads bent. Shortly before twelve o'clock on the night I mention the four Princes of the Blood, in full uniform, entered the Hall and took their places there, standing for some twenty minutes bent over their swords. It was something I would dearly have loved to have seen.

Naturally there was immediate talk about the fitness of the new King to rule the Empire which his father had thought so much about. He had something of a reputation as a playboy, with his night-clubbing, plus-fours and bagpipes, but there was no doubt about his popularity. I doubt whether any member of the Royal Family had ever been so popular at home or abroad, for there was something about his boyish figure and smile which elicited warmth from men and women alike. Everyone wished the young King well, but how disappointed we were soon to be.

38

EDWARD THE BRIEF

In the thirties my Domino Room was regularly enhanced by a most interesting character of great charm called Valentine Castlerosse, actually Viscount Castlerosse, and later to succeed to the Irish earldom of Kenmare. I had seen him in the Domino Room before on a few occasions when he had been brought there by his eccentric uncle, Maurice Baring, the great friend of Chesterton and Belloc. At that time, being so much younger than Maurice, he was shy. He was also no more than tubby, but he was soon to become outrageously larger than life both in physique and behaviour.

At the time of which I am now writing he must have weighed eighteen stones, accentuating his weight in cold weather by wearing a mink-lined overcoat with a sable collar. All his clothes, like his waistcoats which always had lapels, were designed to command attention, and he reminded me of Oscar Wilde in his belief that a man's clothing should express his personality. His head was round, almost bald, his face pink and chubby, his nose long and curved, and his smile usually seraphic especially when he had scored a point with some vitriolic remark or bawdy comment like: 'Anybody can make a mistake, as the hedgehog said to the hairbrush.'

For some years, starting in about 1926, he had written a very successful gossip column in the *Sunday Express*, called the Londoner's Log, which concentrated on Society both of the High and Café varieties. For this purpose, apart from his interest in food and wine, he used the Café Royal quite regularly, but preferred the Restaurant when with friends like F. E. Smith, the Socialist firebrand Aneurin Bevan and, in earlier days, Clarence Hatry. There he was well known for one particular peculiarity. Posing as a connoisseur of food (perhaps likening himself to the Blue Monkey), he insisted on mixing his own sauces at the table. Naturally the great chefs employed by the Café did not approve, and they always tasted the sauces, of which he invariably mixed so much that there was a great deal wasted. Their verdict was that the noble Viscount knew so little about food that his sauces always tasted the same because he overloaded them with Cayenne pepper. The waiters' theory to account for this was that the pepper increased Castlerosse's thirst, for he consumed enormous quantities of champagne, perhaps even infringing Horatio Bottomley's reputation in that respect. As with Bottomley, champagne helped to run him into perpetual debt, a nuisance he shrugged off with 'Oh, I've always lived above my newspaper's means.'

His work for the *Sunday Express* kept him in close contact with its proprietor, Lord Beaverbrook. As a result he would sometimes appear in the Domino Room (which for such a character was his rightful home) with another close friend of the Beaver, Mike Wardell, a former Guards officer with a black patch over one eye which caused him to be referred to as the Pirate and later, when a certain cartoon character became famous, as Popeye. Their conversation was fascinating to me because, in what they believed to be their mutual confidence, they often discussed the private affairs of the Beaver. Not the least interesting of these topics were his love affairs, which seemed to be legion. Having seen the Beaver, with his large head and imp-like smile, I would not have thought him attractive to women, but no doubt they were taken by his remarkable personality and the interesting friends to whom he could introduce them.

It was from Castlerosse that I learned of his manner with new possible conquests when they were first invited to Beaverbrook's country house, Cherkley, near Leatherhead in Surrey. The lady was put in a bedroom next to 'the Lord's' and the connecting door was left slightly ajar. If the lady left the door as it was, the Beaver would attempt to join her. If she closed it, she remained unwooed. I had to agree with Castlerosse that this was 'most civilized'. Castlerosse's own sex life was also of interest, though how he managed with that enormous stomach was a source of wonder to all of us. Perhaps he talked about it more than he performed but talk about it he did, and in the most improper terms. I heard that on one occasion when Lady Astor patted his stomach playfully she had remarked, 'What would we think if this was on a woman?' Castlerosse had immediately replied, 'Half an hour ago it was!'

What interested me most was Mike Wardell's inside information about the new King, Edward VIII, with whom he had been fairly friendly when he was Prince of Wales – as had Castlerosse, though he had never been one of the Prince's 'set' as Wardell had been. It had long been common knowledge that as Prince of Wales Edward, whom his family and friends always called David, had been specially attracted to married women. The first of these to become the subject of public gossip was Mrs Dudley Ward, referred to by her friends as Frieda, whom he met at the end of the First World War when he was very young. It was said that even the engine drivers on trains knew whom he was visiting when special stops had to be made. But Edward was not a promiscuous man like his grandfather, and the only other lady who was mentioned in the Domino Room or the newspapers was a certain Lady Thelma Furness.

So far as those relationships were concerned they were accepted as being in the old Edwardian tradition – no husband was going to cause trouble so that no scandal would ensue. The Prince and Mr Dudley Ward, a Liberal MP, were often seen together and Lord Marmaduke Furness kept his peace. But in 1934, while King George was still on the throne, Wardell had been able to tell Castlerosse that there was a new lady in the Prince's life, a Mrs Wallis Simpson. She was different in that she was American and, most importantly, in that she had been divorced before marrying her current husband, Mr Ernest Simpson, whom the Prince also knew.

I cannot pretend that I paid much attention to Mrs Simpson's name even when Wardell showed such concern about it. For his part Castlerosse, who did not seem to like Edward much, though keen to be photographed with him, was interested only in the possible gossip paragraphs. But over the next eighteen months more and more people began to mention her, particularly Domino Room journalists and writers like Castlerosse and Evelyn Waugh who dined with Lady Cunard, Nancy's mother.

Lady Cunard was a petite American married to the heir to an English shipping fortune, and called herself Emerald, though her proper name was Maud; she was full of gossip about the new liaison and was telling her friends that the Prince of Wales had completely fallen for Mrs Simpson and had dropped Mrs Dudley Ward and Lady Furness 'like hot coals'. Further, the gossip went, Mrs Simpson had her eye on being the future Queen.

At that stage nobody took this idea seriously, especially as there was no publicity about Mrs Simpson in the newspapers. But it soon became clear that something was brewing when American newspapers and magazines on sale at the Café Royal and elsewhere appeared with sections scissored out by a censor, which later turned out to be the distributors who were terrified of being sued for libel. There were Fleet Street journalists among our regulars who had access to the censored parts because their journals were mailed direct to them from America, and they took delight in reading out the offending portions.

It was from one of them, Arthur Christiansen, the young editor of the *Daily Express*, that I first learned that there was a conspiracy of silence on the part of the British press itself, particularly after Edward had become King early in 1936. With his older colleague, the lantern-jawed Scot John Gordon, of the *Sunday Express* he had been called to a conference with Lord Beaverbrook at Stornaway House in St James's, and after their briefing they had then looked in at the Café to discuss its consequences for them. Both showed their extreme frustration at being made to sit on what they called 'the hottest story for years' and at being unable to tell their readers what was happening to their King, while their foreign rivals were having a field day.

'I never thought I would live to see Beaverbrook inflict censorship on his own newspapers,' Gordon said in his broad accent.

'You think it's his fault?' asked Christiansen, who, having been editor only three years, was not so sure of himself.

'I know it. The King roped him in and he talked Harmsworth and Walter Layton into joining him.'

Harmsworth was the son of Lord Rothermere and nephew of Lord Northcliffe, while Sir Walter Layton was responsible for the *News Chronicle*, the Liberal newspaper.

'Well, we are stuck with it until we can get him to change his mind,' Chris said, twisting his right hand round the wrist of the left, as was his custom when not getting his way. 'I'm sure that he's not just sucking up to the King. He just thinks that publicity against Mrs Simpson could drive him further into her arms, and he wants him out of them.'

'You don't think the King intends to marry Mrs Simpson?' asked Gordon, sipping his soft drink, for he seemed to be a teetotaller.

'Frankly, I do. So does Mike Wardell. But the old man doesn't. At least you heard him say he doesn't. But I don't suppose he told us all he knows.'

'You can be sure of that,' Gordon said crisply. 'Anyway, there's nothing for us to do but go on collecting all we can against the day when we might be able to use it.'

As Mrs Simpson was American, the idea of an eventual marriage with the future King of England was naturally of enormous interest on the other side of the water, and though the scandal of the relationship became more and more widely known in London, as evidenced by the spate of smutty jokes on the subject, and was colourfully reported in the foreign press, the British papers continued to remain silenced. One copy of an American paper smuggled across the Atlantic and into the Café Royal flatly declared that Mrs Simpson would not only marry the King but would become accepted as his consort. 'King *will* wed Wally' blared the *New York Journal*, while another claimed that 'The Yankee at King Edward's Court has more British blood than the King', which was probably true.

By that time the Prime Minister, Stanley Baldwin, and his cabinet colleagues were beginning to be deeply worried by the affair. So were the staff at Buckingham Palace. The servant who used to play billiards with King George continued to come into the Café and I heard him complaining about the way his beer money had been stopped as an economy measure while he and his colleagues were required to take presents galore round to Mrs Simpson's London flat.

It was from Valentine Castlerosse that I heard that the issue must soon come to a head.

'Mrs S. is going to divorce her husband and it's going to look very like collusion,' he told his Fleet Street colleague Tom Driberg, who under the pseudonym William Hickey ran a gossip column in the *Daily Express* called 'These Names Make News', and was later to become a Labour MP.

'And is it?'

'Hard to tell, Tom, but I don't think Simpson has been paid off, if that's what you mean.'

'Well, they won't be able to keep the divorce out of the papers,' Driberg said.

'No, but it will be a pretty subdued affair, considering what it could be.'

'You mean the Beaver will keep the ban on?'

'Neither of us will be allowed to comment on it,' Castlerosse said.

'Do you think the other papers will abide by that?' asked Driberg, eyeing a young man at a nearby table, for he was yet another of the Café Royalites addicted to what Philip Heseltine used to call, with such venom, 'joy-boys', and he reminded me of Oscar in other ways, though he was not nearly so attractive a character.

'Probably,' Castlerosse replied. 'The King seems to be getting his way – so far.'

'What about Baldwin?'

'Ah, he's a different kettle of fish. I think His Majesty will meet a brick wall there.'

Castlerosse was right on both counts. When Mrs Simpson's divorce suit was heard in October in Ipswich, of all out-of-the-way places, the police prevented reporters from following her after she had been granted her decree nisi, and knocked cameras out of press photographers' hands. There were no trimmings to the bare report of the case, but by that time Mr Baldwin had been active in telling the King of his fears about what would happen if he insisted on marrying a lady who was going to have two other husbands still alive.

One would imagine that what a prime minister says to his monarch or what happens in a cabinet meeting would remain secret, but it seems that somebody always talks and it is not long before the facts, variegated no doubt, become common gossip. Only a few days elapsed after Baldwin's visit to the King before newspaper editors were discussing the event. From then on newspaper interest was intense, and I eavesdropped on an intriguing conversation between two officials of Lloyd's Bank in nearby St James's, revealing the extent to which reporters were trailing Mrs Simpson wherever she went. She and Mr Baldwin had accounts at the bank, and by coincidence both happened to go there at the same time. The reporters who had followed Mrs Simpson immediately concluded that the bank was being used as a secret meeting place. As their numbers swelled in the street outside, Mrs Simpson had to be smuggled out of the back of the building via the bullion lift!

In November, soon after the Simpson divorce, there was open talk about abdication brought into the Domino Room by lobby corre-spondents, who heard it being discussed by MPs at Westminster. One of them came in with a story alleged to have leaked from the Guards Club, where Ernest Simpson had lunched with the King.

'Wallis will have to choose between us,' Simpson was alleged to have said. 'Do you intend to marry her?'

'Do you think I would be crowned without Wallis by my side?' the King had replied.

The following day Aneurin Bevan confirmed that the King was hoping to reign with Mrs Simpson, at least as consort, when he came into the Domino Room with Frank Owen, a fellow Welshman and at one time the youngest MP.

'I was bidden to Stornaway House by the Beaver,' Bevan related. 'Who should I find there but one of the King's aides in satin breeches and with toy sword and all. He had been sent to ask how Labour MPs would react if the King insisted on marrying Mrs Simpson.'

'What did you tell him?'

'I said that all the King had to do was to ask himself how any middle-class suburban housewife would react.'

'That was sound advice, Nye,' Owen said. 'The Beaver's all wrong about this one.'

Owen was right. It was considered scandalous, even by hard-bitten journalists, that Mrs Simpson should be staying with the King at his hideaway at Fort Belvedere, near Windsor, and one MP tried unsuc-cessfully to prise the story open by asking a parliamentary question about the continued censorship of the American newspapers entering Britain. But what really shocked MPs was the way the King went ahead with a tour of the distressed coalfields of South Wales and, no doubt genuinely overcome by the poverty and unemployment he saw there, promised to get something done about it, while knowing that he could well be abdicating within a few weeks.

We in the Domino Room had a first-hand account of the King's behaviour from Hannen Swaffer, one of the journalists on the tour. 'The King was in tears as he saw the desolation and the loyal people in rags, so pathetically keen to get close to him. I'm sure he intends to prod the politicians into some action. . . .' Of course Wales was not alone in suffering from unemployment. There had been a series of 'hunger marches', involving desperate men from all the industrial areas – one, which ended in Hyde Park, involved nearly a quarter of a million people.

It was at this point that the Café Royal was brought right into the centre of the crisis. The Prime Minister needed to discuss all the issues of the possible abdication with the Archbishop of Canterbury, and he ordered a private suite in the Café to do it. Possibly the idea was to prevent speculation by reporters who might have seen the Archbishop entering No. 10 Downing Street, which was being carefully watched. Seeing them together in the Café Royal should not have occasioned suspicion because they were often seen there. Both were members of 'The Club', a most exclusive dining club founded more than a century before by Sir Joshua Reynolds, the painter, and limited to sixteen members. The Club met regularly in a private room at the Café Royal, and for this reason neither man was a stranger to my eyes. Nevertheless, I made a point of being in the foyer and noticed that they left separately.

As usual the tubby, snub-nosed Baldwin, then in his seventieth year, was smoking his little pipe, filled no doubt with the Presbyterian Mixture to which he later lent his name for advertising purposes. I could never see that advertisement with its caption, 'My thoughts grow in the aroma of that particular tobacco', without recalling that night when my close association with the Café Royal seemed to have dragged me right into the heart of history in the making. Also as usual the Archbishop, Cosmo Gordon Lang, looked sour, stringy and humourless in his gaiters and silk hat.

Of course I tried hard to find out what had gone on in that private room, but I have to confess that I failed utterly. The waiters had been rigorously excluded once they had served the meal, and it was only later that it became clear what must have happened. Nevertheless news of the Café Royal meeting quickly spread, and it helped to strengthen the belief that Baldwin and the Archbishop had plotted to use the Simpson affair to get rid of a King they disliked. To many high Tories King Edward seemed rather radical and prone to interfere in political affairs. To the Archbishop he seemed to lack all interest in religion. The Archbishop had known what was going on from his own sources, for he had received hundreds of anonymous letters attacking Mrs Simpson and including some of the forthright American press cuttings, but had been powerless to do anything. His anger must have been intense for if, as seemed possible at one point, the King intended to marry Mrs Simpson and keep the throne, he would have had to crown him at the Coronation.

In the middle of November Tom Driberg was back in the Café in search of further gossip for his column and with some of his own. He told how his boss, Lord Beaverbrook, had taken off for America in the German liner *Bremen* and had then immediately returned in it, having been requested by the King to do so.

'There's some move to form a King's Party to keep him on the throne, with the Beaver and your father leading it,' Driberg told his drinking companion, Randolph Churchill, the very able son of Winston.

'Where does Mrs Simpson stand?' Randolph asked.

'She knows she can never be Queen so she wants a morganatic marriage. That would make her a Duchess, and she would have all the social and prestige privileges of being the King's wife, but any children would be barred from the succession.'

'No King's Party or anybody else will ever bring that off. It would need legislation and Parliament would never stand for it.'

'Well, that's the plot,' Driberg said. 'And Express Newspapers are to start campaigning for it tomorrow.'

'And I suppose Beaverbrook's real purpose is to bugger Baldwin?' said Randolph, who knew that the Beaver had feuded with the Prime Minister for years.

'Well, your father wouldn't be averse to that, would he?' Driberg asked.

Randolph answered silently with a smile.

At that juncture I was hoping that Castlerosse would come in, because I had heard him say that he knew that Randolph was after his wife. He had in fact openly accused her of having an affair with him during one of the loud slanging matches which occasionally accompanied their meals together in the Café. Lady Castlerosse, whose name was Doris, had been a friend of Gertrude Lawrence and, like that down-to-earth lady, was well capable of taking care of herself in any verbal contest. The sad truth was that Lady Castlerosse was fair game for anybody if they had any money. Valentine knew this, but it was common knowledge that on one occasion he had hidden outside their Mayfair house while a certain baronet was inside and thrashed him with a blackthorn stave when he emerged. A similar encounter with Randolph would have livened things up for us.

The 'plot', if there ever was one, did not get very far. Randolph had been right. Soundings in Parliament convinced Baldwin that there would be no support for a morganatic marriage, which was what Mrs Simpson seemed to be after. Once the King knew that was so, he was determined to abdicate.

In a way which now seems astonishing, the newspapers still declined to tell the public that the King was prepared to give up his throne rather than give up Mrs Simpson, but on 1 December the Bishop of Bradford, of whom few people in the south had heard, inadvertently gave the newspaper the cue they were waiting for so eagerly. In an address to some religious conference he remarked on the King's failure as a churchgoer, and the *Yorkshire Post*, a great northern newspaper, developed the theme, believing that he had been hinting at the danger of a morganatic marriage.

The London papers followed the lead, and soon the whole country knew what I and many others had known for weeks. There was intense resentment at the realization that the King had convinced himself that his personal happiness and Mrs Simpson's mattered more than his duty to his peoples, both at home and abroad. While thousands of couples who would have been happier divorced remained together for the sake of their children, the wretched King was not prepared to make a marital sacrifice for the whole family of nations. It seemed a strange attitude to a throne which some of his forbears had striven so desperately to acquire. The romantic idea of giving up a throne for a woman was all right when the country was some mid-European principality, but when it was mighty Britain it made no sense to anybody.

Among the radicals in the Domino Room there were those who took the line that, as an individual, he should be free to marry whom he liked. Some republicans even welcomed the situation, believing that it would weaken the monarchy, but the great majority, both in the Café Royal and in the country, were appalled at the prospect that a commoner with two other husbands living might become Queen of England. Not one of the Domino Room's dreamy poets suggested that it was understandable that, like Mark Antony, the King should lose his world for love.

Still, every cause, however unworthy, attracts supporters and I saw a few hundred young people outside Buckingham Palace cheering and waving placards proclaiming: 'God Save the King from Baldwin' and: 'We want Edward. Perish all Politicians!' A couple of dozen or so also disported themselves outside No. 10 Downing Street, chanting, 'We want our King . . . We want our King.' They were not helped by the support for the King given by the Blackshirts, then being led by Sir Oswald Mosley. The King's sympathy for Hitler was not popular, especially as it had been rumoured that the Germans were using Mrs Simpson to influence the King in their favour.

The King abdicated on 10 December, and that night there were emotional scenes in the Café. Some jeered at the tragedy, raising their glasses with such toasts as 'The King has ratted. Long live the King.' One man stood up and recited in a sarcastic tone the lines from a poem by the seventeenth-century poet Richard Lovelace:

> *I could not love thee (Dear) so much,*
> *Lov'd I not honour more.*

But on the whole there was a serious mood of depression, with deep concern about the fitness for the throne of the King's brother, the Duke of York, who had a shy, diffident manner and a bad stammer. This was an especially worrying time, with Nazi Germany rearming at such speed. It seemed an odd response with so many radicals in the company, but most of us stood to attention when Douglas Goldring, an habitué since the early twenties, began to sing 'God Save the King'.

On 11 December Archbishop Lang, who had never been a popular figure, gave vent to his pent-up frustration by making a broadcast which rebuked the King in terms which many thought to be savage and uncharitable for any churchman. This led a man called Gerald Bullett to compose a clever little verse which was retailed with glee in the Domino Room:

> *My Lord Archbishop, what a scold you are!*
> *And when your man is down how bold you are!*
> *Of charity how oddly scant you are!*
> *How Lang, Oh lord, how full of Cantuar!*

There was also news of a further poem by another occasional visitor, Osbert Sitwell, though nobody ever seems to have seen it, probably because of the danger of libel. * As soon as the King abdicated he was

---

*Editor's footnote: It is still unpublished.

deserted by most of those who had been his friends, only a very few like 'Fruity' Metcalfe, his boon companion, remaining faithful. So Sitwell was said to have recorded this base behaviour in a poem entitled 'Rat Week'.

Many ardent Royalists were astonished at the way the crisis subsided as soon as Edward left the country to join his beloved lady. The new King, George VI, settled in surprisingly well and we had a new Queen, Elizabeth, whom we could respect and take to our hearts. They and their family were to acquit themselves so superbly that not only was the damage quickly remedied but most people felt that the country had greatly benefited by the exchange. But the Royals must have been concerned about the ease with which the government had been able to get rid of a King who had not happened to suit it.

I heard only two stories told in the Domino Room about King George VI. It seems that the manager of the bank which handled his private account was called George King, and the new monarch derived great fun out of telephoning him on a private line, opening the conversation with, 'Is that George King? This is King George.' He should also be remembered for his name for Manchester, where it seemed there were a number of local dignitaries who bored him on his occasional duty visits. He called it 'The City of Dreadful Knights'.

While reminiscing about the lady love of one King Edward, I should here record that Daisy Warwick, who had been forty-nine when King Edward VII passed away, lived to see his son die and his grandson abdicate, and then to last two years longer. She left the world she had loved well, if unwisely, in 1938 at the age of seventy-six. Comrade Warwick remained a committed Socialist to the last, even though her education had ruined her.

I have to admit that I was among those who cheered when Neville Chamberlain returned from his Munich meeting with Hitler, brandishing his scrap of paper which he sincerely believed had ended the German menace. But I think that most Britons were cheering with me. We had a taste of what was to come, though from a different source, one Saturday evening in June of 1939, when six bombs planted by the Irish Republican Army exploded near Piccadilly. Nobody was killed but there were great piles of broken glass which had inflicted nasty injuries, a sight which was to be common enough once war with Germany was declared in the following September.

The war immediately cost us many of our younger 'members' who joined the Forces, but it brought back some old ones like Zulu

Campbell, 'the Flaming Terrapin', who came all the way from South Africa to volunteer, and Chris Nevinson, who had left us to live in France and America but returned as an official war artist.

With my memories of the First World War neither the blackout nor the early bombing was a novel experience for me. The Café Royal was full night after night with people in need of cheer, and Jimmy Agate did his best to keep us all in good spirits. By that time he was well into the publication of his memoirs, which he presented under the modest title *Ego*. I think they are bitty and so difficult to take, except in small doses, that I am resolved not to present my diaries in that stark form. I must admit, though, that I enjoyed his dedication of *Ego 3* to one of his Hackney ponies: 'Unlike Caligula I cannot make my horse Ego a consul: but I can dedicate this book to him and I do.'

Another journalist, Hannen Swaffer, also gave us great amusement, though his humour was unintentional. After his crusade to introduce Prohibition had failed he became interested in spiritualism, spurred on, I believe, by Sir Arthur Conan Doyle, who was quite convinced that communication with the dead was possible through a sensitive 'medium' and often spoke on psychical research at Café Royal banquets. Conan Doyle claimed that he had received messages from the dead Northcliffe, so Swaffer was keen to experiment himself. Within a few days he became convinced of the existence of the spirit world during a séance when a luminous trumpet danced towards him calling, 'Swaff, it's the Chief. I am so glad to see you, Swaff. . . .' At later séances, Swaffer said, the Chief discussed old colleagues and events in Fleet Street. The result was a book by Swaffer called *Northcliffe's Return*.

As with most of these 'communications', conjured up in darkness which facilitated trickery, the content was all trivia, and most of us in the Domino Room thought Swaff had finally gone off his head. Impervious to the banter, Swaff has remained a spiritualist, doing all he can to secure converts. Many of his famous friends have taken part in his séances, including Beaverbrook. But he failed to interest Bernard Shaw. 'I gave up table-turning in my childhood,' Shaw replied to the invitation. Swaff retaliated: 'Now that you are approaching your second childhood I thought you might like to have a go.' Though increasingly acidulous and cadaverous, Swaff has retained his sense of humour. Foreseeing the day when his flat overlooking Trafalgar Square might be bombed, he quipped, 'It would be a tragedy: Nelson would be the only columnist left there.'

The Duke of Windsor made a few visits to London from France in connection with a wartime job he was hoping to secure, but he was almost a forgotten man. The only time I heard of any interest in him was when it was rumoured that the Gestapo was planning to kidnap him and his wife to install them as puppet King and Queen once the invasion of Britain had been accomplished. I think that was one of the reasons why he was sent to the safety of the Bahamas as Governor.

I noticed that once again, in spite of the seriousness of the situation, the conversation and general behaviour of our crowd became trivial in the extreme, as it had been in the First World War. A steady batch of dirty stories too feeble to remember provoked loud laughter among intellectuals who would normally have disdained them.

In the spring of 1940 James Agate, dapper and pugnacious-looking as usual, stomped into the Domino Room brandishing a new walking stick. Sitting beside Basil Cameron, the conductor whom he had arranged to meet, he wasted no time in showing his acquisition.

'The walking stick of William Hogarth, Britain's greatest painter,' he declared.

'I wouldn't agree with you that he was the greatest, but I do like the stick,' Cameron said.

It was indeed a handsome object, spirally fluted down its length and with the handle decorated with theatrical masks.

'How did you come by it?'

'Bought it from the owner for £5. But what does the price matter?' Agate asked, fingering the fluting lovingly. 'As with all good things, I shall appreciate its value long after I have forgotten the price.'

'No cynic, you, James,' Cameron remarked, recalling Wilde's definition of that superficial type as a person who knows the price of everything and the value of nothing.

'I hope not, Basil. I hope not. Values are what my calling as a critic is about.'

I wish there were more critics like Agate. Having overheard, as well as read, so many of them, they too often succumb to the temptation of using their space to air their own knowledge or search for convoluted, hidden meanings which were never in the author's mind.

A week later Agate came in with yet another stick he had bought – a malacca cane with an ivory handle which had once belonged to Bosie Douglas. As he displayed it with pride I wondered what he would have said had he seen the stick in my possession – the one I bought when Oscar's effects were auctioned. I had a mind to bring it in and show it to him, but I was afraid that he might want to buy it and that

I would be no match for his persuasiveness. Or maybe I was just afraid.

39

UNFATHOMABLE ENDS

Though the Brasserie lacked the French atmosphere of the old Domino Room, it still seemed to me that the horror was greater there than outside when in June France surrendered to the Germans after putting up such a miserable fight. At all levels of their society the French seemed to set such store by their '*honneur*', yet their efforts against the invader were dishonourable and the behaviour of many of them in collaborating with Germany was to prove detestable.

We had, of course, General de Gaulle in London rallying the Free French forces, many of whom appeared in the Café, sailors in their colourful hats with red pompoms, army officers in their *képis*, but the great De Gaulle himself never appeared and all we heard there were stories about his quarrels with Churchill. The one I best remember was told about a meeting of war chiefs chaired by Churchill at which De Gaulle was being difficult, making arrogant demands. In his fractured French Churchill warned him: 'Si vous m'opposerez je vous get-ridderai.'

After the ignominious defeat at Dunkirk, which had been converted into the 'miracle' of the evacuation, Agate told a tale of how one army officer who was exhausted on the Dunkirk beach had managed to haul himself into one of the little boats and collapsed in sleep under a tarpaulin. The boat took him to Dover, but by the time he awakened it was back at Dunkirk!

In September the Blitz came to the Café Royal with the explosion of a large delayed action bomb in the centre of Regent Street. The brave bomb disposal men partially defused it, but not completely, and it blew up, shattering hundreds of plate glass windows. The Café had to be temporarily closed, and I realized what a catastrophe it would be for me if it were destroyed, as the nearby Café de Paris was.

Alan (A. P.) Herbert, who was often in the Café with his ready smile and wit, put our feelings into verse:

> *We have no quarrel with the German nation —*
> *One would not quarrel with a herd of sheep —*
> *But, generation after generation, they*
> *Throw up rulers who disturb our sleep.*

I went down into the Piccadilly Underground once or twice when the siren wailed but, suffering from claustrophobia, especially in crowds, I decided that I would rather be killed at my table or in my bed than be trapped in a funk-hole. The atmosphere of the air raid shelters, which I detested but many came to enjoy, was captured in pencil and paint by Henry Moore, who would join us in the Domino Room after drawing in the depths.

Churchill, of course, was our table talk hero and our British villain was Aneurin Bevan, his foremost critic, whom many of us regarded as a traitor. He made it clear that, for him, the German invasion of Soviet Russia, which had been a staunch ally of Hitler when it suited, had given new meaning to the war. With no knowledge whatever of military matters he carped on at Churchill both in the House and on his occasional visits to the Café, where we agreed with Winston's description of him — 'a squalid nuisance'.

It is hateful to write on the subject of death, but one by one my old friends of the Domino Room were disappearing, some naturally, others — alas — by violence or their own hand. Mark Gertler had already gassed himself, then in March 1941 we were saddened, but by no means surprised, to learn that Virginia Woolf had drowned herself in the River Ouse, having left a note for her doting husband, Leonard, recording how happy they had been. I had seen her on odd occasions, once going into Hatchard's, the splendid bookshop in Piccadilly, and again returning some books to the London Library. She had looked more gaunt and bony than ever, almost emaciated, and very melancholic, in spite of her literary success.

After the publication of her novel *Jacob's Room* in 1922 she had become world-famous, especially in the United States, with a succession of books like *Mrs Dalloway*, *The Voyage Out* and *To the Lighthouse*, none of which appealed to me as they seemed to lack a sensible plot, and for me fiction must have a plot to make a worthwhile read. All this detailed examination of characters in whom I cannot begin to be interested bores me. If one has to drive oneself to persevere with a book, then for me it has failed. Virginia's face, which never bore much make-up, could be animated and she sometimes laughed in what seemed an artificial, hooting way, but she was the kind of person who could never be happy. I have seen so many of them in the Domino Room, introspective souls who are always so concerned with why we are here and what life is really about that they have no time to enjoy it.

Suicide is so often the fate of such people and when they are talented it seems a dreadful waste. To a person like myself, determined to get as much out of life as possible, self-destruction, when death is so easy to encounter by accident or fatal design, seems criminal. I suppose people have some right of decision in this regard, but suicide is an act of extreme selfishness when genuinely loving relatives, like Leonard Woolf, have to bear what must seem to their friends to be the stigma of their inadequacy.

Another of the casualties of the Second World War so far as the Café Royal was concerned was Valentine Castlerosse. A column about High Society, when the nation was fighting for its survival, was not viable, and when Castlerosse succeeded to the earldom of Kenmare he returned to his Irish estates in Killarney. He had divorced the wife who was so generous with her favours, and remarried more happily, recalling to my mind his interesting view: 'Marriage proves nothing: it is only in divorce that proof is necessary.'

He was greatly missed, for he had a marvellous sense of humour. I heard it said that on one occasion when he was in a bunker during an important golf match he clasped his hands and said, loudly enough for all the spectators to hear, 'Please God come down and help me with this shot. And don't send Jesus. This is no job for a boy.' Many no doubt thought it blasphemous, but Valentine prided himself on being a good Catholic and probably was – 'after his fashion'.

As was inevitable with a glutton in the same league as Oscar and Caruso, the sins of the flesh were to kill him. In 1943 he died, at the early age of fifty-two. Considering the enormous quantities he ate and drank it was surprising that he lasted that long. Poor Valentine! Nobody can cheat Death, but he was one of those who helped him. I remain in his debt for many laughs and for memorable additions to my diary like: 'The cruel thing about money is that one must part with it to enjoy it', but I hope, for the repose of his soul, that he repaid his financial debts to the many whom he owed. The one characteristic I disliked about Valentine was the way he felt justified in living extravagantly on goods supplied in good faith by people who often were not paid. It was funny for me to hear him say: 'Not to do a thing you want to do because you cannot afford it is quite absurd.' It was not funny for the people who had laboured to supply his needs and were denied their payment. I see little difference between refusing to pay a debt and stealing. I heard his friends say that Castlerosse would have been bankrupted had not Beaverbrook come to his rescue at his urgent request, and paid his bills so often that he called Valentine 'My never-ending Lord of Appeal'. Let us hope that the final Lord of Appeal has been as generous.

Mosley and his Fascists had quickly been rounded up but we kept hearing one of them – William Joyce, the so-called 'Lord Haw-Haw' who promoted Germany and denigrated Britain from the temporary safety of Hamburg. He was of little interest to us, but another renegade was – our old friend Ezra Pound, who had become attracted to Fascism, and Mussolini in particular, while living in Rome and sent propaganda broadcasts from that city. He had remained an American citizen and most of his barbs were directed against that country, so when Italy was defeated he was indicted for treason by an American Grand Jury in July 1943. He was judged insane and committed to an asylum, which most of us thought was the best solution to his terrible circumstance.

His condition remained the subject of much serious discussion in his old haunt but, as I have said, most Domino Room conversations in the early forties tended to be trivial, in spite of the savage killing and destruction from the air. I remember, for example, a long and heated argument between James Agate and a man who insisted that the moon could well be made of green cheese because there was no proof against it. Jimmy could do no better than claim that he had once encountered a green cheese which was definitely made of moon.

On another occasion in 1944 Agate was enjoying a discussion with some bearded chap about Einstein's theory about time and the impossibility that two distant events could happen at exactly the same moment. Jimmy's final refuge against the scientific onslaught was to quote a limerick I had not heard before:

> *I don't like the family Stein,*
> *There's Gert, there's Ep and there's Ein.*
> *Gert's poems are bunk,*
> *Ep's statues are junk,*
> *And nobody understands Ein.*

My old sculptor friend could not have liked this verse, and time will tell if the opinion is true. As for Miss Gertrude 'A rose is a rose is a rose' Stein, I already agree.

While the Luftwaffe's blitz on London had failed we had to face a further ordeal – attack by robot flying-bombs or doodle-bugs, as they became known. Their engines made such a peculiar noise that as they approached they were easily audible in the Café to those with hearing. We would then sit quietly, waiting for the silence which meant that the bomb was about to dive. Of course I could hear nothing at any time and at first I had to ask my waiter to explain the silence, though later I could discern what was about to happen from the expressions on my friends' faces – attentive disquiet and, in some cases, jaw-clenching fear. While the silence lasted we could do nothing but hope that the bomb would fall somewhere else. Immediately after the bang, which I felt as a vibration when the impact was near, the conversation would immediately resume in relief, little thought being given to those who had been killed while we had been spared. We should have dived under the table to avoid flying glass, but nobody ever did. I suppose we were all too cowardly to let others see we were afraid. The V1s, as the flying bombs were also called, were augmented by V2s, long-range rockets, which arrived unheralded, but we were soon relieved from both as the Allied armies fought on towards Germany.

On 20 March 1945 Bosie Douglas died at the reasonably ripe age of seventy-four. It was sorry news for me, for it meant that another major figure had left us. He had an unhappy life, dying convinced that his talents had not been appreciated and that fate had continued to conspire against him from the moment that he had met Wilde. There could be no doubt that his character and outlook had been monstrously warped by the Wilde affair, with which he was always bound to be associated, but I feel that his nature was weak from the start. Nobody could deny his ability as a poet, however, and I was deeply affected by his sonnet on death which I never read until he had resolved that mystery in the only way it can be:

> . . . *For in the smoke of that last holocaust,*
> *When to the regions of unsounded air*
> *That which is deathless still aspires and tends,*
> *Whither my helpless soul shall we be tossed?*
> *To what disaster of malign despair,*
> *Or terror of unfathomable ends?*

For me, Victory in Europe Night, 8 May 1945, was just a repetition of 11 November 1918, except that the clothing worn by the revellers was different. Here we were again celebrating 'the end of the war to end wars', with Piccadilly the centre of the singing and dancing which lasted until dawn. Some of the songs like 'Roll Out the Barrel' and 'I'll Get Lit Up When the Lights Go On in London' were memorable up to a point, but not to be compared with the classics of the Great War.

I was soon to see celebrations in the streets which appalled me – on the night of 26 July, when the results of the General Election showed that a majority of the nation had rejected Churchill, who had brought them to safety. There were many in the Café who were as jubilant that night as if the millennium had arrived. When I thought of the Labour leaders whom I had seen at close quarters, like Ramsay MacDonald and Aneurin Bevan, I was full of foreboding.

Mercifully Bevan, the 'Bollinger Bolshevik', ceased to use the Café, but I did see him one evening striding out after a meeting with leading doctors in a private room. It had been organized by the British Medical Association to present its case for professional freedom inside the nationalized Health Service, of which he had been put in charge. One of the waiters told me that Bevan had begun by saying, 'The place isn't like it was when Oscar Wilde, myself and a few others made it famous.' He had then ordered a particularly large plate of oysters. I fear the doctors did not get far with him. He divided them and ruled them, and their talks of strike action came to nothing. It was in July 1948, my diary tells me, when Aneurin Bevan made his biggest political gaffe by referring to the Tories as 'lower than vermin'. I was delighted to hear that his London home, near fashionable Sloane Square, was quickly daubed with large black letters: 'Vermin Villa – home of a loud-mouthed rat'. The *Sunday Despatch* followed up with a headline: 'The Man who Hates 8,093,858 People', that being the number who had voted Conservative in 1945. The Socialists in the Café were more angered than the Tories, because they feared that the remark would lose them the next election.

It was regrettable that Bevan, who called profit 'private greed' but had no objection to making one himself, should have had such a log on his shoulder, for he had great speaking talent. I recall one occasion when he was being asked what the government intended to do about the difficulty some employers were having in finding men to do certain jobs. He replied: 'Too many jobs chasing too few men is a headache. But too many men chasing too few jobs is a heartache. I'd rather have the headache than the heartache.' Had Bevan been less motivated by class warfare revenge he could have become a statesman.

I regard it as something of an achievement to have seen George Bernard Shaw out of this world. He died in 1950 aged ninety-four, when I thought he must be going to make a century. I would have liked to have outlived Augustus John, but, ancient and decrepit as he appears to be from all accounts, he still soldiers on in the pubs of Chelsea. After the way he has abused his body he has not deserved to live so long, but I imagine that, as with Shaw and with myself, the fact that he continues to work keeps him going. Tennyson expressed the best advice I have ever encountered in poetry:

> *Unto him that works and feels he works*
> *The same grand year is ever at the doors.*

40

A BURNT-OUT EMBER

The Brasserie, as I shall have to call it here, closed its doors forever in January 1951. I was desolate as I took the Tube to Russell Square on that last evening, then walked to my digs in chilling rain. The walking distance was short, since I had moved to Coram Street, but had become progressively longer in time, the stick which I had always carried for effect having become a necessity.

The closure meant that my social life was at an end and I felt angry and resentful as well as sad. Still, I could not blame the Café Royal management. For reasons inexplicable to me, attendance had fallen away both in the numbers and quality of the customers. So Bohemianism, and the pretence of it, which is what perhaps I had been witnessing for some years, had finally to be buried. No doubt there were still plenty of young artists and writers about, but attitudes had changed and they seemed reluctant to spend time in talk and banter.

Perhaps they deserve a good mark for that, but for me it spelled a savage deprivation after sixty-four years of near-continuous enjoyment, provided free, by what had looked like an unending stream of unwitting entertainers.

The area once occupied by the Domino Room and then by the Brasserie reopened within three months as a restaurant. The Grill Room, with its original Domino Room mirrors and furniture, remains, and I suppose that a few of my old friends still go there. But for me the magic of the place was gone and I have never been near the Café Royal since, for it would be scarifying for me even to see it. Perhaps one day some place like the Domino Room will rise again. There must always be a need for a meeting place where lively minds can abrade each other, like flint and wheel, to strike the coruscating sparks of wit and challenging ideas. Maybe some future Café Royal management will resuscitate it.

I am driven to admit that in some respects the closure was opportune, for at the age of eighty-four, and declining suddenly in health, the journeys to and from Regent Street were becoming increasingly exhausting for me. Now that I am definitely unwell I rarely leave my room, being limited to reliving the past through my diaries. The candle of my life is guttering, which I think is a more appropriate simile for me than Frank Harris's imaginative symbol: 'A man's life starts with a small noise, dancing round and round, throwing off sparks, shining with a circle of magic white light, radiating energy to the audience, then gradually slowing, the sparks dying, the radiance fading, rocking back and forth and stopping, a burnt-out ember in the dark night.'

I have not thrown off many sparks myself, but I have witnessed a unique display of pyrotechnics over what must be a record period of time. That experience has brought me happiness according to my definition of the word. Happiness is no entity that one possesses or does not. It is a state of mind engendered by a lot of little things which have to go on happening. In my case they did so and, even when things were dull, all I had to do was ask myself what I would be doing were I not in my observation post.

My only real sadness has been the passing of so many of my friends, but I look forward to meeting them all again some time soon. And I do mean to *meet* them; to make myself known to them at last.

Now that all my days are the same and getting through them is laborious, I am ready to agree with Swinburne:

From too much love of living
From hope and fear set free,
We thank with brief thanksgiving
Whatever Gods may be
That no man lives forever,
That dead men rise up never;
That even the weariest river
Winds somewhere safe to sea.

I have often wondered whether ghosts step out of those gilded mirrors when the Grill Room doors are closed and the lights extinguished. If so, there will be no ghost with more entitlement to haunt the place than mine.

EDITOR'S EPILOGUE

Mr Terrapin's papers suggest that he had feared death more than he had admitted but he remained independent to the end, concealing his painful and debilitating symptoms as best he could, to avoid being sent to hospital to die. As a result he suffered the indignity, which he had predicted, of being 'found dead' in his bed-sitting-room. Sentimentally I felt that, had he been able to summon up the energy, he might have dragged himself to his beloved Café Royal to breathe his last. So I arranged the next best thing for him.

Mr Terrapin had been cremated and I managed to recover the small urn containing his ashes. Then, one evening, I booked a table in the Grill Room, as is my practice. This was possible only because the Grill Room, along with the rest of the Café Royal, had been saved from demolition and conversion into an office block by that same Charles Forte mentioned almost dismissively by Terrapin when he had opened a milk bar in Regent Street. With no money but supreme confidence Forte (now Sir Charles) offered to buy the Café Royal in 1954 for £450,000, having previously pledged his credit to buy the nearby Criterion building. When the owner found a bank willing to lend the money if someone could be found to guarantee the loan, Forte suggested that the owner himself should function in that capacity. The owner, who hardly knew Forte, was so taken with his boldness and style that he agreed to do so.

Forte was determined to keep the Café Royal as a catering establishment, so not only have the old Domino Room fixtures and fittings been preserved in the Grill Room, together with the Nicols's quality of the food and wine, but the original atmosphere can be recreated in the imaginative mind, especially as famous artists and writers still patronize it.

Before entering the building I walked completely round it, slowly trickling a little of Mr Terrapin's mortal remains from a paper bag into Regent Street, Air Street and Glasshouse Street. I retained perhaps a saltspoonful of this granular, grey ash in a small horn snuffbox. Then, while sitting alone at my table, reflected to infinity by the facing mirrors, overlooked by the 'pure Baroque' caryatids and 'pagan' ceiling, and visualizing, as best I could, little Mr Terrapin sitting at table ten, I sprinkled the contents surreptitiously on the floor.